Stealing Innocence

Sylvia Hubbard

HubBooks, Detroit, Michigan

Stealing Innocence

Sylvia Hubbard

Published by HubBooks Literary Services

All rights reserved. Sylvia Hubbard © 2004
ISBN: 97815495645-4-3

Discover other titles by Sylvia Hubbard at http://sylviahubbard.com

License Notes

For information address:

Sylvia Hubbard | PO Box 36825, Grosse Pointe Farms, MI 48236
Visit her website at: http://SylviaHubbard.com

Author's Note:

If you're reading this version, this would be revision for 2013. Thank you for supporting my work. You are holding a version of the book the bootleggers haven't touched yet and a better version that was edited by Shonell Bacon an excellent editor! I do thank her for all her help and I hope I've justified her editing correctly.

stealing innocence

tying a man down...

to get what she wants...

leads to sweet Pay Back!

Sylvia Hubbard

Chapter 1

Being awakened in the middle of the night was not cool to Kimberly, but Leroy was persistent in his attempt to shake his sister from her slumber. Kim was not an average-sized girl at 5'7", 180, but Leroy was a year behind his sister and six feet two at two hundred and fifty pounds, he could easily move her like this.

"Kimmie, wake," he pleaded in a quiet voice. "I know you're tired."

Kim had always been highly sensitive. Over the years, she had gotten better at controlling her sensitivity to people, but things that wouldn't faze a normal person could send her into a fit of hysterical nauseating tears.

Leroy was not a normal person. Physically he was a large brawny boy, and mentally he was definitely different from others. When he was denied oxygen at birth for almost three minutes, Leroy was brought into this world with a mother who only lived from one high to another, almost starving her children to death before the state took them away and put them in the guardianship of Uncle Charlie, their mother's stepbrother.

"Kimmie, come on," he insisted, rocking her harder.

Kimberly groggily sat up, but before she could adjust her eyes to the dark room, Leroy was yanking her out her bed and leading her out of the bedroom to the upstairs hallway chute, which led straight down to the basement. He covered her mouth to stop any protest she was about to mutter about his rough treatment to make her aware of the deep voices going on two floors below them.

"Now dat Kimmie got her license, I want you to get her a job at the home-" Uncle Charlie spoke. "You said there's a lot of rich old coots who'd love to get their hands on her." His Alabama accent stayed with him even though he had been in Detroit for almost thirty years.

A chill went down Kim's back as she listened to her uncle and his friend Willis Cox talk about her like she was a cure-all for youth to old men.

Willis chuckled nastily. "Seeing as how she's at an age of consent, you damn right. Them old farts won't know what hit them. I gots six in mind she can pick from."

"Pick from? Aw, she ain't gonna have no choice in the matter. The richest fart will do."

There was a lot of cackling going on after that, but she didn't need to hear anymore. Leroy followed her quietly back to her room. She waited until he closed the door behind him and turned on the bedside lamp before she attempted to speak.

"Thank you, Lee," she said stiffly.

"When I heard Willis ask about your school stuff, I knew I should come get you."

She nodded, understanding. Leroy was not the brightest boy in the world, but when it came to her feelings or even other people's feelings, he was tuned in like a radio. She loved her brother very much and each would do anything for the other.

"Is Uncle Charlie gonna hurt you again?" he asked.

She corrected him. "Going to, Leroy. Use proper English. Just because we grow up here, it doesn't give us any excuse for bad grammar. Our father was a doctorate you know." Uncle Charlie loved to boast about how their father got his education and left their crack addict Momma for smarter women. To make Leroy feel better, Kim fabricated a story for her brother to make him think their father was some doctor. The story certainly improved Leroy's self-esteem. Often she told Leroy, "Dummies don't run in our family, Lee. If Daddy could get a college diploma, you can get a diploma from regular school."

Leroy wanted to be just like his daddy or at least the man Kimberly had fabricated. Her brother hadn't put two-and-two together to know Kimberly hadn't been old enough to remember when her father had been around their family since Kimberly was exactly a year older than her brother.

From what she knew of their father, which Uncle Charles sometimes told her in a drunken stupor, her father had tried desperately to stay and support their mother, but she continued to sneak out and get high or just go out and party, not caring about his feelings. Her father had been a possessive man and wanted to keep her mother on a tight leash or maybe he just loved their mother so much he wanted her to do right by him and their children.

Sometimes Kimberly would make up things about their father, putting him together from what she heard about him from Charlie and what she could only dream of a man she would want to be with. Even she would get confused when Leroy went on asking sprees about their father and his characteristics.

"He was real nice and thoughtful, Lee. He'd do the sweetest things for no reason at all. Everyone else thought he was a bad person, but he really wasn't. He had a temper, but when he loved, he loved as fierce as that temper inside of him." For some reason, Kimberly had a feeling their father didn't just abandoned them. She suspected their father probably didn't know where they were.

Whether he was drunk or not, Charles always became angry when she tried to get information from him about their father, especially their father's name.

When their mother could no longer pay to keep her things in storage because sniffed up her money, Charles had her mother's things thrown out of storage because he wasn't going to spend his hard-earned money "on some stupid junk."

That "stupid junk" could've been the key to Kimberly finding more about their father, but Uncle Charles was a selfish man.

When Leroy would ask for a description of their father, Kimberly would answer him with whatever she could imagine or what she wanted. "He's tall, just like you with nice muscles, very nicely built." Yet, she had never seen a picture of their father, so this was all lies, but it was all worth it when Kimberly would see that look of satisfaction and self-assurance on Leroy's face.

At fifteen, Leroy asked her when he was sure Uncle Charles wasn't around, "If I work at it, can I get me some muscles?"

"Sure," she encouraged him.

Leroy began a strenuous muscle building routine, even going so far as to fix up an old weight set in the backyard and work on it when he wasn't doing anything else. With her assistance, he got a job removing bricks and concrete materials from different construction sites at a small demolition company after school, without Charles knowing. Kim had forged his work permit and lied to Charles saying Leroy needed to stay late at school because of his learning disability. Uncle Charles never cared although Leroy's impressive size began to make him uneasy.

Especially when Kimberly's last "punishment" by Uncle Charles rendered her unconscious and when she came to, she found out Leroy had almost killed Uncle Charles with his bare hands. If Willis and a few more guys had not been present, Leroy would have done so.

The cackling downstairs brought Kimberly back to the present and now a new dilemma that seemed to involve her in one of Uncle Charles get rich schemes. Another chill went down her back because none of his previous schemes ever worked.

"Yeah, I just wished our daddy had stayed around and helped Momma out so we could be a big happily family," Leroy continued, as Kimberly crawled back into her bed.

"Together, we are a happy family," she assured him, taking his hand in her own. Their skin tones were the same caramel brown, but that would be the only similarity between the two of them. He had supposedly inherited his father's brownish-red hair and big frame, while Kim was an exact image of her mother with thick black short nape length hair in a feathery cut, big boned, and very slanted chocolate eyes that were very expressive.

"And Uncle Charlie never hurt me. He just wanted to make me understand that not listening to him would lead to pain. I should have followed his words and not my heart."

Speaking about the last beating was painful. She should have never fallen in love with Eli to begin with and none of the events following all of that would have happened. If anyone knew her, they knew she would never leave

Leroy. Eli didn't understand this. He didn't want anyone but her, and if she wasn't willing to let her brother loose, then he didn't want her.

So be it, but there had been the baby.

When Charlie found out Eli didn't have a penny to his name, he ordered her to abort the five-month-old fetus. Kimberly couldn't do that, but Charlie found a way to make her lose the baby anyway and break Kimberly's ankle, too. She had recovered from the miscarriage and the broken bone, but the pain of losing Eli and the baby had been devastating.

Charlie knew this and insisted she start up her schooling again, encouraging her to get her G.E.D., then go for her CNA so Willis could get her a position at one of Henry Ford's new nursing centers for the elderly. Willis worked there as a janitor and what he couldn't steal, he tried to find ways to get.

She had heard them speaking a lot lately about the wealthy that came there to live out the rest of their lives. Willis noted a lot of times how the old men just wanted someone to care about them in their old age. These old men wanted someone to stay by their side until the last breath left their bodies and then the center turned all that money over to the government because most of the "old coots" died without a will or even an estate to leave it to. "It's a darn shame these men can't hand me a couple of million or so, yet the government just waits for them to die, then git it all. It ain't fair," Willie had stated vehemently.

Charlie agreed heartily, and he had found a way to get those men to give their money to him. He would use Kimberly just like he had used her before in other situations, except this time she knew it could be dangerous. And when the crap went down, she would be the one getting in trouble with the law and knowing Uncle Charlie, she would be forced to serve the time, which he probably should have gotten a long time ago for all the stuff he'd done, but gotten away with.

All her life, her uncle used Kimberly in order to get things because Uncle Charlie didn't believe in real work. Anything to get a buck was his motto, which was why she never questioned why Uncle Charles adopted them instead of allowing the state to put them in a foster home. First, it was to get the supplemental aid the state provided Charles for keeping them in his home until Kimberly turned eighteen. Charles was still receiving some kind of disability supplement for Leroy, even though her brother was nineteen, and would continue to receive supplements until Leroy died or Charles miraculously decided to allow Kimberly to become guardian. Kimberly knew hell would freeze before Charles would allow someone else to get their hands on that money.

Charlie was capable of doing a lot of things (except working at a real job) and getting to more money was his ultimate goal. He would do anything to get his hands on a lot of money and like he said, 'the fatter the wallet the better the fart.'

Another chill went down her back.

"I'll make sure Uncle Charlie won't hurt you none, Kimmie," Leroy vowed.

Her mind was so deeply absorbed in the present situation Uncle Charles was planning she forgot to correct Leroy's bad English. "He won't," she assured her brother.

He bawled up his meaty fist. "I'll make sure he won't touch you again!"

She hugged him tightly. "Please don't threaten like that, Lee. It scares me, and Uncle Charlie said if you hit him again, he'd make sure you get put in a home and never see me again. Do you want that?"

Looking in his deep brown eyes, she knew Leroy was in a quandary. Protecting his sister was number one in his life, but if he weren't around, who would protect her?

To Leroy, Kimberly was the best sister in the world and a very good-hearted person. He had been protecting her since they were babies, and he would continue to protect her until they died unless some man came into Kimberly's life that really cared and loved her. Once that happened, Leroy could take a break from protecting, but of course start it all over again when Kimberly had children.

With the way their life was now, Kimberly doubted anyone would ever love her and accept Leroy in their life. Most people felt Leroy should be in a home, but she was never going to give her brother up and if it meant being alone forever, then so be it.

"Please Leroy. Promise you won't hit Uncle Charlie again or they'll take you away from me," she pleaded with him.

Reluctantly, holding her very close, he grudgingly said, "I promise, but it'll be hard, Kimmie. He makes me so mad when he yells at you."

"He yells at you, too."

"But that's just to call me stupid. It don't hurt me none, but when he yells at you, it hurts you so much. I can feel you hurting in me, and I don't like that at all."

Her brother was so wonderful. She kissed his cheek and promised, "I'm going to get us out of here. Now that I got my license, I can work anywhere. We can leave Uncle Charlie, but we have to save."

"I've been putting away the money like you told me to, but I'm running out of hiding places, Kimberly. He keeps tearing the house up and not telling us what he is doing next."

Uncle Charles would constantly change the house around every few months or so. To earn money, he did home repairs and loved to experiment on things around the house. His latest project was the basement. He was adding rooms and sorts. When Leroy was home, he would assist Uncle Charles, but most times Willis was around and Charles would much rather prefer to be in his friend's company even though Leroy never minded to work hard.

"I know and you keep hiding our stuff really good, Lee, because when it's time to go, I want to get out of here like the wind in the night."

He giggled. "Like the wind in the night." Leroy liked when his sister used descriptive terms to give him an understanding of what to do or what was going on. She always tried to make things easier for him to understand, and she knew he loved her very much for it.

Chapter 2

The John Kronk Boxing Center in Southwest Detroit was almost filled to capacity, but Jaelen Gates' mind was oblivious to the world around him as he creamed the punching bag harder and harder, wishing it was his father's face.

Jaelen enhanced the force as he connected his fist more and more with the bag to combat the demons he called his never-ending temper. He was angry and releasing his energy on the punching bag felt almost a little better. Stupid rules! Stupid contract! His father was crazy! Was he supposed to remain abstinent? How the hell otherwise do you prevent unplanned pregnancies? Only date sterilized women?

"Hitting it just a little harder might help," a sultry voice said behind him.

He turned with sweat drenching from his tight muscled body to look at the black eyes filled with mirth. Of course, she would find it funny. Any man in misery and Onyx Heart found it hilarious.

"You shouldn't be in here." He growled. Any other person might think twice about making fun of him or even trying to engage in conversation with him in his dark mood. Onyx was no ordinary person. Just looking at her exuding strength and arrogance, as she stood akimbo smirking again, clearly told anyone she didn't care what kind of mood anyone was in. She was here and didn't give a damn if anyone wanted her here.

"As if they could stop me?" She raised a black brow in amusement. "In any case, I was summoned by your father."

"Oh really? Does he have more restrictions? I can't eat now?"

She snorted at his cynicism. "I don't get paid to take this abuse, Jae. He has his reasons. When a man lays down the law like that, he is trying to make up for his past mistakes."

"By making me pay for them!" he screeched angrily. Jaelen was past the point of caring what attention Onyx and he drew. He knew Onyx alone drew enough by her dark beauty. "Fuck that! You are not about to stand here and try to make sense out that man's insanity. This is all that is. Insane!"

She didn't look the least bit affected by his yelling, but he certainly got everyone else's attention. Folding her arms over her chest, she leaned against the wall near the punching bag. "I am only an ear for you, Jaelen."

"You are one of his paid gooneys. Why should I even be talking to you?" he sneered.

"Because I'm your friend, too. Now are you going to talk about it or hit that bag until you find the right woman?"

"There is no right woman for me, Onyx, and you know it."

"Well if you're going to be pessimistic about it then of course you won't find her. Rest assured there are women out there who will put up with your foul disposition. Do you know in the past three years you have not once cracked a smile?" she asked teasingly.

His frown worsened. "There is nothing fucking funny."

"And you curse worse than a sailor." Her eyes rolled heavenwards in playful defeat.

"If I didn't know any better, I'd say you sound like a bitchy housewife."

"God forbid that to happen to me." She moved up to him and gently pushed him out the way. "And if you're going to hit the bag," she said, moving her fist up in a defensive position, "you need to follow through with your whole body." Quick as lightning, she hit the bag with enough force to puncture the leather casing. Some sand blasted out, almost getting in his eyes.

He knew Onyx was nothing to play with. Standing at only five-feet-four-inches, she could take a man out triple her size with her bare hands. She was black belted in several martial arts techniques and was a military expert on hand-to-hand combat. Weaponry was her second skill, but she didn't need a gun. She was swift and when she came at you, you'd better just surrender before she struck first. They'd been friends since he was seventeen and enrolled in the army. She was a year older, but already teaching classes to the new recruits. Many guys thought she was full of shit, but she wasn't. Just because she looked like she weighed one hundred-thirty, her punches could knock a man breathless or even kill him if she hit him in the right place. With the pitch black hair always tied up in a ponytail, a lithe figure, dark chocolate skin, and those shadowy pupils that looked anyone in the eye and showed no fear, Onyx lived up to her name.

Presently, she was out of the army and ran a security/detective agency with her brother, Lethal Heart. He was another force to be reckoned with, but Jaelen got along with him just fine once Lethal understood Jaelen and his sister were just friends. Lethal was even meaner than Jaelen. That was pretty mean, but this was why Jaelen hit it off with Onyx so well. She knew how to placate her brother and Jaelen very well, especially when their tempers were above the normal level. Onyx would dare them to find humor.

She was on this mission now although punching his only relief sour was not helping him either, which meant he had no call to be angry, and she was tired of standing there trying to placate his anger, but just wanted him to stop being angry.

Jaelen couldn't remember not being angry in his life, and he knew it was a downfall especially in a relationship. He was good at his father's body distribution business. Detroit was a city where citizens took care of themselves very well, sparing no expense. His father had cornered the distribution market in hair care to salons and boutiques. Jaelen had boosted their own line in this past year to a million dollars in profit, and it was looking positive for the rest of this year.

Yet, his father had too many incidences with women in the past that wanted to take him for his business and his hard-earned money. Jaelen's mother, Yvonne Stewart, had been one of them. She had purposely gotten herself pregnant with child to give Maxwell's wallet a hard time. It was all she was interested in from the get-go. Soon as the test results had come in that Jaelen was really Maxwell's son, Maxwell had a vasectomy performed on him at the age of twenty-five so women could not blame him for impregnating them.

Maxwell paid aplenty to Yvonne, but he steered Jaelen over to his side once the boy turned eighteen. All Jaelen's life, he had lived with his father telling him that sex was great, but only needed "to be shared with the woman you plan on being with for the rest of your life because all these other tramps giving it away are nothing but money-hungry whores. They'd do anything to get a piece of the business and their paws in your wallet."

Jaelen had been careful all his life. He lost his virginity at seventeen, yet all his carefulness still didn't pay off when ten months ago, Monica Williams, a good friend of his approached him to let him know she was four months pregnant. When Maxwell found this out, he hit the roof. He went absolutely ballistic.

It was Onyx that found out the truth to Monica's deception. She was hired to catch Monica in a lie. Six months ago, she recorded Monica at the Bloomfield Hills Country Club admitting to her sister, Jennifer, the baby she was carrying wasn't Jaelen's, but Robert Lampkin's, an ex-best friend of Jaelen's. Since Jaelen was worth more and was "cuter", Monica decided the paternity would belong to Jaelen. Maxwell had a blood test done on the child immediately after it was born a month ago, which proved that by ninety-nine percent the child was not Jaelen's

Still Maxwell set down rules for his son and put a clause on Jaelen's ownership of the company. His father decided to divide the shares of Gates Distribution giving Jaelen forty-percent ownership. He could collect on the fifty-percent ownership that was put aside to be routed back into the company only if he did not have a child out of wedlock from an unplanned pregnancy before marriage. In the event if a child or children out of wedlock did surface while he was single, the off spring(s) would receive the fifty-percent ownership profit and control of the company at eighteen years of age. Ten percent of the company's stock would stay apart of Maxwell's estate until his death when this would go to Jaelen. Any legitimate children could claim the profit from Jaelen's stock in a trust given to them at their twenty-first birthday.

This measure was taken by Maxwell to make sure Jaelen didn't sow his oats too plentiful because he knew his son cared a lot about the company and had seen the devastation baby mommas could wreck upon a business and a man's bank accounts.

Onyx wasn't done verbally lashing him. Her interest was piqued to know Jaelen allowed Maxwell's decision to affect him so much. "I agree your old man's as loony as a bird. He's been so screwed over with baby momma drama it's affected his decision to act reasonably in this situation. You're an angry asshole who can't accept Max is going to do anything and everything to make sure you don't make the same mistake he made. Get over it, Jae! He's not going to change, and all you can do is adjust. Use a condom. Hell! Use two for all I care. It don't make a damn difference, but you will not let this menial shit fuck up my day. Get it?"

This was a "mean-it" tip: Meaning she was past trying to coax him out of his anger. He had pissed her off, and she hated being pissed off.

"He's still a crazy asshole," he grumbled.

"Well, you're an angry asshole, and I still love you."

His frown disappeared. "You love me?"

"Shut up." Playfully, she pushed him and walked away.

He punched the bag one more time, forgetting Onyx had destroyed it and cursed as the sand this time successfully got in his eyes. Damn women! All of them. They were making his life miserable.

After washing the sand from his marble brown eyes, he took a nice long shower. Shaving his head bald had been a great advantage for him. Usually he wore eight cornrows straight back to his nape. Onyx said when he wore his hair like that it reminded her of the singer D'Angelo.

This was one of Detroit's hottest summers, and he hated sweating in his hair. Anyone could tell he was a meticulous person. He kept a neat appearance and had distaste for filth on or around his presence.

Onyx called it anal and a way to get women to look the other way. Once she told him, "If you weren't so damn ornery and anal, you'd be a great guy, Jae."

Jaelen wasn't trying to be a great guy. He just wanted to be left alone. Of course, he had needs, every man did, but emotional attachments to the opposite sex was a turn off for him. He didn't want to be with just one woman. Jaelen never believed just one woman could satisfy his needs. That would be impossible. Like Onyx said, who would want someone as ornery and anal as he was?

Chapter 3

Checking his temperature, Kimberly frowned, worried. She had somehow grown close to Wescott Hawthorne, a sixty-eight-year-old elderly man with Native American/African blood. He was so kind to her at times. She would just cry when she was alone at night, knowing she was only gaining his affections because Charles and Willis wanted his money.

It had taken six months to get West, who she fondly called "Big Chief," to propose marriage, yet she lied to Charles and told him Wescott wanted to procreate after the marriage. Even then his health was failing, but Kimberly lied to Charles about the severity of West's health. The elderly man sincerely wanted to marry her, and she wanted to grant him his wish. They had become great friends, and losing him would be terrible for her. Along with his failing health was his inability to procreate, but that didn't faze Kimberly. She didn't care about the money; Only about Wescott. They married on her eighteenth birthday in a nice private ceremony at the nursing home chapel where they had met. Kimberly had been working there for two months before the courtship started seriously.

During the courtship, she continued to work, but after the wedding, she quit to take care of him personally while she continued her studies to become a registered nursing assistant. They stayed at his St. Clair Shore home until a month after marrying when his conditioned worsened and he was taken to St. John's Hospital near Detroit. Tonight was one of the worse nights for him. An infection had taken hold of his only good lung and was slowly making him deteriorate into nothing. His massive shape had been reduced to bones in a few short months, and she worried she wouldn't be able to spend any more time with her husband.

He would love how she would read him stories and laugh at his jokes. She had heard Willis tell Charlie Wescott's net worth in cash on-hand was seven hundred and fifty thousand dollars. In addition to this, a nice million-dollar estate with the two-million-dollar home in St. Clair Shore, a yacht, and two percent stock in Traverse Bay Casino in Traverse City had just been inherited from an uncle that had passed away earlier in the year.

"Hello, Sweet Butterfly," West weakly rasped, opening his old brown eyes.

"Hello my chief," she teased back to make him feel better. His nickname for her always made her blush whenever he said it. "How do you feel?"

"Not as bad as I probably look. You stop that worrying." He knew this by her furrowed brow.

She couldn't help but to worry and fret. Seeing him like this was not good for her sensitive emotions. "Promise me something," he asked, when he was able to draw another breath. The cancer had spread fast in his lungs, and the doctor told them he had no more than two months to live.

"Anything, Wescott. Anything," she said through sobs she was desperately trying to hold back.

"You won't let my nephew get his hands on my money," he whispered.

He had never discussed a nephew before, and this news shocked her. "W-What nephew?"

Wescott was starting to fade away, exhausted by this little reality. "You can't let Junior get my money. T-Take me to your home, Sweet Butterfly, right away."

She had to get up close to him and put her ear to his lips to hear him with his withering voice being so low. "Why?"

"I've told the doctors I want to be released to my wife. Make it so." He was too weak to speak anymore.

Kimberly didn't know what else to do but call Charles. An hour later, Charles had Wescott's release papers approved for the morning if his symptoms improved and took the credit card Kimberly found in Wescott's personal possessions.

By the time Kimberly came home with Wescott in the morning, Charles had set up the bedroom. From the way there was an extra comfortable chair by the bed and some free wild flowers on the table by the window, Kimberly knew her brother had also helped get this room together.

Leroy was most likely at school when she came home so she didn't bother to look around the house for him.

Wescott was feeling much better, but still very weak. Charles purposely made himself scarce because he did not want the man to sense how much power Charles had over Kimberly.

After feeding her husband, who could only lie in bed, she sat by his side. "I know I'm going to die, Kim, but you must go to the Livonia Sperm Center. There, I have left samples of my sperm in the event I ran out of time. Go there and show our marriage certificate and get them to impregnate you. It's the only true way you will hold on to my estate. Junior is not really watching out for my death, but I can guarantee, he'll be looking me up in a couple of years. I have placed him with a tidy sum that should last for the next two years. This should give you more than enough time to carry our child in the event some of the sperm doesn't work."

She started to protest, but he shook his head.

"Tomorrow, Kimberly, go there," he insisted. She knew this was a serious talk when he used her whole first name. "I don't have much time. My spirit grows weak every minute."

She wiped the sweat off his now pale skin. When she had met him, he had been a tanned brown. He was considered a light African American male to anyone who didn't know his heritage well. His Indian blood showed in his light brown skin tone. He looked about a good six feet two, but Kim had never seen him stand. The wavy soft light dark cocoa hair blended in nicely with his soft brown eyes. She had seen the pictures of Wescott when he was young, and he had been a very nice looking young man, strapping and very handsome.

In most of the pictures, he had worn no facial hair, but in the photos where he did have facial hair, she thought he looked rather cruel and strangely dangerous, yet very exciting. If she had known him then, she didn't think she could have been attracted to him because he looked so threatening even when he smiled in some of the pictures. Kimberly would have feared him. She knew some people just looked mean and couldn't help it, but they weren't really. Wescott certainly wasn't. He was kind, sweet, and gentle.

"Promise, Butterfly, you'll do it," he insisted, seeing her reluctance.

"Maybe I don't deserve so much, West. Maybe he-"

He cut her off. "Kimberly, Trust me when I say Junior is a spiteful, greedy boy. He takes and takes, but won't give. He's a possessive maniac, and he doesn't deserve one dime of my money after squandering and gambling away his own inheritance from my brother's death. Will you be my dutiful wife and do as I say?" When she still hesitated, he seemed to read her thoughts. Taking her palms into his frail bony hands, he held them as tightly as a little baby would hold on. "For whatever reason you married me, Kimberly, I do appreciate you making my last days very happy. I wish I could have met you sooner, and then I would have heeded the dangers of what smoking would do to me and want to live longer. You've given me so much time and so many good memories to last me an entire lifetime even if I have only known you seven months."

Reluctantly, she made the promised knowing she would do everything in her power to keep it. Kimberly didn't like to break promises. "I'll do my best, West, now get some rest," she ordered, kissing his forehead.

He relaxed, knowing she wouldn't break her word. "Read to me, love. Your voice soothes my pains that no medicine can."

She blushed at the warm compliment and found his favorite book, Wuthering Heights.

In the middle of the night, Wescott died in his sleep still holding her hand. She cried until the early morning light. This was even worse than losing the baby and Eli in her life. She wondered how far she would sink in this world before better days would come her way. Would she be forever doomed to be heartbroken, weary, and sad? Would some man come to her and allow her to rest her weary head on his shoulders for once in her life and be strong enough to carry her through the worst times of her life? There had to be a silver lining to her dark cloud of life. If she waited and prayed, maybe it would come to her.

She just hoped the silver lining would come soon.

****

Charles helped her the morning after Wescott's passing to go to the funeral home to make the arrangements. Charles instructed the funeral director not to post any obituary. The family would take care of that. He had absolutely no intentions of placing any obituary at all, but the funeral director didn't know this and honored the request. After an exhausting morning, her uncle took her to the Livonia Sperm Center with Willis driving and then waiting in the car while Charlie went in with her.

Leroy had been left at home to clean the house up to remove everything that had to do with Hawthorne. Kimberly had put any really personal items in hiding before Hawthorne passed because she knew her uncle wouldn't let just let her keep anything.

After waiting for an hour, they met with Ms. Collins, the supervisor in charge of the center. The entire facility had just gone through renovations from a fire, and many samples were lost or misplaced. After searching for three hours, Ms. Collins came back with grievous news.

Wescott's samples had been likely part of the damaged samples, but they could not be sure because some of the samples records were damaged as well, and the process was taking longer than usual to match what was there and what was not there.

"When will you know?" Charlie demanded to know, striking a fist on the edge of the supervisor's desk impatiently.

Ms. Collins looked clearly uncomfortable answering Kimberly's uncle. Her eyes drifted briefly over to Kimberly who stayed quiet, almost disgusted about this whole situation, but her fear in Uncle Charlie and his impatience in this whole matter was very evident to anyone who saw her right now.

"We don't know. Call me in a few weeks and maybe then I'll have some knowledge of what is going on," Ms. Collins answered, trying to snootily disregard Charles.

Her uncle grumbled under his breath as he turned away from Ms. Collins. "And you call yourself a supervisor."

Kimberly was looking rather hopeful knowing they hadn't found anything because she wanted the entire scam to end now that Wescott was gone. She didn't want to be deceitful anymore. Right before leaving with Uncle Charles to go to the funeral, she had told her brother they might be preparing to leave soon.

"Get your coat on and let's get the fuck out of here," Charles barked, preparing to leave out the door.

Charlie had warned Kimberly not to divulge of Wescott's death to anyone. Continuing to say he was still serious ill could float with a lot of people. The less people knew of it, the less chance the news had of reaching the nephew's ears. No doubt he was probably as greedy as Charlie. Before leaving the director's office, Kimberly swiped up the woman's personal business card while Charlie had his back to her. Ms. Collins saw her and only winked. She stuffed the card into her pocket before Charlie turned around to wonder why wasn't she following him out. Bowing her head and avoiding eye contact, Kimberly mumbled a "Good day" to Ms. Collins and quickly walked out the office while Charlie followed.

Willis was eagerly waiting for them. Kimberly was glad to sit in the back seat away from the both of them. Sometimes Willis gave her the creeps by the way his large dark brown eyes looked at her from head to toe hungrily all the time.

Charlie let Willis know what was going on as soon as Willis started heading home. Willis wasn't too happy like Charles about the news the supervisor had given them.

"We might end up startin' all over again, but we won't be doing it at the same place. I got some other friends at other old folks' homes who won't mind getting a cut of the deal," Willis said eagerly.

Sharing wasn't in Charles' language, and he shook his head sharply. "We ain't about to start over with another fart. I can't wait that damn long, but I know we ain't gonna be gitting our hands on anything properly if she ain't got no baby. We start spending like we want to, and I think that nephew'll be alerted to someone's spending his uncle's money. We gots to make sure Kim's got legal claim, or the nephew'll get his greedy ass hands on my money." It was amazing how Charlie claimed the money as his so easily. "If he didn't fall ill so soon after she got married, I'd get her to fuck him, shit."

"So what'cha gonna do?" Willis asked.

"Let me think," Charles grumbled.

This terrified Kimberly the most. Whenever Uncle Charles had to seriously rack his brain with an idea, anything could come about. Anything that would definitely mean Kimberly was going to hate what he had thought up.

"I got it!" he suddenly exclaimed, turning around and looking at her, giving her a murky sneer. "I shoulda done dis a long time ago."

"What?" Willis asked, excited.

Charles cackled wickedly, facing the front again. "Let's get on home. We gots lots to do in very little time."

Chapter 4

Checking his Rolex for the third time, Jaelen impatiently drummed his fingers annoyingly on the table of Fishbone's restaurant. On Friday night, the restaurant in downtown Detroit was packed. He'd made reservations a week ago for Onyx's birthday.

Onyx was half an hour late.

His cell phone went off. "Yes," he answered with a growl.

Loud music played in the background as Onyx yelled back, "Get your ass down to club 2-K. I'm being detained in an emergency shift change, and when I get done, I want to see you." After hollering the directions, she hung up.

This was ridiculous. The woman could be exasperating. No doubt she was caught up in an assignment that was running over and decided to involve him in on the fun. Whether he came or not, it wouldn't matter, but she must really want to see him if she initially demanded for him to make dinner reservations for her birthday then demanded for him to come to the club. She knew he was leaving for Canada for one week on a forced vacation his father was making him take.

Getting into his red BMW Z3 Roadster convertible, Jaelen decided to meet Onyx at the club.

****

An hour later, Onyx was still at the club. She had stopped waiting for Jaelen to show up. Too bad. She had really wanted to speak with him before he left on his vacation. She would miss him whether he believed her or not. The ornery cuss.

Her brother came up beside her as she watched the club scene through a quiet raised booth in the back with one-sided mirrors. "Happy Birthday."

"Yeah, I guess," she mumbled.

"What's got your panties in a bunch?"

"You know I don't wear underwear," she snipped. Not once since his appearance beside her had she looked at him. Her black eyes stayed right on the crowd, which danced below her. "Did my replacement get here, or are you the replacement?"

"Yeah. Pete's here. Thanks for standing in on short notice until I could find someone."

Bouncing was just a small section of their agency, and Lethal was trying to phase this section out, but there were well paying clients who demanded only Heart's Agency.

Onyx sighed wistfully and looked seriously at her bullock brother. They were like night and day in sizes, but each possessed a dangerous skill that could be considered deadly to any human being. Lethal was two years ahead of his sister at thirty-five. Having a big brother was like having an unconditional friend in her life. No one could tell her anything bad about him, even if he was always bitching about something. They both possessed the dark looks. Lethal was just bigger and exuded muscles at six feet six, three hundred fifty pounds. His nickname at the gym they owned together with a friend was called "Trunk" because he reminded people of a thick tree stump with thick branches for arms and colossal thighs to hold up the tight body.

Yet, as large as he was and as angry as he could become, he would never harm a hair on his sister's head. She was the world to him, and he wouldn't allow anyone else to do anything to her though Onyx was very capable of defending herself.

"Whatever," Onyx shrugged nonchalantly. "Now I can go home and sleep."

"The party's just started out there. Aren't you going to enjoy yourself?"

"I don't feel like socializing."

"Onnie, what the hell is the problem?"

Onyx decided if anything, Lethal could keep a secret. "I was planning on a very nice birthday with a friend who promptly stood me up."

"Very nice as in what? And who is this friend?"

"Very nice as in getting my grove on and the friend is none of your business."

"Onyx," he warned in a very brotherly tone, which meant he was demanding to know.

She rolled her eyes heavenwards. "I might as well tell you since you're going to bother me to death about this matter." Pausing a brief second to take in his criticism, she mumbled, "Jae."

"Excuse me?" he exclaimed. "I know I didn't hear Jaelen Gates' name come out your mouth. I thought you guys were platonic." He gave her a cold glare. "Onnie, have you been lying to me about your relationship with this twerp? I swear I'll break every bone in his body if he hurt you."

"Oh yeah, right. No man could possibly do that to me." She huffed. "And you won't hurt anything on Jaelen." Onyx decided to start from the beginning. "Ever since his father's decree, he's been pent up like a bomb about to burst. I know he's been abstaining just out of spite, and Max knows this, which is why he forced Jae to go on vacation. He thought it would do him some good, but I know all that boy needs is some relief, and he'll be back to his old grouchiness instead of this new touchiness. He glares, growls, barks, you name it, and he's doing it more and more each day. He's a time bomb."

"Let me get this straight. You were going to give Jaelen some bootie to get him in a good mood? Sister, if bootie would cure that boy's cantankerous disposition, he'd need a quadruple dose in order to get rid of that foul monkey he carries around his back."

"Look at who's talking about somebody's moods. You've got nerve." She poked him in the chest. "And who's to say I wasn't needing some bootie, too, and he was the only one at bat?"

"You? Onyx, I want to say, not speaking as a brother, you've got men lining up to spend one night with you. You're much too fine to give it away to an obnoxious ass like that. Plus, you know you'd only mess up a great friendship."

She sighed, knowing he was right. "Well it was good he didn't show up. He was probably so pissed at me for dissing him for dinner tonight he flew right away to Canada when I didn't show up." She giggled to herself. "I can just see him now grumbling about women and some people having the nerve to stand him up."

"So are you going to party tonight?" he asked.

She still shook her head. "I'm horny as a toad, big brother." Onyx was never shy about what she wanted. "I think I'll go find myself a bootie call and settle down for the night."

"Take care of yourself," he warned.

"You should be saying take care of whoever I choose."

Chapter 5

The rough shaking was pulling her out of a very deep slumber. Kimberly groaned thinking it was Leroy again in the middle of the night. She had just gotten to sleep after being up for three straight days, and her body felt like lead weight.

Going from Wescott's last night at the house, to planning the funeral, to the constant worrying about when she and her brother would leave and the mysterious construction taking place in the basement, Kimberly had too much on her mind to sleep.

Trying to ignore the shaking, she dropped back into the darkness and serenity of sleepy land. Suddenly a hard whack on her leg slammed her awake abruptly, and her eyes shot open because her pupils couldn't focus. There was light coming from the hallway to light the room, but she couldn't find out who had hit her.

"Lee?" she asked, trying to look around and cursing her eyes for not focusing immediately.

"Git your ass up," Charles growled. His voice was coming from the foot of the bed. Her vision came in loud and clear. He was standing akimbo. Willis was now at the door, flipping on the light to her room. She groaned again as her eyes were forced to refocus due to the lighting change.

25

Uncle Charles never made night visits to a room. Once you were asleep at night, any dealings with him for that day were over until the morning. "Where's Leroy?" she asked to give herself some time to fully take in the situation.

"Leroy ain't gonna be waking up for a long while, little girlie." Willis sneered.

Looking at her uncle's scrawny friend who was so dark he looked purple with the lights on, she didn't like that lecherous look in his eyes. Moving her eyes slowly to Uncle Charles, she asked, "What did you do to Leroy?"

"We gave him a little extra to eat at dinner time, so he won't be interrupting what I gots to do to you."

Fear arose quickly in her rich dark chocolate eyes. "What are you going to do to me?"

Sadie Thompson chose that time to come into the room. She was Uncle Charles' girlfriend for six years, but on the side, she was also a prostitute when she needed a little money. "Charlie, I'm all done with getting those clothes off with the scissors and I didn't even cut him none." Sadie was a big woman at five-eight, two-hundred sixty pounds, but she thought she was more beautiful than Eartha Kitt, which she looked as old as. She never told anyone her true age. She wore mounds of makeup all the time. Kimberly was inclined to believe the woman slept in make up because in all the years she had known Sadie, the older woman was never without it. Her hair was always in Goddess Braids bunched up on her head in a crown like fashion. Sometimes it was blonde, most times it was a mixture of black, gray, and blonde. "Did you tell her?"

"Tell me what?" Kimberly demanded to know, terrified for her life.

"Dammit, I was gitting ready to till you interrupted us," Charles said at Sadie.

"It ain't my fault you too damn slow. What's so hard to tell a girl she's gotta a good fuck waitin' downstairs?"

"Get the fuck out!" Charles ordered her.

Sadie stormed out the room, shouting more curses.

"What does she mean, Uncle?" Kimberly asked warily. "What have you done?"

"You and I both know you need to get a baby between your legs."

Kimberly noticed he was holding Wescott's photo album of pictures when he was younger and in his heyday tightly to his side. "I ain't got any more time to explain the matter. Sadie's here to help you, but I did what had to be done."

She shook her head. "I don't understand."

"Get your ass out of bed," he ordered.

Slowly, she stood up and reached for her robe while putting on her shoes.

"You don't need none of that! Get your ass in the basement." He grabbed her arm and pushed her toward the door. They passed by Leroy's room. Even in the hallway, she could hear his loud snoring and knew what Charles and Willis said were true because Leroy was usually a light sleeper.

"Everything is simple. You go down there, get yourself a baby, and it'll be all over before you know it. No one's the wiser and no one's gots to know."

She stopped at the top of the basement stairs. "I don't understand. How am I supposed to get a baby by Wescott if he's dead, and his sample is gone?"

"I found someone who looks just like the old dude when he was younger. Not exactly like him, but had that look about him when he was a young cat." He grabbed her arm and dragged her down the basement. She had come down here last Saturday, and knew instantly they had been back down there since then to rebuild. Where there had been open space, there was a large room built with a door. The walls were thick and she could tell a bathroom was inside from the attached sewage line on the side of it. Charles continued to speak. "It don't look like nothing's wrong with him. We destroyed his car so there wouldn't be any trace of it."

"It was a beauty!" Willis whistled.

"Yeah, but I bet the young cat is making payments for the rest of his life. You ain't got to worry none about what he gots to say about you gitting the job done 'cause when it's all over, he won't have nothing to say anymore." He stopped in front of the door with a small one-way mirror. "You have the option of listen to him rattle on, but you can cover his mouth."

She gasped as a red glow was filtering the room and an unconscious man was strapped down on a full-sized mattress. There were four poles sticking out the ground with holes at the top of them. On his wrist and ankles were handcuffs and the other ends of the cuffs were looped through the top of the poles sticking out the ground. He was splayed wide with his arms reaching off the side of bed and his long legs coming off the bottom of the bed. Four handcuffs were used because it looked as if Charlie had misjudged the reach of the potential victim's ankles. "He's tied down?! You tied a stranger to a dirty mattress so he could get me pregnant? How am I going to do that?"

For the first time in her life, she saw Charles blush. Sadie had followed them down. "Didn't that other buck teach you anything?" she asked gaudily.

"Teach me to rape a poor innocent man? Do you know we could go to jail, Uncle Charles?" she asked angrily. This was insane. "Who's going to take care of Leroy if both of us are behind bars for kidnapping?"

"That's why you gonna go in there straddle him until he pops his cork up in your pouch and do it until I feel like you've got a child up in you."

His description was gross, and she bristled. "I won't. I'm going to the police myself and tell them you've done this," she threatened, only thinking of Leroy's wellbeing and not hers

Before she could blink, his fist slammed into the side of her face by her ear, knocking her to the ground. The steel toe of his boot kicked her right in the chest, knocking the breath from her body.

Sadie came to her side using her own body as a shield against Charlie's rage. "You gonna kill her, stupid!"

Willis was trying his best to hold Charles back, but her uncle was much larger than the skinny friend. Charles was of medium height with a beer belly and strong enough to probably throw Willis out of his way if he really wanted to.

"You stupid bitch. I'll kill you if you threaten me like that again," Charles screamed.

Sadie tried to help her rise, but Kimberly winced and then almost passed out from the pain in her right shoulder, which hit the ground in her fall and now was out of joint. Sadie could see the joint sticking out awkwardly and carefully helped Kimberly to her feet.

Willis opened the door with a key and Kimberly stopped allowing Sadie to help her, doing her best to snatch away without hurting herself more.

"If you don't do it," Charlie sneered, "I'm going to send Leroy to a god awful place, and you'll never see him again for the rest of his life. They'll fill him up with drugs till he won't know what time of the day it is."

The tears welled up in her eyes and began to roll down her soft cheeks. "No! Please, Uncle Charles, don't do it." Her shoulder was forgotten, and she concentrated on her concern for her brother.

"Then get in that room and when Leroy wants to know what's going on, you'd better make up something good 'cause next time that boy even looks like he's gonna take a swing at me I'm gonna shoot him."

A large sob escaped her lips. "Oh Jesus, he's just a baby."

"Then get your ass in there!" he bellowed. "The sooner you get a baby in your belly, the sooner we can all put this behind us."

"I-I can't do anything! I'm on my period."

Sadie hand shot to her crouch to feel the thick pad. "She's right, Charlie. We'd better not give him a bloodbath."

Kimberly sighed in relief knowing none of them had any medical knowledge of how a woman's cycle really worked.

"Then might as well make yourself comfortable with him 'cause you ain't leaving till I know for sure a baby's in your stomach." His patience was short, and he shoved her in the room and shut the door, locking it immediately.

She scratched and clawed at the door, screaming for mercy with her one good limb, begging her uncle or Sadie – even Willis – to open the door. The window was just a mirror, but she could just imagine them all laughing at her.

Turning her back to the sound proof door and leaning against it, she slowly sank to the floor against the wall next to the door. She cried for Leroy to save her repeatedly until exhaustion overtook her and she fell asleep.

****

Pain pounded repeatedly in his temple as he slowly ebbed to reality.

He realized after a while the red glow wasn't his vision, but the lighting in the room.

Abruptly after this, he realized he was chained to some sort of bed. What the hell was going on? He tried to move his arms, but they were held taut by handcuffs. Looking down at his feet, his eyes widened in shock. He was naked. What the fuck? Who the hell would bind and gag him?

Please don't tell me this is some sick Stephen King novel and some crazed maniac will stand above me with a machete and slice me to death. He desperately tried to break free, but the handcuffs were tight, and the poles seemed cemented in the ground somehow. Damn!

Looking about the room, he noticed a bathroom in front of him with shower curtains to pull for privacy. Beside the toilet was a small sink.

The walls were clean and looked newly constructed. One would think it was built especially for him, except for the double handcuffs at his ankles.

His eyes continued around the room until they stopped at what looked to be a head slumped against the wall lowered. He could just make out the head belonging to a female, but he couldn't distinguish if she was dead, sleep, or unconscious and needed some type of medical attention. Whatever it was, he hoped she could help him out of this predicament.

Just as he was about to start mumbling at the top of his voice to awaken her, a door opened beside the female, which he had not noticed when he previously scanned the room, and a large burly young male entered with a boyish face.

Jaelen pretended to be asleep again as the boy hurried into the room, set the tray he carried of warm food on the table beside the mattress, then quickly turned away to go to the female on the floor. Jaelen was a bit teed he was being entirely ignored as if the boy saw a man chained naked every day.

Didn't anyone think it was strange? He wondered if Onyx realized he was missing? He wondered if anyone would notice he was missing? Of course not. Everyone would think he was in Canada for at least a week and wouldn't get suspicious of his disappearance until a week and a half at least when he didn't come back or answer his phone. If anyone knew Jaelen, they knew his cell phone was his life, and if he couldn't be reached any other way, his private number would ring in his side pocket, no matter the time or day.

As big and rough as the young man seemed, with tender loving care, he gently caressed the top of the female's head. A weak feminine voice softly called out something. Her head never moved.

The boy looked very worried as he kneeled down beside her. "Kimmie." He shook her arm.

She let out a piercing scream as reality slapped her hard. Holding her dislocated shoulder carefully, she blocked Leroy from touching her. She looked up into his bleak deep brown eyes filled with concerned.

Immediately, she remembered Charlie's words. "I-I'm fine," she lied, quickly reassuring her brother.

"No, you aren't!" he said angrily.

Jaelen, who was listening, could tell the girl wasn't a good liar.

"Why did he do this, Kimmie?" Leroy reached to grab her, but she knocked his hands away.

"Don't touch me, Leroy! I'm in a lot of pain," she ordered. Fighting the wave of pain, she assessed her situation and fought to control the bubbling hysterical tears that desperately wanted to spring from her eyes. "H-Help me to my feet," she ordered.

Jaelen could hear her voice quivering and wondered what was wrong with the woman.

The young man was amazingly attentive, and Jaelen had to wonder about their relationship. The boy helped the young woman to her feet. She was dressed in a light nightgown of an undetermined color due to the red hue of the room. And she looked under thirty, but that was as much as he could discern unless he opened his eyes up all the way. Her nape length dark hair was combed back and loose. She seemed very tired and weak.

****

It was easy to ignore the man in the bed once her brother was around and she concentrated at how much pain she was in

"I-I need your help, Lee," Kimberly said, gripping his arm for support. "M-My shoulder is out of place. Remember that time when we were young, and I fell out the tree and you had to put my shoulder in."

He nodded. "But I will hurt you, Kimmie," he said, worried.

She stifled a sob. "I know you don't want to ever hurt me. I love you so much, but I-if you don't, Lee, it will hurt even more. Please, honey. I need this. Can you help me?"

Lee listened carefully to her instructions and her orders to ignore her whimpers of pain. Instantly, he put the bone in place. There was a loud popping noise once he did it, and she almost collapsed from the searing agony pulsing through her shoulder, which shot through her whole right side of her body. Yet, instantly she could maneuver her right arm and heaved a sigh in relief.

Thanking her brother, she hugged him. "Is he upstairs?"

Leroy shook his head. "He's gone. Sadie and Willis are in the kitchen. He said I could bring your dinner if I was good and didn't do nothing, but stayed in my room." She knew Leroy hated staying in his room, but she was glad he loved her so much he would do this for her.

"You can't stay long or they'll get suspicious. Have you found a key yet?"

Disappointedly, he shook his head. "I'm sorry, Kimmie. I did mean to find it, but they always around and watching me."

She caressed his cheek, trying to comfort him. "It's okay, Lee. We'll get out of this. Did you bring something for me to change into?"

He excitedly went out the room to return two seconds later with a bundle of towels and another gown.

"No clothes?" she asked.

"Sadie gave me this only. She wouldn't let me bring anything, and I'm to take your other stuff when I pick up dinner."

"What about him?"

"I'm supposed to help you with him."

"Good because I don't think I can handle him alone." She cut her eyes to the bed now and met the cold eyes of the man. Her chest started to hurt and the urge to just throw up returned.

The man looked away as if to clearly showed her she meant absolutely nothing.

This man's proximity brought out a feeling of pure anxiousness and anxiety inside of her.

Searching between the clothes, Kimberly saw there were no underwear and no feminine napkins, but douches and even some baby powder and lotion, which meant Sadie knew her flow had stopped. For a day she had gotten away with not doing what Charlie wanted done, but now...

Disgusted, she looked over at the bed, and then turned away from it before her nerves crumpled and she became a crying mass. She noted the chili on the tray by the mattress and an idea formed quickly. "Leroy, remember the medicine I told you never to go in my room and touch because it will make you sleepy and it might make you die?"

Leroy nodded.

"I need you to get that and put it in the chili. Just half a bottle should do, but don't you dare eat a bowl."

"But I'm hungry," he whined.

"Leroy, don't you dare! Promise?"

He nodded yet again.

The door opened suddenly and Sadie stepped in. "That's enough visiting, Leroy, Kimmie's got work to do, and we wouldn't want to distract her, right, girl? You got so much work to do."

Kimberly said nothing to Sadie, but turned back to Leroy. He could read her eyes and nodded once more before leaving. Being this close to her brother had its advantages.

When Leroy and Sadie were gone, she held the clothes tight to her chest and went to the makeshift bathroom, pulling the curtains shut for some privacy.

****

By this time, Jaelen was incensed. Didn't anyone find it strange to see a naked man lying on a bed chained like a runaway slave?

Just as the young woman finished behind the curtains the door opened again, and the fat lady stepped in the room again.

"You taking all day on purpose, Kimberly?" the fat lady snapped impatiently.

"What do you want, Sadie?" the young woman asked angrily, almost crying. Jaelen could hear a lot of frustration in the young woman's voice.Matter of fact, she sounded as if she was on borderline hysterics.

Jaelen took note of their names for the police later on, if he lived through this.

Offended, Sadie said, "I don't know why you're getting so hostile with me. It ain't my fault you go on and let y'er husband die."

"I didn't! He was ill way before he met me, Sadie. I'm being hostile because you are a part of the horrible plot to take an innocent man, use him, then kill him. Do you expect him to just perform as if everything is all right?"

Sadie narrowed her eyes to slits and balled her fist. "You better make him perform, Miss High and Mighty, or Charlie won't be the only one smacking you around. Do whatever you have to do to get him. The quicker you get the job done, the faster you'll get out of this." Sadie moved over to the mattresses and looked down at the man who lay with his eyes closed. "Maybe after you're done with him, I can take him for a little ride before Charlie wastes him. He's got potential."

The idea disgusted Jaelen, and he couldn't help but allow his eyes to flash open to show his repugnance. Sadie cackled.

"Seems y'er new boyfriend's been listening. This ain't no dumb man."

Jaelen wasn't sure if the first comment about "taking a ride" was said to really irk him or just test to see if he was listening.

"Get out!" Kimberly snapped. "Just get out." Her tone was indignant and definitely stressed.

Sadie just cackled some more as she left, but Jaelen felt the woman was eyeing him like a piece of juicy meat she wanted to eat up. A vile chill went down his spine at the thought of that obese filthy looking woman trying to touch him.

Speaking of touching him, his piercing, marble-brown eyes shot over to the young woman at the end of the bed looking at him accusingly. She had the nerve to accuse him of spying! Wasn't she a trip?

"That wasn't nice," she exclaimed, dramatically folding her arms protectively over her chest.

His eyes slanted cruelly and instantly Kimberly was aware why Charlie chose the man. His eyes alone could sear her with heat. He had that callous look about him just as West's old pictures had been.

She couldn't do this! Not with his eyes pinning her.

Giving him her back, she looked desperately around for something. She had to do this. For Leroy's sake, she had to do this. There was no choice in the matter. Charlie would hurt her and send Leroy away. Picking up the nearest towel, she turned back to him, holding the towel behind her and slowly walking around the bed. Her heart pounded faster as she moved close to him as if he could get up and attack her.

Without that meanness about him, he would actually be quite handsome. He looked devastatingly handsome, even with the frown.

He strained at his bondage, but she only shook her head and put her free hand on his chest. "Stop," she pleaded. "You're going to hurt yourself."

He ignored her pleas and continued until he tired.

She stepped back and watched, mesmerized at the power and strength he utilized to free himself. All the fighting in the world wouldn't free him, but even when blood began to run down his arms, he still didn't stop until he was purely exhausted. A sheen of sweat had started all over his body.

"Are you done?" she asked simply.

He only glared at her, blaming all the tiredness and damage on her she figured because he had no one else to blame.

This she could understand, yet she still didn't like the ruthless look of him. It made her nervous, and she couldn't do anything when her nerves were too highly involved.

Get this over with, Kimberly, she told herself.

"All right, mister, I don't know how to explain this, but since you were eavesdropping, you probably have some idea what I have to do."

He looked even more angrily confused. His brow frowned even harder, and the cool room suddenly seemed much warmer to her.

She couldn't take it anymore and threw the extra-large towel over his face in a hurry and watched as he again strained to throw it off. The black linen was much too thick and large to remove by just shaking his head, but she figured again he was only doing this to show his resistance to the entire ordeal. She had a lot of resistance to this situation as well, but she had no choice. Yet, neither did he. She almost admired his fight and wished she could take some of it and put it inside of herself.

He fatigued again and she watched amazed at the sweat, which now covered his entire body. Her hand again went to his chest, and he stilled, becoming taut.

"You must understand," she barely whispered. "I must do this. They will hurt me if I don't." Kimberly gave into the temptation of letting her hands run down to the rippled belly and was amazed at how the muscles tightened under her contact. "You are beautiful," she said breathlessly. She blushed to herself, not believing she had said this truth out loud, but then feeling a little bit braver once she had confessed this. She liked how he made her feel, the strength and courage he seemed to radiate and how she could absorb his power.

Slowly, her hands moved over the perfect pectorals and Kimberly smiled as the muscles pumped and twitched under her fingers. Her exploration moved on to the broad shoulders.

"Eli never looked like this." She flushed again even though her words would never be revealed to anyone since Charles would take care of him afterwards. "What a waste."

To compare him to her ex-love had been cruel to Eli. This man couldn't help that he was a black Adonis from head to foot and could put almost any other man to shame.

As long as she was taking advantage of this situation, she decided to familiarize herself with the rest of his gorgeous body. The more she studied it, the more she found herself needing the touch of his skin against her palms.

His body recoiled from her touch, and she was glad his eyes were covered because she didn't know if she could take those hard, piercing brown eyes glaring and filled with disgust.

Kimberly had a man – a beautiful man – there to control and take some pleasure, even if it was only visually because she didn't think the physical act of sex was to enjoy.

She remembered Eli's kisses had been pleasant and his touching her chest had also been stimulating, but the actual act of "lovemaking" – if one wanted to deem it as such – had much to be desired.

Initially, she thought it was because it was her first time. In Kimberly's mind, she thought a woman was supposed to have a discomforting feeling for her first time.

She remembered every second.

Eli had begun by kissing her. Nice pleasant kissing, which was deeply satisfying, then his hands fondled her breasts, and she sighed, relaxing and allowing him to move in between her legs, feeling his hardness pressed against her.

"Oh Kim, I just can't wait!" he said suddenly, and then he pushed her legs open wider, and the most jolting pain shot through her groin. The pain subsided, but in all her life, Kimberly had never felt so detached with something concerning her body. Just watching him panting and feeling as though heaven had come to earth made her a bit frustrated because she thought she was supposed to feel like that, too.

Kimberly figured a woman couldn't possibly enjoy her first time because there was so much going on at one time – physically and emotionally – yet when the second time she allowed Eli to "do it," he did the exact same thing. It was as if it was the first time all over again, and she was further disappointed when she looked at the clock afterwards to note the dissatisfying routine had lasted no more than fifteen minutes.

Of course, he was allowed to do this over and over again because she began to feel maybe she wasn't supposed to enjoy it. Maybe women really did fake it to the partners they loved, and this was the sacrifice they had to make to be with a man.

Yet, she had to wonder why afterwards she felt a need … a strong need – as if something was unfinished.

In any case, they must have been doing something right because the desired effect was achieved. By the sixteenth time – yes she actually counted – she was positive that between the eighth and eleventh time she had conceived.

Actually, in all, Eli had "done it" twenty-nine times before he left her.

Jaelen could feel her hesitancy, and he prayed this meant she would stop. The damn towel covered his eyes well, and he was furious at her for making him endure the tortuous fear of "what-is-going-to-happen-next?"

Kimberly wondered a moment how was she supposed to accomplish her feat, but once she had spied on Willis and Charles watching an adult movie and thought it was hilarious to see the woman straddling the man like riding a horse.

She pushed the thought of remembering how the woman looked as if she enjoyed it because of course anyone would when they were being paid to do it.

Moving on the other side of the bed, she saw a thick leather strap with a buckle on the floor, attached under the bottom of the bed. Her quick thinking skills immediately kicked in, and she realized why Charles had this. It looked as if he'd intertwined several leather belts together to accomplish spanning the length he needed. She placed the metal end buckle on the bed beside his stomach and he jumped from the coldness.

He was doing his best not to be afraid, but she could understand his wariness. Quickly, moving back to the original side where she was facing the door, she grabbed the leather with the appropriate holes and kneeled on the bed. He scooted away as best he could, and Kimberly felt a little offended.

Abhorrence of her touching him had not occurred to her, but he did. Hastily, she yanked the buckle over his waist and looped the leather through almost too tightly, receiving a little pleasure from hearing him moan from the squeeze. He then realized exactly what she had done.

The fight in him kicked back in fast and he bucked around so hard she was knocked from the bed on her bottom. It was her turn to wince.

"It won't do you any good," she told him, rubbing her bottom as she stood. He tried even harder to get released. "I like this no better than you."

His head turned sharply to her voice and she could just imagine those cold brown eyes glaring daggers at her. Yes, covering his face had been a very good idea.

Shuddering nervously at the thought of seeing his face, she forced her mind to other things – like the task at hand.

Slowly, she leaned over his body with her back facing away from his head. She knew that if she sat on his legs he would easily be able to dislodge her again and throw her to the floor. Yet, since the buckle was around his waist, it was made difficult to knock her off when she turned this way.

Jaelen could feel her heat on his stomach. She felt about one hundred sixty to seventy pounds, and her thighs were very strong and gripped him as he struggled to fight. Suddenly, he went deathly still. Warm long soft fingers grasped his manhood and held him. He could sense a naïveté in her touch. No, she couldn't be that innocent to what she was doing. The woman looked about twenty-five. Not particularly ugly, but nothing to say she was a beauty queen. On the heavy side if one asked him. Yet, Jaelen had been so picky about women lately he couldn't really count on his eyes to discern if she was just really ugly or not.

Kimberly heard him grunt and almost apologized for squeezing too hard or maybe it was when her nail had flicked around the tip. Gripping the soft member firmly, she was a bit fascinated by its velvety smoothness. With her other hand, she rubbed the thick muscular thigh to see if he felt like this all over, but he didn't. There was brown hair covering his smooth chocolate skin and she was also amazed to note he took excellent care of his feet and nails.

Usually when she saw men's feet, they were horrendous, but this man had excellent grooming habits. Her eyes moved back to the member, and her curiosity peeked to the large orbs underneath, nestled between his legs. Rubbing the tip of her fingers over the skin of them, she was amazed to see they were cool to the touch and thought it was astounding how hot his body felt, yet these small spheres were not affected. She had studied the human body in school and until now, never believed a word the teacher said.

Her eyes shifted back to the silky shaft, which had grown in her hands and she smiled knowing he was only becoming like this from her touch. There was power behind this knowledge that was close to feeling as if she had conquered the world. The shaft was a beautifully-sculptured piece of dark flesh coming alive under her contact and she had to wonder how was she to accomplish her task.

She didn't remember Eli being like this. Although she never had a chance to touch him like she was touching this stranger.

When would she know when he was ready? He didn't feel that he had come to his full potential, but even at this stage he seemed rather large.

Gasping, she chuckled because she could feel his heartbeat surging and then actually see the veins appearing on the side of the now semi-hard member. The growth startled her into dropping it and her chocolate eyes were amazed at how the flesh didn't lay right back down, but pointed straight at her groin as if it knew where it was supposed to be. Kimberly figured that was the signal to let her know it was time.

Picking it up by the bulbous tip, she could see the blood pulsing under the velvety skin.

Becoming even more comfortable with the now fully hardened member, she gently scooped up the inflexible shaft, which pulsed even harder in her fingers. Kimberly felt a surge of exhilaration flowing through her. She loved how his shaft seemed to not care that he didn't want her, but defied his control and answered to her contact.

The man groaned in defeat as she praised the flesh for doing what she wanted it to by caressing her fingers across the pinnacle and delightedly chuckled as it swelled even more. Amazing! Had Eli been this long and thick?

She could grasp this stranger with both her fists and still have room at the bottom for almost another hand and his circumference was substantial; her fingers could barely tighten around him.

Releasing him suddenly, she pulled up her gown and positioned herself over him. She squeezed her eyes tight as she guided the swollen head at her dry opening and moaned painfully as she allowed her weight to lower herself on to him.

Tears swelled in her eyes, but she refused to let him hear her cry. She allowed several tears to fall from her chin to his thighs before she used her arms to wipe her face. The pain was so bad and her soft innards molded against his appendage like a tight fitting glove. She didn't stop until she was almost fully impaled on him and she couldn't take any more.

Jaelen felt the wetness on this thigh. His body was so alert right now; he could feel her own heartbeat racing inside of her through his contact with her. He wanted to know what the hell she was crying for, but that was neither here nor there. He cursed his traitorous flesh for responding so eagerly to her ministration. Being celibate for so long had made him highly sexually sensitive and his control weaken.

Kimberly wiped more tears away, which blocked her vision, gripped her thighs securely against his, and began to move up and down. She could feel more and more moisture enveloping around his firmness inside of her and the aching subsided as she slowly moved upon his body. Closing her eyes again, she pushed all thoughts out her head and concentrated on what she was doing, focusing on the "pleasant sensations" now building within her stomach, then she felt a throbbing reverberating from him and knew this to be him releasing.

Disappointedly, she stopped her motions and moved away when she was sure he was done. His body was still stiff, and she smiled to herself seeing the sheen of sweat covering his chest when she looked back at it and heaving as if he'd done a lot of work. How could he be tired when she had really done all the work? she wondered in amusement. Too bad when he is going to die. She would have liked to have known more about him and if he knew what was supposed to happen after those "pleasant sensations."

Going to the sink, she soaped the washcloth in the warm water and returned to the bed with a bowl left under the sink. Unbuckling the strap first, she let the belt fall to the floor. He was still rather tense, but she had done this many times to restrained patients and cleaning them came natural to her. This also gave her a chance to examine how the flesh began to soften and almost go to sleep.

He heard her chuckle again, and he allowed himself to relax even though he was spitting mad. He couldn't believe what had happened. Nor could he believe it was happening to him. They must know who he was and intended to steal a child literally from him to claim his fortune, then kill him and no one would be the wiser.

What would they do with him? What would they do with his child?

Damn! Not knowing his fate was making him even angrier, and he prayed with every bit of his heart that somehow, some way he would get out of there.

Once she was done cleaning him, she helped him relieve his bladder after she emptied out the bowl. She could tell he was embarrassed, but she remained distant from his feeling. Just as she was done with him and was about to begin on herself, Uncle Charlie came in carrying a sleeping bag under one arm. Sadie was standing at the door.

Charles looked pleased with her, and she had no doubt he had been watching. He laid the sleeping bag on the hard cold cement floor.

"Lay down. We wouldn't want too much spilling out," he said as he laid out the sleeping bag beside the mattress.

She obeyed laying and keeping her eyes from meeting Charles. She was upset and mad. This was crazy and she wanted to say so, but knew being by Charles' feet, it would be murderous to speak. Sadie picked up her old clothes and Kimberly saw her go in the garbage and remove the box where she had put the douche in.

"Should I take the towel?" Sadie asked.

Jaelen recognized that female's voice and shuddered remembering what she had said earlier. The male voice must be of "Charlie," who they were speaking of earlier, he concluded.

He tried to remember anyone named Charles, but nothing came to mind. No one who was close to him and be privy to his whereabouts, would do something so deceitful. He wished he could see something … anything! Where was the young lady? Why wasn't she speaking?

"No," Charles said. "Leave it." He looked down at Kimberly, who avoided looking at him. "Don't move! You ain't through with him. I'll be back in the morning, and you can do it a couple of more times before I go burn the old boy up like I did his car." He walked out the room.

Sadie followed and Kimberly listened for the door to lock, then she heard both go up the stairs and into the kitchen. The kitchen had a squeaky plank next to the clock near the entrance of kitchen leading to the living room. The lights were still on, and she knew what she had to do.

Getting up, she took the towel off his face and went to the bathroom. Jaelen's eyes readjusted to the room's red lighting to find her digging through a small plastic trashcan in the bathroom area.

Kimberly triumphantly pulled out the other douche bottle. Sadie had not realized her mistake by giving Kimberly a twin pack. Looking over at the stranger who saw her holding the bottle, she nodded her triumph at him, and then closed the curtains to hurry up and clean up.

Jaelen knew what the bottle was and wondered if after all of this, her trying not to get pregnant really set well with him. Any other woman would have gone with this plan, yet this young woman wanted no part of him. He almost didn't like that feeling inside of him.

After using the bottle, Kimberly wrapped it in tissue to hide it well. Coming from behind the curtains, she settled in the sleeping bag and lay down. She'd been listening intently to the upstairs footsteps and none of them sounded like Leroy's.

Pretending sleep, she heard some footsteps heading over toward the squeaky plank, and then coming down the steps. There was silence, then the lights overhead went off and the footsteps started back up the steps again, and over the squeaky plank.

Jumping up when she heard nothing, she felt her way over in the darkness to the bed.

Jaelen recoiled from her touch. She hushed him sharply. He cringed as her fingers felt up his arm.

Upset, she said, "I have to find a way to get you released. I am not going through that again, and I have no doubt after they drink and smoke till daybreak, they'll be down here to watch again. So you will have to put up with me touching you, sir."

He was almost insulted. Not only from her tone of voice, but the fact she had not enjoyed herself when he should be the one suffering.

Had he hurt her? Why would she be so against doing "that again?" He really wanted to ask her so many questions.

"You have to groan or moan if I'm hurting you. I have no intentions of taking off your gag and listen to your mouth. It's probably as cruel as your eyes." The last sentence she had muttered more to herself, but he had heard it from her being so close. She tugged on his arm, but gave up when it felt as if he wasn't even trying to help her in the least bit.

"Where are you, Leroy?" she asked herself aloud in frustration.

Stumbling to the sleeping bag, she prayed Leroy would come through before they came back. She hated being here, and she hated this man's presence. He was awful to be around. Even in the dark, where she couldn't see those knife-like, brown eyes glaring at her. Yet, she could still feel the coldness about him.

Jaelen strained to hear in the darkness; he was positive, however, that he heard crying. What the hell did she have to cry about now? He was the one strapped to a dirty old mattress and forced to have sex, which he still couldn't believe had happened to him. He was starving because he hadn't eaten when he was at the restaurant. He was also the one who was going to get burned up in the morning like his car. Damn, he loved that car.

Still she cried – a horrible sobbing he was sure had her shaking. This went on for a while until he fell asleep, hoping they would wake him before they set the bed on fire.

Chapter 6

Someone nudged her, and she opened her eyes slowly, dreading to see Uncle Charlie, but it wasn't. The person standing above her was a sight she praised the Lord for.

Hugging her brother, she pushed her tears out her eyes so she could see his wonderful face. His hands were filled with so much stuff.

"Where's everyone?" she asked Leroy.

"Charlie and Sadie had a fight before he ate, and he hasn't come back, but you know he never misses Matlock early in the morning.

"What time is it?" Kimberly asked worriedly. Charles was known to leave, stay out all night, but he always came home by the time Matlock ran on his favorite cable channel at five in the morning.

Leroy showed her his watch, which read twenty minutes after four.

She sighed and took the clothes he handed her. "Did you get a key?" she questioned.

"Only Willis' car keys. I couldn't find any keys to these handcuffs, Kim."

"Go upstairs and get the clock off the wall in the kitchen. I have an idea on something else, while I look around for something to get these cuffs off," she ordered as she began throwing off her gown and putting on the pants and

T-shirt Leroy had brought her. After putting on some sandals, she looked at the bed, which she had her back to while she dressed. He was awakened and looking very curious. She wondered how long he had been awake, but didn't bother to question him. Instead, she went out the room and looked around the basement for tools that could assist them in getting the man free.

Leroy had come back with the clock and at that same moment, Kimberly found a sledgehammer. They exchanged items.

"Start at his feet and see if you can knock the pole free." While he started, she went to the head of the bed and took his hand. The back of the analog clock, which had the date flip to today's date, had a smooth surface. The clock was stopped because Leroy had unplugged it in order to get it off the wall.

She pressed his hand on the back of the smooth surface then quickly took it back up to the kitchen and replaced it on the wall, but didn't plug it back in knowing Charles wouldn't notice it because he'd be too intent on getting the basement cleaned up. When she returned, Leroy had freed one leg and was working on the next leg. Her brother's powerful body went into each hit.

"Get on the bed and hold his other leg, Kim. Pull it tight to hold the pole steady. This might help in breaking the second one sooner," Leroy suggested.

When she crawled on the bed this time, the stranger didn't cringe she noticed. He must be realizing they were trying to help him.

With her back to him, Jaelen found the position familiar and cursed his manhood for also remembering the moment.

Just as Leroy hit the steel pole with the sledgehammer, Kimberly gasped, feeling the slight hardness under her buttock. She looked back at him accusingly and he tried desperately to look innocent.

She turned away, hiding her blush and encouraging her brother to hurry up. Leroy broke the second pole in ten hits. She crawled off the bed hurriedly and leaned over to hold the man's arm, doing everything possible not to make eye contact with the stranger. She had a feeling he wanted her to look at him, but she refused to do so. Not after that embarrassing moment. The sledgehammer needed almost twenty strokes to break the pole and its handle also broke at the same time.

Leroy took the head of the hammer and tried to pound at the last cuff, but the metal didn't dent a little. "We aren't going to make it," Leroy said hopelessly, seeing it was a quarter to five.

"Yes we are!" she said determinedly.

"This pole's really cemented in, Kimmie," her brother disputed.

"We have to try. They will kill him, Leroy."

"But at least we won't be here."

This was true, but she wasn't going to have the death of this stranger on her conscious. "It's the right thing to do, Leroy."

Leroy gave the metal his best hits, but nothing happened.

She whined angrily and huffed. Holding his arm tightly, she looked at Leroy intently. "Do something, Leroy. We don't have much time."

Leroy looked at the man who didn't look scared, but worried, and they both looked at Kim who looked only at Leroy. Because she was close to him and what her eyes were suggesting, Leroy knew he couldn't protect her if she was in that position, but he needed her to distract the stranger, which she seemed to be doing by leaning over him.

Before Jaelen realized their intentions, severe pain shot through his hand, then his arm and he wished he could die. Without thought, he swung his free hand in the direction of the pain, striking the first object his fist came into contact with.

Kimberly didn't see his other hand coming, but her nose felt the pain as she was hurled off the bed by the force of his punch.

Leroy pulled his hand free of the cuff then went over to his sister who had blood all over her face and chest by now. He grabbed the gown and handed it to her.

Kimberly was crying, but calmed herself down and felt for any breakage. There was none, and then she calmed her brother. "I'm fine," she said, pulling the gown over to catch the blood coming from her plugged nose. It sounded as if she had a cold.

"You're bleeding," he exclaimed, then turned to the bed ready to do more damage to the stranger.

Kimberly jumped up in her brother's way, knowing Leroy was about to attack the man. "He didn't mean to, Lee," she insisted, holding her brother back barely.

"Apologize," Leroy demanded.

The stranger was clutching his broken thumb to his chest. He'd ripped the duct tape off his mouth already and was sitting up. "Hell no," he snarled.

"He's just upset, Leroy. Please!" she beseeched her brother. "We don't have time."

Leroy stopped, feeling the insistence in Kimberly's voice. He went over to the pile of clothes he had brought in and tossed the shirt and pants at the man's lap. "I never forget." Leroy growled.

"Neither do I." The man sneered back, still holding his broken thumb.

"Come on, Lee," she ordered, pulling on her brother's thick arm until they were out the door and Leroy started up the stairs.

"Where the hell do you think you're going?" the man asked after putting on his pants and coming out the room grabbing a hold of her arm.

"Away from here and if you're a smart man, you'd do the same." She tried to wrench her arm away. "Let me go!"

"I won't. Not till the police get here."

"You stupid man! He'll be back any minute. By the time the police get here, there won't be a trace of you around. Now let me go. I won't be here when he gets here."

"No!"

"Let me go before Leroy hurts you!" she said.

"He won't."

She stopped her struggling. This stranger didn't know how crazy Leroy could get when he knew his sister was being hurt, but obviously she needed to make him see. Smiling wickedly, she said, "Just remember pay backs a bitch, mister." She looked up at Leroy who didn't even need to be told and hauled off, punching the stranger in his nose.

He jerked her arm back from the force of the punch, and Kimberly heard the bone pop out of place again. Leroy caught her before she lost her balance and fell.

Blood shot out the man's nose. "What the hell was that for?" he yelled.

"Get out of here before he gets here," Kimberly warned again as Leroy gently helped her up the stairs.

Jaelen didn't want her to leave, and it wasn't just leaving here, but leaving his presence. He had a feeling if she did he'd never see her again. His whole body ached and how he stood and moved around was sheer will. "You can't leave!" His voice sounded so desperate, and the tone peaked Kimberly's attention.

Kimberly stopped almost at the top of the stairs. Looking back at the stranger, she saw the intense look in his eyes. This had nothing to do with the police. This had something to do with what had happened between them. Keeping her wits about her, Kimberly met his eyes with a strength she had found within herself somehow. The cruelty was almost gone about him, yet there was something there that seemed ... wanting. She didn't know what he could want from her. "Our lives are in danger," she said slowly, hoping he understood. "He will do anything to make sure we are here to stay when he gets back. If I don't leave now, I will never have this opportunity again in my life. Do I make myself clear?"

Jaelen understood, but he needed her for some strange reason. "Then come with me."

She shook her head. "He'll find me and bring me back. I can't involve anyone. It has to be just Leroy and me."

"What if there is a baby?"

His tone of disgust was evident, and Kimberly remembered how her touch had sickened him. "Don't worry," she said, drawing on his cruelty. "I will make sure you won't be the father of my first child. I want nothing from you, and I certainly don't want to deal with you any more by having your child."

Jaelen's chest felt strange. He'd never taken harsh words like this before. Usually they went in one ear and out the other, but he didn't like her speaking cruel. It ... hurt him. "You don't mean that."

"I do! ""Leave me alone."

His callousness returned like a drawn weapon. "I'll find you and make you pay."

"You finding me is the least of my worries. I fear Charles more than you."

Leroy helped her up the stairs quickly. She looked back at the stranger one last time. The harshness was there, yet with him standing there topless and the pants unbuttoned at the rim revealing the V of hair coming from his groin, she couldn't help but be affected by the sensuality he exuded, even with a broken nose.

"Leave before he gets back," she warned, before stepping into the kitchen.

Willis was passed out in front of the television with the bowl of chili in his lap.

Leroy grabbed some bags he'd left at the door before heading in the basement, and then helped her out the door to Willis' white rusted Sundance. Leroy knew how to drive, and he knew Kimberly was helpless with her shoulder out of joint.

He started up the car after helping her get situated and drove off. "Will he be all right, Kimmie?" he asked, a little worried.

"He's a smart man. He'll leave." Kimberly pushed the stranger out her mind and prayed they would never be in Charles' clutches ever again. She really didn't care about the money, but knew they needed it in order to survive. "Did you pack my purse?" she asked.

Her brother nodded.

She would give the woman at the center a ring when they rested and see if she could assist in the process of finding her husband's donation.

****

Jaelen grabbed the shirt and the pair of shoes left by the large boy and ran up the stairs, just as he heard the car pull away. Cursing, he put the shoes and shirt on. He was going to heed her words and leave. There was a man on the couch and he went over to him and searched his person until he found a wallet in the jacket pocket. The man didn't awake, and he remembered her telling her brother to do something to the chili earlier. Whatever the young man had used had certainly worked.

A car pulled up in the driveway just as Jaelen stuck the wallet his back pocket. His heart raced and he looked for an escape other than the front door. He found the back door and quietly opened it just as he heard the front door open.

Once he was outside, he ran around in the darkness, staying close to the house until he was in the front of the house. He had to use the car to lean on to quiet his step since it was parked real close to the house.

His legs were wobbly, but fear and determination to live made him run down the street. The handcuffs around his ankles were tucked in the side of the shoes to prevent them from rattling.

Jaelen didn't stop until he was sure he'd run about ten miles from the house. He found a pay phone, positive he was in Detroit — somewhere because the area code on the phone read: 313. It felt like the Eastside, but it was so dark he wasn't sure.

A tired voice answered the line and the computer operator asked, "Will you accept a collect call from Jaelen Gates?"

"Yes," Onyx said, coming awake as she filled with curiosity.

Before the operator left the line, he was screaming, "Help me, Onyx. Come get me now!"

Chapter 7

SIX YEARS LATER

Onyx opened the doors to the federal courtroom. A lot had changed about her, but much of the same things she continued. The business she and her brother had started was fully loaded with cases. The security division was becoming a household name, and the school for martial arts had a two-year waiting list. The siblings had involved themselves in help setting up the Detroit public schools with its first boot camp type charter school. They also provided free self-defense classes for young women when the rash of rapes had terrified many females and parents on their way to school in Detroit a couple of years ago.

She still continued to wear black, representing her name well, but there was maturity about her. At 30, she hadn't aged a day and continued to keep herself in excellent shape.

Her relationship with Jaelen had taken on a twist. After his "kidnapping," he changed, becoming more distant and cold. He ran his father's business with an iron hand and had begun small takeovers of beauty supply stores and shops around the city. He was preparing to open his own shop and supply store, which would feature on the first front level a full line of the Gates hair and body care line. In the back of the first level and the entire second level, he would have a beauty salon and body-care facility complete with massages, pedicures, mud bath treatments and more. He was still planning the third and basement levels, but he had ideas in mind.

Jaelen was on his way up in Detroit's society. He was a bachelor and had firmly committed to being a scoundrel of the heart. He seemed unable to be caught. No woman seemed to catch his fancy, and his affairs were merely for his pleasure alone, nothing else. Onyx had heard on many occasions of Jaelen finding pleasure in a woman's arms, getting them all excited and ready for him, then leaving them wanting. It was as if he found some kind of sick pleasure hearing them beg for it and him offering no release.

Onyx worried about his emotional state. He'd gone to a psychiatrist after the kidnapping for about two years. Sometimes, she would catch him pondering when he was alone, and she had to wonder what he was thinking about. She wasn't the only one who worried about Jaelen. His father, though greatly pleased by his son's business life, was highly irate with Jaelen's personal life. Maxwell and Jaelen often argued consistently about Jaelen's behavior toward women and his one-night affairs.

Maxwell was ready for grandchildren and ready for his son to find some type of happiness outside the office. He didn't want Jaelen to be miserable like he had become in his old age.

Onyx's eyes searched around the filled courtroom and found Maxwell sitting behind Jaelen, who sat behind the federal prosecutor's desk. They were conversing privately, but broke it up when Onyx seated herself beside Maxwell.

Jaelen frowned at her curiously. She had been out of town for the past week and a half, offering no support to his situation and now that she was back had chosen to sit beside his father instead of him.

Onyx thought he had perfected the art of looking disgruntled all the time, but he always found new methods to frown in different ways. Amazing, she thought, wondering were there any categories in the record books for the longest frown. Jaelen would hold it for six years. The man had yet to crack a smile in her presence, no matter how ridiculous she had gotten.

Maxwell leaned over to her to whisper, "You did it?"

She nodded, knowing Jaelen was straining to hear what they had to say to each other. Maxwell only spoke with Onyx when he wanted something. Onyx knew this, but didn't care. Maxwell paid very well for her services.

She handed him an envelope, and he hurriedly opened it to read.

"Does anyone else know what you've done?" he asked excitedly.

She shook her head and smiled. If Jaelen leaned back any more, the entire bench would fall back. "I only said I would do my best. No one knows it's done. Everyone's safe."

"How will you make them believe everyone's safe?" Maxwell insisted.

Onyx patted her chest safely. "I have something to let them know." Don't worry, Max. Are you going to take the letter to him?"

Maxwell was purely frustrated and excited, a state Jaelen had never seen his father in before.

Maxwell went to the prosecution table before the judge came in. Jaelen was dying to know what exactly this was all about, so he turned to Onyx who looked innocent and tight lipped.

"Don't you even think about keeping something from me," he said, sneering.

She pursed her thin lips together stubbornly. "This is a need to know matter, Jaelen, and personally you don't need to know."

"I am the victim here. I deserve to know."

He'd been crying that for the past six years as if immediately she was supposed to be sympathetic to his situation, but she had heard it so much, it sounded like a broken record.

Smiling wickedly, she said, 'We're all victims, Jaelen, but at some point in our lives we must tell ourselves to get over it and go on with life."

"So bringing that son of a bitch to justice is wrong of me? I should have just let it all go?"

"Oh, no. Bringing him to trial was justice. Sending him to prison will be even better especially for your state of mind. You won't be satisfied until this is over."

"It won't be over until they are all behind bars."

"The other two are serving ten years for just helping."

Jaelen smirked proudly. Willis Johnson and Sadie Hutchinson were locked up for their participation in the kidnapping and raping of Jaelen Gates.

The judge would have slapped five more years for the conspiracy to commit murder charge, but Sadie and Willis testified against Charles on his case.

"I'm not just talking about them," Jaelen said.

When Maxwell sat down, he looked at Jaelen with a "don't-get-upset" look."

"What?" Jaelen demanded to know.

"This morning the defense entered their list of witnesses for the bastard. She's on this list."

"What?" he screeched.

Onyx leaned forward to calm him. "Jaelen, this isn't the time to lose your famous temper," she warned. "The prosecution couldn't get her to say a word all week long since she's turned herself in." Charles was pleading not guilty, and the defense would try to prove Charles had no idea what Sadie and Willis had done in his home.

"I'm not going to sit here and let her lie on the stand."

Maxwell huffed. "We all know her testimony, or whatever she says is key to his case. She could take the fall for him."

Onyx agreed. "He'd get off scot-free and she'd serve the time. Her brother won't be prosecuted because they said he was not competent to stand trial. He would go with Charles though."

Jaelen remembered her words. If she didn't get away, she would never get away from him for the rest of her life. Charles had her, and he was going to use her to his advantage and she would let him. Damn!

The judge entered the courtroom and the bailiff called the courtroom to order as everyone stood.

Onyx looked over at Charles, who was smirking triumphantly. She knew exactly what he was planning, but she had a few plans of her own. Sitting behind Jaelen was on purpose. His large frame gave her enough cover until she was ready to show herself.

This would be interesting. Onyx couldn't wait to see the expression on everyone's face when the trial started to go as she knew it would. Just as the defense began its opening statement, Lethal sat beside her. She smiled up at her brother, and he nodded back.

"I did it," Lethal said to her. She hadn't told anyone what she had done, except Lethal. She could never keep a secret from him.

"What took so long?" she asked, annoyed.

"I had to get the popcorn. This is going to be better than a movie."

Onyx almost chuckled as she looked to Maxwell and nodded. Maxwell moved over to the prosecution again to whisper something in his ear. The man nodded and Maxwell put a thumbs up signal to Onyx.

Jaelen glanced back at her with a "what-the-hell-is-going-on" expression on his face.

"At this time, the defense would like to present its first witness, your honor," the defense attorney said. "We call to the stand, Mrs. Kimberly Parker Hawthorne."

Jaelen's full attention followed the bailiff as he opened a small door by the jury stand and a slim woman entered the courtroom. He hadn't seen her since that night, and he immediately noticed a change. He looked away quickly to compose himself, but then looked in her direction as she was being seated and sworn. Her eyes were lowered to the ground, and he could tell she had lost a lot of weight. He remembered her as being heavy built. Her five-foot-eight height seemed not so awkward anymore, and she had come down from her size sixteen to a muscular-toned size twelve. Her hips seemed a little slim, but he figured it was maturity. If she'd had any children, he couldn't tell, but he desperately wanted to know.

The prosecution had hired Lethal to find her, but she had led him on a goose chase around the country for the past two years, then just last week out of the blue she turned herself in at the first precinct downtown with her brother. Leroy was then deemed incompetent to stand trial, and the prosecution dropped its charges against Jaelen's wishes.

Kimberly was denied visitors in jail and waited for trial. Every day Jaelen had read her guards' reports, which only noted the inmate cried at night when she thought she was alone.

He often thought of the night she cried until he had fallen asleep and wondered if she cried for her brother now like she had done before or did she cry for some lost love that was not at her side.

Jaelen had to wonder why Kimberly was being called as the defense's witnesses. He wanted to ask, but he had a feeling if he waited a few moments he would find out soon enough.

Kimberly kept her eyes lowered as she was sworn in and pushed her nervousness and dread away. Kimberly knew he was out there. She could feel his eyes on her. Don't think about it, she told herself. You are here and he's over there. He can't hurt you like he said he would.

As the defense began to ask her questions, she wished she could have seen Jaelen's face when she confessed she was a medical therapist in Davenport, Ohio and that she had twin sons born two years after leaving Detroit. She knew this was key that she said this, so he wouldn't think her twin boys were his.

The defense began to get to the important questions. He questioned first did she live with Charles during that year before Leroy and she left. She confessed truthfully that she had.

"Were you in the home of eighteen-seventy-five Westwood on the night of August seventh?"

She hesitated a bit, but said clearly into the microphone, "Yes, I was. I took a shower around eleven, then fell asleep while watching Jay Leno in my room."

"Do you know a Mr. Jaelen Gates?"

"I know of the family, but I cannot confess to having a personal knowledge of Mr. Jaelen Gates."

Jaelen gripped the bench because his temper was about to explode. Lethal took out his popcorn, and Onyx wondered if she should move near Jaelen so Kimberly could see her.

"Did you see Jaelen Gates on the night of August seventh, Mrs. Hawthorne?"

There was a pregnant silence around the courtroom as Kimberly took a deep breath and slowly lifted her eyes until they met those cold, marbled browns glaring at her. With his eyes alone, he could touch her with a feeling she hadn't felt in a long time. Fear. Even Charlie's lawyer couldn't scare her anymore. This man wanted to kill her and she could feel his hatred like the knife was already in her chest. As much as she wanted to, she couldn't break the eye contact with him, but she knew she had to answer the question. Again she was facing this man, forced to do something she didn't want to do. He wouldn't understand, just as he didn't understand the first time. I HAVE NO

CHOICE, her mind screamed at him, but she knew her thoughts, even if she had voiced them, would fall on deaf ears. He had one agenda. To get her.

Swallowing her fear, yet feeling it sink into her belly and make her body shudder, she licked her lips. Her mind reeled at what to do. She didn't want to say the words they wanted her to say, so what could she do? Her brain reeled with thoughts until she thought it was losing blood flow. The room began to spin. Her mouth had suddenly gone dry, and her head began to hurt under the strain, but she wouldn't break eye contact with him as she leaned forward to the microphone and spoke clearly, "No, I didn't."

"You bitch!" Jaelen bellowed, jumping over the banister that separated the lawyer table. Three bailiff's rushed forward to stop him as Jaelen fought to get toward her. "I'll kill you, you lying bitch!"

Kimberly jumped out her seat and pressed herself against the far wall, terrified and praying the three bailiffs could hold him.

The judged banged her gavel for silence and order. "Mr. Cross, if you can't control your party, I will dismiss this entire courtroom."

Lethal jumped over the banister and grabbed Jaelen out the clutches of the three bailiffs that barely held him. "Calm the fuck down," Lethal muttered in Jaelen's ear.

Jaelen allowed himself to be dragged to the back of the courtroom.

Kimberly was asked if she was all right, but she didn't answer right away. Not until she was positive the larger man who had grabbed Jaelen had a secure hold on him, then her eyes moved over to black familiar eyes She didn't know what to say or do right then.

The judge asked again if she was okay.

"I-I need to go to the bathroom, your Honor. I-I don't feel very well."

"We can dismiss for the day, if it would make you feel better."

Kimberly knew that was a bad idea. To go another day without seeing her children or Leroy was treacherous. "N-No, your Honor. I just need a small break."

The judge conceded. "Thirty-minute recess," she announced and banged her gavel.

Kimberly looked over at the seats to where she saw the familiar face, but she didn't see the person any more. Jaelen was still at the back of the courtroom, glaring at her hard. She followed the bailiff out the courtroom to a private bathroom. Even though the bailiff was a female, she opted to stand outside to give Kimberly some privacy.

Kimberly wondered how she could find a way to see the mysterious person if she was escorted from room to room. Suddenly, the doors to the bathroom stall opened and a woman stepped out.

Kimberly looked into the familiar, cold, raven eyes of the woman and was positive this was the woman that pretended to be a guard at the prison three days ago.

"We meet again," Kimberly said. She had so many questions, but since the woman was here and not where she thought her to be, if she had done what she promised it meant there was really no hope.

"They're safe," Onyx said once she saw the disappointment begin to show on Kimberly's face.

Kimberly brightened, but it was too good to be true. Nervously, not wanting the woman to think she doubted her, she asked, "How do I know they are safe?"

Onyx reached into her inside jacket pocket and pulled out three-baby booties. Upon handing them to Kimberly, the young woman gasped as if she were seeing a pot of gold. Onyx had never seen something so touching as the woman caressed each booty as if it were a precious gem, then she hugged Onyx who just stood there, not used to being hugged. Occasionally, Lethal would give her a noogie, but not this.

Kimberly apologized, seeing how uncomfortable the woman seemed. "I lost myself in the moment, ma'am."

"Onyx," she introduced herself. "They are all safe, and you won't have to lie anymore." The disgust was evident in her voice.

"But I never did," Kimberly said.

Onyx had been about to open the door so the girl could leave out, but stopped. "What do you mean, you didn't? Jae said you raped him."

"The lawyer is the one who messed up. Like I said on the stand, I was awake until a little after eleven-thirty. Uncle Charlie didn't wake me up until about twelve-thirty."

Onyx almost protested with the girl until she realized what that meant. The lawyer had made the mistake, which couldn't discredit Kimberly at all and made her still a good witness – now for the prosecution. "Let me talk to the lawyer. I think if things go right, you can see your babies and brother by tonight."

Kimberly smiled and almost wanted to hug the woman again, but suppressed her emotions enough to just nod. "Thank you, Ms. Onyx."

"Just Onyx, Mrs. Hawthorne. Good luck on the stand." This time she did open the door and Kimberly walked past her, out the bathroom. She told the guard immediately she wanted to see the judge in her chambers. There was a turn of events, and she didn't want to be the defense witness anymore.

Chapter 8

Jaelen sat at the back of the courtroom because the judge ordered him to do so. He couldn't help but become upset. Kimberly's honest testimony could prove all Jaelen had told the police was the truth.

When he'd initially gone to the police, by the time the district attorney finally believed what he had to say, it had given Charles enough time to clean up the basement, wipe down all prints, and remove anything that had to do with Jaelen's imprisonment. When the police were finally given the warrant to search the house, there was nothing in the basement but an empty room clean of everything, which Charles had told everyone he used as his new exercise room.

It was his word against everyone else, and one shadow of a doubt would free Charles from all the charges the federal government was trying to pin against him, which were kidnapping, conspiracy to commit murder, and rape.

His father had to plead for the judge not to fully dismiss Jaelen from the courtroom. This was the judge's condition if he stayed. Maxwell also informed him the judge had suggested to the witness to have a personal protection order placed on him as well for her safety.

"Did she get it?"

"She said she didn't need it. After today, you would leave her alone. She was positive after she finished her testimony."

Jaelen snorted. "She's that sure of herself."

"She called the judge to the chambers. There's been a turn of events, Jaelen." Maxwell was giving him that "don't-get-upset" look again.

"What?"

"She wants her testimony to be for the prosecution."

"So she can lie some more?"

Onyx came into the courtroom. "They're calling everyone to order. The judge is about to come in." She sat down beside Jaelen and assured Maxwell. "I'll stay back here with him."

Jaelen snorted. "I don't need babysitting."

"You do need control," Onyx snipped.

The courtroom again silenced as Kimberly entered from the back room to take the stand. Just as she came in the door, Charles was being told of her plea to the judge. He began to argue with the defense attorney. Their words became quite heated and everyone heard Charles when he said, "Don't let that bitch take the stand, you stupid mother..."

The judge banged her gavel. "Mr. Hoffman, you will silence your client immediately, or I will have him removed from the courtroom as well."

Kimberly sat down after she was re-sworn. She kept her eyes away from the direction of where Jaelen sat now with Onyx by his side, and Kimberly had to wonder had Onyx done this to help him. Whose side was she really on? That was neither here nor there because Kimberly just wanted her babies were safe, yet were they really? Had Onyx let him know she didn't just have the twins? If Jaelen knew this already, he would have been trying to get to her sooner. No one had told her he had tried to visit her in jail, but how was she to be sure?

She could feel his eyes on her. His presence was so formidable she couldn't help but feel his eyes on her watching every move she made and every emotion she felt, which was very evident on her face. Did he see her nervousness? Kimberly decided she would not make eye contact with him because she knew she wouldn't be able to fight her feelings for him.

Onyx whispered to Jaelen, "They're going to try and discredit her."

"She discredited herself by lying," he whispered under his breath.

Onyx didn't comment, positive Kimberly had not done all this to be discredited. The young woman was a quick thinker and would redeem herself soon enough. The only question left was if Jaelen was forgiving enough to hear what she had to say.

Once the courtroom settled down again, the defense stepped to Kimberly, now on the attack. Onyx could tell just from the man's akimbo stance in front of Kimberly, who seemed ready to defend her actions.

"Mrs. Hawthorne, you stated earlier you never met Mr. Gates at your home on August second?"

"Yes, sir, I met-"

"That will be all for this defense," he said, cutting her off.

Kimberly narrowed her eyes and looked at up at the judge. "Your Honor, I wasn't done."

"Your Honor, the defense has nothing left to ask this witness, and since she has not presented anything credible, I am asking for her dismissal."

"That really isn't for you to decide," the judge asked, a bit amused. "You can't discredit your own witness. You should have known before she stepped on this stand what she was going to say. It is up to the prosecution to discredit her."

"She is being a hostile witness."

"She is not, Mr. Hoffman. She has answered all of your questions."

"Correct, your Honor, and we wish nothing else this witness has to say go on the record."

Onyx knew if Kimberly couldn't finish what she said they could easily discredit her.

Kimberly interjected, "Your Honor, I didn't answer the last question fully because the defense didn't ask the question correctly. I wouldn't-"

Mr. Hoffman interrupted again. "There is no more for this witness to say, your Honor."

"Yes, there is," Kimberly disputed, ready to become quite put out at this man. Now that her children were safe, she wasn't afraid of his threats. Looking down at her hands, she squeezed the booties tight in her palm.

Jaelen saw her look down at her hands, and his eyes caught sight of something in there. She held the objects preciously and he was curious to know what it was that gave her some sort of strength to carry on.

"No, you don't," Charles said, standing up glaring hard at Kimberly.

She could see the threat in his eyes, but she was far from worried and would have protested again, but a voice in the back of the courtroom said, "Yes, she does."

All eyes turned to Jaelen.

"Sit your ass down before I do it for you," he growled.

Even Onyx was shocked. This was not the Jaelen she knew.

The judge banged her gavel again, almost flipping it out of her hands. "Both of you shut up." Glaring at the defense, the judge said, "I must take into consideration the witness' statement, Mr. Hoffman, and allow her to proceed. According to my papers given to me, Mr. Gates was kidnapped on the night of August second, yet the police stated that Mr. Gates was held until the morning of August third. Meaning that if Mrs. Hawthorne fell asleep during Jay Leno, she could have been awakened later meaning the next morning. Since the question was not asked properly, the witness does have the option to complete the answer."

"But, your Honor-"

"There's no buts about it, Mr. Hoffman. I understand that Mrs. Hawthorne may reveal information that may be detrimental to the defense, but no one told you to ask incorrect questions and at that point you gave Mrs. Hawthorne the opportunity if she so choose to offer information, which she does in order to answer your question correctly. The only way she can be stopped at this point is if Mr. Cross objects."

Everyone looked at the prosecution, who looked rather laid back and triumphant.

"No objections, your Honor," Mr. Cross said.

Mr. Hoffman did not look pleased at all and stormed back to his chair to argue again quietly with Charles.

"Mrs. Hawthorne," the judge said. "You may continue on with your answer."

Kimberly had not heard one word the judge had said. She was a bit thrown off track because her eyes were locked with those deep solid marbles soon as he came to her defense against Charles. There was that look again she remembered from the stairway that morning. She then began to remember when he had stood there with his pants unbuttoned, no shirt, and a broken nose.

"Mrs. Hawthorne," the judge called again.

Kimberly broke the moment and looked at the judge. "Y-Yes, your Honor?" she asked, flustered.

"You may continue with your answer."

She was too disconcerted to think straight. "Please repeat the defense's question."

The clerk typist repeated, "Mrs. Hawthorne, you stated earlier you never met Mr. Gates at your home on August second?"

Kimberly took a moment to gather her wits and then began to finish answering the question. "Yes, I met Mr. Gates on the morning of August third when my uncle Charles awoke me a little past one in the morning to go down to the basement with Willis and him where I was taken to a specially built room. Mr. Gates was handcuffed to a mattress on the floor, and I was threatened to rape him or risk never seeing my brother again."

The judge smiled, amused. "Since there are no questions from the defense, I am turning the witness over to the prosecution."

Mr. Cross stood as he asked his first question. "How are you sure it was one o'clock, Mrs. Hawthorne?"

"We walked by the clock in the kitchen, and I checked the time."

"Can you tell the court what happened after you were threatened?"

Kimberly began to relive that night to the crowded court, keeping her eyes on Mr. Cross. By the end of an hour, she had finished leaving out only the embarrassing detail of Jaelen becoming aroused when she was trying to help him become free and Leroy punching Jaelen in the nose.

"You stated you put the clock back on the wall after putting Mr. Gates' prints against it?"

She nodded. "If you check the police pictures, you will see there is an analog clock in the kitchen and the time and date has stopped."

"Your Honor, that would be federal evidence number twelve."

There was shuffling of papers. Onyx was passed a folder by Maxwell and opened the folder. Jaelen eagerly looked over also.

"If you check the clock on the wall and look a little below it, you will see the clock is not plugged in. Leroy took this off the wall for me. I took Mr.

Gates' hand and pressed it on the back of the clock to show he had been there at that time and place."

Onyx looked up at Jaelen. "Do you remember this?"

He frowned. Now that it was told to him, he remembered it. At the time it happened, he was so intent on watching Leroy with the sledgehammer, he didn't notice what she was doing to his hand. "I-I vaguely can remember."

Kimberly continued. "Mr. Lethal Heart of Heart's Security Agency with a certified fingerprint specialist can present reports that show the prints found on the clock are of Mr. Gates."

"Objection!" Charles' attorney said. "There's no proof my client was living in the house when those prints were found on the clock."

The prosecutor passed a page to the attorney and then the judge. "Your honor, this is a police report the defendant made five years ago about someone breaking in his house and the only thing stolen was the clock in the kitchen. Lethal Heart can come to the stand and admit the clock was taken by himself and willing to serve whatever punishment for the larceny if the defendant wishes to file charges."

"I'll allow it," the judge said smirking.

Charles screamed in frustration and tried to get out his chair. The bailiff caught him in time and tackled him to the ground.

Kimberly lowered her eyes, trying to hide her joy because at that point she too knew Charles couldn't hurt her or Leroy again.

Chapter 9

The judge dismissed court at three, and everyone would come back tomorrow for closing statements, but there was no doubt in anyone's mind Charles had been the leader of the entire kidnapping of Jaelen Gates. Kimberly was a pawn in his desire to get his hands on her deceased husband's fortune.

Kimberly was just glad because the prosecution dropped charges against her, and her own trial was dismissed. She was a free woman although Jaelen did have the option to request a civil charge against her and Leroy. She hurried out the courtroom, looking around for Mr. Heart, who had given the bailiff a note to give to her as soon as she stepped down.

Mrs. Hawthorne, meet me in back of the courthouse at three p.m. at the private entry. There is someone waiting for you. L. Heart.

Kimberly's heart raced as she saw a black Jimmy with tinted windows pull up and Leroy jump out. He ran toward her, and they hugged for dear life. There was no one around, so they had plenty of privacy.

He was rambling about how much he missed her, but she shook him. "Where are the babies?"

He pointed to the SUV, where Lethal was opening the back doors and three children jumped out and began to run to their mother. The tears of joy filling her eyes made it so difficult to see, but she felt all of their arms wrap around her and hold her tight. She was too happy to see all of their precious faces and kissed them repeatedly to show her love for them.

A voice cleared behind her, and she looked over her shoulder to see Onyx and Jaelen standing there. Jaelen's eyes were directly on her while Onyx looked amusingly at the children.

Using her body to block them, Kimberly immediately ordered Leroy to take them back to the truck to get ready to go.

Of course, Wesley and Thor obeyed because at four years old they adored their uncle Leroy to pieces, but Jason was almost six and tried to be protector; he didn't let anyone mess with his mother. He didn't particularly like the way the big man was glaring at his mother and tried to stand beside his mother to show the man his own frown of displeasure, but Kimberly was pushing him toward his uncle without breaking eye contact with Jaelen or putting any attention on her oldest son.

Finally, she had to practically turn around and snip, "Get to the car immediately, young man, before I become very upset."

"I don't like him, Momma!" Jason snapped.

"I'm fine. Now, please, go to the car."

Jason peaked around his mother's hip with the most vicious frown his five-year-old face could muster, not at all intimidated by this large man.

Onyx almost laughed, but suppressed her amusement.

Jason reluctantly stomped to the car while Kimberly turned back to Jaelen.

"Do you always have people wanting to protect you?" Jaelen asked, sneering.

"Do you always look like you want to kill everyone? If you would just get that look off your face, I wouldn't have this problem," she snipped, taking her upset over her son out on him.

Jaelen was taken aback by her tone of voice and almost struck speechless.

"Now, if you'll excuse me, I would like a private moment with my children and brother, but if you're going to press the issue of making all of this a civil matter, you can talk to my lawyer. He's handled all my husband's and my matters, so what's some more work for him?"

"You don't think I should take this to another level?"

"You can do whatever you want to do, Mr. Gates. The federal prosecutor even said I was an innocent pawn in my uncle's greedy scheme to get my husband's money."

He stepped close to her, narrowing his eyes to slits, but Kimberly didn't step away, yet her pulse raced hoping he wouldn't throttle her. "You may have fooled all of them, but not me. I was there."

"If you were really there, then you'd have seen the obvious. I had no choice. I can't begin to make you see you weren't the only forced because you are too stubborn and pigheaded to see anything else. I don't care what you do because I know I was also the victim. Good day, sir." She turned around to walk away, but he decided to grab at her arm to hold her there.

With the speed of lightning, she yanked at his hold, and Jaelen found himself flipped over her and onto his back.

Onyx's eyes grew wide as saucers. She couldn't believe the woman had studied karate.

Lethal couldn't help himself. His laughter was loud and raw.

Onyx had to bite her lip as she helped Jaelen up who looked even angrier.

"Good day," Kimberly said, again turning her back on them and walking away.

Jaelen had to fight with all of his control to hold back. He didn't want to be flipped again, but he also didn't want her to go away … again. Damn!

Lethal opened the front passenger side door for her and then sat on the driver's side.

"Where to madam?" he asked.

"St Royal Hotel downtown, please," Kimberly said.

Lethal nodded and took off. "He is rather persistent, but I really don't think you have to worry about civil proceedings bombarding your life."

"I am not worried. I am innocent and whatever he thinks he can do, I know I won't be affected. I'm sick and tired of people thinking they can use me to their means. What I did to him, I was forced. I regret it, and I hated every moment of it. Please Mr. Heart, just get me to my destination so I can take a warm bath and put this whole day behind me."

"Yes ma'am."

"Quit calling me ma'am. Kimberly will do."

He only chuckled.

Chapter 10

J aelen went to the construction site where his new venture was in bloom. His offices were finished, and he enjoyed coming there and working, but today his mind was not on his work. On the way there, Onyx drove him and spoke about the civil suit he planned.

"I seriously think you need to just drop it, Jae. She's been through a lot."

"And I haven't?" he asked defensively.

"I'm not saying that." She reached in her leather bag. "Read it and if you still decide when I call you tomorrow you want to continue to press civil charges against her, then so be it. I won't interject, and I will do everything to help you out, but I think what is in this folder," she handed a manila folder to him and continued, "will change your mind."

Jaelen had read it as soon as he sat down at his desk. This was the report Heart's investigator had written on his extensive investigation of Kimberly.

Her whereabouts for the two initial years were undetermined, but it was believed from her association at the homeless shelter that she lived on the street until the Livonia Sperm Center contacted her a year after her departure from Michigan because they had finally located her husband's donated sperm. She then disappeared after this to protect herself from her uncle and her husband's nephew, whom she had found out, issued a death threat against her.

There was a PPO filed against the nephew, Ainsley E. Wescott, signed by a Detroit judge two and a half years ago when Kimberly was four months pregnant. But too afraid the law wouldn't protect her from him, she left and went to Florida to hide. There is no documentation of any prenatal care after that, but she delivered two healthy sons at Tampa Woman's Hospital.

About three years ago, Kimberly's whereabouts were found in a hospital in Tampa, Florida where she surfaced to ask for aid for her three children.

The social worker reported that Kimberly was in the midst of an inheritance case with the nephew of Wescott Hawthorne for his estate, and she couldn't afford to live anymore on the income she was living on with three children and a disabled brother. She was working as a dishwasher in a homeless shelter at four and quarter, where she also lived.

To make extra money, she tutored the children and adults in schools while she also cleaned up the establishment. Upon getting the aid she needed from the state, Mrs. Hawthorne worked cleaning homes for a maid service, continuing her job at the homeless shelter, and also going to school to become a medical and nutritional therapist. She earned her degree in three years and moved her family to Davenport, Ohio, where she worked in Davenport General Hospital.

Only six months ago, the court deemed her the legal inheritance benefactor of the Hawthorne estate, but by then the money was gone from legal expenses and appeals, and all that was left was stock and houses and some warehouse storage facilities on Detroit's eastside. The Bellini Corporation took over the estate and assisted Mrs. Hawthorne in getting a very good price for the home and in buying some of the stock.

Along with keeping the warehouse business, she also kept the stock in the Indian reservation casino and now had opened up two accounts for her sons and put a majority of the profits from the casino she received in those funds as she continued to work at Davenport General Hospital. She took a family leave two months ago and was due to return by the end of the month.

Jaelen read the report again, but something didn't click right. It never mentioned the third child and where he had come from. Her whereabouts for the first two years was undetermined? She hid, of course, but she couldn't have born a baby all by herself on the streets, could she? Maybe the boy was a stray? No, he respected her wishes too much to be adopted. Maybe Leroy hit some girl up? No, the young man was just too childlike to even think of something so ridiculous.

The boy had called her Momma, but was he older or younger than the twins? Damn! Jaelen had not really paid much attention to him because he was so intent on giving Kimberly his full attention.

Going back to that moment when he had walked out the courthouse to see her embracing the three children, he couldn't discern his emotions.

Jealousy seethed through him, but over what? That other males were in her life, or that she was pouring emotions on others and not...

Why would he care whom she poured her emotions over? Damn, Jaelen, you can't get confused now, he thought. Six years you haven't thought ... much ... about her. An hour ... or two ... or five everyday couldn't count as much, could it?

Either way, she raped him and no one was going to distract him from what she had done. She had forced him, his body, to defy his own control and do her will. Her will...

What was her will now? Did she want something from him? Some of her last words had been that she didn't want anything from him and never would. How could he be sure and who was this other son?

Picking the phone up, he dialed Lethal's cell phone number.

"Heart on the line," Lethal said his usual greeting when answering his personal phone. Only close friends and his sister possessed this number, which he kept private from customers and others he didn't want to be bothered with.

Lethal had a short temperament when dealing with others who were not close to him on his own time.

"This is Jaelen. I wanted to know where Mrs. Hawthorne is residing at while in town. I know she won't be here for long, and I wanted to apologize for my actions this afternoon."

"How long did it take you to come up with that shit?" Lethal asked, not believing one word Jaelen had uttered.

"Look, I don't want to harm her."

"I don't want to see her harmed. I don't care what you are to my sister, but to me you aren't anything but a temper-tantrum throwing asshole. If you want to pick a fight with someone, I can find you in about five minutes and beat the shit out of you."

Jaelen was taken aback by this defensive stand Lethal had taken to him over Kimberly. What the hell was it about her that made everyone want to shield her from him. What the hell was it about him that made everyone feel they had to keep her away from him? This made him quite uneasy and almost guilty. "I said I don't want to harm her."

"Kiss my ass, Jae. You can't lie worth a shit. Mrs. Hawthorne isn't your type, and I don't want her to have to defend herself again against your mouth, and if you ever put your hands on her again, I'll make sure when you go down you'll need a stretcher to get back up."

"Do I have you to thank for teaching her that move today?"

"I wish the hell I did, then I would have told her if you'd especially touch her to make sure you didn't get up. Keep your hands off her."

"Is the pussy that good?"

Lethal swore up and down so loud Jaelen had to take the phone away from his ear. When he finally could hear Lethal's voice calm down slightly, he put the phone back to his ear with caution to hear Lethal still going on, "...stupid motherfucker wouldn't know a good woman if she smacked you in your face. Let me see you even near her, and I swear I'll break every bone in your body with my bare hands, you obnoxious, self-centered bastard!"

The phone line clicked, and Jaelen stared at the receiver. Good woman? That was a laugh. Obviously, Mrs. Hawthorne had decided to seduce Lethal to get what she wanted instead of just taking it like she had done to Jaelen.

It didn't matter, he had Onyx, and he just knew she would help him. Her number was on speed dial, and she answered on the first ring.

"What do you want, Jae?" she asked when she answered because she had caller ID.

"Mrs. Hawthorne's whereabouts."

"Oh yeah?" she said, as if she would readily give it to him. "She's at none of your damn business. Anymore questions?"

"Why do I have the feeling I am being pinpointed as some kind of asshole?"

"Because you are. I'm only being honest for your benefit, Jaelen. I can't allow you to hurt her."

He was now at his end's rope about this entire thing. "I don't fucking get it. What the hell is it about Mrs. Hawthorne that everyone feels they have to come to her defense?"

"That's just it, Jaelen. You don't get it, and you never will. You're a self-centered bastard who just doesn't get it."

Surly, he asked, "Have you had words with your brother recently?"

Onyx had enough of him and his victimized attitude. At first it was easy to look over it, but this man was beginning to really piss her off with his snide remarks and selfish manner. She decided to make him get the point. "I don't need Lethal's opinion of you to know who you are. We've been friends too long. I know you quite well without the opinion of others."

He didn't pick up she was peeved. "So we are friends?"

"Indeed."

"Then as friends, why can't you help me out?" he said this as if now was the time to be in his favor. As if she would be doing him a favor by giving him what he wanted. Onyx only wished she was face to face with him so she could light him up with her fist, instead of her mouth.

"Because your intentions for Kimberly are not the intentions I want for her, but you're so caught up with what was happening to you to not see what was happening to her. Don't you get it? She had no choice in the matter. The man was going to hurt her and her brother. He had every intention to hurt even her children if she didn't lie on the stand. Her children, you asshole. She defied him twice to help your ass when at any moment she could have been caught and beaten half to death.

"You don't get that she suffered at this man's hands all her life, mental and physical abuse. You don't get that she did whatever she had to do to get you free that morning. Oh no, not the great Jaelen Gates, all he sees is that some trick tied him to a bed, raped him, broke his nose and finger and then had the audacity to let him go and run from the law for six years.

"Well, she wasn't running from the law. She was running from her uncle because once he found her, he beat her so bad she had to go into the hospital for three weeks with broken ribs, a concussion to her head, a displaced jawbone, two black eyes, a busted lip and nose. All because she wouldn't tell him the location of her kids and her brother, and then she wouldn't take the rap for her uncle.

"He found them and beat her oldest son until she swore on everything that was holy to take the rap. You still don't get it? Then let me tell you what his lawyer's hired goons found women to do to her in prison-"

"Never mind," he said disgusted. "You've said more than enough and when you put it that way, I do sound like an asshole."

"Then you'll understand why I have no intentions of giving you her whereabouts, and she'll be heavily protected until she leaves town in two days because there are several threats other than yours going around to cause harm to her."

The line clicked; he couldn't believe she had hung up on him. He again was left staring at the phone looking rather stupid.

****

Onyx felt almost good hanging up on him. She stepped off the elevator at the St. Royal Hotel in downtown Detroit. Knocking on the appropriate room number, the door opened to Leroy who looked very worried. "I'm looking for Kimberly Hawthorne."

"She's in the bathroom, and she won't come out."

Stepping in the room, she saw the three boys sitting in front of the television quietly. The oldest gave her a curious frown, but that was it before his attention was again drawn by Nickelodeon.

Leroy led her to the bathroom door. "Kimmie," he said, knocking on the door. "There's a lady here to see you. Come out."

A weak voice muffled through the door. "L-Lee, I told you not to answer the door."

"But you wouldn't come out."

Onyx pressed her ear against the door. "Mrs. Hawthorne, my name's Onyx, do you remember me?"

"Miss Onyx ... I mean it's just Onyx, right?"

"Yes, are you all right?"

"I-I feel ..." There was a brief pause. "I-I ... oh God."

Onyx heard a lot of liquid splattering, and she hoped it was toilet catching it. Looking down at the lock, she pulled a bobby pin out her hair and fiddle with it. "I'm coming in," she warned.

"Y-You can't. I locked the … the … the door," Kimberly forced this out just as another round from her stomach decided to come up to join what she had emptied out since entering the hotel room.

Onyx closed the door behind her so no one else could see the distress Kim was in. She really did look horrible. Her eyes were bloodshot, and her skin could almost be deemed pale even though she was a dark complexion. There was a foul odor permeating the room, and Onyx went closer to see the toilet filled with vomit. She flushed it as Kim finished emptying her stomach.

"Not feeling too well?" Onyx asked obviously, sitting on the tub about five feet away from her after turning on the air.

Kimberly only shook her head, not wanting to open her mouth afraid something else would come out.

"Stress?" Onyx tried to guess.

Kim again shook her head.

"Jaelen Gates wouldn't have anything to do with this, would it?"

Her stomach lurched once … then again.

"Yeah, he makes me feel like that, too."

When Kimberly could catch her breath, she said, "Y-You don't understand. I'm not very good at confrontational conflicts." She couldn't help but to start crying, which had caused the initial sickness. Her nerves had been so frazzled by the time she made it up to the room she had started crying as soon as the bathroom door was closed, not wanting to let her sons see how upset Jaelen had made her.

"I think you did an excellent job. That was a pretty good flip. You must attend my aikido class. You'd make an excellent student."

Kimberly cried even more. "I never thought I'd have to use it."

"Well, you did and I'm sure your teacher would be proud. Now, please, Mrs. Hawthorne, stop crying. I can't stand it."

Kimberly couldn't help herself, and Onyx tried her best to comfort her, but it was very difficult when she had never been in the situation of trying to calm down a woman before. She herself had never had hysterics. This was so awkward to her.

Through her sobbing, Kimberly asked, "D-Did I hurt him?"

Onyx snorted. "That uncaring jerk? He couldn't be hurt, even if me and my brother decided to kick his ass."

Kimberly stopped crying to look at Onyx, worried everyone would try to do something all because they thought Kimberly was crying over him. "I'm not upset about him. I just can't stand to be confronted like he was doing. Please don't hurt him because of me. I don't think I could take the guilt."

"I think beating him down to a pulp would be good for Jaelen."

Kimberly wiped her eyes. "You're trying to make me feel better?"

"Is it working?"

"A little. The idea of seeing him beaten to a pulp literally would be very funny."

Onyx laughed a little. "Well, I think I could accomplish it if you wanted me to."

As tempting as it sounded, Kimberly shook her head. "As angry as that man makes me, I don't think I could have it on my conscious to see him beaten to a pulp."

"Oh, damn. I thought I was going to get some good exercise in today."

"You're pulling my leg again, aren't you?"

Onyx nodded.

A wry smile graced Kimberly's face, and then she burst out chuckling. "Thank you for trying to make me feel better."

Onyx passed her some tissue. "I came to check on you."

"Thank you for that, too. I never did thank you at the courthouse after everything was over."

"Well, a lot happened. It's understandable."

Kimberly stood to wash her face and brush her teeth after flushing the toilet an extra time. "I think I'll be leaving tomorrow. I want my life to get back to normal and get the boys in a real school. No more home schooling for them. I'm finally free. Although I do miss Detroit."

"Why don't you move up here?"

"I can't. Not with Jaelen here, and he's not going anywhere. He might see-" She stopped herself.

"He might see what?"

"H-He might see me and want to kill me again," she lied.

"No, he's your last worry, I assure you. If you change your mind, let me know. I know a lot of doctors who could be interested in hiring you."

"Thanks." She felt a whole lot better.

Onyx still considered herself Jaelen's friend, and she thought to express this to Kimberly by saying, "He wants to see you though."

Kimberly didn't need to be told whom Onyx was speaking about. She turned away to wipe her face, not wanting to meet Onyx's black eyes that seemed to see everything. "I don't want to see him."

"I just thought to tell you because he questioned me about your whereabouts. I only knew because Lethal told me. I should let you know Jaelen and I are good friends and that for some reason he wants to see you."

"It's good he has a friend like you. You seem like a nice woman, but I don't want to see Jaelen for any reason. I don't want to see him ever or have anything to do with him."

"Is that why you never told him about his son?"

Kimberly faced Onyx and immediately became defensive. "What do you mean?"

"I was born at night, not last night, Kimberly. I can see Jaelen in that oldest boy, and I'm positive Jaelen probably saw it, which was why he probably wants to see you."

"And as his friend, you intend to tell him?"

"As his friend I want to protect him from harm, which is what his father hires me for, but on a personal level, I know he can be an asshole, and I don't want him to harm you, in turn harming himself."

"Jason is mine. I carried him for nine months, I starved for two weeks to make sure he ate good and had a clean bill of health. I won't let Jaelen take my son from me. I won't." The inflections in her words were hard, and Onyx had no doubt in her mind this woman would do anything for her children's sake.

"He has a right to know."

"He has no rights. His name is not on any birth certificate."

"A simple blood test could change that."

"No!" Kimberly screamed and then covered her mouth as if she had cursed in church. That nauseous feeling was starting again in the pit of her stomach.

Onyx had not come here to have a showdown with this woman, but Jaelen would never forgive her if she allowed Kimberly to leave without making him aware he had a son.

"What if he signs a statement he won't try to take the child away from you? Would you give him the chance to at least see the boy?"

"I don't want him in my life. I want nothing to do with him, don't you get it?"

"You aren't being fair to Jason."

Kimberly turned away. This was all too much. Onyx was asking her to share her parental right with Jason. Her first-born child! A boy she thought she would detest, but learned to love unconditionally. No, this was her son, not Jaelen's, and she didn't want his father to be any part of Jason's life. She could find a good man. A man who would be able love and cherish her children as much as he would love and cherish her.

Jaelen could not be that man. He wouldn't know the first thing about cherishing her, and he definitely wouldn't know the first thing about being a good father.

"We are leaving tomorrow and if you really don't want him to hurt me, then you won't tell him – ever."

Onyx knew this meant she was dismissed. Leaving tomorrow her ass. She'd bet ten bucks this woman would be on the next plane out of town. "Fine, if you feel that way." She left as Kimberly began to brush her teeth.

Leroy came to the door of the bathroom.

"Pack 'em" was all Kimberly said to him before closing the door to take a shower.

He needed no more instructions. Those were familiar words to him and he moved the boys to do his bidding immediately.

Chapter 11

Jaelen sat practically in the dark by the time Onyx burst in the office looking as if she had run up the stairs to the fourth floor. Only the desk lamp was on in the large office, and she almost didn't see him sitting behind his desk in a black T-shirt and jeans.

His tone was still surly as he asked, "How can I help you, friend?" He intentionally emphasized the word, "friend" still upset about what she had said earlier.

"She's leaving," Onyx heaved. "What the hell is wrong with your phone?"

He didn't change his surly tone or unemotional mood. "Off the hook. I decided since all my friends think I'm being such an ass, I could do without friends about now. Who the hell needs enemies when I have friends like you and Lethal?"

Onyx dismissed his mood. "Get your ass up and let's get to the city airport. She thinks she's got me, but I paid a bus boy a bill to tell me her destination. The operator at the hotel told me she asked about the next flight out of Detroit to Davenport."

"Why should I care? Your brother has threatened me with bone breaking if I go near her again."

"This is important, dammit, Jaelen."

He shot out his seat, showing his true emotions. "Important? It was important when I wanted to speak with her, but did you care? No you just decided to shove down my throat what an ass I've been."

She snorted, now calming down, because he was being his usual jerk-self. "But you have been."

"That's neither here nor there. You are my friend, and last time I checked friends were supposed to help each other."

"I am helping you. I'm telling you where she is. Are you going to just stand there with your finger in your ass or get to the city airport before that stupid plane takes off?"

"Why don't we do one better and beat her there?"

Onyx smiled wickedly. Jaelen could be an ass, but he was also clever as hell. "Lead the way."

He stormed past her, picking up his phone to find Armando Bellini, who just happened to call him an hour ago and told him he was in town. They could use the Bellini's private jet to get them to Davenport before Kimberly stepped off the plane. He couldn't wait to see her face. He hadn't felt this alive in a long time.

****

Kimberly handed her bag to Jason. "Stay there, Jason, and make sure your brothers don't go anywhere."

Jason groaned. "Do big brothers always have to watch their little brothers?" he complained.

She smiled. Her son always came up with the most interesting question. She could tell he was going to be a bright young man if she encouraged him. "Yes, and they also have to be responsible for their mother's purse while she goes and tries to find the luggage. Stay by Leroy and keep an eye on him, too. You know he can act just as crazy as Wesley and Thor."

Jason laughed because he knew his mother was only teasing although Uncle Leroy could act pretty silly.

After kissing her son on the cheek, she took the escalator up to the luggage rack to find their bags. The trip was thirty minutes. It was totally impossible to lose their baggage that quickly, but after standing there for fifteen minutes and seeing the same luggage repeatedly, she surmised something was wrong. Going over to the luggage counter, she inquired about her baggage.

The man seemed not to know what she was talking about, and she filled out a report about the luggage, highly upset. Once she joined her sons and brother, they could tell she was not in a particularly good mood and just followed her out the airport.

Leroy almost knocked her down at her abrupt stop near the front doors.

"There's our luggage," Thor said as if no one else saw it either being loaded into a very long limousine.

Onyx leaned against the limousine, her black outfit going great with the color of the vehicle. Kimberly was wondering if the woman wore any other color than black. A few feet in front of Onyx stood her nemesis, looking good as usual in a black t-shirt and white jeans. His hair was corn-rolled neatly, but he still had that cruel look about him.

She looked past him back to Onyx who wore dark shades, so Kimberly didn't know if she was looking guilty. Of course, she wouldn't feel guilty. She was his friend. Kimberly wondered how deep was their relationship. Was she just mad because she had Jaelen's son? What was it to Onyx?

Kimberly ordered her brood to stay there as she stepped forward not really ready to confront Jaelen. Her stomach swirled nauseously. She hadn't been this sick, even when she had been pregnant. Jason tugged on the back of her dress.

"Momma, let's go home," her oldest son urged quietly.

"Soon, baby. Let me speak with Mr. Gates and then we'll go."

"I don't want you to talk to him. I don't like the way he looks at you."

At that point, she could have told him Jaelen was the worst demon in the world, but it wasn't in Kimberly's nature to hate. As much as she thought Jaelen hated her, she couldn't say one bad word to his son about him. "I'll be fine. Leroy won't let anything bad happen to me."

"But he couldn't protect you against Uncle Charlie."

"I told you Uncle Charlie's never going to hurt us again, and we do have Mr. Gates to thank for that."

"I don't want to thank him for nothing." Jason spat on Jaelen's expensive Italian leather shoes.

She gasped, not believing her son had done that. Without thought to what she was doing, she took out a piece of tissue and began to wipe off the shoe.

Jaelen only watched as she bowed at his feet. He almost took a little pleasure at seeing her like this. A plan began to form in his head, and he couldn't wait to get her alone and let her know his intentions.

"I think I like you like that – kneeling at my feet."

Kimberly stood up abruptly. "He's not like that. His teacher's think he's the sweetest. I don't know what's gotten into him."

"Most likely the stress of not seeing his mother for two weeks."

"Most likely." She raised a brow, wondering why he was frowning. "Is there a reason you followed me?"

"I happen to have business in Davenport."

She looked at him as if he handed her a load of bullshit.

He continued. "Onyx graciously told me you were headed here, and I found out your plane landed ten minutes after mine."

"What else did Onyx tell you?"

"That you were suddenly leaving Detroit. She said something about you not wanting anything to do with me. I find that hard to believe."

She was tired of his pretty words. "If you're going to throttle me later, you might as well do it now."

"Throttle you? I'm not one to hold a grudge, and Onyx was nice enough to point out to me I've been holding one like an ass. I can admit when I'm wrong, can't I, Mrs. Hawthorne?"

"What do you want, Mr. Gates? My children are hungry and tired and want to go home."

"That's why I ordered a limousine for them. I thought it would be nice of Leroy to show Onyx around this small town of Davenport while you and I have dinner."

At that point another limousine pulled up. Their bags were in the first one and that driver was ready to go.

Kimberly said with control graciousness, "No thank you. I think I want to just go home and rest."

Jaelen stepped forward a little bit more, but kept his hands behind his back to show her he had no intentions of grabbing her again. "I insist. I think meeting with me tonight will get out the way of a very long court case."

Her eyes widened with horror. Onyx told! He knew? "I really don't feel so well."

"I don't mind talking in the hospital emergency room, but I will speak with you tonight, Mrs. Hawthorne."

Why did she have the feeling every time he said her name like that his tone inflected some kind of disgust? "I don't want to speak with you. You can speak to my lawyer."

"They ruin the fun, but I assure you if need be we can call a transcriber who can get here within the hour with a stenography machine to type this whole conversation."

"I'm sure you can, but I don't want to speak with you at all. Whatever you have to say to me, you can say to my lawyer."

Jaelen insisted, "I don't want to. Now you can either do this the hard way or the easy way, Mrs. Hawthorne, or will I have to have Leroy thrown in jail for assault and battery because you know if I have to drag you to the other limousine he will attack. He already is waiting for the word."

She looked back at Leroy to see him intently staring at them and waiting for Jaelen to touch her. Closing her eyes, facing him again, Kimberly fought the bile rising in her throat. "This really isn't a good time. Can't I speak with you tomorrow?"

"No," Jaelen said emphatically. "I wish to speak now."

"Does anyone say no to you, Mr. Gates?"

"No."

"I'd like to go on record as being the first."

"It's noted, but you'll still walk your ass over to that limousine and plop yourself down in it, won't you?" he said knowingly. "I'll even be nice and give you a chance to tell them how Aunt Onyx is going to keep them company while Mommy handles some important business." Without even waiting for her to say she would, he turned and went to the other limousine. She wished she had a rock so she could flick it at his head, but Kimberly knew she wouldn't do it. Maybe she could get Jason to and just chalk it up as being a naughty child.

No, she couldn't be vindictive, and she certainly wouldn't teach her children to become like that.

Going over to her brood, she said, "Mommy has to attend to some business. Some very important business and Mr. Gates is going to help her."

"No!" Jason said emphatically, almost mimicking his father in tone and stance.

"I will be home late, but I promise I will be home."

"No!" Jason repeated, not caring what she was trying to say to placate the others.

She knelt at her son's eye level. After cupping his face and kissing his brow until that frown of his disappeared and only concern and love filled his eyes, she said, "I love you. I love you very much. You know this, don't you?"

He nodded too filled with emotion to speak.

"Then you'll be good and do as Uncle Leroy says. Onyx will be with you, too, and she also helped Mommy, so we owe her a great deal of respect. Promise me, Jason, you'll be Mommy's good little boy and be your best."

Jason nodded again and hugged her tightly.

Even though Jaelen was in the car and saw the touching scene, he had that nagging feeling inside of him that he didn't like the way she cared for those boys. Then the difficult brat had the nerve to hug his mother and glare straight at Jaelen as if he knew what his mother had told him was a bunch of shit. He didn't like that boy at all. He was too … smart. As if he knew what Jaelen was up to.

Damn brat!

Onyx watched as Kimberly went to the other limousine after having quiet words with Leroy and stepped in, blowing her children one last kiss.

Kimberly seated herself across from Jaelen, making sure her knees didn't rub against his long legs. "I'm not hungry and if I see any food, I'm likely to lose what's left in my stomach, so speak so I can hurry up and get back to my children."

"You want me out of your life, don't you?"

"Yes," she exclaimed.

Jaelen didn't like how serious she sounded. "I'm starving, Mrs. Hawthorne, and really don't care how you feel. Either take me to a restaurant or risk me becoming highly upset."

He didn't care about anything but himself, she told herself. "Peachies," she told the driver. "On the Grand Boulevard."

The driver knew where to go and headed in that direction.

"Talk," she ordered Jaelen.

"It can wait until we get to the restaurant."

"Do you try very hard to be this difficult, Mr. Gates, or does it come naturally?"

He didn't answer her question. Instead, he picked up his phone and dialed a number. "Hello, Mr. Hathaway, this is Jaelen Gates."

Her eyes went wide as saucers. He couldn't be talking to Mr. Arnold Hathaway the Davenport General Head Director.

"Yes, I've come into some funds, which I would like to donate to your fine facility. I have heard of the excellent work it has done with muscle therapy ... Ah yes, Miss Parker is a fine staff person. I understand this, but I also know your facility is in need of the building, which would expand your excellent facility. Tomorrow? Good. I'm sure she will understand. Thank you, Mr. Hathaway. I will be sending over the check in the morning." He cut the cell phone off and looked at Kimberly waiting for her reaction.

"What are you trying to do?" She asked confused.

"Ruin your life. Make you miserable. Make you pay," Jaelen said simply.

"For what?" she asked incredulously, filled with frustration.

Speaking as if she should have known this all along, he said, "Ruining mine for the past six years."

"What have I done to you?"

"Made me damn miserable. Do you know I needed two years of psychiatric treatment because of my emotional state?"

"I don't care."

"That's the problem. No one sees my side of this. No one sees that I was a victim. All they see is you and how helpless you pretend to be, but you aren't. You made it through six years of running and look at you. Fit as a fiddle and a good mother obviously to those boys."

Kimberly stated defensively, "I have worked very hard for my sons."

"See there you go again. Always trying to make people feel sorry for you. That's not going to happen any longer. You're going to feel sorry for me since no one else will," Jaelen stated.

She decided to draw on his sarcasm. "Why should I feel sorry for you? You're the one who had a good time. I did all the work."

"You will feel sorry for me because you'll have no choice. Just like you didn't that night and on the stand. You'll have no choice. You'll make me understand what is it about you that just makes my close personal friend want to protect me from you and you'll also become my own…" he tried to come up with a nicer word, but he couldn't. "Slave."

"I think you need to check the constitution. They outlawed that years ago. Have you lost your mind, Mr. Gates?" she asked.

"Oh no. I'm finding my sanity."

"And not making a bit of sense. You just expect me to do your will."

"I think it's only fair. I deserve one day of slavery from you in order to make up what was being done to me since if I prosecute you, I'll still be the bad person. I want justice from you one way or another, and if I have to make your life miserable for the rest of your life, then so be it, but what is one day of slavery to a lifetime of freedom."

"From you?"

"Yes," he answered.

Kimberly looked very wary. "Let me get this straight. You won't take me to civil court if I allow you to either make my life a living hell or become your slave for one day?"

"Either one, yes," Jaelen answered.

"If I do this, you won't bother me for any reason for the rest of my life. I won't see you for as long as I live."

"I won't bother you, but seeing me is another story. You can't possibly think I won't take advantage of you in the twenty-four-hour period, do you?"

Her mouth dropped open. "You don't want me?"

"You say this like I'm some kind of cannibal, Mrs. Hawthorne. I don't bite, unless you won't me to."

"Was that your idea of charm?" she snorted. "You don't want me like that. I haven't…" She blushed. "I don't do that."

"I find that hard to believe, but that's neither here nor there. You will be doing it come midnight, I assure you."

She hit the seat with her fist. "This is ridiculous. You can't be serious."

"As a heart attack, Mrs. Hawthorne."

Kimberly wanted to die of blushing, but she bit down on her tongue to stop the flush desperately wanting to surface. "Why after twenty-four hours will I want to see you? I think after being in your company for so long, you'd be sick of me. You certainly was before."

"There are more issues at hand other than becoming my slave for one day we need to discuss."

"Like what?"

"Well now that you are unemployed, I would like to know how you intend to care for those children?"

"I have reserves."

"Oh, yes, Mr. Hawthorne's money?"

"That and I know I can get a job."

"You know, Mrs. Hawthorne. I have some friends in high places, and I believe your money was in the First National Bank of Davenport, which is an entity of Bank One out of Chicago. Did you know this?"

"Why would I need to know this information?"

"Well, there's been a … how shall I say it … computer error in the bank's favor. Of course, I spoke to the manager and she assured me, she would get to it, but with it being a Friday and her vacation kicks in Monday, I'm not sure if she'll be getting to it too soon."

Her fist closed tightly and stiffly. "Do you always drive people to insanity?"

"I have a knack for it. How am I doing?"

"Quite well."

"Come here, Mrs. Hawthorne." He patted the seat next to him.

"I'm quite comfortable over here, and I haven't agreed to your slavery yet."

"I want to show you what's in store for you in the next twenty-four hours."

"I like surprises."

"Oh, you're going to be surprised all right, now get over here," he ordered, his eyes narrowing to slits.

Reluctantly, she dragged herself next to his left side and stiffly sat next to him, but refused to look at him. She kept her eyes straight.

He pushed a button to raise the window to give them privacy from the driver, and then he turned toward her. "Like I was saying, now that you are unemployed I have a rather interesting job offer for you."

She rolled her eyes heavenwards. "I don't want anything from you, Mr. Gates."

His right hand came to rest on her thigh on top of her hand.

Kimberly closed her eyes. He was touching her. Dear Lord, help her. Why was he doing this to her?

"Onyx pointed that out to me."

"What else did she tell you?"

"That you had something to tell me that was very important."

She looked at him, realizing how very close he was. His face was just inches from her and at this vantage point, he didn't look so … mean. Matter of fact, he was far from cruel looking and for some reason, she didn't remember his lips looking so delicious. They were covered up that morning. Bite her indeed. She had lost her train of thought again.

"Do you?" he inquired.

"What?"

"Have something important to tell me?"

Had his face gotten closer? Kimberly wondered. "Nothing I can think of right now." This was literally true because she couldn't think at all.

"Accepting employment from me would be very beneficial," Jaelen said.

"It would?"

"Yes."

She liked how he clearly pronounced the last sound on the end of every sentence he spoke. Did he know he did this? His lips were definitely very delicious. Biting her didn't seem like a bad idea anymore.

Kimberly jumped back moving to the far-left corner on the seat to get away from him. "I disagree. It would only make it difficult to live."

"Onyx said you did miss Detroit. I'm giving you a very excellent salary with full benefits."

Curiosity was killing her. "How much?"

"Fifty thousand to start with ten percent salary increments every three months, and end of the year bonuses. Moving expenses, a company vehicle, and free child care."

That was damn good for whatever the position was. "What is the position?"

"Manager of my newest venture. I read your resume. You took cosmetology in high school for two years before you switched to another vocational school to study to become a nursing assistant."

When he paused, she used that time to explain her sudden change. "More money was to be made in that field."

"Of course. You can never have enough money."

She didn't know if this snide comment was aimed at her desire to better herself back then or how she came to become the benefactor of Hawthorne's estate.

He continued. "You then went to several colleges to finish your medical therapist degree and minored in two fields, nutritional and business management. You'd be perfect for my new company."

"I don't have any managing skills."

"You don't need it. You just have to sit there and make sure the managers do their job and the clients are happy."

The limousine stopped. "Would you care to talk about it more over dinner?"

"I'm really not hungry," she insisted. "I'm even more not hungry since being in your company."

"You can order water," he said. "You do drink that, don't you?"

Jaelen was being sarcastic again, but she couldn't take it as being cruel. She was the one now being difficult, but it was only because she knew he intended to hurt her. Maybe not physically, but his plans were to do something to her to make her pay for his anguish.

"Mr. Gates, I don't want anything from you."

"You've already stated that, but you have mouths to feed. This is an excellent opportunity. Mr. Hathaway at the hospital was very upset to see you leave, but he does understand an opportunity like that couldn't be passed up."

"But I haven't accepted it."

"Funny. He thinks you did."

"I don't want it."

"Yes, you do. That's selfish of you not to accept. A parent has to make sacrifices. Going to Detroit is not going to kill them. I grew up there and look at me."

"Now you see why I don't want them there."

"Have we a bit of sarcasm here, Mrs. Hawthorne?"

Angrily she accused him, "You make me like this. You make me say mean things and awful words. You just rub raw on people's nerves until they're mean and cruel just like you. You're like a parasite infecting everyone around you with a frown and horrible attitude. I don't like feeling like this. I don't like feeling so uncomfortable, and you make me feel like this."

Her words had done the same thing they had done on the steps. Actually affected him. Dammit! She's the one who was trying to sway someone. "You have dinner with me, Mrs. Hawthorne, and I'll do my best not to infect you."

"You can't help it. You're just cruel naturally. Can't you see I don't like your company?"

"I find that hard to believe."

"Because you're a self-centered jerk, of course, you can't. Why isn't it possible that I just don't want to be with you? You aren't all that and a bag of chips, Mr. Gates. Your looks may be devastating, but your personality couldn't spark a match."

"What are you trying to say?"

"Like the song says, beauties only skin deep, but ugly is to the bone."

"I'll have you to know, there are a lot of women who find me very attractive and would do anything for me."

"Good. Get them to be your slave. I'm sure they'll jump at the chance."

"I've tried, but it doesn't work. I don't think I'll stop being cured until I have you in my will, and I won't accomplish this until you allow me to be your master."

"Cured? Cured from what?"

Again, he'd somehow scooted close to her and she couldn't scoot away. He was inches from her face and those eyes mesmerized her. "I'm sick, Mrs. Hawthorne."

"This isn't new, you know."

His finger pressed against her lips to quiet her. "Six years, I've tortured women. Bending them to my will. Mastering the art of seducing the hardest women until I had them begging for my touch, then you know what I would do to them once I knew they would do anything for me?"

His palm now cupped her face and forced her eyes to keep contact with his. When she didn't answer, his eyes lowered to her lips, which quivered in nervousness. "Talk to me," he whispered urgently.

"I don't know," Kimberly answered his question.

"Leave them. Leave them needing and wanting me because I knew even if I took them, I wouldn't be satisfied until I could possess the one woman who made my own body forget who the real master was. Do you remember, Kimber?"

The nickname he made up made her whole body shiver. "Y-Yes," she whispered.

"How did it make you feel watching me respond to your every touch, when you knew I didn't want it?"

Her mind pushed the words out her mouth. "Powerful." She smiled a little, remembering the surge of emotions as he came to life under her fingers. "S-Strong."

It was his turn to sit back abruptly, and she realized he had done what she had done to him. Her mind defied her heart and allowed him to seduce those words out. She gritted her teeth in frustration. "I hate you!" Tears welled up in her eyes.

"Stand in line."

She took a tissue and wiped her eyes. "Don't do this to me. I've been through too much."

"What about what I've been through?"

"You got your justice. Charles is behind bars."

"Charles wasn't the one fucking me in a red lit room."

"I don't want to do that again. I hated it. I hated doing that to you. Is that what you want to hear? I'm sorry. I'm sorry I had to do that, but I had no choice. Don't do this. I won't be able to take it."

"You won't? You think I'm going to enjoy it? This is only to get you out my system. I can't go on with my life because of you. I sit up at night wondering. Wondering about what the hell was under that damn white gown that made me feel like that? Going from woman to woman trying to feel like that again, but I can't. I can't find one woman who made me feel like that."

"I didn't mean for it to feel bad. I was just doing what Uncle Charlie told me to. Why would you want me to torture you like that again?"

Jaelen was taken aback. She thought she had done something wrong? Hell no, but … she hadn't felt any pleasure in it, had she? Yes, she was right, she had done all the work, and he had gotten all the pleasure.

Dammit, score another one for her. She had made him feel sorry for her again. "Oh no, Mrs. Hawthorne. I won't be privy to your ways like you've wrapped Lethal around your finger."

"I haven't!" she denied vehemently.

"Then why does he want to break every bone in my body?"

She remembered Onyx's words. "A good whooping would probably do you a whole lot of good for your crappy attitude."

He couldn't believe he felt like laughing all of a sudden. Was this just natural for her or did she make an effort to do this? Was she only doing this to make him forget his present ire with her?

"I won't be swayed. I intend to carry out my revenge tonight once you agree to it."

"I don't understand your terms."

He sat back. "You'll do my bidding for one day. Twenty four hours, then you'll come work for me."

"I don't want either. I accept that what I did to you was wrong, Mr. Gates. I'll even accept the punishment from you on your terms, but I do not think I could stand working for you after everything. It would be unbearable."

"I insist or I'll find some judge in my back pocket and take those children because of an unfit mother, especially when they find out you do have a record for prostitution."

Her mouth dropped open wide. How could someone be so horrible? "I never prostituted myself."

"According to the Detroit police, you did on two accounts. Solicitation does not look good on a record for someone trying to prove they are a fit mother."

"You wouldn't!"

"You want to try me?"

Kimberly was really not feeling well. His revenge was to make her life miserable. Would she rather prefer the frustration of more courtroom drama or this? "I never prostituted. Charles made me trick those guys into thinking they were going to do something and then I'd run with the money. I never sold my body for sex, but one of the men happened to be a police, and I didn't run fast enough for him."

Her explanation meant a lot to him, yet he wouldn't allow her to sway him from what he wanted. "Think hard, Mrs. Hawthorne, because I've had six years to think about making your life miserable. Six long years to ponder how I could exact revenge upon you."

She leaned her face in her palms. This wasn't happening to her. He wanted her to be at his mercy. "How long do I have to decide this?"

"Until the end of this dinner." He opened the door and stood outside the limousine.

Kimberly came to the edge to step out and saw his hand being offered, but she declined and used the door to pull herself out being extra careful not to touch him. She almost forgot how rather large he was next to her five-foot-eight height.

Hawthorne would have been this height as well, and she wondered if her husband were alive now, would she be in this predicament. If he had been stronger, he could have possibly saved her from Charles.

Yet, her words to her son had been the truth. Jaelen had made it possible for her to escape with her brother from her uncle, and she was grateful for that, so granting his wish would show some kind of appreciation and if she really thought about it.

How could a man really recover from a rape?

Women had clinics and therapy, even support groups. Jaelen had his money and business to keep his mind occupied, but he had this demon inside of him. She had violated his body and he had no way to justify it in his mind. His friends liked her too much for him to drag her through the court again, taking away time from her children, and to hurt her physically would just be wrong. All he was asking for was one day of torture with him. Charles had abused her physically and mentally all her life. What could he do to her that had not already been done, that she couldn't live through?

After they were seated inside the restaurant, he had ordered what he wanted. Jaelen could tell her mind was very much distracted as she took a moment to tell the waitress she just wanted water. This gave him time to look at her closely. She had lost a lot of weight, but he could tell she had taken very good care of herself. Her hair had grown, maybe from the pregnancies, in a slight curl right above her shoulders and her face had matured even more. She certainly didn't look twenty-four, and he could tell she was wise beyond her years, yet innocent in so many ways. There was so much in life she had missed, mainly happiness, and he could almost sense the yearning pouring from her. Was this what Lethal and Onyx saw? A young woman in the prime of her life, sacrificing herself for those she loved and cared about?

Her head bowed slowly as the waitress came to take their order. He ordered the special. She shook her head when asked if she wanted something to eat or drink.

When the waitress left them, he leaned over to ask, "You are going to be hungry later?"

She shook her head. "I don't feel I could be comfortable with you, Mr. Gates, ever."

"I'm not a bad boss. My employees think I'm rather good, if I must say so myself."

"They won't have the history you and I have. It won't be the same, and I hope I don't let my personal feelings come in between my business, but dealing with you will be difficult on a day to day basis."

"We'll meet to discuss business. Once you have given me my day, I assure you there won't be anything personal between us. If you put that aside, you won't have a problem. Now do we have a deal, Mrs. Hawthorne?"

She met his gaze as she sat up straight in her chair. "I want the job in writing, signed and notarized."

"Onyx is a notary public. I will present these papers to you tonight. A friend's personal assistant has traveled with us, but she opted to stay at the hotel."

"I want everything you have offered me about the job in writing," Kimberly insisted.

He assured her with a nod.

His food was delivered, and he tucked his napkin in his collar. "Take the limousine back to your children. You need time to pack and do whatever mothers do with their children to let them know they won't be seeing them for the next day."

His tone of disgust caught her ear and she asked, "Didn't your mother kiss you goodbye whenever she went away?"

"Spending my father's money which was given to her for me was too big of a job for her. Letting the nannies and butlers raise her son was her forte."

Kimberly almost pitied him, but fought this feeling away. Having any pity upon this monster of a man would only mean more frustration for her. "Can I at least know what is planned for me?"

"No and Onyx has no idea either, so pressing her with questions will not help. She has no idea what I have planned for you."

Kimberly wondered if she let Onyx know the man plan to enslave her would Onyx disagree. She tried one more attempt to dissuade him. "Do you really have to do this to me, Mr. Gates?"

"I must. For my sanity, yes." He took her hand in his. "I must find some peace in me and having you at my will is more than enough."

What was one more day of what I have experienced all my life? she thought again. "Fine. Tonight," she told him aloud.

He almost wanted to assure her everything would be all right. She acted as if she were going to get her head chopped off. "Until tonight. Midnight."

"Midnight." She left him to his meal and sat back in the limousine. After telling the driver where she lived, she realized today was August second. Did he realize August second was the anniversary to his kidnapping?

Chapter 12

Once she left, Jaelen had time to ponder about the plans he had for Kimberly that night. In truth, he had no real idea what he would do.

On the way to Davenport, he and Onyx had discussed the job opportunity. Yes, he was feeling quite remorseful, but he still felt Kimberly owed him something. More than just an apology.

This was his opportunity to get his cruelty out of his system, pent up inside of him for the past six years.

Yet, now that he knew he had her willingness, he had not a cruel intention planned. This was awkward for him because he was a man who always knew what he was going to do, especially when it concerned women. Kimberly was different from other women. She didn't want his attention. She had experienced so much pain in her life to actually have him even try to scare her was ridiculous. He could intimidate her sometimes, he noticed, but he found she seemed to somehow draw upon his cruelty and would occasionally bite right back. This was what spurred him on, and he actually found it titillating to see her break her kind exterior to shoot right back at him. She had spunk of her own; she just didn't realize it yet.

His friend, Armando, called him on his Nextel at that moment. "How's Davenport?"

"Small," Jaelen complained. "Amazingly, they do have a city airport on the outskirts of town. Are you done in Detroit yet?"

"Oh, no. I have about three days' worth of work to do, so use the plane and my assistant to your advantage, I really don't mind. I was only just checking in on your comfort and if you needed anything else. Did you catch up with the young lady?"

"Yes, and she did accept my terms."

"So, why do I get the feeling you are not satisfied?"

"I've come into a dilemma. She's given me her complete willingness for a full day, and I haven't the faintest idea what to do with her."

"Revenge is an awful feeling, Jaelen, and I can't really understand what drives a man to exact it, but everyone has their reason." They had spoken of Jaelen's desire in depth earlier about why he needed to follow Kimberly when Jaelen had asked him for the use of the plane. Armando had thrown his assistant in with the favor. Jaelen had been a little bit more honest with Armando without revealing Kimberly's name.

Armando continued, "But tying her to a bed and doing the same does come to mind."

"Women are different. She forced me to take pleasure, Armando."

"True, their pleasure during sex is more mental than physical, unfortunately, but you have one day to seduce her mind into defying her heart. You've had six years of practice, Jaelen. I'm sure you can convince her. Raise her expectations, and then exact the revenge you've waited so long for."

Jaelen grimaced, finding gratification at the thought of accomplishing his revenge on Mrs. Hawthorne. He knew Armando would have the answers for him, and he should have called him first. Having a family full of men bent on staying single or exacting revenge on women from crimes of the heart would be his specialty. At least, one or more of the Bellini men were always holding a grudge against some kind of woman in their lives, at one point or another. "I will let you know how it goes."

"Please do, but don't let my wife know I've done this. She'd blast me to death."

"How is married life for a Bellini?"

"Rather interesting. She keeps me on my toes, Jaelen. I tell my cousins they really must get one of these." He spoke as "these" was something one could buy at the store.

"One of what?"

"A loving wife. She completely has me wrapped around her finger, and you know I'd rather be no place else. I find myself sick with puppy love when I realize this thought."

"I just find it sick." Jaelen didn't think it was possible to want to be wrapped around some woman's fingers. If that was love, he could very well do without it. Yet, just a year ago, Armando had been a confirmed bachelor having nothing to do with committing himself to the opposite sex until he was stranded on an island with Faith Patterson. She had captured his heart, and he never regretted becoming the first Bellini to marry.

His marriage was a momentous occasion since the Italian American Bellini men of Chicago were known to be millionaire-confirmed bachelors of the world.

"I'm sure none of them have taken your advice."

"Not yet, but they don't think I see they envy when Fay and I are together."

Jaelen had seen it, too. Even after seeing them together this past Easter in Chicago, they acted as if they had gotten married the day before. He noted how Faith always wanted to touch her husband, and in turn, her husband always wanted to be near his wife. It was almost sickening. Yet, even Jaelen had been affected by the intimacy they shared and wished ... then changed his mind because he figured what Armando had came every blue moon for any man, and in Jaelen's case, his opportunity had passed because of his disposition. "I do appreciate your advice in this muck I've gotten myself in."

"No problem, but make sure you understand it's off the record. I can't taint my law degree over a silly matter of advising my clients to restrain women. Fay might get jealous because I haven't done it to her although the idea about now does sound quite tempting."

Jaelen knew he jest, although his tone did start to sound serious. They cut their conversation to an end. Jaelen had a few ideas in his head by the time he got off the phone. He wasted no time in planning his seduction of Kimberly Parker Hawthorne.

Chapter 13

When Kimberly stepped out the limousine, this time allowing the driver to assist her, he asked her to tell Ms. Heart he would be waiting for her. Mr. Gates had requested Onyx come to the hotel to notarize some papers.

Onyx came to the door as soon as Kimberly stepped up on the porch. Surprisingly Kimberly noticed she didn't look worse for wear, considering other babysitters she had hired who looked ready to drop when Kimberly came in the door. Some would just look as if the back of a car had dragged them. She found it hard to believe three boys and Leroy had not made a dent in this woman's exterior. Kimberly was under the impression there was more about Onyx than meets the eye. This woman was in control of all she surveyed and let nothing ruffle her feathers.

"Is everything okay?" Kimberly asked worriedly.

Onyx only nodded. "They've eaten and are on their way to bed."

"You cooked?"

Onyx snorted as Kimberly walked past her to get in the house. "God forbid. I ordered Chinese."

Kimberly checked the time. Eight o'clock only? Onyx had gotten the boys to actually go upstairs at eight to get ready for bed when Kimberly would be still chasing them around the house to put on their clothes for bed. What had she done to them?

"I probably tired them out. We practiced some martial arts move in the back before dinner. I worked them out until they were sleeping at the dinner table. I should be asking you if you're all right."

Kimberly shrugged. "I'm breathing. That's the best thing happening to me at this moment."

"Then you'll tell me what happened. Did you like the job he offered?"

"It's very interesting, and the challenge of it seems advantageous."

"So you'll accept."

Kimberly wanted to scream 'I had no choice,' but instead she calmly forced out, "Yes." She didn't know whose side Onyx was on, and if word went back to Jaelen she hated the very idea of it all, there was no telling what he would do. Speaking of sides, she asked, "Why didn't you tell Jaelen about Jason?"

"And ruin the fun of seeing you say it?" Onyx teased, then shrugged. "Because I went out on a limb when I even said Jason was his son. I was in pure shock when you made my assumption truth, but now that I've spent time with the boy I can see you've done a very good job. Why hasn't he questioned about his father?"

Kimberly knew Onyx followed her to her bedroom, so she could hurry and pack for tonight. At least Kimberly had gotten a couple of hours of sleep prior to Onyx's arrival so she could have enough strength to deal with Jaelen. "I've managed to avoid questions of that nature, but I think he knows he was not wanted. I try very hard to get him to understand whether he was planned or not, he is here and that's all that matter. He was supposed to go to camp with ... some friends, but I thought keeping him at home for school, although a good opportunity for his education, Camping would be more beneficial instead."

Onyx noted her fluster and wondered if Kimberly was keeping anything else from her. She could tell the home had been just recently moved in, but she couldn't tell if there was more Kimberly was hiding.

"You intend on telling him the truth soon?" Onyx asked, stopping at the doorway to lean on the wall.

Kimberly began to pack an overnight bag. "When I take the job, I'm going to have to explain a lot. Being around Jaelen, I have a feeling my son will figure it out. He's quite intelligent." A look of wonderment filled her eyes topped off with love.

"He means a lot to you. Why is there no record of his birth at any hospital? I checked everywhere."

Kimberly looked slightly triumphant as if keeping the secret so long was an accomplishment. "Because I had labor in the bathroom of a nursing home in New Orleans. That's where Lee and I settled after running away from here the first time. The director and I became close, and she let me and Lee stay in the back of the home and helped me get papers on the birth two years after I had them."

"The twins?"

Kimberly shook her head. "I said him, meaning Jason."

Onyx frowned a bit. She was positive she heard "them," but allowed Kimberly to go on, wondering if she would slip up again.

Kimberly chose her words carefully. "It was a difficult birth. Even though I knew the process of childbirth, actually experiencing it all alone was terrifying."

Onyx had the feeling Kimberly was seriously keeping something from her, but didn't press the issue. She could find out all in due time. Shit always floated to the top sooner or later, and Onyx had a suspicion Kimberly's shit must be a load and a half. "Is that how Miss Collins contacted you?"

Kimberly nodded. If Onyx were up on her game, Kimberly assumed that is when the trail to find her became fresh. Everyone who had been trying to find her were waiting for her to do that because it was no secret Wescott's sperm was there if one did their research right. "I flew up here three months after having the birth and had myself impregnated. By this time, my husband's nephew was running out of money and was sniffing around the home. I was six months pregnant with these twins before he found out about everything."

"Has he confronted you?"

"I've never met him, but I know his name is Ainsley Hawthorne. He has this lawyer who sends my lawyer notices about how Wescott's inheritance belongs to him. I had several close calls that just didn't add up. I knew it wasn't my Uncle Charles because I was valuable alive to my uncle. Killing me would defeat his purposes to get off. I put a restraining order again this Ainsley Hawthorne even though I've never met him."

"So you think he's made threats against your life?"

"He would be the only one who could easily benefit from my death. He would be next in the line to inherit Wescott's estate. My children could be awarded to the state and no one would care. This was why I took self-defense classes. I needed to protect myself if there was danger near."

Onyx felt a twinge of pity for the young lady. She hoped she never had to be in this situation and even appreciated having a healthy brother whom was the world to her.

"I will return tonight, so you may enjoy yourself."

"I will never enjoy myself in that man's presence."

Onyx's mind was almost a million miles away. She really wanted to write down what she needed to take notes on her observations about Kimberly and she knew by the time Kimberly came back from her one day with Jaelen there would be some things Onyx would be positive of.

Kimberly stopped her packing to give Onyx her full attention. She remembered Jaelen saying Onyx had no idea what Jaelen had planned for Kimberly. She was almost tempted again to say something to Onyx, but she felt she'd already turned his friends against him.

Saying something about his blackmail would just make it worse for Kimberly. Jaelen was determined to carry out his revenge no matter the consequences. She also thought to find out just what kind of relationship Onyx and Jaelen had without being too conspicuous. Curiosity about Jaelen made her ask, "What is it about him you like as a friend?"

"I really couldn't say. He reminds me of my own brother, but Jaelen's worse. He grew up listening to his father spout about women and their deceptive ways. I think the only reason he and I do get along is because I'm not like ordinary women."

Kimberly had to agree.

"And I don't allow him to irk me. He's a controller. He always likes to be in charge of a situation. He hates being powerless. We butt heads, but in the end we're back to just agreeing there's no winning."

"And why haven't you been more than just a friend, since you get along so well?"

Onyx really had to think about this one. Six years ago, she would have slept with Jaelen and not thought twice about it. "I would say because Jaelen really does feel like a brother."

Kimberly believed her, yet that didn't mean they were NEVER going to sleep together. Onyx didn't look like a woman who would have reason to lie. Matter of fact, Onyx seemed like the person who loved to shock people with the truth.

Onyx bid her adieu until later. While on her way to the hotel in downtown, she hit Lethal up on his cell.

"Heart on the line."

"Are you busy, big brother?"

"Not too busy you. What's up?"

Onyx heard water running and females giggling in the background. No doubt her brother was "entertaining" company in his own spa with a waterfall inside his home. Lethal loved spending his hard-earned money on extravagant materials for his home on the eastside of Detroit.

"Ainsley Hawthorne, nephew to Wescott Hawthorne."

"Not much to go on."

"Contact Mrs. Hawthorne's lawyer," Onyx demanded. "And give me a call on anything you can find out."

"I love a challenge."

She could just imagine the gleam in her brother's opal eyes. "I know. Got a bigger one for you."

"Do go on. You've turned me on like a light bulb, sister dear."

She chuckled at his silliness. "Nursing home in New Orleans. Mrs. Hawthorne said she worked down there. Think you can find it?"

"That's all she told me."

"She was close to the director and she used to live in the back of it. Had her first son there."

"What about it?"

"I think there's more to the story."

"You think she'd give you a line?"

"I think she'd do anything possible to hide her life from Jaelen. I want to know."

"Are you helping that son of a bitch still?"

"He's my friend, Lethal, and I'm going to do whatever possible to protect him from harm. Even from himself and especially from other women who would want to do him harm."

"Mrs. Hawthorne doesn't want any part of him."

"But you have to wonder why. Besides the obvious, I think there's more."

"And you intend to find it out."

"Can you get it to me yesterday?"

Lethal answered without hesitation, "I'll do my best, but from where I am right now, I ain't doing shit for at least four hours."

"Let me know, Lethal. Have fun."

He laughed more to himself. "You know I will," he said before the line clicked.

When Onyx arrived at the hotel, Armando's personal assistant who had traveled with Onyx told her Jaelen was on his way, but had dictated the necessary papers he needed to have signed to the personal assistant. Onyx placed her seal on the papers, but made an addendum about terminating only if Jaelen found a discrepancy in her work ethic. He couldn't dismiss her for personal reasons or terminate employment in any fashion without giving her a substantial amount of money.

When Jaelen arrived to sign the papers, he questioned Onyx about the addendum. He didn't seem disturbed, but he was quite inquisitive as to why she felt she needed to add this.

"You have your days, Jaelen, and protecting Mrs. Hawthorne from you petty temperament is my bottom line for putting this in."

"Two million? The woman could do anything in her personal life, and I can't fire her."

"As long as it doesn't affect her job, you have nothing to worry about."

"I think this is ridiculous."

"And I think you're only hiring her to control her."

"So you didn't believe me on the plane about wanting to give her a better life?"

"A little, but Mrs. Hawthorne's capable of making it on her own without you. I had you think you came up with the suggestion to give her a better life because you deserve to be in the company of her. I think she'll make you into a better person, Jaelen. You need her, and in turn she needs your strength."

"Matchmaking is not your forte," he snarled.

"I wasn't trying to. I just feel the two of you will be an asset to each other."

"I don't get it. A few hours ago you wanted to protect her from me."

"That's before I realized you two had something in common."

"What?"

Onyx couldn't quite lie so easily to her best friend, and she knew Jaelen knew her too well to note if she did, but she would be damned if she was going to reveal Kimberly's secret. "Like I said on the plane, she has something important to tell you."

"She couldn't think of it when I asked her." He stepped up to her, but he knew Onyx wouldn't be intimated enough to tell him. "If there's something I should know about, why can't you tell me?"

"I don't want to. I feel it is Mrs. Hawthorne's purpose to discuss the matter with you." She tried to step around him, but he moved in her way, again.

"But it is important?"

Onyx couldn't discern the frown. Whether he was mad or just curious was a mystery to her. "Important when the moment is right. If she doesn't think the moment is right, then it is not."

"Yet, you feel we are connected by this information."

"I believe you are. It's up to Mrs. Hawthorne to believe now. If you wish to know it, your attitude toward her must change."

"How is that?"

"She's got to feel she isn't confronting you all the time. I think if you changed your behavior slightly, get her to relax, she'll feel she can relate to you and in turn reveal to you."

"You aren't going to tell me?" Jaelen asked incredulously.

"No, now don't you have something to do?"

"No, not until midnight with Mrs. Hawthorne." He squinted one eye turning away slightly, so he wasn't blocking her way to go into her room.

Onyx stopped in her stride, not at all liking his lightened tone of voice. "She actually agreed to meet with you willing? You didn't browbeat her?"

A look of innocence came into play on his face. "I didn't," he professed. This was partially the truth. Onyx didn't say anything about blackmailing and intimidation.

"She's agreed to fly to Detroit tonight to see the setup."

"Yes, and accept the position once I give her these papers."

"Why do I have the feeling you aren't telling me something?"

"Funny, I get that same feeling from you. You want to explain yourself first?"

"No." Onyx turned to walk away, not wanting to reveal any more than what she had already told him. "Just make sure you don't harm her. I swear I'll break your nose if she comes back harmed – physically or emotionally."

"I'll be on my best behavior."

"That's what has me worried," she mumbled under her breath going into her room and closing the door. Onyx wondered what was he keeping from her.

****

Kimberly sat nervously near the front door, awaiting Onyx's return. The clock in the hallway read 11:30 p.m. It was still early, but Kimberly was too nervous to do anything else. She had prepared everything, made all the necessary phone calls, and changed her plans completely. After putting the boys to bed, she had taken a nice long hot shower to try to relax her, but even that didn't help. Her mind was filled with thoughts of what could possibly be planned for her for the next twenty-four hours.

"Momma," Jason called for her the third time.

"Yes, baby?" She came to the bottom of the stairs to see him crotched in the middle of the stairs.

"I can't sleep."

She knew Leroy was up in his room assembling his model cars he loved to build by hand. He had a great eye for detail and usually listened out for the boys. She had returned the three booties back to him, and he replaced them in his bag he always carried, along with a fourth pink bootie he had never had to relinquish.

Going up to her son, she picked him up and carried him back to his room he shared with his other brothers. He was large and quite heavy, but as a mother, the weight of her son didn't matter. Making him feel better did.

After tucking him in, she asked him what was wrong as she rubbed his brow until the frown left his forehead.

"I miss Nae-nae," he said longingly.

"I bet she misses you, too, but sending her to the camp was an excellent opportunity. I miss her as well, but I spoke to Miss Collins and she said Nae is doing very well."

He nodded in understanding. "Can I call her tomorrow?"

"The next day, I promise. She'll be excited to hear your voice." She kissed his cheek. "I miss her, too, but she'll be with us soon. The summer is almost over."

"Why do you have your bags still packed?"

She almost forgot how observant he was. "Mommy needs to return with Mr. Gates, but Onyx will be keeping an eye on you all for me. Do you remember Mommy's number?"

He nodded, but the frown was returning.

"Have I told you how handsome you are when you don't frown?"

"Yes, but I can't help it, Momma. I worry about you so much."

"You worry too much about everything, Jason. I won't let any harm come to you, and I will always come back to you, I promise."

"We just got you back," he protested.

"I promise I will be back. It's just one day, then I'll be home. Now go to sleep."

"I love you, Momma."

"I love you, too, sweetie."

He cupped his soft hands to her cheeks and gave her a very serious look. "You let Mr. Gates know I know what he's up to, but I won't let him."

"Won't let him what, Jason?"

Jason's frown disappeared and a smile appeared. "Come back safe, Momma."

"What's he up to, baby?"

Jason pursed his lips together, and she knew this meant right now wasn't the time to talk about it.

"Goodnight, Momma."

Just as she closed the door to his room, the doorbell rang.

Onyx began speaking as she stepped past Kimberly into the house carrying a large black bag.

"Thornton Ainsley E. Hawthorne, Jr., son to Wescott's brother ... Thornton Hawthorne, always referred to as Ainsley. A thirty-year-old who is lazy and spoiled rotten as defined by his mother, Cassandra Lampkin who opted not to marry Thornton when she realized she was pregnant, but instead married a Thorin Lampkin, some marine owner in the upper peninsula part of Michigan. He stays in a small two-bedroom apartment in Greektown, which he gets a supplement from his stepfather of sixteen hundred a month.

"He doesn't have to work, but unfortunately he is so deep in debt from his gambling addiction he had to. He's made false claims to the lawyer who's working with Ainsley that whether they win the case or not, his mother will still pay the lawyer fifty thousand dollars upon completion of the whole matter. Every year the case goes on, the lawyer will receive and extra five thousand."

"He doesn't intend to pay it?" Kimberly asked.

"Cassandra has no idea the deal exist. Ainsley's debt is now a quarter of a million to his lawyer alone."

Kimberly felt a little guilty for the young man.

"Don't you dare," Onyx warned. "He dug himself into that grave, now let him lie in it. I'm sure your husband felt he was leaving the money to the right person when he married you."

"But it was Charles that made me even approach Wescott. I would never have married him if Charles had not ordered me to make him think I liked him, but I did actually come to love Wescott and he loved me."

"So, it was only fate that completed everything."

"West did mention Junior was a spiteful boy, and he squandered money on gambling. He didn't want Junior to get a dime. Those were his words."

"So you have nothing to feel guilty about. The limousine awaits, Mrs. Hawthorne. I have your cell number if anything happens. Don't worry. Try to have a good time."

Kimberly snorted. "A good time with that man? You must be kidding."

Onyx only watched her trudge to the awaiting limousine hoping this would change things for Kimberly and Jaelen. She also hoped Jaelen was smart enough to stay out of her brother's eyesight with Kimberly or Lethal wouldn't be accountable for his actions.

Chapter 14

The limousine took her directly to the city airport onto the runway where a private plane that read Bellini Enterprise was preparing to take off. Kimberly was escorted inside and the door shut behind her. Jaelen was on the phone in a deep business conversation. She noted he had changed to a dark blue three-piece suit and looked his usual stuck up self, clean-shaven, and untouchable.

He didn't acknowledge her, but she had a feeling he knew she was present. A stewardess guided her to the seat across from Jaelen and helped her buckle in then gave her quick flight instructions.

By the time she was done, Jaelen was off the phone and staring intently at her looking quite ominous. She looked around to take notice of the luxurious plane's interior, which seated fifteen comfortably, but it didn't account for the space in the back. She refused to believe that was the room for just the bags.

Without being questioned, Jaelen explained what was past the black curtains of the seats.

"A bathroom with a shower, a kitchen and a bedroom."

Her brow rose. "Why would anyone need that?"

"The Bellini family often uses this one to travel across the world. They have a larger one capable to seat fifty with two bedrooms and two bathrooms."

"But why would they need bedrooms? These chairs are quite comfortable enough."

A heated gleam filled his eyes. Could she be that naïve? "Sometimes bachelors like to entertain."

Kimberly blushed, looking away from his concentrated glare. "In a plane?"

"The act isn't always performed in a bedroom on a bed. There are variations, which I'm sure you're well aware of."

Her blush increased. "I'm aware. I watch cable."

He chortled snidely. "I meant to say you should have first-hand knowledge."

Kimberly could immediately tell he was trying to get a rise out of her. Jaelen's whole point in life seemed to irate people. He liked to push people's buttons, and the ones that stood up to his verbal assaults were the ones he grew closer to. Kimberly didn't want any part of this man close to her, but when she had had enough she sometimes forgot caution. "Why do you do that?"

"Do what?" he asked innocently.

"Push people's buttons. Do you enjoy having everyone ticked off at you?"

Before answering her, he pulled out a cigar, chucked off the end, and lit it. Even after that, he took a slow smoke in and let it drag out. He was doing it again. "I enjoy knowing I can do it."

She bristled. "I've resolved to ignore you when you do it, Mr. Gates. You can't help but be a hateful man, and I don't think it was me who made you so. I may have escalated an already present problem, but in no ways will I take the blame for your cantankerous disposition." She changed the subject. "Am I to know what is to be my fate for the next twenty-four hours, or will you watch me squirm?"

"In due time. We'll be arriving in Detroit in less than thirty minutes."

Kimberly didn't dare show her nervousness. His probing, marbled brown eyes seem to be searching for this.

"So Kimber, why on some instances do you use your maiden name?" he asked.

Her new nickname on his lips still made chills run up her back. "Anonymity was crucial in most cases. Miss Parker was a way to blend with the crowd. Hawthorne attracted too much attention."

"I thought as much. Running from the law can be difficult."

"It wasn't the law I was running from." Her mind screamed, It was you at first. Yet, she didn't say it out loud. "Junior, as West called him, had made threats on my life, and my own uncle was going to do anything to get his hands on me. I had no other choice than to hide."

"That seems to be your life story, or shall I say your excuse on all accounts."

"Whether you believe me or not, I was rarely able to make a free choice on my own in the past. I was always coerced, beaten, or threatened to do what others wanted me to do for them." She took a deep breath in relief. "It felt good up until today not to be scared anymore."

He knew she referred to his coercion tactics to get her here. Jaelen looked at the pilot light, wondering when the man would give the green light to take the seatbelts off. "The nephew is still out there?"

"Once the personal protection order took effect years ago, he's been rather quiet. Leroy and I get crazy phone calls, telling us I'll be dead by morning every blue moon though, but we just change the number, make it unlisted, and try to go on. There's not much we can do. If I do come up missing or dead, all fingers will point to him first."

"Then I'll get away with murder?"

Kimberly narrowed her eyes. "You'll be second. Mr. Heart would find out who did it."

"Ah yes, Lethal. You've grown quite attached to him, haven't you? Does he know about today?"

"No and I have no intentions of telling him. If he knew, he would kill you."

"So, you think you're doing me a favor?"

"No, I just don't want you on my conscious anymore, Mr. Gates. I've felt guilty all these years for what I did to you. Lethal said I shouldn't because

I had no choice in the matter. It was either rape you or never see my brother again."

He really wanted to get off the subject because he was already edgy about not getting the green light, and he didn't want her to realize his present ire. "Have you ever met Junior?"

She shook his head, noting he'd changed the subject; she assumed bringing up that night had him upset. "I've met his lawyer. Sometimes others who work for him – mostly bums willing to do anything for a hundred bucks – come up to me representing him and scaring me. This was why I took up the defense classes. I needed some way to protect myself. Leroy took up a few hand combat courses as well because I feared they'd try to hurt him in order to get what they want from me."

"Which is?"

"My children's inheritance. West wanted children to pass on his bloodline. I granted an old sick man his dying wish, but in turn I was granted children, which I love dearly. It's been wonderful being a mother to them."

A twinge of jealousy shot through his chest again, and he had to bite his tongue not to shoot off his mouth once more, yet the effort was extremely difficult when the acerbic tongue came natural to him. He could tell his questions about everything else made her a little bit comfortable and in that regard he felt he could get her to open up. Jaelen needed her to put her guard down in order to get to her.

"Is there anything you wish to know about me, Mrs. Hawthorne?"

"No." Her tone was a definite flat refusal.

"You mean nothing comes to mind," he said, hoping she had just meant something else.

"I mean the less I know about you, Mr. Gates, the less I will have you on my mind."

"Getting to know me means you won't be so uncomfortable around me."

"Keeps me on my toes."

He couldn't believe for one moment what she was saying. "So for six years you haven't wondered about me?"

"I won't lie. My curiosity had piqued of your whereabouts and well-being. I was surprised to find out you could be looked up so easily on the Internet." She wouldn't confess this was a weekly obsession of hers.

"Was this your way of keeping in touch?" The remark was filled with sarcasm and her expressive, brown eyes told him so, but she only bucked under his intense stare.

"You could say that. The gossip mills were dreadful about you though."

"Gossip mills?" He seemed curious.

"Oh, yes. Things about you breaking hearts, driving women insane. You seducing mothers and daughters in one night." She clicked her tongue in disappointment.

"And you heard this all the way in Davenport about me?" An inquisitive brow shot up, and Kimberly looked away trying to ignore how the more immensely handsome he seemed to get, the more she noted his facial expressions weren't always frowning all the time. She liked it when he frowned because it made her not see those delectable lips of his that begged for attention. On top of all this, he was acting strangely ... nice.

Kimberly didn't know if she liked him like this or not. Was he humoring her or setting her up? She wouldn't trust him as far as she could throw him. "I did have associates who kept their ears open and their mouths shut."

"So you knew of my seductions that I told you about in the limo?"

"I didn't blame myself for them at the time because you seemed..." She fought for the right word. "Content."

"Content?" He snorted. "Far from it."

The pilot chose that time to let them know they were in the air and was free to move around. He popped his seat belt off so quickly as if he had wanted to burst from the chair.

"Don't like being confined?" she asked, knowing this was a dig, but tried her best to look as innocent as possible.

Jaelen cut his eyes so sharply she gasped quietly as the look that glittered in his eyes at her. She could tell he wanted to throttle her.

This time she snorted. "I can see you expect people to have a sense of humor about your remarks, but you can't take the heat when you're in the kitchen."

"You're trying to push my buttons, Mrs. Hawthorne. I can forget how nice I'm trying to be and go toe to toe with you, if that is what you desire."

"I don't desire to confront you verbally, Mr. Gates. You made it evident you can handle yourself very well with your mouth."

Jaelen pushed the salacious thoughts out his head. Using the word desire and mouth in the same breath made him think of other things than revenge.

Standing up and moving beside her, he pulled the armrest up, so there wouldn't be any barrier between them. When she reached over to unbuckle her seat belt, he covered her hands to stop her. Raising her eyes reluctantly to meet his, she could have sworn she saw amusement for a brief moment, but pushed it out her head because this man couldn't have a funny bone in his body.

"I prefer you like this," Jaelen stated.

"Confined?" she asked.

"In my control is more like it."

She forced herself to relax and not show how irate she was with him.

He checked his watch. "Do you realize what you've agreed to, Miss Parker?

"It's Mrs. Hawthorne," she corrected him stiffly.

"At this point, I can call you anything I want."

"Are there any names you wish to call me that you feel would be more appropriate?"

"Nothing I can think of right now, but I don't like calling you by your married name."

"I had a feeling you had a problem with my married name. Why is that?"

"Marriage to anyone for you is not befitting."

"I made a wonderful devoted wife to my husband," Kimberly said proudly, rubbing the fact in she was married, which to no end seemed to annoy him. She had caught on quite well how to hit right back verbally.

Jaelen didn't know whether to be proud of her or burst her bubble. He pondered this as he also noted how alert his whole body seemed to feel. Just like that night so long ago. Sensations he never thought to experience again were coming to the surface of his mind and heart and that need, he felt so long ago filled him.

Kimberly noticed how taut he became. He turned his face away, and she had to wonder if her barbs had actually made a dent in his stony reserve.

"I'm sorry," she couldn't help saying.

He looked at her now sharply. "For what?"

"I shouldn't do that."

"Do what?"

"Sink to your level," popped out her mouth before she could stop it, and then covered her mouth in shame. "I did it again," she mumbled through her fingers.

Jaelen couldn't help himself and smirked. She really was that naïve and she took everything to heart. No wonder she couldn't handle herself around him without becoming upset. "You really shouldn't take everything I say or do so seriously, Miss Parker."

She almost wanted to correct him again, but bit her tongue.

"You are right about one thing. My callousness does rub people the wrong way, and I do it intentionally for the rise I get out of people. It's comes so naturally I can't help myself." He couldn't help his hand as his fingers moved to touch her cheek and noted the softness under his contact. She was very vulnerable, and he understood how people took advantage of her open heart. "Do you always want to protect and help everyone, Miss Parker?"

She shrugged, trying not to be affected by his touch and warm voice tingling her eardrums. "I can't help it. I want everyone to be happy around me."

"Jason doesn't seem like a happy boy."

Kimberly stiffened a bit more. Why would Jason be on his mind? "My son is temperamental."

"He couldn't have gotten that from you. Was his father like that?"

He didn't know? she thought. "Sometimes."

Jaelen didn't know why he thought of the boy with the constant frown.

"He told me to tell you something, which he feels only you would know what it means."

His hand was now moving slowly down her face and his thumb rubbed over her lips. "What was that?"

Clearing her voice, Kimberly almost whispered, "He said, he knows what you're up to, but he won't let you."

Jaelen's frown returned as he drew his hand away. "He won't let me what?"

She shrugged, hoping he would be able to figure out what her son meant. "He wouldn't say anything more after that."

He looked quite disturbed at this.

Kimberly thought she should explain her son's uniqueness. "Jason has always been observant to other people's emotions even if they weren't about him. I'm sure he knows you have something planned for me, and he is aware of your animosity for me."

"Does he actually think he can protect you from me?"

Again, she shrugged. "Jason talks like he's ten feet tall sometimes."

He was not about to let that young man spoil his revenge. If he wasn't scared of what Lethal would do to him, no five-year-old was going to take away his intent to get to Kimberly. "My question was never answered."

"What question?"

"Do you know what you've agreed to?"

"Not really, but I figured whatever you plan for me or want me to do, I have no choice in the matter. I just hope you use good judgment and think that I have a family to return to."

"Meaning?"

"I have people in my life that have to look for me for strength. I hope I won't shame myself ever in their eyes, but what I owe you I feel I must allow your every wish to be granted within this period. Maybe then I won't feel the guilt I always feel for you."

He didn't like her feeling guilty for him, but knowing what she had done to him bothered her gave him pleasure. "I won't do anything your children will be ashamed of, I will assure you, but I will instruct you that the word, no or anything in the refusal family won't be in your vocabulary today." He took her hand in his and looked deep in her eyes. "I want to hear you say it, Miss Parker."

"Say what?" she asked.

"You'll be mine for twenty-four hours."

"I agreed to it."

He leaned closer to her and she wished the arm barrier was there to offer some protection from his proximity.

"I want to hear those sweet lips say it."

Kimberly knew this was just another way to break her down and damned if she wanted to resist him. "I'm yours to control."

His smirk was triumphant. If only she knew how much joy those words brought him. "Again."

"I'm yours to control."

"Now kiss me," Jaelen ordered, feeling very lightheaded.

She tried to yank her hand away, but he held her tighter. "N-"

He covered her mouth with his index finger. "You weren't about to use the n-word, were you, Miss Parker?"

If her eyes could get any wider, they'd be big as saucers. Oh yes, this was going to be fun, he realized, torturing her from one moment to the next.

"I can see why you were beaten. You don't follow orders very well."

This was an intentionally cruel remark. "I can obey you. Your request caught me off guard."

"How so?"

"That's not something I thought you'd expect of me."

'It isn't and I would have stopped you had you obeyed, but I was just testing you and of course you failed."

"Am I to expect this verbal abuse for this entire day?"

"My cryptic remarks are to be ignored."

"It's difficult to ignore it when everything that comes out your mouth is cruel."

He didn't know if he liked her pointing out his faults. Onyx did it occasionally when he perturbed her to no end, but no one else dared. "You don't like me do you, Miss Parker?"

"Not particularly, if I can be honest, but if I was to appease your male level of testosterone high for the day, then I'd have to say you knock my socks off, or was this another test I failed?"

"This is not a test. I just wanted your honest answer."

"Well then you have it. I don't like you. I never have. From the moment I saw you, I didn't like you."

"You didn't know me. I didn't say one word to you if you'll remember."

"You didn't need to speak to show your cruel side, Mr. Gates."

"Call me Jaelen," he ordered.

"I'd prefer Mr. Gates."

"It's not a request."

She giggled more to herself. "Then Jaelen it is although it does sound too intimate."

"Why do you want to distance yourself from me so much?" Jaelen asked, trying to hid his annoyance with her confession.

"Do I have to repeat myself all the time? I don't like you."

"You find me handsome," he pointed out from their earlier conversation.

"Yes, I do," she agreed. "But I never judge a book by its cover."

"Oh, please. Women do it all the time."

"I don't," she emphasized. "If you would stop being stereotypical, you'd see that." She waved the thought away. "I forget you're Jaelen Gates, the most stubborn man alive." She let out an exasperated sigh. "You could drive the mentally insane crazy."

"You don't know a thing about me to presume I'm stubborn."

"I don't? If that's what you think." Now she knew why Jason was so stubborn. It was definitely his father's side of the family. Amazing how her son took on qualities of a man he had never met.

"Just because you fucked me doesn't mean you know me," Jaelen said, sneering.

The assistant decided to clear her throat to make her presence known. Kimberly blushed clear to her toes knowing the assistant had heard Jaelen's last statement.

Jaelen didn't even bother to look behind him at the assistant. "Yes, Miss Caruthers?"

"We'll be landing in fifteen. There's a downpour in the city, but I have your limo awaiting as we speak at the Detroit airport, and your car will be taken to the address you specified. Will there be anything else?"

"Did you make contact with the institute?"

"Yes. The director assured me she's sending over one of her best instructors. The guards will let her in, and Edward is waiting at the airport with further instructions in hand, which he assured me he's already started."

"Good. Thank you, Ms. Caruthers." He reached inside his jacket and pulled out an envelope.

The assistant smiled gratefully, but made no move to take the envelope. "Mr. Bellini has well compensated me for my time and trouble, sir."

"I know, but this is just a tip."

Ms. Caruthers didn't want to argue and accepted the envelope and left.

Kimberly was so highly embarrassed she didn't know what to do. "May I be excused?" she insisted in a low, controlled voice.

"You aren't going to throw up, are you?"

"Onyx told you that?"

"She said you don't handle confrontations very well."

"Only with you, Jaelen."

He liked his name on her lips. "I think you handle yourself quite well, Miss Parker."

"I have to use the little girl's room," she urgently insisted.

With a quick flick of his hand, the seat belt released her, and she couldn't move fast enough to get away from him. Once she had taken the pressure off her bladder, she felt a little better. Running cold water, she splashed it on her face several times. "You can do this and live," Kimberly convinced herself.

Returning to her chair, she was glad to see he had moved back in his chair. "I hope this won't be a habit," he snipped.

"I was hoping you'd leave me alone after the trial was over, but we can't get everything we hope for, can we, Mr. Gates?" She bit her tongue. "I apologize. I meant to say, Jaelen."

"Do you often punish yourself when you know you did something wrong?"

"Only when I really didn't mean to." Automatically, she strapped herself in.

His cell phone went off, and she was relieved to see him highly interested in the conversation and not her. This gave her time to note how he had changed over the years up close. There was more expanse to his chest, and he seemed meatier, but far from fat. No, this man, as before, kept himself in excellent physical condition. Her eyes drifted down his body and for some reason settled on his crotch. Unconsciously she licked her lips. There was a slight twitch in the general area and her eyes went up to meet his.

She realized he knew she was examining him, and she busied her eyes elsewhere almost feeling his smirk. The stewardess came around to let them know the captain was about to land. She asked him quietly if he needed assistance with his seatbelt, eager to be of help. Kimberly could see the stewardess' eyes eating him up like he was a biscuit.

He waved the woman away, but snapped his finger at Kimberly who gave him an I-knew-you-would-ask look.

There was no need to interrupt his conversation in order for her to understand what he wanted. Reluctantly, she removed her straps and stood in front of him. He moved his arms out her way and waited patiently for her to do the honors, while he continued his phone conversation.

Kimberly steadied her fingers as she grasped the buckle and pulled it over to his lap. She forced her eyes to keep from wandering to his crotch, which she was now very close to. Just as she snapped the seatbelt in place, she snuck a peak at his face, remembering the buckle Uncle Charlie had on the bed. He wasn't looking at her, but down at her shirt. Being bent over him made her blouse open further and revealed her dark red, laced, wired bra that barely covered her chest. Looking accusingly back at him, she knew why he held that weird smirk on his face; she gasped and sat, angrily pulling her seatbelt over her.

If she could have thought of an awful name to call him, she would have, but none came to mind. It just wasn't in her nature to do it. He got off the phone per captain's instructions and only watched her with a look in his eye, which she couldn't quite discern.

Avoid looking at him, she thought, but that made it even harder not to look at him. Why did he have to look so damned good?

Upon landing, he escorted her to an awaiting limousine. Jaelen dragged her through the rain as he walked at a fast clip.

There was a young man inside the limousine, who only gave her a minute glance before he turned his attention onto Jaelen with the deepest blue eyes. For a white guy, Kimberly found the young man rather handsome in a cruel sort of way. She could see the arrogance dripping off him and wondered if Jaelen influenced him to be that way. Jaelen had a way of bringing the worse out in people.

"You never cease to amaze me, boss. Is she the reason I received a strange list of things to do?"

"Is it complete?" Jaelen snapped.

"Most definitely. Does this mean I get the day off?"

"No, but nice try. You just haven't checked your e-mail yet. Before I left Davenport, I sent over another list."

The young man groaned. "No rest for the weary."

"You knew that before you took this job."

Edward winked at Kimberly to show he was only kidding. "Good thing you pay me well."

Jaelen was not in the mood to mince words with his assistant, who couldn't take death seriously, let alone anything he said. "Where can I drop you off?"

Edward chuckled at his boss' underlying meaning of wanting to get rid of him. He hadn't seen Jaelen this edgy around a female ever. He wondered who the young woman was, but he didn't ask questions. He would eventually find out. "Same place you're going. I have my car parked in the back. I've informed the construction company they have the day off, and the food will be delivered to the appropriate locations. I'm still working on the last item of the list as we speak."

"You have four hours."

"If you haven't noticed, it is the middle of the night, boss."

"Did Ruby pitch a bitch?"

"And then some."

Jaelen sighed. "This ought to be interesting."

Kimberly was wondering who Ruby was and why Jaelen seemed a little nervous about Ruby's attitude. Once she assessed Edward was of no interest and their conversation had nothing to do with her, she stared out the window watching the streets go by, missing her children and her brother.

Once they stopped in front of a large building still under construction, Jaelen seemed a bit more moody, if he could actually be. She didn't know if this was because of Edward or herself. Most likely his temperament was because of her. When had she not made him angry for one reason or another?

Again, she didn't allow him to assist her out the limousine and was very aware how closely Jaelen was behind her as she walked into the building.

Kimberly assumed it was an ingrained gentleman trait that made Jaelen open the door for her to allow her to proceed through into the lobby. Edward followed behind them, but stopped at the stairs they proceeded up, which led to a studio in the completion stage. She noted how everything was dimly lit, creating a very amorous mood. All five senses were heightened as Jaelen guided her into a beautifully-decorated room filled with exotic purple flowers, which she had never seen before. Standing at the foot of a masseuse table was a woman in her forties, laying out some bottles on a table nearby.

Kimberly stopped dead in her tracks at the doorway and looked at Jaelen, her eyes filled with questions she didn't know how to express. "What is this?" was all she could come up with without jumping to conclusions. For whatever reason, as much as she wanted to despise him, it just wasn't in her nature to do so.

"Are you resisting?" he inquired.

"Can I be honest and fail another test?"

That weird smirk, she was really starting to hate, came on those luscious lips. "Were you expecting something different?"

She kept her voice low, so the woman wouldn't hear them. "A bed and lots of handcuffs came to mind."

His voice became strangely deep. "That's much later, Kimber." His nickname was driving her senses crazy. "Right now, you've had a stressful week. I figured you needed this."

"You're being considerate?" she asked suspiciously.

"Is that so hard to believe?" he asked, annoyed at her distrust.

"Yes."

"Do you accept my generosity?"

She would be crazy to pass up a nice massage. "Yes," yet to keep him guessing, she added, "only because I have to do whatever you desire." Moving past him, she went to the masseuse instructor and introduced herself.

"Hello," she said.

"Hello, I'm Patricia, and I'm here to instruct Mr. Gates," the woman said.

"What do you mean instruct?" Kimberly asked, looking at Jaelen, who was removing his jacket and rolling up his sleeves. He cracked his knuckles, and Kimberly's heart raced.

"It means you take yourself over to those curtains and get undressed and then you'll join us back here while I massage you or were you not accepting my generosity."

A horrible wretched gurgle came from her throat as she stiffened like a board and traipsed behind the curtains in the corner. She could hear them whispering, but she didn't care. No matter how good this instructor was, she would not relax. He was going to massage her. Jaelen was going to touch her.

Kimberly held her stomach, praying she wouldn't vomit. Her head felt light.

"Procrastinating is not going to make this any easier, Miss Parker," he sang on the other side of the curtains.

Angrily, she wrapped the towel about her and stomped out the curtains. She laid on her stomach carefully without revealing herself to him. She tried to relax, but nothing could help. Not when she knew at any moment, he would be putting his hands on her. The towel was moved down to the lower part of her tailbone.

If she could turn red all over, she would have done so. This was the most embarrassing day in her life.

Patricia's voice was calming as she placed her hands high on her back in the curve of her neck. "Miss Parker, I'm not going to bite," Patricia teased. "You'll enjoy this if you don't think about it."

That was impossible! He was standing behind her. She would die to know what he was thinking. Don't perspire, she ordered her body. Closing her eyes, she tried to do what Patricia said to do. The warm hands soothed her whole body as she felt the stress from the past two days leave her body. Patricia's hands drew what stiffness was left completely out her body, and she sank deeper in the heavenly sensations. Even when the strength of the massage changed, Kimberly didn't notice. She had never had a full back massage before, and now she knew what was so wonderful about it as Patricia's hands attacked her lower back. Kimberly had given a lot of massages to patients being a physical therapist and knew the healing effects to the mind literally, but she had never experienced the feeling for herself.

A moan escaped her lips as she felt more than just a week's worth of tension leave her body. This was a lifetime of stress floating away, taking her far away from the world around her. Kimberly didn't realize the soft humming noise she vibrated throughout her whole body as the strong fingers kneaded the muscles of her buttocks.

"Lord, have mercy," she whimpered under her breath as those fingers and wide palms relaxed her to no end.

Kimberly paid no mind as the towel fell to the floor and the hands moved down to her thighs. Beautiful, she thought, loving how the hands found the overwrought points and alleviate the muscles until they were like Jell-O.

The hands kneaded her calves and moved down to her feet and Kimberly's moans became louder as extraordinary techniques were applied to the sole of her feet, causing a burst of endorphins throughout her body as the hands moved high to her other thigh.

"How does it feel, Miss Parker?" Patricia asked over her.

"Wonderful, don't ever stop," she murmured softly.

"Mr. Gates is a wonderful student."

Kimberly stiffened as she realized now these were no woman's hands that touched her. For how long had he been touching her? Had she been that oblivious to her surroundings?

"Do you think so, Kimber?" he asked, noting her sudden stiffness, but expertly rubbing that from her body. He saw goose bumps come on her arm when he said her name and wondered what she was thinking. The moaning she had previously surrendered herself to had been encouraging as it showed her weak spots. Patricia had pointed them out very well, and if he wanted to, he was positive he could get to her again.

Kimberly didn't even know Jaelen nodded Patricia out the room. She was concentrating on his hands and the diligence of how he had mastered relieving tension in her body. What made it worse was that she enjoyed it and really never wanted him to stop, but didn't want to admit what good it had done to her.

"You're good for the first time," she forced out.

"You noticed? I am a quick learner though. I never thought I would receive pleasure in doing something of this nature, but I must admit knowing you enjoyed it has made me relish my expertise on the matter. Maybe you could teach me more."

"What makes you think I enjoyed it?"

"You were purring like a cat a few minutes ago."

Kimberly was glad he was behind her because then he couldn't see her blush.

"Relax Kimber," he whispered near her ear. "I won't bite … yet."

Not one muscle of hers could defy him. Before she knew it, her mind gave in as well. Yes, she had a long stressful life, and his fingers were doing a wonderful job in making the burden on her shoulder go away.

Chapter 15

Coming awake abruptly, she sat up. No longer was she in the beautiful smelling room but a pull-out sofa bed in an office. The sun shone brightly though the windows behind the desk, which was sitting in front of her. She heard Jaelen's voice in the direction of the desk and knew he sat with the chair facing the windows talking quietly. He turned around as if knowing she was awake.

His eyes were instantly on Kimberly, and he stopped speaking. "And with that, Mr. Cadolsa, I bid you adieu." He hung up the phone for a brief second, but picked the receiver back up and dialed someone. "Miss Parker has awakened, Ruby." When he put the phone down this time, he sprung from his chair and rounded the desk. "Feeling better?"

She stretched longingly. "Is my slavery over with?" she asked, hopeful. Her body felt as if she had slept for days. "How long have I been sleep?"

"It's about ten now. Ruby is on her way up to treat you to a full day's spa treatment, get your hair done - you know the usual. During this time, she'll be discussing what her intentions of the salon area will be about. She's taken great pains to make sure everything is perfect and has worked very hard to make the spa a success. My goal is to make sure she and you get along.

Don't bother to extol her with any of my bad qualities. She knows me quite well to not listen to your complaints."

She gasped. "I don't complain!"

He leaned against the corner of his desk with that strange smirk on his face. His eyes were indiscreet as she forced herself not to seem conscious under his intense stare. "All right, whine is more like it."

She was about to complain, but he quickly said, "That's neither here or there, but you really need to get dressed before Ruby comes in."

Kimberly looked down at her body to see she only wore her slip from under her dress. If she could blush any harder, she would have definitely succeeded this time, fully knowing he had dressed her.

"Could you give me a minute to myself so I may get dressed?"

"Shame is not an option, slave," he reminded her. "There isn't anything I haven't already seen." His tone was completely nonchalant as seeing her would not affect him at all.

Angrily, she jumped up, finding her clothes in a chair and practically shoved them on. Yet, as angry as she was, modesty won out and with care, she kept her back to him, without showing him anything pertinent.

Jaelen was most disappointed, but too amused by her anger to really care.

Ruby arrived just as Kimberly was through combing her hair. There was still a slight curl at the tip where the hairs just barely touched her shoulder.

Jaelen made quick introductions. Ruby was a short woman of medium size girth. Her bossiness was evident even before she spoke, but she had a motherly nature and an eye for detail, also. Kimberly observed this as Ruby spoke to Jaelen about his state of undress and the bed being pulled out. Jaelen was not wearing his tie or his jacket.

Due to the woman being older than Kimberly and out of respect, Kimberly insisted on calling the woman Ms. Ruby.

"You need to go home and actually get some real sleep, Jaelen, instead of bunking at the office all the time," Ruby complained.

"And miss your bitching about me needing an actual home? What on earth would I do with myself if I couldn't hear you complain all the time?" Jaelen responded with feign audacity.

Ruby laughed wholeheartedly, not taking his sarcasm serious. "If you didn't sign my checks, Jaelen, I would definitely find a way to put you over my knee. Your mother should have given you more barnyard whoopings when you were younger."

"I rather enjoy my sour disposition," he placated.

"It's fine for you, but misery loves company, don't it?" she asked Kimberly.

"And he spreads it around so freely," Kimberly spoke gravely.

Jaelen narrowed his eyes cruelly at Kimberly with a look of warning.

"How can you sleep at night when you've taken away such a beautiful smile from Kimberly's face?" Ruby teased.

Kimberly smirked. "Yes Jaelen, how can you sleep at night?"

"I don't sleep, so I feel no guilt, Miss Parker," he remarked.

"Of course not. A man like you all wrapped up in yourself has so much to ponder late at night, don't you, Jaelen?"

He only gave her a Thank-goodness-Ruby-is-here look.

"Miss Ruby, give me a moment with Mr. Gates, and I'll be down in a second," Kimberly graciously asked.

Once Ruby was out the door, he shot out the chair, came around the desk and straight to Kimberly. She didn't flinch, but she did brace for a physical blow. He stopped two inches from her face.

"A slave never shames her master in public," he seethed angrily. "You need to understand your position."

"When I'm not used to being a slave?" she countered.

"Not according to your life with Charles," he shot back.

Kimberly calmed down instantly. "My life with Charles was torture, if you must know."

His hand came up and cupped her cheek. "Is that what you want from me, Kimber? Do you want me to torture you?" His voice wasn't hard anymore, but deep and deliberately soft.

Yet, again the nickname only he called her did things to her body she couldn't understand.

His touch was warm and gentle, and she was almost tempted to lean her head into his palm, but she resisted this urge. Jaelen moved his other hand up and gently caressed her shoulder, arm, then cupped her breast. He never broke eye contact with her and the alarm and fear that appeared in her soft brown eyes was quickly subsided as he spoke. "Is that the only way you will obey me?" he asked, moving so close she could feel his body's heat. His thumb aroused the nipple through her clothes, playing havoc on her senses.

Kimberly wanted to lean into his body. He created a need between her legs that surpassed anything Eli could have accomplished. Damn her stubborn pride! Damn him! Biting her lip, she remained still as his lips now caressed her neck, suckling her ear, sending sharp twinges of pure lightning from her head to her toes.

Jaelen waited for the moment she gave in, when her body took over her stubborn mind and leaned into him and her head arched back to give him free reign.

As soon as she tilted back, he released her, stepping away and watching as she fought the passion haze cloud with a look of confusion and frustration.

"I can torture you, Kimber, but you won't like it."

Her body had been on the brink of exploding before he stopped. Now mental and physical yearning hit her at the same time, and if Kimberly didn't have enough malevolence for him in past, she detested him even worse now.

"I hate you, Jaelen," she said disdainfully. "With every fiber of my being, I hate you. I wish now I had let Charles kill you."

You want me dead?" he asked, a sneer marring his handsome face.

"Yes!" she said vehemently.

"Stand in line, Miss Parker, because my enemies are everywhere." He sat back at his desk and put his hands behind his head as he leaned back in the chair. The nefarious smirk on his face was nerve racking, and Kimberly had to fight the overwhelming urge to smack it off his face. She had never been a violent person, but he was capable of driving her to that point. He reeked of evil, and he could be called the spawn of Satan, but he would probably find that amusing.

"Scoot, little slave, and be back in three hours - no more or I'll torture you again. I'll have you begging until you are so hoarse, you can't speak for days."

Kimberly forced herself to swallow the scream bubbling inside of her. She had no doubt he would do as promised as he now wore a demonic look on his face.

Leaving out, she wanted to swear for revenge, but Kimberly was not a vengeful-type person. She could easily stop this all and take a cab to Lethal's office, but what was twenty-four hours to give in return for a very well-paying job and being back in Detroit where she could disappear in a crowd and where she wanted to be back.

Ruby didn't say anything about what had happed in the office, but she suspected something wasn't right between Kimberly and Jaelen.

Kimberly could see the older woman was dying to know, but Kimberly didn't want to speak on it at all to anyone, so she decided to only talk business with Ruby.

For the next three hours, Kimberly learned of Jaelen's new business venture, and if she wasn't so angry with him, she could almost admire him for his vision. Ruby spoke highly of him, but said, "I find it amazing a man so cantankerous could possibly understand women so well."

Kimberly laughed with relief at that comment, glad she wasn't alone in feeling her employer was that way.

Chapter 16

During that time away, she was treated to a facial, manicure and hairstyle. Ruby took her to another salon Jaelen owned out in Southfield. Kimberly was pampered beyond belief including with a full body mud bath. She did, however, have an argument with the torturous woman who had made it her mission to get all unsightly hairs off of Kimberly's body including between her legs. Of course Kimberly knew women did this, she had just never gotten the time to have this done to her with the children and Leroy always around and needing something. As grateful as she should have been, she wanted to throttle the woman that had worked so hard to make her beautiful.

Ruby then decided to tackle Kimberly's hair. The thick mane had always given Kimberly trouble, and most times she twisted the hair into a neat style away from her face, leaving the back hanging down to touch her shoulders. Ruby lifted her hair, after washing and cutting the damaged ends, sweeping the thick, dark chocolate strands into a beautiful French roll with ringlets in front of her ears.

Kimberly couldn't believe that was her face that stared back at her in the mirror, and although she should have felt relaxed and beautiful, all she could think of was, What would Jaelen would think?

That thought was rudely interrupted by the rumbling of her stomach, yet now that she was finished with her makeover, she was shown to another room where breakfast was ready for her. Despite her hunger and the delicious food, she was too overwhelmed to stuff herself.

"The limousine is here to return you to Detroit," Ruby said.

"You aren't coming?" she asked with disappointment.

"No, I have some things to tie up here for Jaelen, but we'll have lunch by the end of next week."

Kimberly returned to Jaelen's office where she met two other assistant managers and office assistant. Just as that meeting was ending, Edward came in the room and handed her a long black mackintosh coat consisting of the finest materials.

Waiting until they were alone in the room, Kimberly asked bewildered, "What's this for?"

Edward looked at her filled with curiosity, as if there were a million questions he wanted to ask, but wouldn't dare to ask.

Kimberly wondered exactly how close Jaelen was to this young man. "He said to tell you to be wearing only the coat along with shoes when you get to his home." Edward gave her a shoebox. Upon opening it, there were four-inch, patent leather, black, stilettos.

Flushing in embarrassment at the humiliation Jaelen wanted to put her through, Kimberly really wanted to protest, but that knot in her stomach formed and she just decided to complain about her safety. "I could break my neck," she mumbled.

"I don't think he much cares," Edward said simply. "Would you like to change here or in the limousine?"

Kimberly didn't answer him, but instead went into Jaelen's bathroom and changed her clothes. Upon coming out, she saw Edward abruptly jump up from Jaelen's desk. The young man was working on the computer, and she wasn't sure if she should be suspicious of Edward or not. He seemed like a bright young man but liked people to think he was some kind of lackey, but there was something in his cool blue eyes that reminded her of Charles, and this terrified her beyond what Jaelen could do. She would keep an eye on this young man. She wondered if she should take the initiative and warn Jaelen.

She decided not to because it was none of her business unless it concerned the business Jaelen wanted her to be responsible for.

He moved real close to her at an uneasy proximity "Are you ready?" he asked.

"As I'll ever be." She had the coat closed up tight all the way to her neck.

Edward reached out and touched the lapel of the mackintosh. "You know, Jaelen's never taken a woman as serious as he does you. What do you have the others don't?"

She stepped back. "I don't know what you mean, but I would like to be taken to Jaelen right away."

"You are beautiful," he said, moving back to her and wrapping his arms around her waist. She put her hands up to his chest to push him away, becoming highly nauseous. "I can't deny that, but you aren't Jaelen's type. He likes his women dumber. You've got way too much brains."

"I've also got enough balls to kick you in yours if you don't get your hands off me," she threatened, raising her leg slightly.

Edward released her rather quickly and gave her that curious look again as if he were trying to figure her out. "All right, Miss Parker."

"It's Mrs. Hawthorne if you must know."

"Miss?" he asked.

"Yes. Widowed, but I won't give up my husband's name just because Jaelen doesn't like calling me that."

"Jaelen does have his eccentricity, but that is what's to be expected from the rich while the poor still struggle."

"Are you jealous of Jaelen's fortune?"

"Why should I be? I work for him." Edward quickly dropped the subject, as if he were going to say something he shouldn't reveal to anyone, and walked out the room. She followed, going down the stairs with him to the front of the building. He passed her an envelope before she got in the limousine and said, "Please give this to Jaelen when you see him and let him know there are still some things I am working on."

She nodded. "Goodnight, Edward."

He only dipped his head once sharply and walked back into the building. As the driver proceeded to Jaelen's residence, she checked the time. There was thirty minutes to spare; she relaxed. Why she feared the punishment

Jaelen had promised to deliver if she was late she didn't know. Why she even cared that he felt he needed some justice from her she couldn't figure out. Why she was even going along with all this she couldn't answer herself.

Kimberly would just resolve to herself that she was only doing this to get him from exacting a worse revenge. It was just her time, and in the end, she would have a good job although if she really needed Hawthorne's money to live on, she could, but she wanted to save this money because the guilt of having it by deceit in the beginning still bothered her. The money was really for Hawthorne's children, and she wasn't going to spend that money unless she really needed it.

To date, the total in the account was about one million dollars and growing. By the time the twins were older and ready to go to school, they would have nothing to worry about. If she wanted to, she could take the money out, but Jaelen had said he had the account frozen, so right about now, she wouldn't be able to get anything until her twenty-four hour service was complete.

Picking up the manila envelope she had tossed on the seat from Edward, she saw that Edward had not sealed the back, so she decided to open the envelope to see what was inside.

Inside the envelope were canceled checks, a balanced checking account and other financial information. It looked as if Edward was Jaelen's personal assistant who handled different affairs for Jaelen such as paying off creditors and making sure personal bills were paid. Jaelen's life, from his personal finances, looked as if he lived simply, and he was hardly home. There wasn't much to say for groceries except recently and a maid was hired also for Jaelen's residence. She wondered had he made these provisions for her since it looked as if he had made these changes recently.

Kimberly put the papers and receipts back just as Edward had put them in the envelope and set the envelope down, not wanting to handle it too much anymore so he would suspect she had looked inside at his business.

Arriving at a newly renovated townhouse in the New Center Area, she was escorted in by the driver. Obviously, he had been told previous instructions because the driver went to a shelf in the hallway and took an envelope then bid her adieu, leaving her standing in the hallway all alone. She looked around the expensive decorative foyer. Original artwork lined the beautiful peach walls even going up the staircase that was near her, but she didn't dare go up there. Why help him out when she really didn't want to be there? Yet, even though her mind said this, goose bumps came on her skin at the anticipation of seeing him again.

Soft music played behind closed doors in front of her; she slowly entered the front room of the home. The decor of the room was mildly relaxing with soft blues and whites. A full entertainment center drew her attention to the farthest corner, which was where the music radiated from the waist-high speakers. Carefully placed mirrors lined the wall, making the room look larger than what it was, and a fireplace burned low, knocking off the September night chill as she came in the room and closed the door behind her.

She noted there was a doorway beside the entertainment center, which she assumed was where the pleasant fumes were coming from. Going over to the fire on the mantle were many pictures of Jaelen at a different age. She saw he was very full of himself and there were only two other pictures that had someone in them. One was with his father, which she could tell immediately because the older man resembled Jaelen very well. The other was with Onyx and Lethal. In the picture, all of them were wearing army fatigue, holding long rifles and all with serious expressions on their faces.

Kimberly still questioned Onyx and Jaelen's relationship but was too stubborn to ask about it.

"You obey very well, Miss Parker," Jaelen said from the other open doorway.

How long he had been standing there was a mystery to her, but she wouldn't allow that to faze her. She was going to get through this night and find a way to get through the job situation. Ruby had told her he wasn't such a bad boss and rewarded good employees. His other employees talked well about him as their boss and said he was a very hard worker.

She turned to face him saunter into the room with his beautiful, hard, muscular body oozing sexiness like an ever-pouring fountain. To hurry and get it over with, she decided to start unbuttoning her coat.

He caught her hands. "No, Miss Parker," he said, licking those delicious lips greedily. "I want you to go slow, so I can enjoy what you denied me from seeing so long ago." He touched the lapel of the coat and that made her think about Edward and his sordid advance.

She searched his face to see his reaction to her new look, but he showed no approval or disapproval. Kimberly decided against mentioning Edward had been trying to come on to her. Jaelen probably set that up to see what she would do.

"I won't enjoy this, Jaelen," she said honestly, fighting back the urge she had to scream until she was hoarse.

Stiffly, he said, "This isn't about you. It's about me and the pleasure I'll get seeing you suffer."

Kimberly became afraid of his intentions. Her lips became dry, and she was sure as her tongue licked the supple skin there were cracks already surfacing. His proximity made breathing difficult, and she prayed she wouldn't get nauseous again. The back of her mind was pleading with her stomach to stay calm.

"I don't see why you think I have to suffer, Jaelen. Don't you think I've endured enough?"

He waved her upset away like an annoying fly as he went to the other side of the fireplace to a convenient waist-high brass bar. "You aren't allowed to ask questions, Miss Parker." He began to pour himself a sifter of brandy.

His back was still to her when he asked, "Do you partake in spirits, Kimberly?"

She crossed her arms over her chest, extremely vexed by his disregard to her situation. This man cared absolutely nothing about the past suffering she had endured. He could give a rat's butt if she had lived or died back then by Uncle Charles. On top of that, not once had he questioned if there had been a baby from the union.

"If you're asking me if I drink alcohol, the answer is no," she gritted acrimoniously. "I've never enjoyed the taste of the poison."

Jaelen faced her with a nefarious grimace, his eyes belying the truth to her with a strange look of pleasure. He took great gratification in her discomfort, and she hated him for it. The grimace he wore made him look even more sinister, and she would swear he was Satan's spawn.

"Poison?" He held up the sifter briefly. "You sound like a Christian woman, Miss Parker, but anyone knows a woman who would rape a man is certainly not Christian." Again, that surety saunter came as he approached her like a panther stalking prey, and Kimberly certainly felt as if she were about to be eaten.

His eyes glistened and danced in their sockets as he stared deep into her own. "There aren't many people I allow here, Kimber." His voice was deep and reverberating, making her breath catch in her throat.

"Should I thank you for making an exception to your rules?" she clipped, hoping her tone and attitude would certainly provoke him to get this over with.

He didn't answer her as his eyes traveled down her arm to rest on her hands, annoyed. "I thought Edward gave you specific instructions to take everything off."

"I did," she said in frustration, wondering why he was trying to find something wrong with her so he could exact punishment.

He grabbed her wrist and held it up to her face. "Then what's this?"

She looked at her watch baffled. "A lovely timepiece that was on sale at Wal-Mart last Christmas. It's not clothing," she said, defending herself.

I said only the coat and heels. You must enjoy my chastisement." A look of great pleasure illuminated from his eyes.

Her heart raced remembering that frustration he had caused this morning then remembering the threat knowing he would have an immense amount of delight causing her to suffer.

Panicked, Kimberly said, "It's not in your way. It's not bothering anyone."

"It is a distraction. I don't want you to concern yourself with how long your time is or when you'll be returning."

"You want to control me."

"I thought you knew that all along."

She huffed angrily, wanting to call him horrible names, but was too upset to even think of any. He was a horrible person, but the worst thing about it was that he knew he was a terrible person and wouldn't have cared if she had called him a name. That is, if she had made the effort to think of one because any name she chose would be true about him.

He took the watch off her wrist and tossed it into the fireplace.

Kimberly seethed. "Well, in that case, there's a few bobby pins in my hair to hold it up. Would you like me to yank those out as well? They might be distractions, and we wouldn't want that."

"Go ahead." He took a calming sip of brandy.

Angrily, she yanked the pins out sending her curled hair all over her head. He stood there, amused by her maddening antics.

"Are you happy now?" she exclaimed.

The smirk he wore suddenly disappeared and that cold-blooded look turned even worse on his face. "I'll never be happy, Kimberly, until I know I control all of you."

Kimberly was confused by what he meant, but his look was so serious she didn't dare question his intentions. He moved around her to sit in a large chair facing her and the fireplace.

"Take the coat off slowly, Kimber." He lightly stroked an index finger around the top edge of the sifter. "Reveal yourself to me slowly, inch by inch."

She looked down in defeat, fighting the tears that wanted to flow from her eyes and the outcry of emotional pain she was suffering at his hands, trying to break free.

"Look at me, Kimberly. I want to see your face. I want you to look at me, so I can revel in the torture I am putting you through."

She obeyed as her fingers slowly unbuttoned the coat. There was no cold in the room for her to catch a chill and if she was alone this would be a lovely room to undress in, lie on the very soft carpet, and relaxed in front of the fire.

Kimberly dropped the coat to her feet and stood as proud as possible. "You're despicable, Jaelen Gates."

This didn't affect him just as she had predicted. His eyes traveled down her body, stopping only briefly at her stomach where she knew the silver lines were.

"You're not the first woman to call me that, but I figured you would at least keep that information to yourself, knowing slaves don't speak like that."

"Will I get another punishment?" she asked.

"Are you doubting I will do it, Kimberly?"

"I'm this close to telling you where you can put your punishment, Jaelen Gates. Do to me what you will, I won't care."

He was spurred by her defiance. "I knew you had a backbone in that weak body of yours, Kimber, but I didn't know you also had a temper. Don't try me because you've already earned my ire."

"I'm at a point where I really don't care, Jaelen."

"Good, then get on your knees and crawl over here."

It took a moment for what he said to register in her brain. "You want me to do what?" she asked.

"I am not a tape recorder, I don't have a rewind button, Kimberly," he said shortly. "I expect you to listen or has Uncle Charles hit you so many times on the side of the head your hearings been affected?00"

"I can hear just fine."

"Then you heard what I said, what's taking so long to do it?"

Kimberly huffed several times to make her anger known as she sunk slowly to her knees and placed her hands in front of her. Being upset with him made her almost forget her nakedness, but it was too difficult to think she was alone in the room with a man who intended to rape her. What she couldn't figure out was why did her body become excited at the thought of him touching her when he upset her so much.

Remembering to look in his eyes, she slowly crawled toward him until she reached his feet.

He sighed impatiently. "Closer, Kimberly."

She moved past his knees, but stopped.

"Closer," he ordered.

She crawled up into the chair with him until she was inches from his face. The soft chair was large enough to hold his large body and give her enough room to rest her thighs beside his. Sitting naked on a man's lap was absolutely the most erotic thing she had ever done in her life. Feeling the silky smooth material of his suit pants pressing against her womanhood soothed her.

"Kiss me," he said softly. His body had made no move to accept her into his space. He was stiff as a board, and it seemed almost as if he was repelled by her closeness.

Tilting her head to the side, she softened her lips as she pressed them against his. It had been so long since Kimberly had kissed another man; she wasn't sure what to expect.

Her blood felt like hot lava rushing through her veins on a speed trip to anywhere in her body. Her body seemed to purr with electricity as she pressed more on his lips and felt his response slowly come around. That sense of power encompassed her as one of her arms came up and moved to the back of his head, holding him there and enjoying the touch of his mouth against hers. He seemed to be lost in the moment as he gently guided her yielding body closer.

Kimberly moved her legs completely around his waist as he leaned forward holding her tightly. Before she knew it, she was lying on her back under him, enjoying the taste of his tongue.

She was in nirvana, never wanting to let go as he began to taste not only her lips, but her neck, then moved down to nuzzle his face in each breast, lavishing unbelievable attention upon them with his mouth and hands. Kimberly closed her eyes luxuriating in the pleasure he gave her as her body felt like rockets were about to go off inside of her. She opened her legs to the pressure of his hands and cried out as his fingers entered her womanhood, sending her almost over the edge. She wantonly gyrated her hips to the rhythm of his hands, needing him to give her the ultimate joy she had waited so long to have. Was this it? Was he going to show her what was after the top of the mountain? She could feel her body edging closer, and she wasn't scared.

Kimberly wanted to fall into that blissful pool of sexual enjoyment, but she needed him to take her there, and she didn't care how much she hated him, or how much he made her angry, she needed him right now, like a starving man needed food.

His mouth returned to her neck then her lips and she kissed him with a frantic desperation, wanting him to hurry up. Just a few more seconds, she told herself. Just a few more...

He stopped suddenly. She opened her eyes, so alert and hyper-sensitive to everything that touched her skin. Looking around the room, she tried to see if someone had walked in. At this point and time, she wouldn't have cared much, but she wanted to give him the benefit of the doubt that he hadn't stop on purpose.

"What?" she asked, breathless.

"There is no what, Kimber. You've just experienced your first punishment for disobeying me."

She had started shaking her head wildly, even before he stopped talking. "No, Jaelen. Please." She gripped at his shirt. "You can't do this to me."

"Remember, Kimber, you have no choice in the matter."

The tears sprung from her eyes, "Please," she begged, not caring about her pride.

He laid his body on top of hers, a sense of satisfaction about him. Even though she was upset, she held him close, needing the touch of him. He was careful not to lay his entire weight on top of her. "Then you really don't want me to say what I have to say, do you?"

"Will it help take away this frustration?" She pouted.

A genuine chuckle came from his lips, and she couldn't believe how handsome he was when he didn't smile. She couldn't help but think about how Jason favored his father. "No, Kimber." Jaelen lightly kissed her brow, then playfully brushed his lips against hers.

"What is it, Jaelen?" she asked, full of curiosity.

"I'm not done."

"Not done with what?"

"With your punishment."

The groan she expressed was mildly suppressed by him kissing her lips as if he knew she was going to do that and didn't want to hear it.

"Just tell me how long, Jaelen?" she begged to know.

"There are no clocks in here. You wouldn't know when it was almost through."

"Just for a little peace of mind, please, Jaelen." Her nails dug into his chest through his shirt.

He paused for a moment before answering her. "An hour…"

She moaned so sorrowfully anyone with a heart would have felt mercy for her.

Jaelen didn't like that she was able to make him still feel sorry for her, so he added, "…or two."

"No, Jaelen!" This was a demanding tone. Kimberly had started to get angry and began to try to push him away. "I won't do this any longer. I won't!"

He didn't budge and tired of her hands hitting his chest and took them, raising them above her head so she was powerless to do nothing to stop him.

Chapter 17

For the next two hours, Jaelen did as he promised. Torturing her until she was a whimpering mass of sensitive nerves. Kimberly was so angry by the time he left her alone, she wouldn't look at him and laid on the floor so still because every move she made she thought about her need. He had made her make promises to be obedient until she had become blue in the face. She would have made promises of complete slavery for the rest of her life if he would just give her what she wanted.

He was unremorseful, she told herself. He couldn't have subjected her to this torture if he felt bad about it.

Matter of fact, Kimberly was so lost in emotions, it took a moment to realize he had gotten up and went to the bar to get a drink. By now, he was shirtless and through her squinted eyes, he stared down at her as if she had done something wrong again. He looked very bothered by something, but Kimberly knew it couldn't have been her.

"It's time for lunch, Miss Parker," he said.

She closed her eyes tighter, hoping that maybe if she closed them hard enough, he would just disappear into thin air.

He repeated what he said, then ordered, "It's time to get up and eat."

"I'm not hungry," she forced out in a hiss, not believing he could be thinking of food at this time, when her body was on the borderline of madness.

"I am, and as your master, I request that you feed me my lunch."

"Only if it's boric acid," she whispered.

"What was that?" he asked, crouching down near her.

She forced her sweetest smile to her lips. "Nothing, Mr. Gates."

He downed his drink in one gulp. "I thought so. Are you going to lay there or are you going to come and feed me?"

"Why should I?" She sat up. "There's nothing wrong with your arms."

"Are you defying me, Miss Parker?"

She growled her defiance and stood up, grabbing the coat to put on.

"No, Kimberly. I didn't tell you to pick up the coat."

"Don't I need something to wear?"

"Are you cold?" he asked simply.

"No, but I don't want to walk around like this," she exclaimed.

He pointed to the couch where a mid-size white box was gift-wrapped. She had not noticed the box when she had come in because the furniture in the room was white as well, but she didn't think she had been that engrossed by him to the point that she didn't notice that was there. Yet, he had never left the room.

She looked back at him, clearly saying with her eyes that she didn't trust him.

"Open it," he ordered.

Picking up the box, keeping her back to him, she pulled the top open to the box. Underneath the tissue paper was a beautiful green, ankle-length, silk gown. The material was so thin she would swear it was as see-through as the tissue paper it was wrapped in. There was a matching wrap to go with it along with soft satin slippers for her feet.

As she stared in fascination at the gift, he said, "There's a bathroom out those doors and up the stairs to the right. You can get yourself together in there and come back. There's a phone in the hallway. Call your home and check on your boys, then come back in here."

Looking over at him, the delight showing brightly for what he had given her was worth its weight in gold, but Jaelen refused to become elated for her.

His stony look didn't change as he turned out the room and exited out the doorway he had entered through. He desperately wanted to take a cold shower, but he didn't dare let her know he was wanting her just as much as she wanted him. He had desired so desperately to ease her frustration, but he fought the urge to take her out of her misery until he couldn't take it any longer.

Any other woman, he would have gone on until they would promise him the world, but hearing his name on her sweet lips had made his manhood respond so hard he thought he would go blind from the pressure.

Going into his kitchen, he opened the freezer and took out the leather bag of ice he had put in there earlier. Leaning his head against the refrigerator, he placed the pack on his groin and took a deep breath of relief, using every concentrating skill to get some kind of physical alleviation.

Chapter 18

Kimberly didn't know what to think with this gift Jaelen had bestowed upon her, then his thoughtful gesture to call her family. Why did he do things like that? One minute he was this big jerk, then he would turn around and do something so nice she ended up reconsidering the big jerk thing. He would always be mean and cruel, but when he did these things to make her see a different side of him, she couldn't help but fight her feelings for him.

She didn't doubt there was a sexual attraction to Jaelen. How could she not? Jaelen was a specimen of male that other men would die to be like and look like. Those beautiful lips and stony-featured face, with the most sensual dark brown eyes, made her heart race whenever she looked at him.

She would have sold her soul just a few minutes ago to have a piece of him, and his relentless behavior and own control was a turn on in itself.

Going into the bathroom, she quickly washed up and changed into the beautiful gown, loving the feel of the silk on her skin. There was even a matching scarf in the pocket of the robe she could use to pull her hair back and out of her face.

Once she was complete, she went to the phone in the hallway and dialed her friend's home. She ended up leaving a message on the answering machine to let her know not to call the house until tomorrow night. After leaving the message, she called her home.

Onyx answered the phone on the third ring. "How's everything?" she asked after answering Kimberly's questions about the boys and Leroy.

"It's fine."

"So you're going to accept it?"

"It's a good opportunity, and I'd be a fool not to accept it unless something better comes along," Kimberly said.

"Nothing's better than Jaelen," Onyx said proudly.

Kimberly really wanted to know if Onyx spoke of the job or the man himself. "I hope to be home tonight."

"Take your time. The boys and Leroy are very independent although Jason still looks at me like I did something wrong. It's going fine. I do find it fascinating how well you keep secrets."

Nervously, Kimberly asked, "What does that mean?"

"I mean when you have a secret you know how to keep it. I like that. You're secretly deceitful. Jaelen's going to have a field day with this one because I can't even figure this one out." The amusement in Onyx's tone was mildly humorous.

"Are you suggesting something?"

"Look, lady, I'm not one to mince words or even beat around the bush, you've got one of the best investigators in the world stumped because I know there's something you're keeping, but that's okay because I still have cards to play in this little game you play. Like I said, shit always floats to the top, and I can't wait for it to start smelling."

Kimberly wasn't going to answer Onyx's suspicions, and Onyx really hadn't expected Kimberly to answer by the next statement.

"That's all right, Kimberly, but you must invite Lethal and I to the show when Jaelen gets all this."

"I don't find your humor very amusing."

"I didn't ask you to, but if you're not going to invite us, can you please take pictures?"

"Goodbye, Onyx." She hung up, very disturbed by that woman who found humor in the weirdest things, but Kimberly was positive Onyx had not discovered her secret and this pleased her greatly although she had to wonder what card Onyx held.

Returning to the front room, she saw the furniture had been moved out the way and a very beautiful thick white rug laid was placed in front of the space by the fireplace. Jill Scott played softly on the stereo system, and there was a layout of fruits and sandwiches on a tray near the blanket with two glasses of champagne.

Kimberly warily circled the blanket, wondering what punishment Jaelen had planned for her now.

His body came behind her suddenly as his hands rested on her hips to keep her from moving away. She was still a little sensitive to touch, and her arousal returned immediately as her senses were heightened by his closeness.

"I thought you would deliberately take a long time," he whispered in her ear, his lips brushing lightly against the skin of her earlobe.

She could barely speak and forced out in a shallow voice, "I'm a fast learner."

"Pity," he said, moving his thick strong arm around her waist, drawing her closer until the back of her was molded against the front of him. She was almost mindless again and hated him for arousing her so quickly just with simple actions. "I did enjoy seeing you suffer at my hands, Kimber."

Kimberly felt like ripping her nails through the skin on his arm, but she didn't. Jaelen's need for revenge would soon be over and she would try not to remember this.

He moved around her, lay on the rug, then patted the space beside him. She took off her slippers and knelt on the soft rug in front of him. He situated her until he could rest his head on her lap, as she sat up above him. "Feed me, slave," he ordered.

She really wanted to protest the word he had called her, but decided against it. Like she had told him, she had learned her lesson about opening her mouth. He wanted a docile woman and until the end of the day, he would get what he wanted, but she couldn't wait until tomorrow.

"How do you expect to be my boss when you've seen me naked, Jaelen?" she asked, picking up a juicy piece of seedless watermelon and placing it on those beautiful lips of his.

"Easily," he said after biting into the watermelon and licking her fingers clean. "I can be professional when it's needed and having you as my manager will be even easier. Will I make you uncomfortable?"

She barely heard him from the heady cloud of passion surrounding her brain from thinking. Seeing his tongue come out from between those sensuous lips and lick slowly and carefully every drop from her fingers had been a new and erotic experience for her, but also flamed the fires of desire.

He had to repeat his question for her when she actually looked confused.

"I-I don't know," she stuttered. "I don't think so. I've never slept with the boss before, so I'm not used to this."

"Then you'll enjoy the havoc we can play on each other's senses, won't you?"

"I don't like to play games when I'm at work. There's a time and a place for everything."

"I agree." He nodded toward the food.

She picked up a bite-sized cube of ham and fed this quickly to him, making sure she kept her fingers to herself.

"Next time use the sauce," he ordered.

She did and this gave him another chance to lick her fingers. Kimberly didn't think she could do this much longer before giving in and replacing her fingers with her mouth. Jaelen seemed almost amused at her quandary of emotions that passed in her eyes.

When he was full, he made her switch places with him. She mumbled protest that she wasn't hungry, but obeyed. He didn't let her lay on his lap, instead he had her lay beside him on her back with her head on a pillow so it would be slightly raised, while he laid on his side, using his palm to hold his head up, steadied by his elbow.

He picked up a grape and placed it on her lip. She opened her mouth and allowed him to place it on her tongue, but he didn't. The cold wet fruit was first delicately stroked against the bottom edge of her lip, from corner to corner, then he did the same to the top. When he finally placed it into her mouth, the tip of his fingers followed and he waited until she closed her mouth before releasing the grape.

Kimberly felt almost like a queen as he placed food in her mouth, feeding her slowly and sensuously as if each bite would bring her closer to fulfillment. He knew he was turning her on. Every move, every gesture he performed was made to excite and titillate her. The thought of this turned her on even more, knowing he had spent years learning to do this all for her made a warm glow blaze in the bottom of her heart for him.

Kimberly began to do as he had done to her. Licking the tips of his fingers and watching passion burn in his dark eyes, she was encouraged by his response to continue to learn from him how to seduce. She put her finger in the sauce and placed a little on his neck. Her mouth attacked the spot immediately as her hands moved down to begin undoing the buttons on his shirt. He pushed the straps off her shoulders and placed a little of the sauce on her collarbone. He licked it off just as quickly, his arousal pressing against her thigh.

Their game continued until he was undressed completely and she found herself holding him again. A little frightened, yet her arousal encompassing her fear, she massaged him gently as he lay on his back.

The innocence in her eyes told Jaelen she had never done what was on her mind, but he could tell she wanted to. To show her eagerness to learn, she pressed her lips gently against him so light and sweet he barely felt the touch, yet where she had placed it was the most sensitive spot on him, and he couldn't help but become affected by what she wanted to do.

He instructed her in detail on how to please him with her mouth and just as she had said before, she was a quick learner. She followed his instructions to the letter. Jaelen could feel himself being taken away and wanted so much to drown himself in the voluptuousness of her lingual ministrations.

When he couldn't take it anymore, he stopped her completely. The tone of his voice was sharp, and Kimberly thought she had hurt him or she hadn't done something right. He refused to look at her as he sat up. His eyes remained on the fire, and when she was about to speak, he held up a finger to stop her. She obeyed and watched as the muscles in his body tensed then relaxed, but tensed right back up as if he were fighting something very painful. In her innocence, Kimberly didn't know what she had done to him, but what she had been doing had been very pleasant for her and she wished she could do it again.

"Go upstairs to the room at the end of the hall. Stay there until I get there," he ordered quietly, not even looking at her.

She wanted to speak, but knew disobedience would not be tolerated, and he was looking for an excuse to punish her again. Kimberly didn't want to go through that without knowing she would get release from the continuous sensations he was able to illicit from her body.

Going to the doorway, she paused when she heard him call her nickname so quietly she almost didn't hear him.

"When you get in the room, don't turn on the lights. Just wait by the closed door for me," he ordered.

Chapter 19

Reaching the door at the end of the hall, she opened it slowly. A warmness hit her skin like a soft kiss as she entered the room. Her eyes were immediately drawn to the small fireplace burning low to the left. From the low light flame, she was able to determine this was the master bedroom by the size of it, along with what seemed like a closet and a private bathroom, which was the only door opened. Then there was another door near the bathroom; she couldn't determine its use. In the middle of the room was a California king-sized bed with black silk bedding on it. The bed looked handmade, very well crafted redwood, but she didn't move from her place by the door.

A minute or so passed as she examined the room and wondered why the bed kept drawing her eyes to it. It was beautiful and large, but the posts on the bed seemed oddly placed. There were three posts at the head, but the middle post wasn't placed in the center, but more to the left. She couldn't figure out why this post would be off centered. At the end of the bed was an unusually large redwood box connected to the footboard with the hinges on the other side as if there was something inside that connected to the bed.

The door near the bathroom opened and he came in wearing only his pants. A strange black leather bag was in his hand; he set it on the end of the bed. There was a strange high-pitched clinking noise as he set it down, but that didn't unnerve her - much.

Jaelen came around the bed and leaned against the post and crossed his arms.

She started to approach him, but he held up a hand to stop her where she stood.

"All this time, I've waited for this moment, Miss Parker. I've planned on it down to every second."

Kimberly was hoping he would say he didn't think it was right and that she could leave.

He continued, "I want this time to be so fulfilling for me that I'll never feel this way again. You don't know the monster I've become because of the hatred and revenge that's been welling up inside of me since that night." He looked back at the bag. "If you only knew how much this was going to mean to me, you'd almost be happy for me."

Impatiently tapping her foot, she said, "I'll never feel anything for you, Jaelen."

That strange frown of disapproval came to his face. "Lie on the bed, Kimberly, after you undress, and lay your gown over the chair by the bed."

She went over to the chair, which was partially behind him. He didn't turn to watch her, but once she had laid on her back as instructed, he turned around with a satisfied smirk.

"Are you going to fight me, Kimberly?" he asked.

"No, Jaelen," she said impetuously.

He clicked his tongue as if he would enjoy this with a fight inside of her as he went over to the leather bag and took out metal cuffs with rubber edges.

A frigid chill slowly went through her entire body as she looked at the cuffs, knowing what they meant. He was actually going to tie her down just the same as he had been, so many years ago. Kimberly wanted to beg for him not to do it, but she knew her imploring would fall on deaf ears. She decided she would keep her pride and keep her mouth shut.

Once he took out the four cuffs, he came to where she was laying and placed the cold metal on her stomach. "Put them on," he commanded quietly.

Kimberly looked at him as if he had lost his last marble inside his head. "Jaelen, you can't-"

"Can't is not a word in your vocabulary, slave. You have no choice. Now do it or would you like to be severely punished? I could make this morning's punishment seem like walking through the golden gates of heaven compared to what I will do to you, Kimber."

She trembled, more in excitement than in fear, but she didn't want to go through that again with no relief in sight, so she picked up the cuffs and clasped them to her wrist like bracelets. The coldness against her skin made her flinch and then she sat up to put the brace around her ankles. The terror welling up inside of her was slowing building, but she fought hard for him not to see this by not looking in his face.

All this had been done on purpose. He wanted her to want him, just like she had made him want her. He had won, but the torture wouldn't be over until he crumbled every resistance in her body. Would it stop at her body? He had to know there was more to a woman other than sexual pleasure. True, women could be physically attracted to a man and give control to a man physically just as men could do, but would he know to really break a woman, a man needed to get to her mentally.

Even though Kimberly realized this, she certainly wasn't going to inform him of the realization. Why give him another edge to get to her?

He checked to see if the cuffs were closed tightly enough. When he was satisfied with all of them, he went to the head of the bed and reached behind the headboard beside the off-centered post to pull a chain from what seemed like nowhere and she knew her experience be the same as his.

She gasped not believing her eyes as he clicked a wrist clasp onto a small hole on the chain and then repeated this on her other wrist from the outside post.

"I won't fight!" she promised, trying not to strain her voice.

"Doesn't matter."

"So there is no need to restrain me," she said in the calmest tone possible, despite the panic and fear welling up inside of her.

"It does." He leaned over the bed coming inches from her face. "You will suffer what I suffered emotionally, Kimberly. You will know the feeling of being restrained until I know for the rest of your life you will never forget it."

"What makes you think I have forgotten?" she hissed. "This will only make me hate you, Jaelen."

"And you don't hate me now?"

"I'll hate you even more."

He shrugged nonchalantly. "Stand in line, Kimberly," he said as he snapped the last anklet cuff to a chain coming from the bottom box at the foot of the bed. It stretched just enough to make it difficult for her to only slightly pull her leg up.

She tugged at her arms and her legs. He had made it so she was completely imprisoned on the bed and the thought of it made her very terrified.

"Jaelen, I'm scared. Are you happy now?"

"No." He laid a hand on her stomach feeling her body tremble. "You'll know when I'm happy."

"How?" she exclaimed.

"When I let you go."

Kimberly swore on her life when this was over, she would loathe this man for the rest of her life. She had never wanted to hate a person, even Uncle Charlie after all he had done to her, but for Jaelen Gates she would abhor until the day he died.

"When this is over, Jaelen, I won't accept the position."

"You have no choice, Kimberly. Once you accepted to do this, you accepted the position, or I will still make your life a living hell."

She bit her lip to suppress the curse that wanted to be released.

His hands traveled down to the soft thatch of hair and his thumb teased the sensitive nub. Kimberly struggled desperately to get away from his touch and he laughed this odious sneer that sent trepidation through Kimberly like a dark shadow foreboding over her soul.

She stopped struggling for a moment to catch her breath. A sheen of sweat lay over the top of her skin as she realized the trepidation he must have suffered that night. Whether she had no choice in the matter or not, he was a man and had not known her, but he knew what Uncle Charlie's plan was and still she had raped him.

"Jaelen, please don't!" she cried out now, letting the tears burst through because even though she wanted to be released, she still wanted him. Damn her pride! It was a repulsive feeling to simultaneously crave and be disgusted by his touch. She wanted nothing to do with him, but her body would clearly call her mind a liar. He had created some kind of sick need in her to make her body defy what her mind fought to resist.

He reached in the bag and took out a roll of duct tape. Her eyes widened, aghast, as he ripped off a piece and before she could scream her disapproval, covered her mouth with it. The fight in Kimberly returned full-fledged as she twisted and turned, arched and strained until she was exhausted once more, but the fight was unyielding in her body and when she saw he was taking off his pants she struggled even more, not caring if the cuffs injured her. She wanted to be let loose, but she couldn't even verbally protest what she felt because of the tape over her mouth.

Kneeling down under the bed, Jaelen tugged on something out of Kimberly's eyesight that was long enough to reach up to the top of the bed as he stood up still holding it just out of her peripheral vision. Jaelen reached over in the cover to a slit that had been made earlier before she had entered the room and partially down into the mattress to pull out a steel buckle. Kimberly did her best to keep him from fastening the buckle across her waist knowing this would definitely hold her down, but his arms were too long and her fight did absolutely nothing to stop him.

When he reached in the bag for the last time, he pulled out a black face towel and held it up. "The piece de resistance, Kimber. Remember?"

She shook her head wildly as she struggled as hard as she could. Unable to scream or cry, all she could do was struggle weakly against him putting the towel over her face. When she couldn't see, all the heightened senses were now ten times more powerful. She could feel that he had moved away from the bed, but the thought of never knowing when he was going to touch her was the most terrifying for her.

His fingers finally touched her upper thigh and she flinched hard against the thick leather belt over her waist. He didn't stop there. His hands seemed everywhere and despite her stubbornness and anger and fear, she found her body responding to his touch and reveling in it. Kimberly wanted to die. Her body refused to listen to her mind as he used everything available to him including his hands, his body, and then...dear Lord, his beautiful glorious mouth sending her above any reality possible.

No man had created the vehement fury of titillation inside and out her. When his manhood finally pressed between the folds of the hyper-delicate flesh, Kimberly rose into a bliss of the most beautiful beyond known to her senses. She was flying and falling all at the same time, never wanting it all to stop as waves of ecstasy hit her senses repeatedly from every angle possible.

And as he joined her in the nirvana he had created, he held her close, whispering a curse in her ear for doing it again. She didn't know what "it" meant, and at that point and time she didn't care.

Moments seemed like hours as he held her close and when he did push away, it felt so wrong to be somewhere else other than with her. She closed her eyes hating her body for defying her and too ashamed to look at him because of what she had so blissfully enjoyed when she knew she would have sworn on everything that was holy before all this, she detested every bone in his body.

"Open your eyes, Kimberly," he ordered, standing beside the bed after he had released her arms and legs from the cuffs completely.

She shook her head. She wanted to cry, but she was all cried out and couldn't have shed a tear to save her life.

"I want to see your eyes, Kimberly. Open them," he demanded.

Slowly, she elevated her eyes until she was drowning in the dark sensual pools of his own. She wondered how could a man so handsome be so cruel?

"Is this the part you break my nose?" she asked weakly in an almost whisper.

A genuine laugh burst from his lips again, turning those handsome looks up ten times the effect they had on her. She told herself she would never want to make him happy because she would certainly lose her mind to this man and wouldn't care if she ever found it.

Calming down, he caught a hint of surreal fear in her eyes and wanted to know what she was thinking, but he wouldn't ask. "No, Kimberly. Gather yourself together and then get some rest."

She wondered how in the name of crazy did he expect her to get any rest in this room after what had occurred. How was she actually supposed to close her eyes in sleep when he could just come in here and tie her up again? Yet, a yawn did escape her lips and as he turned to leave her alone from the room, she found she could barely keep her eyes open. Kimberly told herself she would get up in a moment to freshen up, but even before the door closed behind him, she was fast asleep.

Chapter 20

Awaking to the fact that she was still in that large, king-sized bed, she jumped up from it in fright almost falling over in the chair that she had laid her gown in earlier. There weren't any clocks in the room, so she wasn't sure what time it was or how long she had slept. She couldn't believe she had actually gone to sleep in the horrible bed in the first place.

Putting on the gown, she went into the bathroom and took a warm shower. Upon coming out, a deep blue Donna Karen suit had been laid out on the bed, along with shoes and underwear. Beside the outfit was an overnight bag that had all the necessities she would need to finish getting dressed.

He was doing it again, she told herself. Being wonderful and thoughtful when she knew he was not that type of person.

After dressing, she put her hands in the jacket and found a small card with a rose in the corner. His writing was like no man's writing - neat and very clear. "Meet me in the front room once you are dressed."

Going down the stairs, the doors to the front room were open and she stepped into them. It was dark outside and by the clock on the mantle it was a little past nine o'clock at night. He was sitting on the couch next to her coat and she wondered if he had looked through the pockets to her wallet she had placed in there before leaving his office this morning.

Jaelen held his sifter of brandy as he stared into the fire looking very bothered. Her coat was probably the farthest thing from his mind. He was still in the same clothes. His shirt was slightly opened to reveal the cut of his chest muscles and his tie loosely hung around his neck. He was wearing the same pants, but they weren't belted. She noted some sauce near the inner thigh and blushed knowing her hands had been in the general area of his body along with her mouth.

"The car is outside. It will take you to the airport to return you to your family." He still hadn't looked at her and to her it seemed as if he were clutching the sifter.

"You aren't going to Davenport?" she asked.

"I have no need to go. Onyx will catch the flight back. In three days, you'll receive tickets for your family to fly up here. I will expect you to be in my office in three weeks. That should give you enough time to pack up your home."

"What about my children's funds?"

"They've been released as promised," he said.

She wanted to say thank you, but the words just wouldn't come out. All he had done to her, she still couldn't forget the shame of it and didn't want to thank him for anything he had done for her even if it was with good intentions for her and her children.

"Don't fail me, Miss Parker. I do know how to count the days, and I don't think you want me to come and get you," he threatened.

Not bothering to respond to him or even say goodbye, she left out the house to get into the limousine. It was a different driver, but he already knew what to do when he told her the private charter was fueling up as they spoke and would be ready for take-off by the time they arrived at the airport.

Kimberly was just grateful to be going home, and she couldn't wait to see the children and Leroy. Afterwards, she would partake in a long hot bath and sleep until the cows came home.

When she arrived at home and greeted her children and brother properly, she took a private moment with Onyx in the dining room while Leroy took the boys in the backyard to play. The limousine that was waiting when she got off the plane took her straight to her home and was now waiting outside patiently for Onyx.

"Just to let you know, I never told Jaelen about Jason."

"You will eventually, I know you will."

Kimberly shrugged. "Why should I? He wouldn't care."

Onyx chuckled. "That's where you're wrong, Kimberly. He would care and I think things would really change for him if he knew. He's a restless soul."

Snorting unladylike, she said, "That man has demons tearing from inside to out. Nothing can make him a better person."

"Do you see Jaelen or do you see the person he wants you to see, Kimberly? You aren't going to tell me after you spent twenty-four hours with a man that not once was he nice or thoughtful to you."

Kimberly had to reluctantly agree with Onyx, but should she tell Onyx about the handcuffs, the punishments, the horrible torture she had endured? No, she wouldn't, not because she was trying to keep Lethal from breaking every bone in Jaelen's body, but because she had accepted the revenge, and she would live with what she had asked for. Yet, along with that, for the time being she would have to deal with this man who would make her miserable emotionally every hour on the hour. Even when Jaelen was not around, she couldn't stop thinking about him, and this drove her insane because she felt if she had no mental attraction to this man--why would he always be on her mind?

Turning her back to Onyx so the woman couldn't see the troubled thoughts she was thinking, she said, "I don't think it will ever be a right time to tell Jaelen."

"Fine, but I think I should let you know in one month Jaelen's father is having a birthday surprise for his son. Their birthdays fall on the same day."

Cutting Onyx a sharp look, she asked tiredly, "What does this have to do with me, Onyx?"

"Only that Maxwell's going to let Jaelen know before the celebration he's dying of lung cancer. He's kept his illness a secret from his son for two years. At the celebration, he'll be inviting the most beautiful women around to gain his son's attention." Onyx stopped, gauging Kimberly's emotions.

Exasperated, Kimberly asked, "Again I ask, what does this have to do with me?"

"Jaelen's going to have to settle down soon. He needs to anyway, but Maxwell would like to see a child before he dies."

"No," Kimberly exclaimed, knowing full well where Onyx was going with this. "You are not going to use a dying man's state of health to make me reveal anything."

"Maxwell doesn't know about Jason, but it would make him happy. Otherwise, he'll go on Jaelen's pity and make Jaelen marry the first woman he sees and get her pregnant."

Kimberly pounded the table angrily. "So I should be sorry that son of a bitch has a conscious and would make sacrifices? What about my sacrifices? What about what I had to endure for my children? No, Onyx. I could care less about that man or his sick father."

"Think about Jason," Onyx reminded her. "Maxwell would be the perfect grandfather to that boy. He'll love your son, and he won't let Jaelen hurt you for keeping the truth. You'll be well compensated for what you've sacrificed."

Kimberly put her hand up to Onyx in disgust. "It's not the money. It's the man, and you know it."

"If you hate his father, does that mean when Jason grows up, you'll hate him for being like his father."

Obstinately, Kimberly said, "That won't happen to Jason."

This time Onyx snorted rudely. "Don't give me that shit. That boy is an exact replica of Jaelen down to those damn frowns. To be only six, he's already got the weight of the world on his shoulders. I bet if Jaelen sees how that boy acts, he certainly won't be the sourpuss you think he is."

"That's what you don't get, Onyx. I could give a fig of making that man's life better. I've got my own problems."

Onyx came up to her, standing akimbo. "Think about, Kimberly. Think about telling the truth because I can't keep Maxwell in the dark too long. He's a dying man, and he pays very well. I like him and I like his son a lot. I don't know how long I can keep my mouth closed."

"If it's money you want, I think I can afford to give you the amount you would request to keep your mouth closed."

Onyx held her hand up to stop Kimberly from going any farther with her bribery. "I can't be bought on this matter, Kimberly. Like I said, you've got a month. No more. I'll personally send you an invitation." She grabbed her bag and walked out the house.

Kimberly really wanted to scream, but she didn't want to alarm her boys or Leroy. Slamming the front door to her home, she buried her face tiredly in her hands and took deep breaths to calm her nerves. What was she supposed to do?

Jaelen wanted her to be in Detroit in three weeks to work for him, then this? Was this the card Onyx had mentioned? It was a good card, but Kimberly knew she could play one better. That woman was a headache in her own right, and Onyx cared much too much about Jaelen for Kimberly not to think that the two must have been lovers at some point.

On top of that, she still wasn't out the woods with Ainsley, who would love to see her dead.

Her thoughts wandered to what Onyx had just said. Jaelen getting married. That was ridiculous. He would make a sacrifice for his father to grant a dying wish. It didn't sound like the man she had come to loathe, but it did sound like the man she didn't dare try to imagine.

First things first, she needed to get Ainsley off her back, so she told herself that after she told the boys about the move, she would place a call to Lethal to help her out. While she was arranging all that, she would go ahead and make plans to be in Detroit by next week. There wasn't anything for her here anymore, and she was almost very eager to start her new job. It was a wonderful opportunity, and she could apply her nursing and therapy skills to give customers extra care.

Lethal didn't seem surprised that she would ask him to find Ainsley for her. He even volunteered to make the young man's life very difficult just to please her. She insisted that he only deliver a message that she wanted to sit and speak with the nephew and his lawyer about terms of the money she had left.

As the week passed, she threw herself in getting the house moved. She worked herself into exhaustion each night just so she wouldn't have time to think about Jaelen, yet the strange gnawing in the back of her thoughts continued to annoy her.

By the end of the week, she called Ms. Collins and let her know of her plans.

Ms. Collins didn't sound too happy about the decision to move to Detroit. "Aren't you worried it would make it even more easily for Ainsley to get to you?"

"I'm working on Ainsley as we speak, but I think it will be safe for Nae-nae to come home. I've found a great place in Detroit for us. It's a four-bedroom home with a great school nearby. I had to pay a little extra for the home to be ready in time, but it didn't need much work."

"I see Hawthorne's money does help in some ways," Ms. Collins said.

"In dire situations, but that's it. I don't want to use the money too much. I want to support my family with money I make, and I think with this job that I can do that. Plus, I can get Leroy into a better school and with vocational school he could actually learn a trade. He loves to work on cars, and Leroy's present employer has been wonderful in teaching him so much down here. I think we're going to do well."

"At least, I'll get to see the children more."

Kimberly agreed with Ms. Collins. They spoke a little more, but Kimberly declined to speak with Nae-nae because Kimberly didn't want to get her hopes up high if things fell through. Nae-nae was used to disappointments.

Jason came to her room on the last night they were to be in the home in Davenport. It looked as if he couldn't sleep. "Momma, are you sleep?"

She turned on the light for him then beckoned him to enter. "Come in, Jason. What's wrong?" She felt his head for a fever, then felt his neck for any temperature. He felt fine to her, but Jason sometimes caught her by surprise with any sickness.

"I feel okay, Momma. I was worried about you."

Kimberly frowned. "What do you mean?"

"You've been gone."

"I've been here the whole time, Jason. What are you talking about?"

He clasped his hands to her temple and looked into her eyes. "I see you, but sometimes you aren't here. You're somewhere else."

The understanding dawned in her eyes instantly, and she wanted to hug him ten times harder than what she was. How could he have known she was thinking so hard of Jaelen?

"I'm sorry, baby," she said, kissing his brow.

"Don't be sorry, Momma. I just want to know who made you unhappy."

"No one, baby. Momma's just got a lot to think about."

He knew she was lying, and Kimberly knew her son knew this knowledge, but he didn't address it. He knew he would eventually find out the truth. Kimberly couldn't get anything past her oldest son.

She invited him to crawl in the bed with her, and he fell asleep once he was in his mother's arms. Staring down at him, she gently brushed his cheek and wished his father could see how extraordinary Jason was, but she knew Jaelen would never see that. He cared only about himself, and she didn't want her son to get hurt by a man who wouldn't know how to be a father to the best son in the whole world.

Soon, she fell asleep next to her son in the comfort of his unconditional love.

Chapter 21

Jaelen received word Kimberly was in town and had contacted Ruby for another appointment. The grand opening wouldn't happen until October, so she still had two months to plan. He was excited about this happening, but couldn't really tell if he was more excited about Kimberly being a part of this or just the club opening.

"If I didn't know better, I'd say you were thinking about Kimberly," Onyx guessed leaning casually in the chair across from him at the restaurant they'd chosen to have lunch together.

"No," he lied quietly.

"Liar," she stated, sitting forward and leaning on the table toward Jaelen. "You've been daydreaming a lot since spending time with the woman. Are you getting fresh on her?" She picked up the hot bread delivered freely to the table and just started picking it apart dropping tiny crumbs in the saucer in front of her.

"No, Onyx." He frowned in disapproval. "When are you going to find your own life so you can stay out of mine?"

"Why should I when yours is more interesting? Plus, Lethal's getting ready to go to Chicago and close on the St. Royal security deal. I think that would be great for our company, don't you think?" She leaned back in the chair and put her feet on the table.

Many people around them looked at her in disapproval, but Onyx never cared about anyone else's opinion of how she handled herself. Especially in public.

He shook his head and then tapped her thick black Timberlands. She smiled and put only one foot down. Jaelen wasn't going to argue with her. He had been trying his best in this past week to not let the minx get on his nerve, but she was doing her best to try to get on his nerve.

Jaelen checked his Pulsar watch for the umpteenth time.

Onyx chuckled. "It's been two days, fourteen hours and fifty-three minutes since she has been back in town, Jaelen. Aren't you going to call her?"

"No. There's no reason to contact her until I feel like it. Plus, I figured she's still getting used to the city."

"Actually, she moved in pretty fast if you asked me-"

"I wasn't asking," he said in a near growl, cutting her off.

Onyx continued as if he had said nothing. "She even enrolled the kids in school yesterday. You've got to meet those kids, Jaelen. They're great."

"Why would I care about another man's kids?"

A strange smirk came to Onyx's lips, and she changed the subject. "Are you going to the gym?"

For brief minute, he looked through some reports that he had snatched off Edward's desk to keep himself busy, so he wouldn't be bored waiting for Onyx before she had arrived at the restaurant.

"No, not today." He frowned as his eyes quickly scanned some reports he had never seen before. These reports didn't look like the reports Edward had turned in.

"What's up?" she asked, seeing he was bothered by something else.

"This morning, I got the strangest message from a bank personnel. She was a teller, so I didn't think it was of any import until I went to tell Edward what she said."

"What did she say?" Onyx asked.

"She said that my personnel accounts needed adjustments before the end of the month."

"What does that mean?"

The grimace of confusion was evident. "Right after I told Edward, he said he had to run a personal errand, but that I shouldn't be worried about anything. He adjusted the account just last night and most likely it was a bank error. So when you called to confirm our lunch date, I decided to take the books away. I've been so busy with the opening, I haven't paid much attention to my personal books, but Edward's been doing a good job."

"Do you trust him?"

"He's been with me for two years. Why shouldn't I trust him?"

Clicking her tongue, she turned the journal around so she could see the entries herself. "When the cat's away, the mice will play. Didn't they teach you at your fancy college? You should always have checks and balances."

"I've had the checks and balances, and I tell you there was nothing to worry about. I think if I can run a two-million-dollar a year company, I can keep track of a rent check."

"Not according to this," she said, looking into the book even deeper.

He snatched the journal away and looked where she was going. Cursing under his breath, he saw the negative symbol. The second curse was much louder as he jumped out the seat and prepared to leave.

"Where are you going?" Onyx asked. "We haven't eaten yet."

"The bank and who cares," he said, answering both the questions in one sentence. "Make it to go and I'll catch you later." Without another word, he left to catch the bank before it closed.

Onyx watched him leave and wondered would he ever realize he was feeling differently about Kimberly. Although she figured when they worked together, they would spend enough time with each other to see what was meant to happen.

Her cell phone rang, and she answered it.

"You were right, she does keep a lot of secrets, but that cat Ainsley sure wasn't hard to find," Lethal said on the other line. "I just left the Park Condominium's on the Riverfront, and Mr. Hawthorne has taken residence in a female lawyer's place."

"Did you approach him?"

"No. I had the doorman deliver the message she wanted to speak with him. She's asked me to be a part of the meeting and I'm going."

"I'm going to," she declared.

"Oh no, you're not. I need you in Chicago. The Bellini family is setting up for the Christmas celebration, and they've invited some special guests. I would like you out there to discuss all the security details with Taylor Bellini. She's the third most powerful female in that family and as annoying and spoil as she acts, I don't think I could do a meeting with her without throttling the pestering little girl."

Onyx chuckled. "And you think I won't kill her?"

"You won't. I know you enough. You've got much better control when it comes to females than I do."

****

Jaelen arrived at the bank just as it closed. On his way home, he checked the account on the phone, but the computer was not registering what he had seen in Edward's private journal.

Once he entered his home, he sat in the chair in front of the fireplace. His housekeeper had left a note that she would be returning Monday to speak to him. Ms. Nolan didn't say what was it about, but he wasn't worried about it. Most likely she needed time off with the holiday months approaching.

Being alone gave him time to start thinking about Kimberly. As much as he tried, he couldn't stop thinking about her. He wanted so much to call her up knowing she was in town, but he knew that if he did she would become uncomfortable.

When the hell had he started caring about what anyone else thought?

Going to the bar, he poured himself a shot of whiskey. It was going to be a long night, and he needed something to put him to sleep other than jerking himself off thinking about her.

Chapter 22

Kimberly was caught off guard by the knocking on the door. Checking the clock on the wall in the kitchen, the digital display read ten p.m. As she was walking to answer the door, Jason beat her and opened the door for her. The security gate was secure, so she was fine with him doing so because Jason knew not to let anyone in.

As soon as the boy opened the door, he closed it right back before Kimberly had a chance to see who it was.

"Jason, that wasn't nice," she scolded him. "Go back up to your room."

He didn't speak, but a very dissatisfied sneer was clearly on his face as he stomped up the stairs. Kimberly made a note to check on the boy when she was done to see what was wrong with him and why was he acting so strange.

With one look at who was standing out on the porch, she knew immediately why her son had acted that way. Jaelen's disgruntled look would have been if she wasn't shocked to see him standing on her porch.

She didn't know how long she had stood there staring at him with her mouth wide open, but it was long enough for him to come to the conclusion she wasn't going to invite him in anytime soon.

"Are you going make me stand here all night?" he asked angrily.

Kimberly looked down at her wrist to check the time again, but then remembered she didn't have her lovely timepiece. The burnt scraps were probably still in his fireplace.

"Shouldn't I?" she questioned sarcastically, opening the security door and letting him in.

He stepped in, brushing past her, and Kimberly had to still herself from that upset in her stomach. He didn't see the effect he had on her because he was too busy looking around the place as if he was just trying to find something to criticize on, but she had to disappoint him. Despite the boys and Leroy in the house, Kimberly kept a tight ship in housekeeping.

"Would you like me to take your coat, Mr. Gates?"

Jaelen turned to her give her a look of clear disapproval. Kimberly was dumbfounded as to how she had gotten his ire up, but when was Jaelen ever just satisfied, let alone happy with something or someone. If that moment ever happened, Kimberly bet she would have to look outside to see if pigs were flying and a blue moon was occurring.

"No, and don't call me, Mr. Gates," he snipped.

"I would like to keep our relationship from now on professional, and calling you Mr. Gates allows me to keep our relationship that way. I've decided Jaelen is just too intimate, and I think you should allow me to do this considering our past."

"You act like it happened years ago, Kimberly," he exclaimed.

Kimberly wasn't used to his booming voice in the house, and she knew Leroy would find it just as disturbing, so she motioned him to follow her. When he just stood there with a stuck on stupid look, she sharply pointed him into the living room where - once he reluctantly went in - she was able to close the doors to keep their voices somewhat muffled.

"Did you come over here to yell at me for some reason?" she asked calmly, refusing to raise her voice.

He paced back and forth in front of the couch like a caged animal. "No, but you act like last week didn't happen."

"Why should I, Jaelen?" she asked, hand on hip. "Does it bother you that I'm trying to act like that? If I don't, I'll go insane trying to discern everything."

Jaelen cursed under his breath. He had not meant to admit that it bothered him she pretended nothing happen, but being here - now with her, what he wanted to discuss with her had gone out his mind as soon as he saw her. He didn't like this feeling encompassing him when he was around her, but he knew if she could act nonchalantly, he could do even better.

Forcing himself to calm down, he placed his coat on the couch, then he looked back at her after removing a large yellow envelope from the inside pocket of his coat.

Kimberly could actually see the man changing right before his eyes, and she wondered had God given her Jason so she could understand Jaelen. Was Onyx right? Having Jason in Jaelen's life would make him a better person? Having Jason in her life made her see a different side of Jaelen, which was probably why she wasn't so terrified of him as much as she had been in the beginning.

"No, I didn't come over here to get upset over something so trivial." Those cold, brown eyes looked her over from head to toe before coming back up to give her direct eye contact. "I heard you were in town, and I thought to drop off this package."

Hesitantly, she stepped toward him as if he were going to bite her and even that thought had her thinking about those delicious lips she had kissed not too long ago. You will not do this to yourself, she thought. Looking inside the manila envelope, she pulled out a set of keys, copies of some paperwork she had already turned in for her own files, and a payroll check in her name.

"There are keys to the office, your first paycheck including a bonus for moving expenses, copies of our agreement and so forth. Everything I think you will need for the office, with a listing of all employees already hired and what positions you need to fill before we open in two months," he explained.

She placed everything back in the envelope. "Thank you, but you could have waited until I came by the office."

"I could have, but I didn't think you should be in town any longer than you had to without getting a reminder of our deal." He stepped a little closer to her.

"Do you actually think I'd pack my family up in a week to run away to Detroit? How stupid do you think I am?" she asked incredulously.

"I plead the fifth, Miss Parker." He walked by her toward the door.

"Plus, if you didn't know, I've been working. I met with Ruby when I got in town, and I met with the Newman construction foreman. He predicts they'll be done in less than six weeks. I was going to suggest an early grand opening inviting the crème de la crème in the metro area."

He had thought of the same thing and was almost filled with pride that she had been on the same track. "I know you've been working."

"Oh, I forget, you know everything. So why visit this late at night, Jaelen? Don't you know people do have other lives that don't evolve around you?"

"I decided I wasn't going to wait until you get around to coming to see me because I'll be leaving out of town tonight."

If Kimberly's foot could have fit in her mouth, it would have fit quite nicely. Had he deliberately made her angry knowing she would say something stupid? Had she fallen into one of Jaelen's pre-dug graves that he loved to trap people in?

The room was quiet as they stared at each other as if waiting for something to happen.

She turned to open the door for him now that he had calmed down. She needed him to leave before she was unnecessarily apologetic because she didn't want to apologize. He was a mean-tempered, conniving bastard, and he didn't deserve an apology when it was probably all intentional because he got a rise out of getting people to look stupid.

When he was gone, she leaned against the door, wanting to beat her head against it.

"Trivial?" she said aloud. Now that she knew how he felt about what had happened, she could get some much-needed deep sleep. So why did it feel like she never wanted to sleep again?

****

Jaelen went back to the club before going home. Just as he stepped into the doorway of Edward's office, he saw Edward closing several drawers as if looking for something.

Holding up the journal, he said, "Were you looking for this?"

Edward seemed slightly uncomfortable. "Yes, sir. I was going to catch the accounts up this weekend. I just received the bank statements and with all the extra responsibilities you've put upon me as the opening draws closer,

I've been too busy to keep accurate records, but I have made sure all the bills were paid, sir."

This was a legitimate excuse and maybe Jaelen was just being paranoid over something silly. Edward had worked for him for over two years, and the young man had never done anything to make Jaelen think he could not be trusted. Jaelen had to admit, however, that sometimes, Edward seemed almost envious of what he had accomplished.

Edward had come to him begging for a job with hardly a good shirt on his back. He tried to hang with wealthy friends, and he probably told those friends that he made more than what Jaelen was paying him or that he was in some type of upper management position at Jaelen's company. Jaelen had also noticed how sore Edward looked when Jaelen had not even approached him about the management job at the club, but then the young man seemed content where he was at and was going above and beyond the call of duty to assist in making Kimberly's new job comfortable.

It would be foolish to suspect Edward of anything when there was nothing really to suspect him of. Jaelen had been putting a lot of responsibility in his hands, but now that Kimberly was smoothly taking over tasks and duties to free up more of Jaelen's time, Edward shouldn't worry about that.

"Use this weekend that I'm out of town to catch this journal up, and I would like a current bank statement as of last Monday on everything," he ordered.

The young man seemed relieved at this opportunity. "Thank you, Mr. Gates, I won't fail you."

Jaelen placed the journal on the desk and then left out of the office, putting his own mind at ease. Having Kimberly in his life had made him a little bit wary of all people, but he figured he could get through all this if he kept their relationship purely business. He had slept with a lot of women whom he had worked for, so this relationship should be no different.

He was positive he wanted nothing to do with Kimberly sexually anymore. He didn't care to kiss her soft beautiful lips, or stroke the angelic face of hers, nor hold that full voluptuous body of hers either while suckling the perfect dark caramel skin with his mouth. No, he didn't want to, so why when he thought of it, his damn manhood was hard as a rock?

Chapter 23

Kimberly went to work the next morning even though Jaelen had outlined in the plan she could work her hours however she wanted to, as long as it did not affect the business. Before the grand opening, she wanted to make sure everything was going to go off without a hitch. She wrote out the plans and what checks needed to be written and for whom by Monday. There was an email for her to keep her schedule open for the birthday party from Onyx and Kimberly wondered how did the woman get her email address, but then again Onyx worked in the information business, so getting the information needed for Onyx wouldn't be hard.

Kimberly had to wonder did it piss Onyx off that she couldn't figure out if Kimberly was keeping secrets. When she arrived home, Leroy let her know Mr. Heart had come by, but Leroy persisted in telling Kimberly that he didn't open the door because the house rules were if they didn't have a key, he didn't need to be opening the door for anyone. Mr. Heart wasn't upset and said he would stop by later to speak with Kimberly.

She had hired Laura Collins, a very nice young woman of twenty, who also had a slow mentality like Leroy, but she was a little bit more intelligent. Kimberly liked her a lot, and Laura had helped her brother get his high school diploma, but then Leroy turned around and helped Laura learn how to defend herself against some bullies at her community college.

Laura and Leroy were becoming best friends, and Leroy was delighted when he found out Laura would be a live-in helper while Kimberly was at work when they moved to Detroit. Laura had also encouraged Leroy to go to community college. It was so good to see her brother learning new things, and she prayed he would be a better person with Laura's help.

Once the boys were in bed, Laura and Leroy went in his room to study just as Kimberly got a call from Lethal, who said he was in the area and wanted to drop in. She invited him on over and fixed coffee for them.

Lethal was handsome Kimberly had to admit. He was a large man and though his size was awesome and almost fearsome, Kimberly had come to see he had a softer side, but didn't like showing it to many people. While she and the boys were in the defense's custody, he stayed with them even though he could have hired someone to sit with them. He taught the boys a little karate and also helped her teach their home schooling, so they wouldn't get behind in regular school. At first, Kimberly had thought he was around to help Uncle Charlie, but then he revealed he was here in her best interest and she came to believe him and trust him. He had taking a liking to the boys immediately, but even Lethal didn't know her secret because she had taken care of that before he even found them.

A brief hug was given to her as he came in the door. "You look well, considering who you work for. I don't see any bite marks on you."

She giggled at his teasing as she led him into the living room. "I am faring well."

"How's the son of a bitch?"

She blushed, forgetting how Lethal could curse like a sailor especially when he was comfortable with someone. "He's fine as far as I know. He went out of town this weekend on a convention."

"How's he treating you?"

Kimberly shrugged. "Like a boss should. I've come to realize this is a wonderful opportunity for me, and I love my job. I also see why he hired me. He was concerned about making sure his clients' heath was in check, and even though he could have hired anyone to run this club, he needed someone with some medical background and nutritional knowledge." She sighed excitedly.

"He plans to run a full health club inside the city limits. It will be the first of its kind anywhere. A full body emporium you could say, and I think his dream is wonderful."

"And what do you think of the man?"

Adjusting her weight uncomfortably, she said, "I don't wish to answer that."

He looked slightly amused. "I don't know what it is about you, Kimberly, but I can't help to find you mysteriously amusing."

She smiled, rolling her eyes heavenwards. "You have a weird sense of humor to begin with, Lethal."

He chuckled in agreement, then took out a long manila envelope. "Here's your information you requested."

Inside the envelope were several computer-generated documents and pictures.

Lethal began to explain everything. "Ainsley lives in the city. I've got a man on him morning, noon and night. When you go meet him tomorrow at the Marriott Courtyard downtown, I'll have three men on you to protect you if needed."

"Really, Lethal," she said rather amazed. "I should be fine. He wouldn't think of killing me in public."

"He wouldn't, but there's no telling who he hired to take you out, and he'll still look innocent. This guy is about as slimy as they come along with his friends. I also found out his lawyers hired another detective agency to start researching you."

She almost choked on the coffee she just sipped. "Why would he be researching me?"

"I don't know, but Del, who happens to be my cousin, said they told him to stop researching after some guy you used to date named Eli." He took out a recent picture of Eli, and she couldn't believe how homely he looked. Certainly not the well-kept person she had dated and loved so long ago.

Lethal found a toothpick he regularly kept in the breast pocket of his shirt and put it between his teeth. She knew this was a deterrent to him from smoking those stinky cigars in her presence. "That one is a trip, according to Del. That boy would sell his mother for the right amount of money."

"Eli? He wasn't like that when I met him."

"Time changes things, and it changes people, Kim. You best remember that."

"If that's so true, why does it still feel like Jaelen still hates my guts?"

"If he hates you so much, why would he give you this great job?"

"I've been trying to figure that one out myself, but I can't come up with anything." Except the fact that he knew she disliked his closeness and wanted her to be under his foot for the rest of her life, but she wasn't going to say this to Lethal because she didn't want Lethal to know Jaelen had done all this for revenge.

A page came in for Lethal, and he looked rather irritated about the call. "I have to go, Kim. I'll call you tomorrow early in the morning, and I'll be taking you to the Marriott."

"Thanks for all your help, Lethal." She hugged him goodbye.

He kissed her cheek gently. "If that boss of yours even gets on your nerve, let me know. I'll get pleasure ripping him a new asshole."

"I'm sure you would love to for no reason at all."

"It might make him a better person."

"I don't think you tearing him from limb to limb will make him a better person. It would definitely make him dead though."

He chuckled lightly. "Like I said, a better person."

Kimberly laughed at his silliness. "Good night, Lethal. I'll see you tomorrow."

When he was gone, she ran herself a long bath and relaxed for a while. Her thoughts were mostly on Jaelen and about this job opportunity. It was a wonderful vision, and she didn't think she had ever told him. She needed to speak with him and find out how he felt about her working for him, yet how did she get him to admit how he felt without asking him right off?

Heck, how did she even manage to talk to him when all she thought about was being with him?

Trivial. That was what he thought about it all. Now that he had his ultimate revenge, he didn't think twice about what had happened. Why should he when all he cared about was himself?

Lying in bed, she stared up at the ceiling until she fell into an exhaustive sleep.

****

Lethal called her at eight Sunday morning and she was ready by eleven. Noon was the meeting time in the Courtyard's dining room, and her stomach turned over a thousand times before she made it there with Lethal.

He parked on the side of the hotel so no one would see her being dropped off. "Del called me last night. He told me they instructed him to start up the investigation on you again. Ainsley wants to make sure there is no one to claim the inheritance or the children if you die."

She swallowed hard feeling, the nausea build up. "I don't have any more relatives, but there are guardian papers. When I knew I was pregnant for sure with Hawthorne's children, I borrowed the money to have them drawn up. The children would go to Miss Collins."

"The woman who helped you in New Orleans?"

"Yes," Kimberly said, wondering how much Lethal knew about her and if he was still fishing for information. She disregarded this distrusting nature of hers. It popped up at the most inconvenient times. "She has a daughter almost as old as Leroy with the same condition as Leroy, but not so severe. Miss Collins moved back up to Michigan three years ago and has been a big help when I've needed to get to my lawyers."

Strangely, he dropped the subject and Kimberly was glad. In no way did she want Pamela Collins to become involved in all that was going on in Kimberly's life. She was already doing above and beyond the call of friendship for Kimberly.

"What could Ainsley be searching for? My mother had no other relatives except Uncle Charles after she died. Trust me, I did all the searching in the world. I didn't want to be in Uncle Charles' care at all, and I definitely didn't want Leroy in that situation either."

He answered her initial question. "Your father."

She frowned. "My father? No one knows who my father is. Charles met him a couple of times, but then he said the man disappeared when he couldn't get my mother to change her drug ways. I don't blame him, but his name never went on our birth certificates, and he never came back for any contact."

"Maybe because of this. Del found it in some old papers of your uncle's. He stored your mother's personal papers in a safe deposit box.

"How did Del get to it?" she asked suspiciously.

Lethal chuckled, slightly amused. "Del can talk a nun out her underwear whenever he does use his mouth and these lawyers are paying him big bucks to get this information."

She blushed at this. "I don't think I want to meet this cousin of yours." Looking down at the crumpled piece of paper, she noticed her mother's handwriting. There was a lot of scratch outs and corrections, but she was able to read the letter aloud. "Dear Thor, I want you to know that in no way is it your fault, but I wanted to let you know that there's nothing for you to feel guilty anymore. Kimberly died in her sleep two weeks ago. Charles felt I should write to you and let you know that. The doctor said it was SIDS even though she was almost two years old, but that it was still a high possibility at that age. Now there is no reason for you to ever come back because your love for me died a long time ago. Goodbye. Alicia"

Lethal explained it. "She lied to him, so he would never know about you and Leroy. I have a feeling your father left not knowing she was pregnant with Leroy and to be spiteful she lied to him about you, so he would have no reason to come back."

Kimberly didn't know if she should hate her mother for keeping her father away because she had a feeling the man would have come and saved Leroy and her if he had known they were alive and their mother was dead. "Where was this letter sent to?" she asked.

"Don't know," he said. "Del said he would let me know, but of course for a hefty fee like I've never helped the son of a bitch out before."

Kimberly flushed remembering Lethal called almost everyone he knew very well a son of a bitch as if it was an endearment. "I'll pay whatever he needs."

"Don't let him know that. Del is all about the Benjamins and will take all he can get."

She handed him back the letter, but he told her to keep it.

He gave her last-minute instructions including the hand signals when she felt things were not going right and then he pinned a beautiful diamond broach on her blouse.

"What's that for? Luck?" she asked.

He snorted. "You could say that, but it's a camera complete with audio intake. As a last backup."

"Aren't you a little paranoid, Lethal?" she asked.

"Yes and proud of it. I saved the Pope's ass because of it."

"You saved the Pope?"

"When he was here about ten years ago," he said proudly. "All you have to do is call my name, Kimberly." The intense gaze in his opaque eyes clearly told Kimberly how serious he was.

Getting out the black Expedition, she headed in the dining area of the hotel. The hostess was at the doorway.

"Mrs. Hawthorne?" the hostess asked.

Kimberly nodded. "How did you know?"

"Mr. Hawthorne described you perfectly. Please follow me."

She was led past crowded tables, directly to a man looking about his early thirties. Hard liquor and tobacco seemed to disguise his age though. Ainsley Hawthorne had an after-five shadow, but she was still able to see some of Wescott's features on the man. Strong after five shadowed jaw, small intense eyes, and hard potent features that brought out a boyish handsomeness, but looking into his light brown eyes, she saw something very mistrusting and deceitful about him. He was a bomb waiting to explode given the right power and money - the money she possessed.

His voice was rather rasped as he made introductions. "You're even more beautiful in person. Now I see why my uncle was so infatuated with you." He took a long drag on his cigarette before drowning it in the glass ashtray.

The waitress came by, but Kimberly refused to have anything to eat. Her stomach was so upset and the thought of eating made her even queasier.

Ainsley ordered a pasta dish with extra cheese on top. Kimberly sipped her water to calm her stomach and clear her mind. When the waitress left, she quickly addressed the business at hand.

"Ainsley, I know that you are upset that the court gave me the rest of Wescott's assets, what little was left, and you feel that I was wrong to have them."

"My uncle was not in his right mind when he bequeathed everything to you. As family I was looking out for my blood," he falsely seethed.

She rolled her eyes at that load of bull crap. "I only granted a dying man's wish to have his children and keep the money away from you. Wescott wanted that. He made me promise."

"My uncle loved me. I was his only nephew," he said angrily.

Kimberly was not going to argue with this idiot. Leaning forward, with her most coquettish look, she said softly, "I've come here today to make a deal."

He seemed to warm to her charm immediately, and Kimberly knew given the chance, this man was the type that didn't take no for an answer. The lecherous gaze coming at her made her hair stand on end in wariness for her safety. "I'm listening, Kimberly."

"What if I gave you half of the assets that I've earned? It's a large chunk of change that would keep you very comfortable if spent right."

This time he leaned forward sneaking a look down her blouse. "What's a chunk?" he asked, almost salivating at the possibility of dollars. Picking up a glass of wine already on the table, he sipped it calmly, eagerly waiting for her response and trying to seem nonchalant about what she would tell him as if he already knew.

She swallowed the bile that was rising in her throat. "One million dollars."

Liquid sprayed out his mouth onto another table. Heads turned in their direction as he choked on the alcohol that went down the windpipe. Waiters came to assist and clean up the mess and bring out new food and place ware. Kimberly remained placidly seated throughout this commotion.

When things died down again, he rasped out, "Where the hell did you come up with that kind of money?"

"Once the court granted me the assets, Ainsley, I pushed them into mutual funds, international stocks, off shore, high interest banking accounts. High returns with, high-risk stocks that would be beautiful if I won and horrible if I lost. By the grace of God, I was always the winner, but I never touched the money. I made do with my two hands for my children and I didn't touch one dime unless times were really bad."

"Which is why it made it so hard to find you? Here we were thinking you were living the high life when in truth you were living beneath the gutters."

"Something like that."

He started up another cigarette. "You're a very smart cookie, Kimberly. I must admit. All my money and time was put into making sure you didn't surface."

She couldn't tell if he was dealing her a compliment or was pointing out something that pissed him off.

He continued. "You're like a roach, you know. All you skanks are alike. Take some down, twenty more pop up and when I flick the lights on, you all run like crazy and hide."

Kimberly's senses were definitively on the high caution side. "You'll take the money?"

"When there's more behind all of that?" he asked as if she thought him to be crazy. "I know you got more for me."

"I'm telling you we can split it or are you so greedy you don't want to handle that? Is it that you want all of it?" she asked, wondrously not believing he couldn't just take what was offered.

"You came to pay me off, lady. You should have been prepared to pay the maximum, right?" he asked. "Hell yeah, I want it all because I deserve it and you don't. Neither does those two brats that think they're my kin."

"I don't let them know of their despicable cousin. Fostering hate at that age would definitely be deadly for you."

He leaned even closer, blowing the cigarette smoke in her face. "Watch your back, whore, 'cause when I'm done, those bastards of yours will be mourning by your graveside while that retardo brother of yours is locked so far away from them, you'll be praying I come and save them."

"I will never need you or your help, Ainsley. You stay away from me and my family."

For a moment, Ainsley almost saw a glint of death in her eyes, but she knew he thought of her as a weak frail looking woman and couldn't possibly be serious. He snorted this brief moment of fear off and snickered. "You really almost had me, slut, but don't worry. Your death will be mourned before I turn custody of the children over to the state and take the money I was meant to have." He tossed the butt of his cigarette in her water.

Kimberly stood up, too angry to sit another moment in his presence. "I withdraw the deal off the table, Ainsley. If you aren't going to be reasonable, then you get nothing."

Just as she was about to turn away, he grabbed her arm, digging his nails in her skin. "You're dead, bitch," he seethed through clenched teeth. "You'll be sorry you ever met my uncle."

She snatched away and scraped at his face. "I already am, Ainsley." Drawing her arm to her chest, she turned around before he realized the four scratches she had left across his cheek with her own nails.

Lethal was waiting in his vehicle for her as soon as she stepped out and she jumped in. He took off immediately. While driving, he checked her arm and issued out orders in a headset near his mouth for someone to stay on the target, while the others returned to base.

"Are you okay?" he asked.

She nodded. "He just dug in a little, but I was frightened." Desperately, she looked for something to vomit into.

Lethal saw this and pulled to the side of the road, jumping three lanes to get to the edge. Kimberly opened the door and emptied the contents of her stomach out on the ground. He rubbed her back for comfort, and Kimberly burst in tears.

I need to get better at confrontations, she thought as she buried her face in Lethal's chest.

Chapter 24

All weekend long at the conference, Jaelen made calls. He had pulled Edward's file and done a lot of background checking, but he couldn't find anything unusual about Edward's past to make him think that there was something he should suspect.

Getting on the plane to return to Detroit, he was seated near a window. A woman, well dressed and a couple of years younger than Jaelen, sat next to him. Every once in a while, she gave him a strange look.

"Do I know you?" she asked, just after the take-off.

Jaelen rapidly took off the seatbelt once the captain pushed the button. He didn't answer her, not wishing to make conversation with a complete stranger and certainly not interested in meeting a woman. For some reason Kimberly was still fresh in his blood, and he couldn't seem to get her out.

"You ever been to Chicago?" she persisted.

Jaelen didn't want to be outright rude to the woman, so he answered gruffly, "A couple of times on business."

She narrowed her eyes at him sharply. "You know the Bellini family?"

"Who doesn't?" he wanted to say, but then his curiosity about the beautiful dark olive skinned woman piqued. "I've been introduced to a couple of the Bellini family members."

"Who? Armando? Alejandro? Or the head bastard himself?" She snorted.

Jaelen could immediately sense a sort of animosity about this woman for the Bellini family. They were a powerful Chicago family that owned an international chain of hotels, motels, bed and breakfasts, and resorts. They catered the world in adult vacation spots and from what Onyx had told him recently, they were looking to corner the ethnic market in adult vacations. Solely owned by family members, not only was the family known for great investments in adult vacations, the family was also known for their real estate business as well. This wasn't what made headlines though. The men in the Bellini family were notorious rakes, all of them single up to date and all of them, except Armando, swearing off marriage like it was an imprisonment.

"Well, I don't think they are all bastards," he said.

She opened up a bag of nuts and bit into one with this serious intense look in her eyes. "You're right. It's just Dalton. I wish he would eat shit and die, if you want my opinion." She held out her hand in introduction. "Sharlie Costello, I work for the Chicago Herald."

The name rang a bell. He had seen some of her work in the New York Times and Detroit News. "You do freelance work as well, don't you? You're a business writer and Chicago's society beat writer."

She smiled. "I'm also working on a biography about the Bellini family."

"Aren't there enough books out about them?"

"Yes, but none of them are about the scandals, and secrets the Bellini family don't want the public to know about. I'm doing an unauthorized version of that family, and I know it will be big because what I have to tell the world about that family will blow lids, especially the son of a bitch that heads the front of them." She looked so pleased with herself it made her features even more beautiful because she didn't look like a woman who usually smiled. Matter of fact, she looked like the type who did a lot of vindictive things to make herself happy. She reminded Jaelen of himself and the person he had become because of Kimberly.

For some reason he felt close to Sharlie because she was a kindred spirit in the revenge life. He let her go on for an hour, spouting how she hated the Bellini family and soon she started concentrating on just the business-head of the family member, Dalton. No matter that he was an internationally known billionaire because of his real estate savvy, he was a personal fuck up in the intimacy department. "He can't keep a secretary let alone a good woman to save his life."

"Do you mind me asking if you and Dalton Bellini were personal?"

She sipped bourbon the attendants had served off the liquor wagon. "I don't care to answer that question, Mr. Gates, but I can tell you something." She leaned very close to Jaelen and he knew she had already too much to drink. "The son of a bitch will shoot bullets when my book is published next year." She giggled. "I wish I could see the look on that bastard's face when it all hits the fan."

Jaelen knew he wasn't going to get her secret out if he continued to ask questions, but he had to wonder what it was. "How did you know I'd been in Chicago?"

Sitting comfortably back in her seat, she said, "You've attended Bellini functions or parties or something where a Bellini was present. I never forget a face." She drunk the last of her drink and then sat back in her seat partially closing her eyes. "I'll never forget how he..." She was fading off to a deep drunken sleep. "He broke my heart."

Jaelen pushed her dark shoulder length out her face and studied her features, wondering when he slept did he look so peaceful. Yes, she had a vendetta, but does a heart stay broken forever? Do the memories continue to hurt a person? Or do they just let it go, so the heart could heal?

He didn't want to hate Kimberly. Not like Sharlie hated Dalton. He wanted to ... damn he didn't know. He didn't know what he wanted from Kimberly, but he didn't want her hurt, and he didn't want her to hate him. He didn't want her to go far from him either, which was why he had given her the job although it had amazed him at how good she had turned out to be.

The plane landed in Detroit, and Sharlie gave him her card thanking him for listening to her. He didn't know if fate had thrown Sharlie in his life to make him see what he could become if he continued on his vengeful path. Or if this was all just a way for destiny to wake up and tell him what he had gotten was not a night of rape done to him, but a woman who could sooth the troubled demons inside of him, if he only gave her a chance.

"If you need anything, Jaelen, please don't hesitate to call me," Sharlie's parting words were.

He wanted to tell her not to hate anymore, but he didn't think it was right to pass out wisdom he didn't listen to. Not until he got his own life together did he think he would find Sharlie Costello and tell her what she needed to do.

For right now, he needed to set aside his own vengeance and get on with his life. He needed to see what was it about Kimberly Parker Hawthorne that made everyone like her.

When he landed in Metro Detroit airport, he was greeted by Edward who showed him the complete journal along with a bank statement attached to the end of the pages. Edward let him know Kimberly had come in over the weekend and did some work for the company and left him some work to look over.

"I took the initiative and brought it over for you to look at," Edward said. This took his mind off the journal for a moment as they arrived at the office. Edward had asked him if he wanted to go home and shower from such a long journey, but Jaelen had decided against that. He wanted to see Kimberly before he rested. He wanted to see her face.

"Order me some breakfast, have my suitcase taken straight to the cleaners, and make sure my car is delivered here by ten o'clock so I can take myself home," he ordered. "I'll look over the journal after I have eaten."

Edward nodded. "Thanks for understanding what I've been going through, sir," he said rather flushed. "I'll make sure from now on that all the work you assign me gets completed immediately."

"With Mrs. Hawthorne on board, you won't have so much to do for me anymore, Edward. From now on I think I can handle my personal accounts and I was going to suggest why don't you think about taking a couple of days off."

The assistant looked very grateful.

"Starting today, Edward," Jaelen ordered. "After you have completed the assigned task, put in a vacation slip on my desk for a week off. Has Mrs. Hawthorne arrived yet?"

"Yes, sir. She's been here for the past hour. She arrives every day on time."

"Have you been watching her, Edward?"

"I've been making sure she does what she is supposed to be doing, sir." Edward seemed only slightly nervous.

"Hurry up with the food, Edward," he ordered, dismissing the young man by turning away and looking out the large window behind his desk, deep in thought.

Chapter 25

Edward walked out and Jaelen watched him out of his peripheral vision. Kimberly came to the doorway, giving Edward a strange look. When she closed the door behind Edward, Jaelen addressed the mistrusting look she had given Edward.

"What was that look for?" he asked.

Kimberly gave him a rather flustered look as if she was caught red-handed doing something wrong. "Nothing," she lied.

"Clearly," he said. "There is something going on between you and Edward."

"No, there isn't," she said defensively. "I just don't feel comfortable around him."

"Edward has worked for me several years. I trust his exemplary work ethic."

Kimberly only shrugged. "He just doesn't seem like the type that can really be trusted. He reminds me of the kind of person that would take candy from a baby when the mother isn't looking."

Her description reminded Jaelen of Edward's added responsibilities he was given since Jaelen had been trying to start up the club. He made a note to himself to check all of Edward's work because Kimberly seemed to have a good judge of people and had always been honest in her feelings toward people.

"Do we have an appointment?" he asked.

"No, Mr. Gates," she answered.

"Then why are you here?" he asked defensively.

"Mr. Gates," she said, taking a deep breath. "There are some things I think we should talk about."

"Do you?" he asked skeptically. "What other things do you think we need to speak about? You work for me, you do your job, and you go home."

He was already starting the day out being a jerk, but she was not going to let that impede on what she had to say although now she didn't think he deserve it. Coming closer to the desk, she licked her lips to fight off her nervousness. "Before we go on any further in this business relationship, I need to let you know some things. I've been doing a lot of thinking over the weekend about our past, and I've come to the conclusion that I've never really spoken to you about the past, except under duress or when I've been threatened."

She cleared her throat and proceeded. "I realized this weekend that I never really addressed what happened directly in terms of an apology." She paused to see his reaction, but the look on his face was complacent as if he were on the borderline of pure boredom. Kimberly continued, "I wanted to say, without the conditions of being browbeaten, threatened, or blackmailed, that for all it's worth, I am sorry for what happened to you. When you gave me that experience of what you suffered, I was able to understand it all and why you were so angry with me. I understand you and your problems a little bit more." She was not going to tell him that having Jason in her life also made it a lot easier to understand him, too.

"What do you mean by problems?" he asked.

Kimberly fumbled for a word to describe what she meant, without insulting him. "I mean the way you act, and why you're so hard on everybody when you really are a rather … good person, in a way." These words were forced out, but she honestly meant it.

His look now spoke of skepticism. "And you think I'm good after what I've done to you?"

"Like I said, what you did to me made me understand you a lot better and why you have a lot of animosity toward me."

"And you don't have any animosity toward me?" he asked.

"NO...yes!" She took a deep breath to calm herself. "Not really animosity. I think it's because before all that, Jaelen, you had to be a jerk."

This time he only raised a brow, but she couldn't figure out what he was thinking.

Kimberly felt like a child in front of his unwavering glare. Any other person, she would have been able to spit out the reason quickly, but having Jaelen's eyes on her, she was consumed with the thought of their night together. She knew Jaelen wouldn't understand how she felt since he thought of their night as trivial.

"Jaelen, I just want to say how sorry I am about Uncle Charlie's treatment and what I was forced to do to you. On top of everything that has happened between us, I wanted to let you know that I appreciate the opportunity you have given me and my family to come back to Detroit and to work on this incredible vision that I think is just a wonderful idea."

He only looked partly amused. "Does that make me a wonderful jerk?"

Kimberly blushed. "No, it doesn't make you wonderful at all. I just think your idea is."

"So, that still makes me a jerk?"

"Yes, you're still a jerk if I should be so honest with my boss."

"I value your honesty, Kimber."

A shudder went through her body as she met his eyes. Did he have to look so serious and say her name like that using the lowest bass in his voice. She blushed profusely and fought her shyness, remembering how she would keep their relationship professional. "I should be going now."

"Is there anything else you wanted from me?"

"No," she said turning away, but then changed her mind and turned back to him. "Except one thing. Did you really freeze my accounts?"

Jaelen gave her a boyish, wicked grin. "Not really."

"What does not really mean?"

"I lied," he said, simply as if it were nothing major. "I hadn't frozen your accounts."

"And if I had challenged you?" She came back up to the desk and leaned over.

"But you didn't."

"But if I had, then what?"

He shrugged. "I don't know, Kimberly. It was all thought about at the spur of the moment. You didn't pull my card and that's all in the past. I won because I had the best poker face."

"Do you always win, Jaelen?"

"As often as possible."

Kimberly decided if she continued this conversation, she would easily start remembering what a big jerk he was. Just as she stormed out his office, her pager went off. It was Ruby calling 911. She went to her office and called Ruby who seemed quite upset.

"Has Mr. Gates come back in town, yet?" Ruby asked.

"Yes," Kimberly answered. "I just spoke to him in his office."

"He has a lot of explaining to do. I just found out that the payroll check he issued last week bounced."

Kimberly adjusted the phone to make sure she was hearing her right. "What do you mean bounced?"

"I mean bounced like a ball," Ruby exclaimed. "I just got my bank statement back and the overcharges made my account overdrawn."

"I'm sure there's just been some accounting error. Jaelen can explain everything," Kimberly assured her.

"I sure as hell hope he can because not only did my check bounce, but all the other payroll checks bounced."

Kimberly was in disbelief of what she was hearing and the possibility of what was going on. "Ruby, are you serious?" she asked to be sure.

"Serious as a heart attack."

"As the manager, let me go in and ask him what is going on," she said. "I'll call you back as soon as I know anything, Ruby."

"That's fine, then I won't come up there until you call me back."

Kimberly hung up, then picked back up the receiver, flipped through her Rolex deck to find the number to her bank in town she had used Jaelen's check to open the account with.

Going back into Jaelen's office, Kimberly noticed it looked as if Jaelen were preparing to leave, but upon seeing her, he put his coat down and gave her his full attention. "Are you here to talk about the past again, Kimberly?" he asked.

"No, Jaelen, I came to speak about an important matter. Ruby just called me and said that the payroll checks issued last week bounced."

"What do you mean bounced?" he seemed to growl.

"That's the same question I asked her. But it's true."

Jaelen slowly sat back in his chair as if in slow motion someone had knocked the breath out of his face. Kimberly did not like the dazed frown on his face, as if he knew something horrible was going on.

"Jaelen, what's was wrong?" she asked.

"I don't know," he said too honestly. "And that's the problem." He stood up and went to his desk. After shuffling around some papers, he headed for the door. "I'll be back in a couple of hours."

Quietly, Kimberly asked, "Do you want me to go with you?"

He stopped at the doorway, but he didn't turn to look at her. "Yes," he said in a rather strained matter as if he desperately needed her in his life at that moment.

Kimberly didn't bother to get her own coat because she had her keys in her blazer pocket that she wore. She picked up his coat he had mistakenly forgotten, and followed him out the door.

"Damn, my car isn't here," he gnarled.

She handed him the keys to the company white Ford Explorer and led the way to where she had parked. He handed her the brief he had jammed the journal and bank statement in as he let her in the SUV on the passenger side. Kimberly didn't know if he was being a gentleman on purpose or if the action just came natural. His mind was a million miles away, and Kimberly knew this was just ingrained into him, but she was still honored by the treatment.

As he started toward the main bank branch in downtown Detroit, she opened up the brief.

"Do you mind?" she asked, to gain permission to look at the journal.

"Go ahead. Maybe you'll see something I don't see."

"I did work at a branch for a short time while I was on the run," she said proudly as the bank statement mistakenly fell on the floor by her feet. She

195

picked it up and without even examining the printout, she frowned at the statement itself.

"What's wrong?" he asked, looking over at her, then at the road repeatedly.

"This statement is a false one. This was made on the computer they usually use for training tellers." She tore off the paper it was attached to. "The white paper behind the statement probably hit the watermark the computer always puts on the paper," she explained, holding the paper up to the windshield so he could see it.

"Fuck me," he cursed. "I'm going to kill him." Taking out his cell phone, he directed it to call Edward's phone, but no one picked up the line.

"Edward must have had an insider at the bank," she said as Jaelen found a place to park and then came around to open her door and help her out.

They went inside together and waited for someone to come and assist them. Jaelen tapped his foot, which was quite a distraction for Kimberly, and she was glad when the woman finally called for Jaelen. He stood and waited for her to stand as well. Kimberly hadn't any intentions of going all the way to the desk with him, but it seemed as if he was insisting upon her to know everything as well.

The woman assisting her reminded Kimberly of the Betty Crocker picture. She was so nice looking and very kind. "How may I help you, Mr. Gates?" she asked, a bit unsure seeing the venomous glare Jaelen had on his face.

On the woman's name tag it read, Maria, so Kimberly used the woman's name to get her attention from Jaelen's deathly gaze. When they sat down, Kimberly handed the woman the false bank statement, and then asked, "Maria, can you tell me where this was generated at?"

"Yes," she said, looking at the corner edge of the paper where some strange numbers were listed at. She wrote the numbers down and did some separating, then typed something into the computer.

Jaelen annoyingly drummed his fingers on the desk. Calmly, without looking in his direction, Kimberly placed her hand gently on top of his to stop him. This was their first time touching since that night, and the electricity surging from the palm of her hands moved up through her arm streaming straight to her brain, then spread through her body like a tsunami.

Slowly, Kimberly looked at Jaelen and the powerful heated cinnamon gaze was evident to her that he felt the same way. Her breathing became shallow, and she licked her dry lips.

"Mr. Gates," Maria said, shocking them out the dimension they had been about to fall into. "These papers were drawn up at the training computer of one of our eastside branches."

Flustered, trying to regain her composure, Kimberly asked, "W-Would it be able to tell us what teller did this?"

"Yes. That would be the teller code in the last six digits," Maria answered, typing in something else and the dot matrix printer beside the desk started going off. "I could find that information out for you," she offered.

"Before you do all of that," Jaelen said, "I need to find out how much the account is in default."

Maria gave him a that-would-be-no-problem look and began to busily type on her computer again. "Are there any other accounts with this one?"

Jaelen opened his brief and handed her a list of bank accounts. "I would like you to check them all out."

Kimberly braved herself and looked at him worriedly. He didn't look at all pleased and stood up walking away from the desk to make a phone call on his cell phone.

"Are you, Mrs. Gates?" Maria asked as she busily typed.

Kimberly blushed. "No, I'm not, Maria. I'm his newly hired club manager. He's been planning on opening the club for the longest as I've heard. It's his dream."

"I thought…" Maria stopped herself. "I mean you have so much control over him and that temper of his."

She frowned, but didn't respond to Maria's statement although she did wonder what did Maria mean by it, yet this was not the time or the place to get into what control she had over Jaelen. Maria was just seeing things because Kimberly knew Jaelen didn't like her at all in that way. The man could barely stand her. So why was she here? And what was that look of his for?

Before she could answer those questions for herself, he sat back down beside Kimberly. "No answer at Edward's home or his cell phone. I called Onyx and asked her to go over to his home and then give me a call when she arrived."

"You didn't want her to be here with you?" Kimberly asked, but then wished she could have taken that question back.

"No. She's much better on the street than being cooped up somewhere." He looked directly at her. "You on the other hand don't mind being tied down somewhere."

She gasped at his double meaning. "This isn't the time or the place to be discussing that, Jaelen."

The wicked amusement in his eyes was evident, and Kimberly realized he was doing that so he wouldn't lose his temper in public. She debated continuing to sit beside him and taking his glib remarks or to go and wait in the car.

"If I don't discuss something, Kimberly, I'm going to break something," he warned.

"Then find another subject," she snapped.

"Fine," he agreed as Maria tore off the printout and handed it to Jaelen. The deadly frown instantly returned as he only took a glance before he swore viciously, heating Kimberly's ears and making Maria turn bright red.

Kimberly took the paper from him and gasped in shock. The accounts added up to five hundred thousand delinquent.

"Are there any checks on any of these accounts that haven't been cashed, yet?" Kimberly asked.

"Yes," Maria said reluctantly, and pointed to a listing of checks. "That doesn't account for the monthly regular withdrawals either." She pointed these out to Kimberly as well.

"Dear Lord," was all Kimberly could say as her mind began to total the negative accounts. "Why wasn't he notified that these accounts were like this?"

Maria looked at her screen. "Well, it seemed like the accounts didn't all update until today. The accounts were put on hold as if the money was there, but would be paid on a later date and many of the checks written out to others were postdated, so the totals wouldn't be in until last Friday." She typed rapidly to update her computer. "It seems the funds were withdrawn just this morning all from one account funneled there Friday." Staring at her screen hard, she said, "I think this could have also been an inside job."

"From his company?" Kimberly assumed.

"No," Maria said in disappointment. "From ours. Hold on for a second while I call the branch that printed out this."

Kimberly looked at Jaelen. "How much, Jaelen?" she asked. "How much could he have taken in all from all these accounts?"

Jaelen had an expression on his face as if he were totally whipped. Kimberly had never seen him like this and didn't know how to handle him. She wished Onyx were here.

Shaking his arm to get him out the daze he seemed to have fallen into, she asked her question again.

"Almost about two million, I would figure if he also took payroll and the weekend drops." He cursed viciously. "He deliberately waited for the weekend drops, the bastard."

Just then Jaelen's cell phone went off. He stood up and went away from the desk to answer it. Maria got off the phone, but she didn't look please. "The teller who generated this report is named Angela Barnes. They're faxing over all her transactions from the past week. I can't personally access them from my computer."

"What does this mean?" Kimberly asked Maria.

"You want the worst scenario?" Maria asked, glancing over to Jaelen who was pacing while he was talking on the phone.

"Yes," Kimberly replied.

"He's bankrupted. If they don't catch whoever did this with the money, Mr. Gates, can consider himself bankrupted."

"But the club and all the assets," Kimberly pointed out.

"He'll have to sell all he can in order to just break even. He took out a substantial loan in order to get the club built according to the records. With the personal lawsuits by employees for bounced checks and the other bills, he needs to pay, this young man is looking at having absolutely nothing when this is all over."

"What would be a quick fix?" Kimberly asked.

Maria snorted in amusement. "Unless you've got two million just lying around in the next twenty-four hours that's about it."

Kimberly bit her lip, thinking hard about the decision she would have to make. She believed Jaelen would be successful in this venture if it could be completed, but then the fact that this man hated her guts and would probably refused to be indebted to her if she made the offer to him. If this happened, should she waste her time to try to convince him that borrowing from her would be the best decision, or should she just wait until he had no other option.

Wescott would understand her decision in this matter and would have supported this decision. Besides the animosity she had for Jaelen and the person he was, his business savvy was incredible and what he could do with her investment for the future of her children would be better than anything, and Jason could have at least part of the business. But Jaelen would immediately think she only did this when Onyx decided to butt her nose into Kimberly's life and make Kimberly tell about her past.

She bit her lip even harder. Jaelen would definitely think he was shortchanged in the matter when she told him about what had happened. But he should have expected it and it should have been the first question he should have asked when he saw her. He had been so consumed in his hatred for her and his own selfishness that he had not cared.

"You act as if you're confused about something, dear," Maria said worriedly. "Is something else the matter other than this?"

Kimberly shook her head.

"If you bite your lip any harder, dear, it will start to bleed."

She stopped biting her lip and made a funky face when she started biting the inside of her mouth.

"Oh, please stop that and just tell me," Maria insisted.

"Maria, if I thought it was just that easy to tell you and make me feel better I would, but I don't think I can feel better as long as that man is in my life, to be perfectly honest."

Maria didn't press the subject as the fax machine went off and she went to get the fax off the machine. Jaelen sat back down and the expression on his face was even grimmer.

Kimberly didn't know if she should ask any questions because she knew Jaelen would speak on it eventually. He would either speak or curse. Either way he would get it off his chest.

"He's gone," Jaelen said in a very forlorn voice. "Onyx found out from the landlady that he packed his things up yesterday and moved out. Most likely he headed for the nearest get out of town spot as soon as he left the office this morning."

Gasping, Kimberly drew her brows together. "Does that mean you won't get your money back?"

He only nodded, but this horrible spaced out look was in his eyes and Kimberly desperately wished for Onyx to be here because she would know how to handle this mood.

"What Jaelen? What does this really mean for you, not just the business?"

He met her eyes directly and closed his briefly before speaking. "I've failed my father. He sweated blood and life for this business and now that I've taken it over, I've driven it in the ground trying to go for my dream. He didn't support me doing this, but he gave me his blessing." Jaelen ran a frustrated hand through his hair and leaned forward staring at nothing. "The hardest part will be telling him and seeing the expression on his face."

Kimberly knew the old man was sick and this could probably devastate him and make his condition worse. What would happen then? Jaelen would blame his father's failing health on himself. Could she live with herself if she never made the offer?

Onyx walked into the bank and then headed straight toward them. Kimberly wondered if Onyx's wardrobe was filled with all black items and if the woman wore a dress at all.

Just as she came up behind Jaelen to make her presence known, Maria returned to her desk with the fax. Kimberly watched as Jaelen and Onyx only made eye contact. They didn't greet like Kimberly would have thought past lovers would greet - a hug, a kiss, or even touching. Why did this make her a little happy?

Maria began to read from the fax. "Tonya Blackman. She's been a teller about two years. There's been no suspicious activity to note the reason why she did this, but according to the manager's note, she didn't come back from her fifteen-minute break this morning after she pushed all of your accounts together, Mr. Gates, and then your accounts were closed by you."

"What do you mean? I never went to the bank this morning," Jaelen protested.

"According to the computer, you closed the accounts at a Westside branch not even associated with the eastside branch about an hour ago and you signed all the documents," Maria said. "The teller verified your signature with your original signature card, which was faxed over to that branch."

"But we must assume that someone else has done this," Kimberly interjected. "If we say it was Edward, he probably forged everything."

"I have sent people to the bus station, both airlines, and the train station," Onyx said. "They are looking for Edward, and I'm also seeing if there are any credit card transactions in his name anywhere, so he if uses anything with his name we'll be notified."

Kimberly shook her head. "Onyx, I think you're looking for the wrong person."

"What do you mean?" Onyx said angrily. "We know Edward did this."

"Yes, I won't say he didn't, but he probably knows how good you all are at trying to find people."

"You're talking crazy, Kimberly," Onyx said.

Jaelen took Kimberly's hand because Kimberly was about to stop talking since it seemed that what she was thinking really might be crazy. "Kimber," he said calmly. "What is it?"

"They should be looking for you. If he could get the withdrawal by using your signature, then he could obtain documents that said he was you."

Onyx began making phone calls like crazy to help stop any fake transactions Edward could have made or could presently make.

Jaelen gave Kimberly an appreciative grimace if that could be a smile as he released her hand. "Maria, have everything investigated. I want to know every transaction this woman did in the past two years. I want to know every keystroke she performed that had to do with my account mainly. I want answers to all of this, do I make myself clear and I want them by the close of business today." He stood up with his brief in hand after passing Maria his business card and started walking toward the exit.

Kimberly followed him because Onyx was already walking beside him. She didn't know where they were going, but she figured with Onyx's presence, she should address the subject. It was now or never.

"Wait!" she called as they were standing in the parking lot.

Both of them turned around and looked at her impatiently. Kimberly waited until Onyx finished her phone call before she started speaking again.

"Before we go any further, I need to know what will you do, Jaelen?"

Jaelen looked at Onyx and took a deep breath as he looked back at Kimberly tiredly. "I have no idea. If we don't catch him, which I think is a possibility, I'm bankrupt," he said disgustedly. "We might even catch him and find the money gone. There is no way I'll be able to borrow the money from anywhere and even the money my father has put away in a trust for my children can't be touched, but they can touch his money and he'll be bankrupted, too."

Kimberly paled slightly. "Trust?" She looked at Onyx.

"That's none of her business, Jaelen," Onyx said angrily.

"I think it is, Onyx," Kimberly said angrily. "What trust is he talking about?"

"It's nothing!" Onyx snapped. "Like he said, he can't touch it and he won't." The fierce look in her eyes was clearly telling Kimberly to keep her mouth closed about the children.

"What the hell is going on here?" Jaelen demanded to know seeing the women practically squaring off.

"Like I said," Onyx said, waving her hand in the air like a fly was in her way. "Nothing."

Kimberly took a deep breath. What game was Onyx playing and why didn't she want Kimberly to reveal knowledge that would save Jaelen? She knew. She knew what Kimberly was planning to say. But why would Onyx want something bad to happen to Jaelen?

"Then why are we standing here like idiots in a parking lot when we could be doing something to find that bastard?" Jaelen bellowed.

"Because Kimberly has something to suggest, and I think you need to listen, Jae," Onyx said.

He looked at Kimberly for her to hurry up and spit it out.

"I'll give you the money, Jaelen," Kimberly said bravely.

He narrowed his eyes so thin she could not see his eyes due to his long dark lashes. "What the hell do you mean you'll give me the money?" he said through gritted teeth breaking the space between them in one long legged stride.

203

Kimberly was forced to strain her neck to look up into his eyes. "I'll allow you to borrow the money. Maria said herself this would be a quick fix."

"And you have two million dollars sitting around?"

"Yes … well I would have to contact the lawyers, but I'm sure as long as I'm doing it as a wise investment it would be nothing to have the money in the proper accounts and even enough to cover the damage done to employees."

A long sullen frown now graced his features for a long moment before he stated emphatically, "No!"

"What?" Onyx said incredibly.

He looked over his shoulder. "I said it clear enough for even you to hear, Onyx. No. I won't accept her offer."

"But you need the money!" Onyx protested. "How could you be so stubborn, Jaelen?"

"Did you really think I would accept being indebted to her?" he asked, facing Onyx, giving Kimberly his back.

Kimberly moved around to face him, drawing his attention to her. "If you were not an ass in the past, Jaelen Gates, you are being the biggest ass now. You would rather disappoint your father than to be indebted to me?"

"I would rather go to hell and back a hundred times than to owe you a penny, Kimberly."

She gave him her most loathsome look. "I hate you, too, Jaelen. I hate you with every fiber of my being, but it's not you who I care not to see hurt. This goes much deeper than your inflexible selfishness."

"What do you care, Kimberly? Why should you give a damn that I'm going to hurt my father?"

Kimberly wanted to scream the truth, but she knew she didn't want to. Onyx was still at her back and it was no telling what the woman would do to her. Calming herself down, she stepped back to get Onyx within her sight. "I believe in your vision, Jaelen. I told you this before all of this happened. I want to see it happens." She had to force herself to speak the next part. "What happened to you personally doesn't matter to me, but I believe making the loan to you would be a wise investment to my children's future." Stepping closer to him and softening her features as if in a coy plea, she said almost in a whisper, "Take the money, Jaelen. Let's go back in there and work it all

out. I swear I'll still work for you in whatever capacity you want and there won't be any changes. You will be free to do whatever you want with the money and the business. I won't use this to…"

"Enslave me?" he asked, but his tone was not vicious.

She nodded. "This has nothing to do with the past, Jaelen. I swear to you, I won't."

"But in the back of your mind, you'll always know I'll be indebted to you. Even if I pay back this…" He looked disgusted to say it. "…loan, the knowledge that you saved me at the worst time in my life will feed your animosity for me even more."

"Jaelen, I am not a vengeful person. You do see that, don't you?"

"What I see is a woman trying to take advantage of a man who is in desperate need of a solution."

"I am not trying to take advantage of you. Why can't you just see that I just want to help you? There are no strings attached. Plus, I thought the worst time in your life was being strapped to a bed and being raped," she said, blushing furiously not even believing that was coming out her mouth.

Onyx couldn't help but snort a chuckle and received a heated glare from Jaelen. "You've got to admit that was funny, Jaelen," Onyx said obviously.

Kimberly drew those hot, reddish-brown eyes back to her when she spoke. "Forget the past, Jaelen. Just for today and think about the opportunity I'm posing to you. I'll keep it all business if that's what you want. I will not even try to tell you how to run your business. All I'll expect is that you not only pay back the loan, but with a bit of interest. I'll even make it your decision for a reasonable rate and payback period. Who else could give you this opportunity in this short of time? By the morning you'll be running at normal."

The defeat in his eyes showed clearly, and she knew she had finally won. Kimberly almost wished he had fought just a little bit more, but then he was right. Knowing he was now indebted to her did go to her head some, and she had to fight the smile that wanted to burst forth on her lips.

Except, Kimberly realized that as Jaelen led the way back into the bank, it wasn't the fact that she had convinced him to turn to her in his time of need that made her happy. It was that for a time, Jaelen would be a real part of her life where she would have some kind of control.

Chapter 26

As they walked into the bank, neither saw the wicked smile on Onyx's face. Her brother came up beside her. He had been privy to the verbal exchange through the ear receiver in Onyx's ear, which she now took out.

Lethal casually asked, "Do you actually think he won't be spitting mad when he finds out about the boy?"

The smile immediately left her face. "He'll be mad, but I think I've got everything worked out. Don't worry you'll get the best seat in the house along with the popcorn when the shit hits the fan, otherwise quit bursting my bubble, little brother." She headed for his car with Lethal beside. "This cupid's stuff almost too easy."

"I don't think he deserves someone like Kimberly, Onnie," Lethal grumbled.

Onyx stopped in her tracks and faced her brother. "Do you want her?"

"Would it stop you in this silly game?"

"Maybe."

"No, not like that," he said disappointedly. "I don't like her like that. Kimberly's one of those gals you have to settle down with." He adjusted his pants just as one beautiful young lady walked by and his eyes followed her backside. "And I'm definitely still sowing my oats."

"Then why are you so uptight about this? Jaelen's ready to settle."

"Is he or does his father want him to?"

Onyx shrugged. "Maxwell only does things that's right for Jaelen."

Lethal looked very skeptical. "The boy's too damn selfish and ornery, sister. He'll break her heart, and that would give me a good reason to break his neck. Is that the chance you're willing to take?"

She shoved him playfully. "You keep your hands to yourself. Plus, it is better to have loved and lost, than never to have loved at all. They have the boy between them, and Jaelen will see they have to come to some common ground for the child."

"And you think our little Kimmie's just going to settle for that? Onyx, whether you see it or not, that girl's got a fire that could match Jaelen's when provoked."

"She may have, and having Jaelen around will certainly bring it out."

"Is that a good or bad thing for them?"

"Either way, I'm just trying to give her leverage over him. The more she has, the more Jaelen will be persuaded to fall in love. To be in his servitude as his manager just didn't sit well with me knowing Jaelen's temperament and wicked tendencies."

"Funny you having a conscious all of a sudden. And him owing her big time is okay with you?"

"For now." Her phone went off and when she got off, she said, "We got a lead on Jaelen's credit card being used at a gas station headed for Lansing and Tonya's credit card was used yesterday on a rental car from Enterprise on the outskirts of the city."

They started toward Lethal's large Expedition again. "Tempest is in the Lansing area, I'll give her a buzz and see if she can be on the lookout for the car. She has some state police connections up there."

Onyx wrinkled her nose at the mention of her cousin, Tempest Heart. She didn't care for the loud-mouthed woman who was as old as Onyx, but a big showoff. "I'll call Jaelen and tell him to cancel all his credit cards and make a fraud alert."

****

Upon leaving the bank, Jaelen was quiet, but he seemed to be quite perturbed. Matter of fact, the more they went through this, the angrier he seemed to get. When they were back in the Explorer driving toward his home where he had left his own vehicle, Kimberly started to think that maybe she had made the wrong decision in helping Jaelen, but did she really expect him to be gracious about this decision. The man had been cornered. He had no other decision to make but to allow Kimberly assist him, yet by the way he was gripping the steering wheel, Kimberly would swear he had done it kicking and screaming.

It reminded her of Jason and the horrible bath times when he would go kicking and screaming. The thought of his father acting the same way made her chuckle to herself as he drove.

"What's so funny?" he casually asked.

"I was just thinking of something. It's nothing, Jaelen."

He looked annoyed that she was shutting him out, but Kimberly had a feeling he would be annoyed at anything she did.

"Are you trying to pick a fight with me, Mr. Gates?" she asked.

"Can I?" he asked.

She sighed. "Jaelen, what happened back there does not make you indebted to me."

"It doesn't? You saved my ass. You saved my company. What does that make it to you?"

"That I'm helping someone in need. You don't even have to be reminded that you owe me if you don't bring it up."

"But the point is, Kimberly, I am indebted to you."

"Do you want me to take the money back?"

"Hell no," he grumbled, "But quit acting as if it's pocket change."

"I need to tie it up anyway. My lawyer notified me when I called him from the bank that Ainsley Hawthorne's lawyer is looking to tie up the money again in court. With nothing in the accounts, he won't be able to. So in truth you helped me, too, Jaelen."

"Don't placate me, Kimberly." He stopped in front of his home and Kimberly was forced to remember the last time she was here. "You'll have dinner with me," he ordered, throwing the car in park.

"I should get home."

"Need a babysitter?"

"No, I'm sure Leroy won't mind watching the children-"

He cut her off. "Then you'll have dinner with me."

"I need to get back to the office and get my briefcase," she lied.

"We'll go back after dinner. Are you trying to avoid me, Kimberly?"

Kimberly flustered, evidently telling him she was without actually saying it. "Do I have to be honest?"

"Yes."

"It's not that I'm trying to avoid you, Jaelen."

"Then what?"

"Your company is just not preferable at dinner time to me. Matter of fact, I don't like your company at all."

"Did you have to be so honest?" He sneered.

Kimberly wanted to scream at the frustration that he was giving her. "Can I leave now?"

He put her keys in his pocket. "A drink inside then. We can toast our partnership."

"I don't drink."

He growled. "I'll serve you apple juice." He came around and opened her door.

Glaring at him, she got out. "One toast, then you'll give me the keys, so I can leave?"

Jaelen didn't agree or disagree, he just escorted her to his door and inside. Kimberly shuddered as she walked inside the townhouse again. It was just as she remembered it.

"Why do you have this large home, Jaelen?"

He went over to the bar in the front room. "Actually it was a gift from my father. I guess this was his idea of a hint. What do you think?" He faced her, sipping the gin and tonic he had just poured for himself.

She started to sit in the large chair, but decided against it and sat on the couch. "Where's my drink?" she asked.

He sighed, setting his drink down and going into another room. She rushed over to a mirror and reapplied her lipstick and then patted down her hair. Kimberly sat back down just as he came back in the room.

Taking the glass of juice out his hand standing up, she downed the drink in a rush. "Well, that's about it. Goodnight, Mr. Gates," she said, after handing him back the glass then she headed for the door, but he called her name and she stopped at the doorway to the front room, facing him.

In three strides, he was in front of her. He paused one moment before he swept her up in his arms and connected his mouth to hers. The taste of the alcohol was still on his tongue as she felt him tasting her and her mouth responded to his kiss and enjoying it as her arms encircled his neck. Her body crushed against his.

She felt her back being pressed against the wall by the doorway, and he pushed the blazer off her shoulders. Kimberly was lost in those beautiful lips that seem to make her forget her hatred for this man and create a deep ache inside that only he could cure and she wanted that cure so badly that she didn't care how she was relieved. Just that he did it soon. So, when he drew away from her to carry her to the couch, she was in her slip, underwear, stockings and heels.

His lips attacked her neck and moved down as she was being laid under him on the couch.

"J-Jaelen," she said breathlessly.

He groaned. "Don't think, Kimberly. Don't think about it," he ordered, kissing her briefly.

She didn't want to, but she couldn't help it. Shaking her head, she was trying to clear away the cloud of passion befuddling her emotions. "W-We can't, Jaelen."

"Yes, we can, Kimber." He attacked an earlobe passionately and Kimberly almost forgot herself until he had to reach behind her to remove her bra.

Shaking her head harder and cupping his face, she said, "Jaelen, do you understand what is going to happen?"

"Don't do this, Kimberly. Just tonight. I swear," he begged, burying his face in her neck still trying to ease his hands behind her while his other hand moved down between her legs. She gasped as he found that she was wearing garters and was able to press a finger deep inside her wetness, pushing away her underwear.

Kimberly was having trouble fighting him anymore when she could barely fight her own body. His hand brought her to full arousal, and Kimberly forgot herself and where she was as she called out his name as her peak exploded, sending billows of passion rushing through every inch of her body. When her body was nothing but a willing pile of flesh, he was able to get up and undress, then join her again to make love as if it were his last time. Kimberly couldn't believe the gentle passion that this man exhibited as she felt like a queen in his castle of love.

"Just tonight," he had said, and repeated throughout the several hours of lovemaking as if convincing his own self he would only need this night to satisfy himself, but Kimberly had a feeling it wouldn't be just one night and she didn't want one night. She wanted Jaelen more and more as the seconds turned to minutes and the minutes turned to hours. His body coveted hers as he made love to her, needing her response in order to be fulfilled himself and finally taking her to a pinnacle she never wanted to leave joining her in the heavenly plateau.

His head rested against her chest, listening to her heartbeat as it still pounded in her chest. Kimberly stared up at the ceiling, not believing she had allowed her emotions to take over and that her body had defied her own reasoning. All she could think about was the fact that she had to face him in the morning and what she would say or do. Why did this have to happen to her?

On top of that, she couldn't blame Jaelen. He hadn't forced her, but he was irresistibly delicious and trying to resist him had been like trying not to drink when she was dying of thirst. Even now being this close to him brought a sense of rightness in her that she didn't want to let go, even though she knew she should feel repugnant.

Braving herself, she readied her emotions on the roller coaster ride she knew would happen, as she tried to get out the door and away from him.

"Knock, knock!" a soft feminine voice came from the hallway.

Chapter 27

Jaelen looked toward the door and cursed under his breath. Jumping up from the couch, he grabbed Kimberly's clothes first and handed them to her before he grabbed his own.

"Jaelen, are you here?" the voice persisted in the hallway.

The front room door was partially closed, and this gave her enough time to at least get her shirt and skirt on. When the door did open, she was gathering her underclothes and was looking around for her shoes. He had put on his pants and went to the doorway.

"What the hell are you doing here, Monica?" he demanded to know.

The tall woman dressed to a tee with her hair and makeup perfect, pushed past him, smiling coyly, but when she saw Kimberly she hesitated, but then proceeded on into the room. "I saw the door open and I thought-" She looked Kimberly up and down. "Was I interrupting something?"

"No," Jaelen bit off.

"Yes," Kimberly said in unison with Jaelen's no. "I was just leaving."

"No, you weren't," he protested to Kimberly.

"In that case, I'll pour us some drinks," Monica said, going over to the bar.

Kimberly moved toward the door where Jaelen was standing. Before he could speak another word, she held up her hand, dropping some of her under things.

"Don't!" she ordered sharply. "If I stay here one more second, I'll scream, Jaelen. We both know this was a mistake and to even stand here and argue over it all would be futile when we have to work together." She swiped up most of the things she dropped and stormed out the room.

Jaelen went over to his shirt and hurriedly put it on to catch up with her.

"Jaelen," Monica said, sipping her vodka, "If the girl doesn't want to be bothered with you, why on earth would you go after her? We both know you can't be a one-woman man."

Glaring at her hard, he replied, "Unlike you, she can be a one-man woman."

Monica actually had the nerve to look hurt. "Well, if you're going to be like that-"

"I can be however the hell I want to be, Monica, because this is my fucking house."

"It was given to you by your father when he thought you and I were going to be married," she pointed out.

"Well, you ruined those plans, didn't you? Are you here to ruin my life some more?"

"You should be glad I wasn't pregnant, Jaelen. You weren't and you will never be ready for children!"

"Dammit, Monica. I don't have time to discuss this."

"Why? Because you actually care that you hurt her feelings?" she asked in disbelief. "You've never cared about anyone, except yourself."

Moving close to her, he forced her to look up at him, holding her shoulders so she couldn't look away. "People change, Monica. Especially when the people around them influence them. Maybe Kimberly influenced me to be a better person, and you're just jealous that you didn't."

The hurt was evident in her eyes as a throat cleared by the doorway. They turned to look at Kimberly, who had walked back in.

Kimberly saw the partial embrace and tried to blink back the devastation in her eyes. "You have my keys," she said in an almost whisper.

Tearing her eyes away from them, she saw Jaelen's coat near the door and picked it up, reached inside, and got her keys.

Jaelen realized why she was acting so stiffly. He released Monica and moved to Kimberly, ready to explain whatever he needed to explain. Although he reached to grab her and force her to listen to him, Kimberly avoided his touch as if it were fire lashing out at her.

Seething, she said through clenched teeth, "Don't touch me! Ever again!"

He started to speak and Kimberly did the only thing that could make him shut up, slapping him with the palm of her hand as hard as she could, then running out the home. Using the electronic pad on the key ring to open the doors and start the engine, she took off, immediately heading home. She couldn't think - she didn't want to think as she wiped her eyes from the tears that blurred her vision. All she wanted to do was get home and forget what just happened between Jaelen and her.

Before going in the house, she did her best to wipe her eyes dry and compose herself. Never would she submit to Jaelen ever again. Never.

****

Jaelen smote Monica with his reddish-brown eyes when he returned from outside where he watched Kimberly burning rubber. If fire could come out his eyes, it would have burned Monica to a crisp.

"What the hell are you doing here?" he yelled.

"I only came because I heard you were having the biggest grand opening anyone's seen this side of the Detroit River and I was not on the RSVP list." She shrugged nonchalantly. "I figured I would get a personal invitation from you."

"I'm not in charge of that anymore." He poured himself a scotch and downed the hot liquid straight, then immediately poured himself another one. "My club manager is in charge of all of that."

"I'm surprised, Jaelen. You usually handle all your own business. You were a workaholic when we were together. You must be getting old," she teased to cajole him. Monica looked pleased. "Can't you just call them tonight and arrange for them to put me on a list of some kind?"

He shook his head. "She's not home yet," he said in a mysterious calm tone.

Monica started to relax, deceived by his state of strange tranquil composure. "And how do you know this?"

Jaelen hurled the glass in the fire, booming at the top of his lungs, "Because she just left, you stupid cunt!"

Her dark skin turned bright red and she flustered to speak; it was difficult with Jaelen's temper so volatile. "I-I should leave."

"You should have never come!"

In her defense, she said, "Jaelen, I just figured we could be adults about this whole situation-"

"Get the fuck out before I lose what little control I have on my temper, Monica," he snarled.

Monica didn't say another word as she hurried out the door. Jaelen poured himself another scotch and downed that just as quickly, relishing in the heat and distraction it provided for now, but what he would do later he didn't know and how the hell was he going to undo the damage he had done? What the hell was he thinking?

Angrily he threw this glass in the fire, cursing sharply, while grabbing the bottle of scotch and heading upstairs. Stopping in the hall, he saw the dark pink material on the floor and picked it up. Kimberly's scent was all over it and he couldn't help but become aroused. Drinking straight from the bottle, he took the underwear upstairs with him. Since that night with Kimberly, he had slept in the guestroom because he found himself unable to sleep in the room that held so many memories he tried not to think about.

Tonight, he found himself sitting in a chair, in that room nursing on the bottle of scotch knowing he would have a horrible hangover in the morning, but not really caring.

Chapter 28

Kimberly checked Jaelen's office to see if he was there; she breathed a sigh of relief when she didn't see him and went back to her office to get her own work done. At noon, she told the temp she was going to the nearby Coney Island to get herself a salad.

Upon coming out the Coney Island, she was faced was faced with a familiar face, but he didn't look at all like the picture Lethal had showed her the other day. This Eli looked like the old boyfriend she had dated, but was more mature looking.

He recognized her at the same moment she recognized him and hugged her closely. "Kimberly, you look beautiful. How have you been?" He wore his most charming smile and kissed her cheek.

A little confused at being this close, she pushed away from him, smiling warily. "I've been fine. How have you been?"

"Great! Were you headed somewhere? Would you like to sit down and have some coffee?"

When she started to say no, he said, "Please don't refuse. I might not ever get this opportunity again."

She conceded and followed him back into the Coney Island, sitting with him in a booth. After he ordered coffee for the both of them, he asked, "How long have you been in Detroit?"

"Just a couple of weeks actually. How did you know I left?" she asked, warily remembering what Lethal said about him.

He flustered a bit, then said, "I went looking for you a while back, to catch up on old times, and I was told you didn't live with Uncle Charlie anymore."

Kimberly wanted to scream at him so loud her voice would never be used again. If he had really loved her, none of this with Jaelen would have ever happened. "I had to leave."

"Kimberly," he said sincerely. "I know I probably hurt you real bad in the past." He took her hand in his. "I want you to know I still love you and what I did was wrong. I've been thinking a lot about you and the baby."

"There was no baby." She withdrew her hand, feeling cold and clammy all over when he touched her. "I had an accident and lost the baby."

He seemed hurt. "I didn't know."

"Of course, you didn't. You weren't there, how could you?"

The waitress came with the coffee and then left.

"How is Leroy?"

"He's great. We're still together. He helps me raise my children."

"Are you married?"

"I was. My husband died."

"Did he leave you with any money?"

Kimberly hesitated a bit, then said, "A little, but what business is it of yours?"

"None at all. I shouldn't be in your business like that. I'm sorry." He poured sugar in his coffee. "How have you been otherwise? Have you found good employment here?"

"Yes. In management not far from here, but enough about me, Eli, what about you?"

He smiled sheepishly. "It's been rough, but I'm doing some investing here and there. I'm hoping they will pay off soon." His natural, light brown-hazel eyes danced with delight.

She pushed the coffee away slightly because the smell of it was making her sick. "I should be getting back to work. I've got so much to do."

He put five on the table and stood with her. "Please let me walk you back. I want to know so much about you, Kim."

She conceded and he asked more questions. She allowed him to know how many children she had and that she was living on the Westside. As they neared the entrance of the club, he asked what did she do and she told him a little bit about her job and only assured him that it paid well. When she persisted that she needed to get into work, he seemed almost desperate to see her again.

"Can we have dinner sometime?" he asked, taking her hands in his and standing quite close to her.

Just at that moment, she saw Jaelen's silver Jaguar pull up right behind Eli, followed by a very large custom modeled black Expedition with Onyx behind the wheel. Kimberly was not surprised to see the woman wearing an all-black leather body suit with matching boots, but at least these had three-inch medium heels. As usual her hair was swept back in a tight ponytail and tucked under to disguise its true length. She walked like she was ten feet tall and was ready to take on the world.

"Dinner would be fine," she said, offhandedly as she looked at Jaelen getting out with sunglasses on and a long dark blue mackintosh with a matching dark blue suit. He paused a brief moment and looked at Eli then at her, then he walked inside. Onyx stood by the entrance with a highly amused smirk on her face as she crossed her arms and leaned against the wall.

"Tomorrow night?" he suggested.

Coming out of her brief daze, she nodded. "Yes, that would be fine. Pick me up here at about six. We can go right after work."

He kissed her cheek one more time and then left, going in the direction they had come. She turned around to face Onyx.

"What?" she snapped.

Onyx looked at the back of Eli, then looked over at Kimberly. "What the hell are you trying to pull?"

"Nothing. It's an old friend that has nothing to do with all of this."

"Really? I saw the pictures of him on Lethal's desk. He cleans up well, but I guess with all your money I'd clean up, too."

"He doesn't know about my money. Why don't you stay out my business?" Kimberly snapped.

"Anything that has to do with Jaelen is my business."

"I wish to God I didn't have anything to do with him."

"Is that why he went into a drunken stupor all night long? I had to drag him out the house."

"Am I to blame for this, too? It's amazing how I'm always doing things to Jaelen when I have no choice or I'm nowhere around."

Onyx smiled triumphantly. "You weren't there last night?"

Kimberly flushed. Of course, he would tell Onyx all his business. "What we did last night was just as trivial as before."

"What before? You mean when you raped him."

Kimberly bit her lip and rolled her eyes around. "I'm not discussing this anymore with you, Onyx." She started inside, but Onyx blocked her way.

"You've had sex before this?"

"This is none of your business."

"Answer the question, Kimberly." Onyx's voice was threatening, but her eyes were more menacing. The look said she had ways to make Kimberly tell her the truth.

Kimberly had a feeling even if she lied Onyx would know, so she decided to just slightly avoid the subject by directing it back at Jaelen. "Why don't you go talk to Jaelen? He tells you everything anyways." She quickly went around Onyx and headed straight for her office.

Onyx decided to do just that. Entering Jaelen's office, she saw that all the window shades were drawn shut, and he was lying back in his chair. She couldn't tell if he was awake or sleep because he still had on the dark sunglasses, but she would find that out very soon as she kicked the back of the chair.

"Leave me alone," he grumbled.

"What does Miss Parker mean when she says when the two of you have sex it's only trivial? When was the last time you fucked her?"

He tipped his eyewear down a tad, peeking at her over the rims, then he looked around the room for Lethal just in case. Looking back at Onyx who actually looked perturbed, he said simply, "You didn't think I would keep her here the whole day and not do anything to her for what she did."

It took Onyx a very long moment before she realized what he said. With one jerk, she grabbed the arm of the chair and in two seconds, Jaelen found himself flat on his back. Before he could recover from that, she grabbed his arm and yanked him up to his feet. He was able to avoid two quick jabs before she got one in the chest, then his shoulders. He basically tried to defend himself, but being hung over and fighting Onyx was impossible to do. Soon he tired of trying to defend himself and ended up flat on his back with the feeling of his teeth in the back of his brain while Onyx stood above him calling him every name in the book.

Kimberly heard the commotion along with several other employees. She rushed to his office, closing the door behind her.

"Get up, you son of a bitch. Get the hell up!" Onyx kicked him in the side, but Jaelen stayed flat on his back with his eyes closed.

Kimberly gasped and came up, pushing Onyx to the side. Kneeling down to Jaelen to see if Onyx had killed him, she asked Onyx, "What is going on?" Kimberly looked up at Onyx when Jaelen didn't open his eyes to her persistent shaking.

"I'm going to kill him, that's what's going on, but I want him to be man enough to stand up so I can."

"You aren't going to kill him."

Onyx stood baffled. "He raped you. He did to you what you were forced to do to him and you're defending him?"

Kimberly stood up shouting, "I told you before this has nothing to do with you. Don't you think if Jaelen was wrong and had actually forced me, I would have told you when I came back to Davenport?"

The outburst shocked Onyx and now she knew what her brother meant by Kimberly being able to handle her own.

Kneeling back down to Jaelen, Kimberly tapped his face gently.

Jaelen was only a bit disoriented as he opened his eyes and looked up at her.

"Are you all right?" she asked, filled with concern.

"Do you care?" he grumbled.

She sighed with relief. "You're fine," she said, getting up. "Could you please take this outside next time, so you won't disturb the office? This is a professional environment."

He snorted and tried to get up. Even though Onyx hadn't cracked any bones, he felt like he'd been run over by a Mack truck. Onyx came over to him and grabbed his arm, yanking him up.

She still looked as if she were ready to kill him as she released him too fast and the room began to spin. When had he ever been in Onyx's good favor? She was always pissed about something he did or said.

He fixed his chair upright. "Why don't the both of you leave me the hell alone?" he yelled, flopping back in his seat with a groan of pain.

"I'd love to, but as you can see I have a job I'm obligated to," Kimberly said flippantly and left the room.

"I ought to kick your ass," Onyx boomed.

"You just did," he moaned, leaning back in the chair and closing his eyes.

"How could you, Jaelen? I trusted you. That's the reason why she hates your guts. I wouldn't tell you shit either if you did that to me."

"She hated my guts a long time ago."

"How do you know that?"

Jaelen looked at Onyx now with a look of dread on his face. "She told me she wanted nothing to do with me anymore after she rescued me from the basement."

"Who's to say she even meant that? Have you thought of that?"

"The woman aborted my child. I know she wants nothing to do with me."

Onyx looked at him confused. "She told you that?"

"She told me, I wouldn't be the father of her child. I knew she had to be pregnant. She was just coming off her period when … when it happened. I knew she had to have had a child, but she made sure I wasn't the father."

"And how do you know that?"

"I think she would have told me if I was the father."

Onyx didn't know what to say. The two of them were so mixed up about each other that it was ridiculous. She decided not to even address him about the subject. "Just don't let Lethal find out about this. He won't just kick your ass. He'll try to kill you."

"Just tell him to stand in line."

His nonchalant behavior worried Onyx. "Jaelen, I think you need to speak to Kimberly before your birthday."

"Why? What good will it do me?" Before she had a chance to answer, he growled. "She'll only say something to piss me off." He turned around, intent on blocking Onyx out.

Angrily, she slammed out the office and headed straight to Kimberly's to get some answers. Kimberly was meeting with three employees and gave Onyx only a partial glance then completely ignored her.

Impatiently, she waited until Kimberly finished with everyone. With the grand opening in less than two weeks, she was kept very busy, but she seemed to be on top of everything. Jaelen didn't know how lucky he was to have Kimberly working for him. She was a dedicated hardworking employee who seemed to enjoy her job.

"You do your job well," Onyx complimented, after the last employee stepped out the office. She closed the door to the office to give them privacy.

"Thank you," Kimberly said as she signed off on something hoping Onyx would go away soon.

Onyx sat in front of Kimberly's desk and propped her feet on the corner.

Kimberly only wrinkled her nose in disgust. "You're going to talk to me, right?"

"No. I'm going to sit here and listen as you tell me why you never told Jaelen about being pregnant by him."

Shifting her weight uncomfortably, she sat back in her chair composing herself. "This isn't the time or the place to discuss this."

"We can go anywhere you want, but I intend to speak about everything now because that man is in there thinking you got rid of the pregnancy."

Kimberly's mouth dropped open in shock. "I never said that to him."

"Did you give him the impression at any point that you wanted nothing to do with him?"

Biting her lip deep in thought, she said, "I may have said I wanted nothing to do with him when we departed that night and when he asked me about children, I could have spoken in anger about him not fathering any child of mine, but that's not something he should have taken to heart."

"Not when any other woman would have given their left arm to bare him a child?"

Kimberly frowned, confused.

Onyx sat forward. "You never knew about the agreement, did you? Jaelen was forced to sign an agreement drawn up by his father that if he bore any children out of wedlock he would lose control of the business to the child."

"I didn't know and I'm sure Uncle Charles didn't know either when he kidnapped Jaelen, but now that I know-"

"You own the business," Onyx stated, cutting her off. "Now that you've given him the loan and with Jason you own everything. He has nothing without you in his life."

"Would it be significant for him to know this?"

"I think it would if you intended on getting revenge for what he did to you," Onyx answered.

Kimberly leaned forward slowly, deep in thought. "Are you a devil's advocate or are you working in his best interest?"

"Bottom line, I'm here for him and his father. What do you plan to do with this knowledge, Kimberly?" Onyx asked.

"Let's see," Kimberly pondered, sitting back with a smirk on her face and putting her hands behind her head. "I could take apart his company little by little until there was nothing left after I buy out his father and destroy Jaelen for the jerk he has been, or I could pretend I don't care about this information you've given me and keep doing what I'm truly enjoying."

"Which one?" Onyx asked.

She gave Onyx a look as if she should have known. "The last one. Revenge has no place in my life like Jaelen's. I'm not a vengeful person, and I don't care that you think I might do something. I'm not planning any mass conspiracies. Can't you people just trust?"

"When the entire world is such a deceiving place? Kimberly, you're alone in that department that Jaelen just wouldn't shop in. Jaelen doesn't trust anyone. Neither do I. And if you aren't so deceiving, why do I have the feeling you're keeping something from me?"

Kimberly deliberately avoided those cold black eyes that seem to see through her. "My protection, I guess. With all that's going on in my life, it's hard for me to…" she was lost for words.

"Trust?" Onyx asked, helping Kimberly end the sentence.

In her defense, Kimberly said, "You don't have people trying to kill you."

"True, not right now, but have I really hurt you, Kimberly?"

"You aren't trying to be a friend to me for yourself, Onyx. You are his friend. You're looking out for his best interest, not mine," Kimberly said defensively.

Onyx didn't want to speak on her friendship with Jaelen. "So why didn't you tell him about the pregnancy?"

"Because I knew there was a lot of abhorrence for me. He would have tried to take custody from me."

"And you don't think he still won't when he finds out the truth?"

Kimberly stood up, quite disturbed by this conversation, turning her back slightly away to shield her open thoughts in her eyes. Not wanting Onyx to see what she was thinking, she said, "That's because you've given me no choice in the matter."

"What about Jason's choice? Don't you think he deserves to know his father?" Onyx stood up and moved behind Kimberly. "You're going to deny both of them the chance to know each other. You need to tell Jaelen soon before the end of this week preferably, before the party would be better, instead of in public. I'll send you an invitation, but I do expect you there."

Kimberly swallowed the lump of frustration building in her throat. Onyx was laying the guilt heavily on Kimberly's shoulders. All the guilt Kimberly did her best not to think about because she felt she had done her part by not terminating the pregnancy.

Yet, it always nagged her that Jaelen would never know the special-ness of parenthood, but then she didn't want Jaelen to think this had been a ploy to have him in her life or even to gain some kind of sympathy from him as his hatred for her mounted. There was no doubt in her mind that he was a very handsome man; along with his personal strength, he would make a wonderful father no doubt, given some kind of patience.

Why couldn't things just be easy for her? she wondered.

"You have until the end of this week or I will tell him," Onyx warned again.

Kimberly really loathed Onyx for her blackmailing tactics and was glad when she heard the office door closed from Onyx's exit. Sitting back down behind her desk, she went deep in thought. What was a woman to do?

Chapter 29

For three straight days, Jaelen observed as Kimberly steered clear of him. Messaging and emails made it easier for her to keep in contact about her job and responsibilities, but also keep her distance.

Even phone calls she made with him were kept brief and sharp. His sarcasm and off-colored remarks were ignored because she seemed to be distracted by other things on her mind. She always seemed to be busy or in meetings. He was beginning to hate how she allowed her job to consume her life, but she had made time for that man Eli. When Jaelen had questioned Onyx about this man, Onyx acted as if she didn't know whom he was speaking about.

As he observed her, he realized having Kimberly around freed him to do other business and to catch up on a lot of work he could never get to. There was no doubt in his mind having Kimberly working for him was an asset to his company and his business life, but his personal life and peace of mind were shot to hell.

Within the past three days, Kimberly and this Eli had met twice for lunch and every night after work for dinner, "catching up on old times." Jaelen had followed them and watched as she laughed so carefree with him and allowed him to touch her hand and arms, then even give her a kiss on the cheek.

Jaelen watched as on the fourth night of them being together, they sat in the parking lot in front of the club, after having dinner, talking for what seemed like a very long time. He cursed that this man was trying to romance Kimberly right from under his nose.

Jaelen wanted to speak with her about what happened that night with him and Monica showing up at the most inopportune time, but he just didn't know how to broach the subject with Kimberly being so distant.

It was on the third night Onyx caught up with him on his cell phone. Jaelen had been keeping to himself.

"Where are you?" she asked, quite concerned.

It was strange hearing concern in her voice like a real sister actually affected by his unusual behavior. Almost touching, if she didn't work for his father and was getting paid to look in on the son. "What does it matter to you?" he asked in a monotonous tone.

"You sound like shit, Jaelen, and you haven't been home in four days."

"You sound like you care."

She sighed, exasperated. "Don't start that I work for your father shit again."

"So why the hell are you calling me?"

"Don't play dumb," she snipped.

"Or you'll what? Kick my ass again? I'm sober this time, Onyx, so it'll take a lot more to get me down."

"You're too tired to put up a fight this time. I can tell it in your voice, but you were sober when she kicked your ass at the courthouse, too," Onyx dug in, knowing she was hitting way below the belt.

"Is there some other reason other than pissing me off that you called?" he asked through gritted teeth.

"Sunday night, you'll be there, right? The Karas House with all your father's friends and business associates. He'll be expecting you."

"Is that all?"

"No. Kimberly called me this afternoon. She asked me to speak with you about your behavior."

"What behavior?" Onyx seemed a bit hesitant to broach the subject. "I told her she was crazy when she told me what she only suspected you were doing. She had no proof."

"Cut the fucking crap, Onyx, and tell me," he ordered harshly.

"She said you were following her around."

When he didn't answer right away, Onyx exhaled as if she knew the idea was hilarious. "I told her she was mistaken because you wouldn't do something so ridiculous."

"How long does she think I've been following her?" he questioned quietly. There was an odd, almost disturbing calmness to his tone of voice.

Onyx realized he didn't answer her question and immediately became very wary by his bizarre behavior. "You aren't stalking her, Jaelen, are you?"

"How long?" he repeated his question.

"Oh Jesus! You've gone mad, haven't you? You have never been this obsessed about any woman, Jaelen." Her voice was getting higher and higher in disbelief. "You can't go around-"

"How fucking long?" he bellowed into the phone.

"She said a couple of days. I thought she was crazy, but I'm calling the wrong person out. Jaelen, you've got to stop this. Go home and get some rest," she pleaded.

He was quiet for a long moment before he said, "I can't seem to breathe, Onyx. I think about her morning, noon and night."

"That's what love is, Jaelen," she said simply.

He snorted. "Is that what it is? I thought I was dying." He paused a moment, taking a long dreary sigh. "It's like your heart starts beating especially for them and your whole state of mind just changes. I can't explain it, but I want to touch her and hold her and see her for every minute of the day, Onyx."

She chuckled. "You should tell her, Jaelen. Tell her how you feel."

"Have you ever been in love, Onyx?"

"No. Lust, but no love," she said honestly.

"Why didn't we ever hook up?"

Jaelen's erratic behavior worried Onyx, but she still answered his question, thinking about the night he was kidnapped and how her plans for them would have changed this whole situation.

Onyx felt almost a little jealous. Jaelen was a passionate man who could get so angry, but loved just as intensely. This was just what playing cupid accomplished and Onyx knew Kimberly would make him very happy.

"I guess our friendship is so wonderful we probably thought fucking would screw it up, literally."

"If I didn't love her so much, I think you'd be the next best thing to be the mother of my children."

"Well, you see there?" she said, matter of fact. "I don't like being second and I'm certainly not ready for children."

He jumped subjects again. "I think I'm going to kill that son of a bitch she's with."

"If you do that, you'll never spend time with Kimberly because you'll be in prison. There are other ways to get rid of pests."

"And you know the solution?"

"Trust me, Jaelen. Lethal's working on it as we speak. Now, I want you to call her and tell her you'll meet her tomorrow for breakfast, lunch, or dinner - anything and then you'll tell her everything then, Jaelen. Everything that you just told me."

"Will she want me, Onyx?"

This was the first time she had heard Jaelen sound really worried about something. He had always been confident about all the things in his life, but it seemed Kimberly kept him so on his toes, he didn't know what she would do next and was really unsure about himself. Hopefully tomorrow, Kimberly would reveal how she felt as well and all of Jaelen's worrying would be over.

"I think if the two of you just talked, Jaelen, things will work out for the best. Make the call and then go home and get some rest."

"Thanks, Onyx." He sounded so relieved. "Goodnight."

When the line clicked, Onyx wondered if things would really work out for the better. And if the better meant they would be happy with each other or would it be best staying apart.

Calling her brother at his home, she asked him as soon as he picked up the line, "What have you found out about that teacher?"

Immediately, knowing whom his sister was speaking about, he said, "He hasn't asked for anything. He's just been asking a lot of questions, but we don't want to assume."

"Lethal, it's been three days. You're going to tell me you don't know anything?"

"All Del knows is that he's dirty, but trying to get behind the scenes in this guy's life has been harder than looking up a nun's dress."

She liked when her brother used ridiculous terminology when he was trying to get a point across. "So how long does she have to do this in order to get something?"

"Not much longer. Don't worry, I've got the best man on it."

"Blaze is not your best, brother. That cousin can't keep the eyes off women to watch the target," she snipped.

"You're just pissed because he almost got you shot."

"Because he was supposed to be watching my ass."

"Well, trust me, he's keeping his eye on Kimberly like white on rice because I told him if he lost her I'd tear his eyes out his sockets. You don't have to worry. Any sign of danger, he'll pull her out. He's just that close."

"Close enough to know Jaelen's been stalking her?" she asked, thinking he wouldn't know that information.

"Of course, but I told Blaze he was lovesick and pathetic, so he shouldn't be bothered."

"How'd you know?"

Lethal snorted. "I figured with all your easy cupid playing, the poor sap wouldn't last that long."

"Why didn't you tell me?" she asked, upset.

"Because, I personally don't like the son of a bitch, and I didn't want to hear you revel about your cupid accomplishments."

"You're some kind of brother, Lethal," she said sourly.

"Being your brother doesn't have anything to do with hating Jaelen's guts. I still say the son of a bitch doesn't deserve her, and if he hurts one damn strand of hair on her head, I'll take great pleasure in breaking every bone in his body."

"He doesn't know yet. He won't hurt her, and once he finds out about her pregnancy-"

"He doesn't know, yet?" Lethal cut her off.

"She plans to tell him tomorrow."

"How do you know?"

"I mentioned she should, and I know Kimberly's a smart woman. She'll do it."

"Did you blackmail her?" he asked suspiciously.

"She just thinks I'm going to tell Jaelen if she doesn't, and she doesn't think I would tell him properly."

"You're almost as pathetic as Jaelen is," he quipped. "But just remember what I said, I'll break him without so much as a blink of an eye."

She had no doubt Lethal could accomplish this if he was serious, but she also knew he was aware Jaelen meant too much to her and to hurt Jaelen would mean to hurt his sister, and Lethal would never do something like that.

With the warning in mind, she said, "I know he won't hurt her," she assured her brother again. "I'll put my own life on it."

She disconnected from him and hoped Jaelen had taken her advice. Just in case, she would go by his house and see if he was there.

Chapter 30

When Jaelen felt himself going crazy with indecision, he decided to just call Kimberly on the cell phone.

She picked up on the second ring. "Yes?" her soft melodic voice said softly as if she knew it was him.

"Were you busy?" he asked.

"Would it matter?"

"No," he said honestly. "I wanted to speak with you."

There was a bit of panic in her voice when she said, "Now?"

"No," he answered, wondering why should she be nervous if he decided to see her this moment. "Tomorrow after lunch or did you have plans with your new boyfriend?"

Again just like she had been doing in the past week, she ignored his snide remark. "Not if you wish to see me, Jaelen. Will this be at your office?"

"Did you have another place in mind?"

Kimberly was glad they were on the phone because the blush came fast remembering what happened the last time that they were alone. "No other place came to mind," she lied. "Tomorrow after lunch, I'll be in your office."

He hung up before he changed his mind and told her he would see her tonight. Onyx was right, he needed to rest, to get his thoughts together and then make the biggest change in his whole life tomorrow.

****

Kimberly put the phone back in her purse, then faced Eli. "I'm sorry for the interruption. What were you saying?"

"Well, these past few days have been wonderful for me and I hope for you, too," Eli said, scooting even closer to her.

"It's been pleasant, Eli. I was able to get a lot of things off my mind and really understand about myself and get my emotions clear about a lot of things." Especially now that her mind was set on Jaelen even though she talked with Eli.

"I know I can never say enough how sorry I am about the past, Kimberly," Eli said. "But I would like to take forever to make up for it." With that said, he reached in the inner jacket pocket and pulled out a red velvet box. Opening the box, she gasped at the large diamond on a platinum band that must have cost him an arm, leg and a chunk of his side, too.

The gorgeous ring was almost too captivating for words, and its brilliance and beauty stunned Kimberly.

He continued, "Kimberly, I want you to be my wife. I was a fool when I was young, and I want to raise your boys like my own. Leroy can live with us, too, I don't care what it takes to have you in my life. I want to do it all for you."

Kimberly felt awful because he was pouring his soul and heart out to her and all she could do was wish Jaelen would say those same words to her. Choosing her words carefully, she said, "Eli, I am touched you still love me after all these years."

"This past few days have been pure soul searching for myself. I'm mature now to know to lose you again would be stupid. Fate has given me a second chance with the only woman I know now I will only truly love forever."

She covered her mouth in disbelief, not really knowing what to say as she stared down at the engagement ring. Slowly, removing her hands, she licked her suddenly dry lips and spoke. "Eli, it would be wrong of me to accept this ring when my heart belongs to someone else."

"Who?" he asked. "You haven't mentioned anyone else these past few days."

"I've been denying it myself because I didn't want to believe how I felt was true. It wasn't until this moment, Eli, when you asked me to marry you, that I realized that I love him." Kimberly couldn't believe what she had said and didn't know if this was an act that she was putting on. Her words sounded too sincere.

He closed the red velvet box. His face was filled with disappointment as he put the box away. "Are you sure, Kimberly?"

She took his hand in her own. "Eli, when you left, I thought I knew what heartbreak was because I thought I loved you. Really loved you, but I was wrong. Jaelen has taught me the real meaning of love, my body and soul, and to lose him would be to lose life itself."

"Your boss?" His brows drew together very troubled. "You're in love with your boss?"

She didn't remember telling him Jaelen was her boss, but it could have slipped in their previous days' conversations. Although she had been very careful about what she revealed to Eli, she had Jaelen on her mind so much, she could have slipped.

Turning forward, she said, "Yes, Eli."

"Surely Kimberly, you have to say this has got to be an infatuation. A man like that wouldn't give a fig about you and your three children."

Kimberly was really starting to feel uncomfortable. How would he know about Jaelen's temperament if he didn't know Jaelen? Did someone tell him? He definitely didn't get that information about Jaelen from her. "It may be all a silly notion, but you've thought me to be silly before, Eli."

He changed the subject seeing her upset. "You know what, maybe I'm rushing everything," he said, patting her knee.

She checked her wrist to see what time it was, then groaned remembering what happened to it and not minding at all that Jaelen had destroyed the watch. "It is getting late. I should be going." She was going to have to tell Lethal she couldn't do this anymore.

When she started to get out of the car, he added pressure to her thigh to keep her there. Looking back at Eli, she saw he still had that disappointed look on his face. Kimberly hoped this didn't mean he wanted a kiss. The past ones - even though they had been on her cheek, forehead or the back of her hand - had left her cold and disgusted.

"I have a surprise waiting, but I was going to do it if you said yes." He paused and she patiently waited for him to continue speaking. "Well, I still want to do it."

Kimberly frowned meshing her lips in distrust, but she had just devastated him with her admission of loving another. Relaxing her hand back from the door, she gave him her most beguiling smile. "What is it, Eli?"

He reached in the back seat and Kimberly braced herself as he dug under the seat then relaxed as he pulled out a bottle of sparkling apple juice and two champagne glasses. As corny as it seemed, it was rather sweet of him to be so thoughtful knowing her aversion to alcohol. Why couldn't Jaelen be so sweet?

She bit her tongue to keep her thoughts on what was happening and not on the total jerk who didn't mind his ex-girlfriend interrupting them or having his ex-girlfriend then call Kimberly and ask to be hooked up with tickets to the grand opening, of course, per Jaelen.

What had Jaelen been trying to pull having Monica call her up to ask her for tickets?

She agreed to a glass and hurriedly sipped it. She wanted to tell him how late it was getting, but he decided to speak again.

"Even though you've rejected me, I hope this doesn't make us any less friends."

She found herself drifting off and immediately shook herself. "No, it doesn't, Eli." Her mind wandered just a little bit as he continued to talk. Kimberly really didn't feel well as all of a sudden her vision was becoming spotted and dark.

"Are you okay, Kimberly?" he asked. Even though he was close, he sounded so far away.

"I'm fine," she heard herself say, but it sounded as if her voice was echoing inside her head until the throbbing inside her skull felt like a bomb ticking so loud, she really wanted her head to explode.

Opening her eyes wide she saw him speaking but couldn't hear what he had to say. She felt so hot and cold at the same time.

Staring at his lips, she saw him say the word "home," and she nodded, too terrified to speak.

Her vision was blurred and it took all her effort to keep herself upright.

Trying to find the lock to open the door, she knew that if she could just get some air that everything would be all right.

Damn, Jaelen, would wonder why she was in the car so long.

Get out! her mind screamed. Too foggy! Too hard! Please Jaelen, please still be out there stalking me. This was the last thing she remembered thinking before unconsciousness enveloped her like a warm blanket.

Chapter 31

Jaelen watched the car for a few more minutes, wondering why she didn't get out the car, but he fought the urge to go over there and yank her out. Instead, he followed Onyx's advice and drove away heading home.

When he got home, he immediately cut off his phone and went straight to bed to get some much-needed sleep.

****

Onyx didn't receive a page from Lethal until nine that night. He only left two words on her voicemail, "Come now." The firm tight voice rang so many alarms bells in her head, she didn't grab a jacket and took only ten minutes to get to his home when it usually took twenty minutes to get to his Westside Detroit's self-designed house - or mansion as others would call it.

Striding into her brother's home was like stepping into a whole New World from the surrounding neighborhood. There was a tropical feel using plants and design to the three story high waterfall in the middle of the family room, which pooled at the feet of people entering the house under a thick glass floor in the foyer.

Walking down into the living room, she quickly went past the beautiful hand stitched leather furniture and walked over handcrafted wooden floors, and pushed against a brown wall panel.

She was probably the only one other than Lethal who could find the secret compartment that opened to an electronic fingerprint and eye key. Everyone else who knew about the secret office used the buzzer underneath the table by the panel.

Leaning forward, she allowed the computer to scan her left eye, while at the same time pressing her thumb to the electronic board. The computer beeped and then a click on the floor sounded before a larger part of the wall opened up with the table holding a very expensive Ming Dynasty vase. She stepped into the newly made doorway to Lethal's at home office. Five server computers lined the walls always on, always reporting new information and printing out reports. She was always impressed at how her brother could multi-task and work so hard.

He had taught her the security business and if anything ever happened to him - God forbid- she would step in and get behind the desk. Yet, being behind the desk wasn't for her, and Lethal knew this, so he ran the office while he sent her to do most of the footwork.

As she walked in, Lethal was at the phone center off from the middle of the room where a large oak desk sat. He had three phones going at the same time. His hands-free phone was on one ear, another receiver was on the other ear, and he was holding a conversation with someone on a speakerphone.

When he saw her, he motioned her to come to him. He finished his conversation quickly, but was looking none too pleased.

"What is it?" she demanded to know.

"She's gone. Kimberly can't be found," he said, very pissed off. He was on the brink of losing what little control of his temper he had left.

"What?" Onyx shrieked. "I thought you had her covered. You said Del was on her like white on rice."

His voice was slightly raised when he said, "He was. He still is hopeful because I can't find or contact him or Zeke. They haven't reported to me in five hours."

"You should have called me sooner."

"And see you react this way when I think I have things under control."

She chortled, exasperated. "If you have things under control, you'd have your ass out of here and knowing where Kimberly was, big brother." She picked up his desk phone and started dialing Jaelen's number.

Lethal came over and took the receiver from her, hanging the phone up. "Don't call him. Not until I know what's going on. I don't want to deal with his temper until I know for sure what's really happening."

"He'll kill me if he knows I didn't come get him."

"I'll kill him if he even thinks of going off on me like you just did and don't even say he won't. You, I will allow, but Jaelen would be missing a mouth when I get done with him."

Onyx knew her brother's temper wasn't as severe when she lost her own temper on him, but he took little flak from anyone else. She also knew if Jaelen was here, Lethal would have knocked him out by now.

"Fine," she agreed.

He moved over to the speakerphone and dialed a number. "This was the last message I received from Del's cell phone." He pressed a couple more buttons before their cousin's silky deep Barry White like voice came on the line, but there was a lot of static. "Lee, Blaze hit me up and gave me coordinates to ... going there now. Sounds like trouble ... the target disappeared ... Eli is taking..." The line cut off.

Lethal turned off the message saying, "I don't think Del knew he was in a bad area, but I've pinpointed his direction to Downriver before I lost him. If Del and Zeke are together, then I'm sure Kimberly can't be far from them."

Only family members referred to Blaze as Zeke because he didn't favor the name and preferred family call him Zeke.

"And if they don't know where she is, then what?" Onyx questioned with doubt in her deep opaque eyes.

"Then Del and Zeke won't be coming back. She's their target and they will do whatever is necessary to protect the target."

The buzzer on the outside of the secret panel sounded. Looking at the camera, Lethal pushed the button to open the secret panel to their female cousin, Tempest Heart.

Although she was family, Onyx couldn't get along with her. Even as children when Tempest played with the Barbie dolls, Onyx wanted to go with the boys and play GI Joe.

Tempest had more thick features, but she had gained the family's height of five feet eleven. Still, she was more feminine than Onyx cared to be as she strode in wearing a light green-pastel, leather skirt and jacket with matching camisole, pumps, and bag.

Onyx sucked her teeth in annoyance as her brother gave his sister a "play nice" look. In Tempest's case, looks were definitely deceiving. Tempest carried herself confidently, but very well portraying a fragile female unlike Onyx whose toughness could be seen in her walk, talk and every gesture.

"Looking good, cuz," Lethal said, giving her a hug.

Tempest smiled. "So are you, Lee." Turning to Onyx, she knew by the cold glare in her ebony eyes that there was a still bad feeling between the two of them. Tempest's warm honey-brown eyes twinkled in amusement. "You're looking bleak as usual, cousin. I really can't wait until you get a man; then maybe you won't look like you're attending a funeral every day."

Onyx only sucked her teeth again.

"What's the pleasure of your presence?" Lethal asked, drawing Tempest's attention before his sister said something to start the two of them arguing.

She reached into her leather bag to pull out a folded manila envelope. "Zeke came to me after his trip to the UP. He said something about Hawthorne this and that, which of course I half-listened to because when is Zeke ever happy. He also gave me this to hold onto and said if crap ever hit the fan to get this to you. I found it strange since he works for Del when he's not under the hood of a car in Red's garage."

Red was their youngest cousin who had chosen not to go into the security business, but ran a fix-it garage on the East Side of Detroit.

Tempest continued, "It's not a completed report, and it's even handwritten. Del sent Zeke up there to look into somebody's father. Zeke hated it up there because … well you know and was so jumpy by the time he got back I couldn't get anything from him." She sat in the closest chair by Lethal's desk. "Most of it's on the information he found out about the girl's father, but there is some strange notes he made about her stepbrother for some odd reason."

"Kimberly doesn't have a stepbrother," Onyx protested.

"Well, then I guess it's just nonsense he wrote down, or I don't know how to read," Tempest said sarcastically.

"I would definitely pick the latter," Onyx said, just as sarcastically.

Lethal looked through the envelope, scanning each paper quickly. "Kimberly Hawthorne's father was found? How did Zeke find him?" Lethal asked, shocked.

"Read it all. He has it all detailed," Tempest said. "Since, I don't know how to read." She was a little ticked at Onyx's retort.

"Damn! Damn! Zeke had all the information right here to connect everything together. Fuck!" He shoved the papers at Onyx, then went to get his jacket, laptop and GPS system. "Watch the phones for us, Temp. If you have to leave, give me a call, but hopefully one of your brothers will call before then. Hit me on the cell if you hear from them."

"I will, no problem," Tempest sang. "Glad I could help."

Onyx was right behind her brother as he went out to her vehicle. As if rehearsed, she tossed him her keys and moved to the passenger side.

He handed her the laptop and GPS then drove out the driveway, picking up speed at a very rapid pace. Onyx scanned through the papers and saw the name of Kimberly's father. "It's a small world, isn't it?"

"Too small if you ask me," Lethal said, anger lacing his words. "I can't believe how all of this is coming together."

"Do you think Ainsley knows this information?"

"Most likely, but my guess is Ainsley has to cover his ass whether he knows this or not and with so many debts, he's got to make sure nothing comes back to haunt him. He doesn't plan to just kill her, but he's got to take those kids out, too."

"Why'd you bring the laptop?" she asked, figuring Lethal was headed to Kimberly's home.

"Because you need to access the server. Whether you noticed or not, Del referred to Eli as Elijah in the telephone message. I just realized it would be very easy for him to change his name." He handed her some papers from his jacket. "This is the skinny on the boy. Check out his father's name. I thought about this when I was looking at Kimberly's information just now."

Onyx's eyes widened in horror. "That's why Del couldn't find him." She immediately booted up the laptop and plugged it into the terminal installed in her SUV.

Soon she was downloading information on the search she asked for. "I'll have an address and credit card statements along with his TRW in twenty minutes."

"Good. We'll scoop up the kids and her brother then be on our way to a safe house by then."

Arriving at Kimberly's home, Onyx instantly knew something was amiss when she saw the front door kicked in. Lethal pulled out his revolver with the silencer already attached as he entered the home, his sister in tow on high alert.

They heard movement upstairs and after making sure there was no one on the first floor, they headed upstairs. Moving stealthily, the siblings were able to come up on the two male perpetrators who were searching around the room in the dark using a flashlight to riffle through everything.

The men didn't hear Lethal and Onyx until it was too late, but immediately drew guns and fired toward the door dropping the flashlight in fright.

Lethal ducked for cover while Onyx crouched down to avoid several shots going over her head. Rolling to the left, she shot up, spun around to avoid a bullet, and gave two back kicks in rapid succession to the perpetrator who was shooting at the doorway while elbowing the other one in the nose.

Lethal grabbed the gun she had kicked out of the man's hand, then punched that man dead in the face. His skull instantly crunched from the impact and he fell to Lethal's feet. Two sharp blows were delivered to the other man by Onyx who then dropped to the floor semi-conscious.

She picked up his gun and tossed it to her brother, who only gave her an "Are you crazy?" look. Yet, he knew his sister was just as loony as he was and he didn't even ask. She would always do what she was trained to do.

Lethal grabbed the man Onyx had taken down and shook him hard. "Where are the kids?"

He moaned, disoriented, as Lethal shook him repeating his question. "Got away," he mumbled before losing consciousness.

Onyx went to Leroy's room. His closet was wide open, and she could tell there were bags missing from there. Leroy must have gotten worried and left with the kids, but Onyx has no idea where he could have gone.

She went back in Kimberly's room where Lethal was tying up the two men. Both were still out of it, but Onyx didn't need to question them. She knew what was happening.

After Lethal got off the phone, Onyx explained. "Leroy has taken the kids in hiding. There must have been some kind of signal or something didn't seem right, and Kimberly trained Leroy to take the kids to safety."

"Where could that be?"

Lethal looked very doubtful. "It could be anywhere considering Leroy has become an expert at it, and we could spend another six years trying to find him."

"Kimberly would know. There could still be time."

That doubtful look didn't go away in her brother's eyes and even Onyx wasn't sure if Kimberly was still alive.

When the police arrived, Onyx left her brother to speak to them while she went to her Expedition to see if any information had come back from the server.

Surprisingly, there were some printouts, and she almost shouted in excitement. There had been several activities regarding the account she had inquired about and this was always good to go on.

Going to Lethal, who was finishing up, she ordered, "Let's roll on Downriver. I'll explain on the way."

He nodded and followed her back to the Expedition. "Call Jaelen, see if he can get over to Kimberly's house to see if Leroy might come back."

She called Jaelen's number, but the digital answering machine picked up, then she called his cell phone. There was still no answer. Knowing how exhausted he was, she ended her call and reminded herself to call back as soon as possible. She also tried Del's and Blaze's cell phones, but she received a computer prompt from both of their lines saying, "The caller you are trying to reach is out of the subscriber area." She figured aloud, "If Blaze and Del are in the Downriver area together, they must be somewhere a cell phone's reception is overrun by a much higher and more powerful signal. Jaelen didn't answer, so I'll call one of our on-call security personnel to go over and keep an eye on the home."

"So what did you find out on the printouts?" Lethal asked.

"You were right. Eli changed his name and used his father's middle name and social security number. According to this, he had warrants in seven states under the name Elijah Phillips, the second, and is suspected of heroin trafficking in Detroit. He used Elijah Phillips to get into Wayne State Pharmacy program, but dropped out in his third year in order to make better money on the street as Eli Phillips."

Lethal chortled, amused. "So instead of becoming a legitimate pharmacist, he decides to become a street pharmacist. That's rich, Onyx. I guess crime does pay."

"Well, it's paying in full because Eli Phillips purchased a lot of property in and around Detroit." She started looking down the list of properties.

"Let me see that," Lethal said, and he turned on the inside light.

She wasn't worried that her brother paid little attention to the road because Lethal was an excellent driver and a wonderful multi-tasker. Others would cringe at his driving, but Onyx trusted her brother very much.

"Ainsley's got to be behind all of this," Onyx concluded.

"I suspected it from the beginning when Eli showed up out of nowhere. Ah ha!" he exclaimed. "No wonder we can't reach Zeke and Del. Eli owns a radio station in the Downriver area."

"That could be what's blocking the transmissions of their phones," Onyx realized.

"You keep trying their phones, and I'll head in that direction. Let's just hope we're not too late."

Onyx wished the same thing too; she also wished Jaelen would answer his line.

Chapter 32

Jaelen arose late and saw it was two hours before noon. How the hell had he slept so late? Jumping out of bed, he saw the glass of Brandy next to the bed and knew it had been the alcohol that had knocked him into a coma.

After dressing, he called his housekeeper and ordered her to get rid of every drop of hard liquor in the house. On his way to his office, so consumed with his own thoughts, he realized he had not picked up his cell phone and had not checked to see if anyone had called.

Arriving at his office, he noticed the staff seemed very preoccupied and didn't notice that he even came in. Going straight into his office, he called into Kimberly's office, but there was no answer. It seemed odd, and he decided to call Ruby's office.

"Is Miss Hawthorne around there?" he asked. Ruby's office was located on the first floor in the back of the club behind the salon area.

"Kimberly never came into work," Ruby said. "We assumed she was with you since she hasn't call."

"She never came in at all?" he asked, shocked.

"No, and there's no answer on her cell or home phone, but Lauren, Kimberly's temp said she thought she saw Kimberly's car still parked in the parking lot."

"Let me check everything out, and I'll call you back," he told her.

Just as he was about to get up, he froze as he met the beautiful soft eyes of a six-year-old replica of Kimberly standing at his office doorway. How long she had been there was a mystery to him, but her precious smile drew his attention and tugged at his heart, making him forget what he had been about to do momentarily.

"I know who you are," she said, coming around his desk and looking up into his eyes as if he were the eighth wonder of the world. "You're Mr. Gates. My mommy told me all about you. She told me how you look and you look just like she said." She smiled even brighter if that were possible. "You are very handsome - just like she said."

"And who is your mother?" he asked with a deep frown, bothered by what conclusions his mind was drawing.

"Kimberly Parker Hawthorne," the child said proudly. "Jason says you won't treat Momma good, but I told him he was wrong." She leaned close as if she were telling him a secret in a room full of people. "Even though I never met you, Mr. Gates, I know Momma's too good for anyone to be mean to her." Her eyes were wide in concern. "You wouldn't hurt my Momma, would you?"

"No, I would never hurt her on purpose," he reluctantly admitted.

She smiled so wide that Jaelen knew instantly he would promise this child the world if it kept her smiling like that. He then knew why he was so enchanted by the child. She was a miniature version of Kimberly.

"Jaenae, you're supposed to be in the lobby," a young gruff voice said at the doorway.

Jaelen didn't even have to look where the voice was coming from to know who it was. His disgruntled frown returned. Still, he looked past the child to see Jason looking as mean as possible, and he groaned internally. The boy was a pain in the ass, and he hadn't even said anything to Jaelen yet.

"See, Jason, I told you he wouldn't hurt Momma." The little girl beamed at Jason. "Momma always says never judge a book by its cover."

"Momma also says don't believe everything you hear from other people." Jason snorted.

She was insulted by this comeback and stood akimbo, facing her brother. "The best answer to anger is silence."

Jaelen was shocked that this young child had quoted a German proverb, but was equally amazed when Jason shot back, quoting Samuel Johnson, "Advice is seldom welcome. Those who need it most like it least."

She was quick to retaliate with "Many receive advice. Only the wise profit by it."

Obviously, she had just stumped her brother. "Where did you get that one from?" he asked in disbelief.

"Publilius Syrus. I read up on it in the library by Miss Collins' house, brother. You are getting lazy," she sang triumphantly.

Jaelen was blown away by the genius level of these children and couldn't be more proud of Kimberly for raising the two of them on her own. He still wanted to throttle the smart-ass boy, but restrained himself.

Jaenae turned toward Jaelen and cupped her small palms to his face. "Jason, how could you not trust face like this?"

Jason snorted rudely, and Jaelen really wanted to put the little boy over his knee to beat that smart-ass attitude out of him. Where the hell did Jason get that kind of language?

"Besides," Jaenae continued. "I think the only one who could frown as bad as you and Mr. Gates is our daddy." She leaned toward Jaelen again as if telling him a secret, whispering, "I haven't met him either, but my momma says he frowns like there's no tomorrow."

"Shut up, Jaenae," Jason snapped, coming up to his sister as if he could protect her if Jaelen decided to hurt her.

What Jaenae said had not registered in Jaelen's mind until she protested with her brother by saying, "But look at him, Jason, he even has your look when he frowns."

"Shut up, big mouth!" Jason ordered.

Jaelen looked at Jason, who all of a sudden avoided looking at him, then he looked back at Jaenae.

"Who is your daddy?" he asked her.

She shrugged, but a touch of sadness erased the humor she had just had. "Momma says he's never met us, but if he ever did, he would fall instantly in love with me because I'm cute and smart."

Jaelen couldn't believe the conclusions he was drawing in his mind. Sweet innocent Kimberly could not be cruel enough to terminate the pregnancy. Monica could, but not Kimberly, especially after she found out she was carrying twins.

Why hadn't she told him? How difficult it must have been to struggle all by herself. The hardships, the sacrifice, the love she must have felt to give them a good life.

"Where is your mother?" he asked both of the twins.

They looked at him as if he should know the answer.

Suddenly, an older woman appeared at the door in a nurse's uniform, exclaiming Jaenae's and Jason's names. "I told the two of you to stay in the lobby."

"It was Jaenae's fault. She was being nosey!" Jason accused, pointing a finger at his sister.

Jaelen stood up to greet the older woman, who excused and apologized for the twins,

"I'm Miss Collins, a good friend of Kimberly's. I've been trying to wait for her all night."

"Miss Collins told Leroy that Momma must be with you since she likes you so much and you must be giving our Momma some good loving, but I don't know why Momma can't just get good loving from us. We give her a lot," Jaenae burst out.

Ms. Collins and Jaelen flushed. Now Jaelen knew what Jason meant about Jaenae having a big mouth because even Jason sighed heavily at his sister. Jaelen gave her a disapproving frown as Ms. Collins flustered about what to say next.

"There you go again, big mouth! She wasn't supposed to know we were at the door listening," Jason snipped.

Jaenae protested, "I don't have a big mouth, do I, Mr. Gates?"

Jaelen was honored the child looked up at him. He knelt down to her eye level. "You do, but it's probably the prettiest big mouth in the world."

Jaenae instantly flung her arms around his neck and kissed his cheek. "Then I don't care how big my mouth is," she said, laughing.

Jaelen was almost tempted to chuckle at her infectious silliness, but stifled the urge while Jason joined in his sister's laughter.

"Jason, could you take your sister back to the lobby, so Miss Collins and I can talk?" Jaelen ordered.

Jason looked up at Ms. Collins, who nodded her approval. Jaelen was positive the boy did this on purpose to piss the hell out of Jaelen. When the twins were gone, Ms. Collins said, "I just spoke to Ruby downstairs, who said she hadn't heard from Kimberly since yesterday. Leroy was spooked when she didn't come home last night and caught a cab all the way to Southfield where I live. I know she has recently spoken of her attraction to you, so I figured the two of you must be together and time got away from her."

"No, she was not with me, Miss Collins," he said brusquely. "She was probably with that old flame."

"Elijah, you mean? She was only seeing him to get information for Mr. Heart. There weren't any real feelings for him, like she has for you."

Jaelen couldn't believe what Ms. Collins was trying to tell him. Kimberly couldn't possibly have any deep feelings for him. That was too impossible as mean as he had been to her.

"Go check on the children while I make some phone calls. There's got to be a good reason she didn't come home."

Ms. Collins nodded in agreement to this and left. He dialed Onyx and was immediately blasted by her voice across the phone.

"Where the hell have you been?" she demanded to know. "I've been blowing you up since last night."

"Out of it, literally," he said. "Have you heard from your brother-"

She cut him off. "Kimberly's missing!"

"What do you mean missing?" he asked.

Onyx started at the beginning, speaking as quickly as she could, before concluding with, "We found Del and Blaze last night in the vicinity of the radio station Elijah owns under his false name. Blaze arrived first and was positive he saw Elijah carry Kimberly from his car into this building and take her to the basement's back office. Del had suspicions that Ainsley was trying something, but we didn't know if Elijah was in cahoots with Ainsley. He told

Blaze to be on high alert for anything suspicious, which is why Blaze stayed on Kimberly so well until she was carried in the radio station. If Ainsley were in with Elijah, Ainsley would know Kimberly was well protected and take special precautions to get rid of her. Lethal was suspicious about it all when Elijah showed up all of a sudden and probably somehow Ainsley convinced him to kidnap Kimberly while Ainsley was conveniently out of town with his folks in the UP."

"She's kidnapped?"

"When Lethal and I arrived late last night, we found Elijah's car still in the parking lot of the radio station. All Blaze could tell us is that Del made some calls and then said he was going in the radio station and for Blaze to get in touch with us, but by the time Blaze was able to get a signal to us, Del had disappeared. There were traces of drugs in the car and in some glasses left in the seat along with the bug Lethal planted on Kimberly and her purse and cell phone.

"We couldn't get a search warrant until early this morning, but somehow they got her out. Del has got to be with her, making Elijah think he's on his side, which enforces our belief that Ainsley would be involved. We're still down here looking the place over inch by inch, but have yet to find anything. We just started fingerprinting."

"Give me your locations. I want to be there."

Onyx told him the address.

"I have the children here with me at the club, but I'm going to send them over to my place. Can you get Blaze over there to keep an eye on them?"

"That's great. He'll be on his way while you are on your way here," Onyx said.

Jaelen rushed out, but not before giving Ms. Collins the keys to his place and telling Ruby to make sure the kids were taken care of with anything they needed.

Chapter 33

Onyx greeted Jaelen in the radio station's parking lot and got him through the police lineup and reporters.

"You know," she said, "all of this must have been planned a long time ago if Ainsley was involved."

She took him into the back basement office. "Like I said before, Blaze is positive Elijah carried her in the back basement office. Del disappeared as well, but we found his phone in the office on the couch. We believe it was dropped by mistake. Blaze is positive no one could have left or came without him knowing."

"Have you thought about a secret passage way?" Jaelen asked.

Lethal was in the room and answered him. "Yes. We've searched all over the building, but we couldn't find anything out of the ordinary."

Jaelen looked around the room. It was a normal office and nothing seemed out of place. He knew Lethal was a genius at hiding spaces. Anyone could get lost in the maze Lethal called a house, but there had to have been a way for Elijah to get Kimberly's body out without leaving this building, so if there was a hidden exit it had to have been big enough to get in and out.

A chill went through his body. Had Kimberly been alive when Eli left?

"Have you checked for blood?"

"Yes," Onyx answered Jaelen. "We're starting fiber analysis after all this is done."

Jaelen tried to push the worse out of his mind and think what could have happened.

"Look!" Lethal said as he knelt to the side of the desk.

The fingerprint technician brushed the corner of the desk, took a sample, and got out the way.

"It could be prints from when the desk was moved in," Onyx assumed the worst.

"I doubt that. Those are fingertips," Lethal observed. "And their skinny. That's female."

Jaelen knelt down to get a closer look at the prints. "As much as I would love to disagree with your brother, Onyx, he's right. And ten million says those are Kimberly's because there is no way a female could have assisted in moving this desk in here."

"You haven't met my cousin, Tempest." Onyx snickered.

Jaelen studied the fingerprints a little closer turning his head to the side, while Lethal gave his sister a playful poke in her arm. "A-I-R," he spelled out.

"What does that mean?" Onyx asked.

"Air," Lethal said.

"I know what he spelled, smart ass, but what the hell does that mean?" Onyx asked.

Lethal and Jaelen looked at each other then looked up at the walls. Jaelen saw there were no air conditioning ducts on the walls, but there was a large fan in the corner. Lethal searched one side of the room while Jaelen searched the other side.

"Behind the couch," Onyx said, figuring out what they were looking for. "There is a waist high out vent behind the couch."

"That's my girl!" Jaelen said proudly.

"Your girl?" Lethal protested.

"Don't start," Onyx warned the two of them, moving the couch out her way. She had on plastic gloves and touched the corners of the vent, but the metal was solidly on the wall paneling.

Lethal ordered a technician to dust the walls and the vents around the entire back of the couch walls. A few minutes later, the technician revealed a set of prints on the border near the floor. After the technician took samples and confirmed it was Elijah's prints in just moments with an electronic scanner, Jaelen put on some gloves and placed his hand on the border. The entire panel shifted and the steel vent released from the wall. It was a 4x4 space and Jaelen took off his suit coat and prepared to go in.

"Where the hell do you think you're going?" Lethal asked, grabbing his arm.

"I'm going to find Kimberly," he protested, snatching away from Lethal.

"What the fuck do you care about her? You're just involved in this to make sure you don't lose the money she invested in your company."

"That's not true, and you know it. I love her."

"That's a fucking lie, Gates. You don't even love yourself. Give me one good reason why I should involve your ass in this?" Lethal demanded to know.

"Because she's the mother of my children, you asshole, and I love the hell out of her, and as soon as I get her out this mess, she's going to be my wife!" Jaelen exploded.

"Children?" Onyx asked. "I thought it was just Jason."

Jaelen turned to her. "You knew?"

Onyx flustered a bit. "I kind of had my suspicion, but all you had to do was really look at the boy and see yourself in him."

"I paid little attention to the constantly pissed off brat," Jaelen spat.

"I wonder where the hell the little shit gets it from?" Lethal snorted.

"Are you going to let me go with you or not?" Jaelen asked, tired and exasperated.

Lethal paused, deliberately keeping Jaelen waiting. "Fine, but I don't want you bothering me or trying to get in my way."

Jaelen handed a technician his coat and followed Lethal as they crawled through the ducts. About twenty feet into it, as Lethal guided with a flashlight between his teeth, they came to a ladder. Crawling down the ladder, Jaelen realized Elijah would have needed help getting Kimberly through all of this, if she were unconscious ... or dead. Again, he had to shake off that horrible gut feeling that something terrible had happened to her. Kimberly had to be alive.

Chapter 34

T he darkness was all around her, and Kimberly faded in and out of consciousness, fighting to stay awake, but the drug they had given her was too powerful, and she was having a difficult time trying to maintain her equilibrium.

She had recently heard men arguing, but before all this, she knew she had been taken to a strange office with a cold cement floor. Eli was the only one in the room, but instead of alerting that she was conscious, she saw the desk right next to her and left a clue for Lethal who was hopefully in hot pursuit. Jesus, she hoped this was all a dream.

Leroy, please tell me you've gone with the kids, she thought, hoping her prayers would be answered.

After someone else arrived with the deepest voice she had ever heard on a man, she was poked with a needle and then passed out again shortly after. When she awoke, she felt badly bruised and was covered and tied so tight she could barely breathe.

She was in a vehicle. Someone was smoking smelly cigarettes that made her eyes water, and played music loudly.

Only the deep voice and Eli's voice were recognizable. They drove the longest time before the car stopped. She started to get scared as Eli asked,

"Where the hell are we? In the middle of fucking nowhere? I thought you said we were going to see Ainsley."

"I'm here," she heard Ainsley's voice.

Kimberly was sure she was going to hyperventilate.

"Where's my money? I've been waiting too long for this," Eli demanded.

"You stupid fool. If you had gotten her here earlier in the week, you wouldn't have had to wait so long. You think I care how long you waited? You think I wouldn't find out you were trying to get the money for yourself?"

"I don't know what you are talking about."

A tape recorder that sounded close to Kimberly played a conversation she had with Eli earlier.

"You son of a bitch," Ainsley said. "You're trying to screw me, weren't you?"

"I would certainly agree," the deep voice said.

"I don't know what you're talking about. I was just seeing how her feelings were to me before I brought her here, so you could kill her ... and ..." Eli stuttered.

A loud shot rang out, and she heard a thud against the car. She wanted to scream, but her throat was too dry and the gag would only muffle it. Was she next? Dear Lord, please don't let me die today.

"Cheating son of a bitch!" Ainsley shouted. Five more shots rang out, then a whole bunch of clicks followed. There was a pregnant moment of silence until she heard Ainsley tell someone to get rid of the body.

"What about the girl?" the deep voice asked.

"Take her to the barn up over that hill. There's a door in the floor in the right hand corner under the bales of hay. Take her down there and leave her there for me."

"What about me? I need to get back to the city, but I need to get some rest before I go," the deep voice said.

"Dump this car in the river by the road leading to the barn and take this. There's a hotel about two miles down this road. Get out of town as fast as possible," Ainsley said.

"What are you going to do with the girl?"

"That's for me to know and you to never find out. I'll take care of her. My parents will be leaving early in the morning to go to Muskegon. I'll take care of her then if the night's cold doesn't kill her."

"What about the kids? Want me to keep a look out for them?"

"Yeah. Do that for me. There's an extra tip if I can have them, too, as soon as possible."

Kimberly heard someone get back in the car and the engine started up. She relaxed as the car started moving knowing that the deep voice was carrying out the instructions. It wasn't until she was being lifted out the car gently by the deep voice man did she start to panic and began to twitch and try to fight.

"Calm down, baby girl," he said soothingly. "You just don't know how lucky you are."

She felt like a sack of potatoes as she was carried over a large shoulder for a ways, then set down against what felt like a tree. She was freezing and knew it was night, but she wasn't sure how long she had been out. There was some tearing before the frigid wind hit her face.

Looking up, there was a dark figure in front of her, but he walked away to an old gold Cadillac Seville. After he took some things out the trunk, he shifted the car to neutral, jumped out, and let it roll into a lake. He then returned to her and began to untie her quickly. When she was a loose, he took his jacket off and handed it to her. All she could do was stand there stupidly and watch him as he took some things out of his bag and took the coverings she was wrapped in. Though she had never met the man, at that moment, he was all she could trust.

"Baby girl," he called to her. She came forward and he handed her a phone. "Call Lethal and tell him where you are. That's one thing about that old ass flame of yours. He had a good phone."

She did as the man instructed, wondering how he knew Lethal while the man made up some makeshift body using leaves, covers, old towels, and a small balloon filled with water to give it weight.

"Heart on the line," Lethal said.

"Mr. Heart, it's me Kimberly!" she said excitedly.

"Where the hell are you?" he bellowed.

"I don't know," she answered. "There's this man here who saved me and we are in the middle of nowhere." She remembered Eli's words and began to cry in relief that she wasn't dead. "Elijah's dead, I think, and Ainsley had me kidnapped. Please come and get me, please."

"Is the man there calling you baby girl?" Lethal asked.

"Yes," she said, shocked.

"Put the son of a bitch on the phone."

She handed the phone to the man who took it. After a moment, he told Lethal where they would be in about an hour. When he got off the phone, she wanted to fall into his arms, but restrained herself.

He looked around the area, then asked, "Stay here. I'll be back in about fifteen. If a car comes, go behind the trees and keep low until I get back."

Kimberly nodded and watched as he took the bundle he just wrapped up and walked toward the barn a distance away. She ducked behind a tree just in case anyone came while she rested on the ground. He was good on his word in coming back. He looked down at her feet.

"You think you can walk two miles in less than an hour?" he asked.

"If I could take off these shoes, I could probably jog it in thirty."

"A brisk walk should be all."

She nodded and started walking with him. Kimberly would walk to the end of the earth if it could get her back with her children and brother. She also longed to see Jaelen and decided that not another moment would pass before she let Jaelen know that she was in love with him. She knew she was because there was no other place she wanted to be except in his arms.

It was a good thing she had worn low heels because by the time they reached the motel, her feet were screaming. She took them off as soon as they were in the room. He allowed her to go to the bathroom first and she quickly relieved herself then let him have a turn.

"What's your name?" she asked when he came out.

He only frowned as if it were a sin to ask, but then mumbled, "Del."

Kimberly could tell he wasn't much of a talker, but he was nice looking. No, that word didn't do him justice because when he took off his turtleneck black sweater, muscles abounded this man like he had the largest mumps all over his six and a half foot brawny body. She looked away, embarrassed to see him like that, then noticed there was one bed in the room.

Looking back at him, she saw he was making himself comfortable in a chair and put his feet up on a low dresser. He waited until she crawled in bed and pulled the covers up to her neck before he turned out the light. The outside lights illuminated the room. She watched through partially closed lids as he pulled a gun out from behind him and placed it on his lap. He just stared at the door as if waiting any minute for someone to bust through the door.

Exhaustion finally took over and she found herself in a deep sleep, wishing Jaelen would come also.

Chapter 35

A weight pressed down on her chest, and she thought for sure she was back, tied up and covered waiting to die and the long walk she had taken last night that now had her legs burning had all been a nightmare. She struggled in her sleep then suddenly felt warm soft familiar lips kissing her own, then her neck and all over her face.

"Kimber, wake up, please," a familiar voice whispered in her ear.

She opened her eyes slowly, not believing what she was hearing, to focus on the face in front of her, which she couldn't believe she was seeing.

"Jaelen?" she asked to be sure.

He kissed her long and hard. "Are you okay?" he asked.

Kimberly couldn't believe this was the same man. He wasn't frowning at all. Matter of fact, he actually looked concerned. She blinked several times to make sure that what she was seeing was real because it was too good to be true. "Did my wish come true?"

"What wish?"

"I wished for you."

His smile was startling as he brushed his lips lightly against hers. "Yes, your wish came true, Kimber."

If this were a dream, it was the best dream she could have ever wished for. Jaelen being nice to her. That was definitely a dream.

A voice cleared across the room, and Jaelen groaned under his breath. Kimberly looked over his shoulder to see Onyx, Lethal, and Del standing at the end of the bed, looking down at them.

Onyx was smirking in satisfaction while Lethal frowned in discontentment. She pushed at Jaelen's shoulders to get him off her and reluctantly he moved growling at Lethal, "Don't you have something to do other than stand over people and clear your throat?"

"Only when I want to annoy the hell out of you."

"Don't I at least get a minute alone with her?"

"What the hell for? She's my client. She's only your office manager."

Jaelen jumped out of bed, ready to swing at Lethal for being the biggest ass in the world.

Onyx jumped between them.

"Boys, now that we're done comparing the size of your cocks, can we get back to business?" she said. "We've got three fucking hours to set up and get all this done before the sun comes up."

"Is Ainsley going to continue to try to kill me?" Kimberly asked.

"From what Del has told us, I wouldn't count on it, and he taped the entire thing. Ainsley won't be able to touch you with a ten foot pole from now on because he'll be serving life in prison for killing Elijah," Lethal assured her.

She put her head in her hands, wanting to cry in relief and feeling almost a little bad for not wanting to cry at Elijah's murder. He would have turned her over for money. That's all she was worth to him and this thought angered her a bit.

"Since it seems Miss Parker is all right, why don't we get set up in the barn?" Onyx suggested.

They started to leave out until Kimberly called for Del, who turned to look at her.

"Thank you, Del. For all you've done," she said.

He only nodded and left out, following Lethal and Onyx.

"He's never been much of a talker," Jaelen explained, sitting next to her.

Kimberly almost felt uncomfortable under his concern gaze. Warily, she asked, "Why are you being so nice to me?"

"Because I have reason to be," he said.

She stood up, now very uncomfortable. "You've never had to in the past. What has changed?"

He avoided her question. "Put your shoes on so I can take you to the hotel," he ordered.

"What hotel?"

"There's a St. Royal resort near Muskegon, and Lethal was given several rooms to accommodate us."

She put her shoes on, reluctantly feeling her feet cry out in pain. "You didn't answer my question."

"Let's just get to the hotel. Aren't you dying for a bath?" Jaelen asked.

Her body was screaming for a hot bath, but she also knew this was a ploy to make her forget what she had been trying to speak with him about. Jaelen's behavior was too weird for words, and she wanted to know why he was acting this way, but arguing with him would probably make it a longer wait for that bath. Kimberly allowed him to escort her out the hotel room to a rental Chevy Lumina in pristine condition.

The luxurious furnishings of the hotel room impressed her.

Jaelen deliberately rushed her into the bathroom and allowed her to bathe for as long as she could, but Kimberly really couldn't enjoy the bath with him on her mind wondering why was he behaving like this. Her bath ended up being short and fast in order to find out what was going on.

When the attendant left them alone after Jaelen issued out some orders for items to be brought immediately to the room, he spoke to her. "Ruby's taking care of everything at the club and…" He fumbled for the name, "Lauren? I think that's her name, is taking care of the RSVP and grand opening arrangements. I was updated that you left detailed instructions for her and Ruby and the only thing on your desk was the urgent matter to meet with the Newman Construction foreman? Once we were assured you were okay, I pushed this meeting for you to next week, but I told them you would call to confirm. Is there anything else you need? I was going to give you some privacy-"

"Jaelen, I want to know what's going on," she demanded.

"What do you mean?"

"Why are you being nice to me?"

He sighed, knowing he couldn't avoid this discussion. "I think I should be a little nice to the mother of my children."

Kimberly felt her chest almost collapse. It seemed so difficult to breathe, and when she tried to swallow, the largest lump seemed to be in her throat. He knew! He knew and he ... wasn't upset?

She stepped back, too astounded for words. Was this one of his tricks? Did he really have plans to take the kids away and keep them in his revenge against her?"

"Where are my kids?"

"They are being protected at my home. Ainsley's goons tried to get to them, but Leroy had already gone into hiding before they got there to kill them."

She sighed in relief. "And what do you plan on doing?" Kimberly had to know.

"I plan on marrying you, Kimberly," he stated.

Now she was taken aback, and she could have been knocked over with a feather. "Marriage? You? You're too selfish to share your life with anyone, Jaelen, and especially me when I've received nothing but contempt from you," she protested. "You are the most egotistical, obstinate, belittling asshole on the face of this planet, and you would not bestow your love and affection to anyone let alone a person who tied you up, raped you, and then ordered to have your hand broken. That doesn't make any sense at all, and I think-"

He grabbed her and gave her a long hard kiss, cutting off any speech she was making or even about to make. Kimberly believed the room was spinning or was it her senses? Being in his arms, feeling that delicious mouth attack her like there was no tomorrow, was sweet heaven. She couldn't help but to accept and enjoy his kisses, wanting more and more.

Jaelen swept her up in his arms and carried her to the bedroom. Before she could think about protesting, he was kissing and touching her all over. Kimberly forgot about how much she hated this man and relished in his touch, wanting more and more as the minutes passed and they made love so deeply, Kimberly cried as she reached pinnacle after pinnacle.

When it was all over, they laid in each other's arms. He kissed her forehead and held her close. Kimberly feigned to fall asleep and waited until she was positive Jaelen was slumbering deeply before she attempted to move out the bed.

As exhausted as she was, Kimberly couldn't sleep at all until she saw her children. She quickly dressed and quietly left the room, going down to the lobby. Before leaving, she went through his wallet and took out all his cash, which totaled sixty dollars. Just as she stepped off the elevators, she caught sight of a familiar face.

Before the familiar face looked her way, she ducked swiftly behind a large plant, lowering her head. A female companion was with him as he walked by Kimberly.

When the coast was clear, she went to the front desk and told the male clerk with the most cheerful smile what room she was staying in.

The clerk was eager to help her out. "How can I help you?"

"How would I go about renting a car? I need to drive back to Detroit immediately."

He started clicking on his keyboard. "Mr. Heart already has two rentals at his disposal," the clerk noted. "He didn't pick up one of them, yet. I can have the valet pulled the vehicle around to the front for you."

She wrote Lethal a quick note. "Good. Make sure this gets to Mr. Heart." As a last-minute request, she asked, "While the car is being pulled around, can I use a phone real quick instead of going back up to my room?"

The clerk handed her a cordless phone and said, "Dial nine to phone out."

Stepping slightly away from the desk for privacy, she called Jaelen's Detroit home number and was so relieved when Ms. Collins picked up the line.

"Are the children okay?" she asked.

"Yes, Kimberly, how are you? Where are you?" Ms. Collins asked, sounding very concerned.

"Horribly emotionally, but physically I'll live." She told Ms. Collins everything that had happened and even though Ms. Collins was startled over Elijah's death, her friend listened and sympathized with open ears.

"So Mr. Gates wants to marry you?"

"Only because of the children. You should have seen the look in his eyes when he said proudly that I was the mother of his children. He gleamed like sunshine." Just thinking about that moment had her panicking and looking around. Now that Jaelen knew they had children together, she had a feeling he would never leave her alone. Whether that was bad or good, she didn't know, but she knew it was just too much to handle right now.

"I'm leaving the hotel now, and I should be there in a short while," she promised.

"Good, we'll be waiting for you," Ms. Collins promised.

She quickly left the lobby going to the front of the hotel, where a valet attendant handed her the keys to a Chrysler Concorde. She would make it into the city by eight o'clock in the morning if she made good timing and hit good traffic.

Chapter 36

Lethal handed the binoculars to Onyx who raised them to her eyes to peer at the main house. At tall, well-built man stepped out the front doors and carefully made his way down the porch to put some bags he was carrying in a new model brown Cadillac Deville.

"Do you think that's him?" Onyx asked.

"I don't know. I don't have my DNA glasses on to clarify," Lethal replied, snorting. "Call up Jaelen and tell him to have Ms. Parker ready to leave. I want you back in Detroit by sunrise."

"Why?" she asked, her brow furrowing in confusion.

"Because I would think she'd want to be in Detroit as soon as possible. She hasn't seen her children in a couple of days."

Onyx snorted. "Are you being sensitive to her needs?" his sister asked, her tone filled with sarcasm.

He only cut a don't-push-my-buttons glare as he grabbed his cell phone that was vibrating in his back pocket. Lethal pushed the speakerphone so Onyx could hear the conversation.

Tempest was calling from the office. "Got a hit off the fax from a Michigan State Police buddy about that Edward character you were looking for."

"Really? Where is the hit from?"

"Muskegon, Michigan. A blue sedan was stopped with him as a passenger." She quickly rattled off the plate and the description of the female driver. "It didn't match the girlfriend, but the description of the passenger fit perfectly of Edward, but his driver's license read Eddie Smith and there's a hotel reservation at the St. Royal. I sent the information to the server and you can download it when you need it."

"Thanks, cousin. Is that all?"

"Well," she said, as if she didn't know if the information she was about to give was important enough. "You received a fax from a Louisiana hit on an Elizabeth Collins. She's wanted for heroin drug trafficking."

The news was shocking to him and Onyx. "Are you sure that was Elizabeth Collins?"

"Yes, she skipped bail about four years ago, and there's a warrant out for her arrest. This is an answer from a hit you put out about her to the New Orleans Police Department," Tempest reiterated.

He looked at Onyx. "Talk about a small world. You need to get to Detroit with Kimberly, but don't tell her what's really going on. I don't want her to panic, but you need to get there as soon as possible, do you understand?"

Onyx only nodded.

"I'll get in touch with Zeke and let him know to keep an eye on the babysitter," he informed Onyx. "Hey Temp, can you swing over to Jaelen's just in case and let your brother know there's an alert out, without putting anyone on alarm?"

"No problem," Tempest said. "Give me the address and I'll be on the way."

Lethal gave her the address, then disconnected.

"I'm on my way, but what about the cars?" Onyx asked.

"Take Del with you back to the hotel and get the extra rental. The keys should be still at the front desk." He held his sister's hand extra hard. "Hurry."

She knew this meant to be careful by the worried look in his eyes and she would most definitely.

****

Jaelen came awake suddenly by the pounding on the door. He looked around the room for Kimberly, but she was nowhere to be found. He noticed his wallet was out on the dresser, and he knew he hadn't put it there. Kimberly must have gone through it, but why would she have to do that?

The pounding again jolted him back to reality. He went to the door to let Onyx and Del in. "What the hell is your problem?" he asked as Del pushed past him and went into the bedroom and then the other rooms to look around the suite.

"Where did Kimberly go?" Onyx demanded, highly upset.

"What do you mean? She hasn't gone anywhere." He looked at Del who was shaking his head.

"She's not here," Onyx exclaimed, going over to the phone. She spoke to the manager down at the desk and asked him to release the last number called from this suite. When she was told that no number had been called, she told Jaelen this.

He cursed under his breath. "She could have gone home," he said.

"But you aren't sure?" she interrogated.

Frustrated, he admitted, "I fell after I thought she was sleep."

"Was she upset?"

"She didn't look it, but she was a bit bothered that I asked her to marry me."

Onyx's eyes narrowed in suspicion. "Did you really ask her, Jaelen?" she asked.

"Not really, I told her." He looked flushed. "I figured she wouldn't accept if I ask."

Onyx groaned. "Get dressed. She's got us beat by two hours."

"What's going on?" he demanded to know.

"I'll tell you on the road," she said. "Give me your keys and I'll get the car to the front. Hurry up." She walked out with Del in tow after she got the keys.

Jaelen cursed again under his breath. He dressed quickly and met Onyx in front of the hotel. Soon as he jumped in the car, she sped off. "Lethal's been trying your house, but there's no answer and Blaze isn't picking up the cell phone. He tried to warn Tempest, but he can't get through on her phone either."

"I take it today is not a good day for cell phones." He smirked.

"I'm going to take it as this whole damn week is going to be pretty fucked up if you asked me the way this case is going." She jumped on the highway and pushed the accelerator down to increase her speed. With it being so early in the morning, she was able to get good time on the highway. "Elizabeth Collins was working at the sperm donor center where Hawthorne had stashed his sperm. We were able to determine that, but when the sperm could not be found, Kimberly had given up on having Hawthorne's children, but she and Elizabeth became good friends. Elizabeth helped Kimberly hide from her uncle Charles for a long while, but Elizabeth was dealing prescribed drugs and was getting ready to be caught, so she quit her job.

"She probably told Kimberly there was a better life in New Orleans where Elizabeth had some connections to the underground world. She was able to help Kimberly give birth to your children and then with her contacts still at the center, Elizabeth was notified that the sperm had been found. So, she arranged for Kimberly to come back up here, get inseminated and then come back down to New Orleans, where she also assisted in helping Kimberly give birth.

"Somehow - we don't know when - she was contacted by Ainsley, who probably offered a great deal of money or even blackmailed because she left Kimberly in New Orleans to come back to Michigan and take up a new job at St. John's Hospital. Obviously at some point, she started working for Ainsley because charges of drug trafficking in Michigan were mysteriously dropped when Ainsley's attorney appeared in court for her two years ago. She had to have been working for them then, but wasn't turning Kimberly into them.

"Why she waited so long before turning on Kimberly I'm not sure. Probably because Kimberly never really told Elizabeth her whereabouts and Kimberly never let Hawthorne's offspring out of her sight, but she had Jaenae to stay with Elizabeth to keep up her studies."

"So all this time, my daughter was close to me, and I didn't know?" he asked.

"No one knew. Kimberly had a lot of reasons for not confessing to anyone about who the father was to Jason and Jaenae. Until recently Charles would have used this information to hurt you financially, and anyone else would have used it to hurt Kimberly."

"Why didn't she come to me?"

"When she thought you hated her the most?" Onyx asked him.

Jaelen knew the answer to his own question. It wasn't as if he had been the nicest person to Kimberly. Her actions were only because of her fears and her need to protect her children. She had sacrificed everything to make sure they were safe and loved and would do that until the end. "So you think Ainsley is now aware of our ambush?"

"We have to assume that." She sped-dialed her brother's phone. "I'm going to find out if Ainsley made any attempt to go into the barn to the ambush Lethal and Del have set up."

"And if he doesn't show?" Jaelen asked.

"It means he knows the gig is up and will have to take care of everyone, including Miss Collins."

Jaelen didn't know what he would do if he didn't have Kimberly in his life. Even if she hadn't had the kids, he knew his obsession about her didn't have anything to do with revenge anymore. It was love. "How long until we reach Detroit?"

"I'm going to try to make it in four hours and hope we are not too late," Onyx promised just as Lethal picked up the line.

Chapter 37

Being without license or identification in her rush to get back to Detroit, she was eventually pulled over by the state police- a lean one and a chubby one. It took her thirty minutes to explain who she was and what her rush was, then another hour to explain all she had gone through in the past forty-eight hours. The officers looked at her as if they couldn't believe what she was saying and was on the borderline of accusing her of drinking too much so early in the morning until she finally mentioned Lethal Heart's name.

A look of deep admiration appeared in both of their eyes and the chubby one, who sat in the passenger seat said, "Let's just call his office and see about all of this?" He didn't give her a chance to speak again until he made several phone calls. By now, they had handcuffed her and taken her to the squad car to "talk," as they put it.

It was almost nine in the morning, and she prayed Lethal would have some kind of answering service to direct callers in an emergency to him.

Disappointedly, the chubby officer said, "There's no answer, ma'am."

"I have his cell phone number." She quickly rattled it off, hoping it was right and praying Lethal would answer.

"Mr. Lethal Heart?" the officer said over the phone. "We're calling about a Mrs. Kimberly Parker Hawthorne, your client, sir?" The officer actually sounded nervous. "Yes sir, a gold Concorde … one moment." The officer got out the front to the vehicle and came into the back. He quickly removed the cuffs from her and handed her the phone.

"Where the hell are you, Kimberly?" Lethal's voice boomed over the receiver.

There was a lot of static over the line, and Kimberly wasn't sure whose phone was to blame. "I'm thirty minutes away from Detroit."

"I ought to ring your neck … leaving like that …" He was cutting in and out, and Kimberly checked her phone, but it was getting a good signal. "…Go to Jaelen's house. Did you hear me?"

"I think so. You're cutting in and out, Lethal. You said go to Jaelen's home and do what?" She put her finger in her other ear so she could hear better.

The phone decided to increase the static over the line, so whatever Lethal was saying was partially lost, "…go to Jaelen's home, there's-" The line went dead. She tried to redial, but there was no signal all of a sudden. "I think he wants me to go to my original destination immediately," she told the chubby officer.

"Do you think we should follow you, ma'am?" he asked.

"Maybe," she agreed and thanked the officer.

Kimberly made it to Jaelen's house in forty-five minutes. Seeing the front door cracked and a footprint on the bottom portion of the door, she stopped dead in her tracks, her heart going off the charts at the idea of something bad happening to her children and her brother. Silently, she motioned for the officers to proceed, indicating the tell-tale signs that something was wrong.

They drew out their weapons and cautiously entered the townhouse. Kimberly wanted to scream in frustration. Her heart was dying to know what happened to her children, and the long minutes she had to wait while the officers checked out the house were like centuries to her.

The chubby one had a note with him, which he handed to her. He indicated, "This was found on the floor next to a stain of blood and a bullet hole in the wall above it. Someone's been here, and it looks like there was some kind of struggle by the way the front room is messed over."

The lean officer went to call for assistance and to try Lethal on his cell phone again.

She read the note:

Kimberly,
The safe house on Mount Elliott. Meet us there. Trust no one.

EC

She was familiar with Ms. Collins' handwriting and knew exactly what old warehouse was being referred to as the safe house. It was one of Hawthorne's properties used as a storage, loading and transferring faculty during the summer months for the railroad. Otherwise, it was kept closed. It was also a backup spot for Leroy to go if he couldn't get to Ms. Collins' home or couldn't find Kimberly.

She told the officer this information, giving him the address of the warehouse. "We need to get there immediately," she said. "I'm sure they are safe."

He shook his head. "I think we should wait for backup, Mrs. Hawthorne. That note was left out in the open and whoever broke down this door saw the note. Who is to say they haven't figured out where the property is?"

"Because Hawthorne has five properties over in the area, and I know which one they would be at." She also trained Jason alone to take his siblings and hide with them there as well in an old furnace that's never used. "Plus, if whoever broke in here has figured it out, that means I need to get to my children even faster without alerting them."

The lean officer returned. "Backup is on the way. I got through to Mr. Heart, but there was still a bad connection. I did understand that he was on his way here, and we are to stay put until he gets here. Then the line disconnected again before he was able to tell me anymore, but I did find out that his sister arrived earlier in Detroit and two of his people were taken to the hospital, but he cut off before I could hear anything else."

Kimberly huffed in frustration, feeling the need to scream almost overwhelming her. How could Lethal ask her to stay put when her children's lives could be on the line? She needed to know. She had to know!

Watching them as they kept an half eye on her, she slowly edged to the car she was driving, clutching the keys praying no one would ask her to give them up. Ten minutes later, the distraction of two city police cars and one state police vehicle pulling up gave her enough time to get in her car and sneak away. She didn't know if they had noticed she had left the scene, but once she turned the corner and didn't see any police vehicles behind her, she took off heading to the warehouse.

It was a fifteen-minute drive from Jaelen's townhouse, and driving up in the parking lot behind the building away from the main street, she saw Onyx's SUV. Touching the hood, she noticed it was still warm. She then saw Ms. Collins' Chevy Caprice station wagon parked close to the building next to another car. What was alarming was that it was neatly parked, but there seemed to be signs of a large struggle and the back hatch was still open. The hood of the car was cold and so was the other car. Looking at the ground in the back of the Caprice, she noticed four different sets of small footprints, but they were at a run.

Raising her head, she looked up at the two-story building and wondered if she had made a foolish decision by coming by herself. Going back to Onyx's vehicle, she took the chance of checking to see if the alarm was on the car. The doors were unlocked, and she took the chance of setting off the alarm and alerting whoever was in the building of her presence. Quickly, reaching up the steering column, she jerked the cords to the alarm. Leroy had told her how to disconnect the alarm, which she did quickly and looked inside the SUV. If she knew anything about Onyx it was that this female didn't carry around a weapon.

Onyx may be good at physical combat, but she wasn't stupid to think that she could dodge all the bullets. Someone like her had to have a backup.

Kimberly found a loaded Walther PPK Beretta and a Remington short barreled shotgun. Underneath the back seat, there were three sheeted five-inch blades around a Velcro band. She strapped this high on her thigh underneath her skirt. All the while she was looking, she kept her eyes on the only back entranced doors and used the large vehicle to hide what she was doing. She tucked the Beretta in the back of her skirt using her stockings to hold it in place and pulling out her shirt to hide the budge of the gun in the back.

In her search in Onyx's Expedition, she found a grenade. Carefully she used her stockings to hold the grenade in place. Then she tied the other end to the crowbar that was placed on the accelerator while the vehicle was in park and looped through to the door, so if someone opened it after she closed it wide, the vehicle would explode. She was hoping the vehicle would implode upon impact of what she was trying to do so she could get an even bigger distraction. After jacking up the vehicle quickly, Kimberly placed the jack on the accelerator, then started toward the building.

Keeping the larger gun out, Kimberly proceeded toward the entrance, praying for strength and hoping that the cops had followed her eventually and would be arriving soon, but she wasn't going to wait. She was going to find out where her children were and hope they and her brother were fine.

She didn't make her entrance until the SUV revved into the side of the building giving Kimberly enough time to get inside and stick to the dark. The vehicle had crashed into a pole in the far corner of the warehouse and shut down.

The first floor was filled with large truck/train containers. The ceiling was about thirty feet high, and the only way to get to the second floor was a set of stairs. The elevator shaft was shut down in the building when it was not in use, but there was a loader rail from the second floor if there was product one needed to get down to the first floor immediately to put in the truck/train containers.

The place was dusty, and she could see mice scrambling here and there about the floor, but that wasn't what made her heartbeat hurry up. It was the fact that the place was so quiet.

Slowly going up the stairs to the second floor, she pressed her back to the wall of the stairs, her ears straining to hear something. There was a light at the top of the stairs lit up and as she made her way to the top, she held the Remington in front of her, waiting to shoot at anything larger than a midget that moved. She had to blink several times to see what was going on.

Onyx had her back to Kimberly, but there was a man who she had never seen lying unconscious at Onyx's feet with the front of his face bloodied.

Jaelen was holding his hands up with a gun at his feet and Leroy was lying face down at Jaelen's feet, also unconscious with blood gushing from the back of his head.

Her breathing was erratic as her eyes were then drawn right over Onyx's shoulder where Ainsley stood holding a gun to Ms. Collins' head. From what Kimberly could assess, it looked as if Onyx had taken out a man, and Jaelen had been about to take out Ainsley until he decided to hold Ms. Collins' hostage.

This could be wrong, but Kimberly felt that nauseous feeling pile up in her stomach and the words, "Trust no one" ringing in her ears from the note she had seen in Ms. Collins handwriting. Why had she written those words? Kimberly wondered.

Chapter 38

"Glad you could join the party, Mrs. Hawthorne," Onyx sneered, not even looking around to see who it was.

Kimberly wondered how Onyx knew as she came all the way to the top of the steps. "Where are the children?" she demanded, looking straight at Ainsley.

"Put the gun down, Kimberly," Ainsley ordered. "I've won and when they find all your bodies, I'll be miles away from here. They still think I'm in the U.P."

Kimberly raised the shotgun higher and held her finger tightly on the trigger. The words "Trust no one" echoed in her brain repeatedly, and she felt the stomach contents coming up. Swallowing quickly, she concentrated on Ainsley as he jammed the gun into Ms. Collins' head.

"Why don't you put the gun down, Kimberly?" Ainsley ordered. "I'll release your friend."

"Where are my children?"

"He doesn't know," Onyx said.

"Shut up!" Ainsley ordered.

"They must have escaped and are hiding somewhere in here. That's the gist of what I got before they shot Leroy," Onyx continued, ignoring Ainsley.

"Shut the fuck up, you bitch!" Ainsley ordered. He aimed the gun at Jaelen, but held Ms. Collins close to him. "Put the gun down!" he ordered Kimberly. "Put the fucking gun down, or I'll shoot your lover, bitch."

Kimberly hesitated, wondering if she should try to get a round off before he surrendered. She needed some kind of distraction.

Obviously, Onyx was thinking the same thing. "What I wouldn't do for another distraction so I can take you out," she said to Ainsley.

"Shut up," Ainsley yelled.

Kimberly realized that Ainsley never pointed the gun directly at Onyx, and when she looked up in the rafters, she knew why. There was a man up there with a gun trained on just Onyx. They knew Onyx was the real threat in this situation, but for some reason, Kimberly felt so powerful.

"Careful what you wish for, Onyx," Kimberly said. "There just might be one real soon."

Onyx smirked as Kimberly moved beside her. "A big one?"

"Maybe. How good are you with throwing things from the behind me?" she asked under her breath.

For the first time, Onyx took her eyes off Ainsley and looked towards Kimberly. "The best," she mouthed without making a sound

"Nice collection you have in your truck."

"Hand made for accuracy."

Ainsley put the gun back to Ms. Collins' temple. "Hurry up and get your ass over here, Kimberly!" His demand sounded almost paranoid.

Kimberly moved in front of Onyx to block the shooter in the rafter's view of her. "How good is Jaelen at shooting?" she whispered.

"He's a crack shot. One of the twenty best in the country with any gun."

Kimberly smiled proudly as she hesitated for a moment, then stepped forward toward Ainsley. "What are you going to do, Ainsley?" she asked. "You can only shoot one person at a time."

"I have back up," Ainsley said proudly.

Kimberly took another small step forward, still in the way of the shooter in the rafters. There was a creak on the stairs, and everyone looked except Onyx who carefully used Kimberly as a shield until the time was right.

Two other men stood behind Onyx by the stairs, aiming their guns at Jaelen and Kimberly's back. Ms. Collins looked terrified.

"Now who's in control?" Ainsley asked proudly. "Put the gun down, Kimberly, or your friend dies. You think you're making a sacrifice for your brats, but remember she's got a retarded kid just like your brother. Who's going to take care of little Pamela with the two of you dead?"

Kimberly hadn't thought of that. Pamela would be locked up for the rest of her life, just as they had always threatened to do with Leroy. She couldn't do that to Pamela, and Elizabeth had been such a good friend. Kimberly had tried so hard not to involve Elizabeth in all of this mess.

"You'll give me your word you'll let her go when I put the gun down?" she asked Ainsley.

"I give you my word I won't be the one to kill her."

"But you just threatened to kill us all. Who's to say you won't keep your word?"

"Because if she ever thinks about telling what I've done to her, I'll find her and kill her, won't I, Bethie?"

Elizabeth nodded, moaning in fear.

"Now put the gun down," Ainsley ordered Kimberly.

Kimberly started to kneel, then said abruptly. "Wait! I just forgot something. I rigged Onyx's vehicle to explode. Someone needs to go down there and stop the detonation."

"You're lying!" Ainsley said.

"I swear to you," she said. "Onyx has enough explosive in that car to blow up this entire building."

Ainsley pointed to one of the men behind Kimberly and Onyx. "Go check it out."

Kimberly listened as the man went back down the stairs, and she could hear the click of his heels as he walked under them in the direction of the car. Slowly, to keep Ainsley's eyes on her, she began to kneel, knowing if the shooter in the rafter saw what Onyx was holding, he would instantly pull the trigger.

Kimberly knew the instant the man below had reached the Expedition and the clink of the door opening was like the explosion itself. Just as she collapsed on her stomach, she heard the shooter in the rafter's scream, "Gun!" but that was the last thing he said as Onyx tossed the gun to Jaelen while she turned and shot a knife into the heart of the man standing on the stairs. Half a second later, Jaelen shot the man in the rafters, taking him out with a bullet right between the eyes.

Ainsley had released Ms. Collins to run for cover as another knife whizzed past his ear. Kimberly jumped up, grabbed Ms. Collins, and ran in the opposite direction to the small office nearby on the second floor to avoid the gunfire on the floor as Ainsley started shooting back at them.

"Where's Pamela?" Kimberly asked Ms. Collins after they hugged in relief.

"She just happens to be at home. I heard someone come in the door while I had all the kids and Leroy in the back by the kitchen. We heard shots being fired, and I hurried everyone out the back. I remember this was one of your backup places you taught Leroy to go to whenever there looked like trouble, while you were staying here. Ainsley must have followed us here because as soon as we got here, Leroy and I had to struggle with them while the twins made their escape and hid. Where could they have gone, Kimberly?"

"The cellar," Kimberly admitted. Taking her hand, they stayed low as Kimberly went into the closet where there was a dumb waiter elevator. Ms. Collins crawled down with her all the way to the first floor to the first floor elevator.

Kimberly went under the large desk where there was a door. She gave the secret knock. A few minutes later, it clicked and Jason popped his head out.

"I'm sure glad to see you, Momma," he said, throwing his arms around her neck.

She quickly helped them all out. "Let's use the back door to get out of here." Reaching in the bottom drawer, she found a set of keys. "Keep low, everybody, and we're playing the quiet game."

Jason and Jaenae were familiar with what could happen, but the younger twins weren't. They were great at following orders, however. She went over to a file cabinet and pushed it out the way.

"Where are you going?" Ms. Collins asked.

Kimberly answered, keeping her voice low, "There's another door behind this file cabinet. We can get to the front of the building and get out before they know where we've gone."

"No. Don't you think we can make a better escape to my car through the back?" Ms. Collins urged. "Especially with the children not being able to run as fast as us."

Kimberly considered this, then nodded. She was too stressed to really think anything through with the knowledge that Leroy could be laying upstairs dead, so she allowed Ms. Collins to lead the way, crouching from the office and through the first floor containment units. At first, it seemed as if they were going in circles and with the gunfire going on upstairs, Kimberly wasn't thinking straight because she was worrying about Jaelen and Onyx. It sounded as if Ainsley had brought additional backup.

"Didn't we just pass this container?" Jason whispered to his mother.

Kimberly looked to her left to see that the office door was right there. Ms. Collins had led them in a complete circle. Even though Kimberly hadn't been in the warehouse in years, she could easily tell where the exits were because of the sunlight coming through the back doors and the new entrance she had blown. So why hadn't Ms. Collins realized this? She was a reasonably intelligent woman.

She told the children to hold up and stand near the container. Kimberly knew with a snap the children would be able to scatter and hide when there was danger, but she didn't want to think she couldn't trust this woman who had been her friend for so long.

"Where do you think you're going?" Kimberly asked Ms. Collins.

"I thought I saw someone, and I was circling around just in-"

A click behind Ms. Collins made Kimberly look around to see Ainsley pointing his gun at the back of Ms. Collins' nape.

Kimberly knew she didn't have to snap. Jason saw danger immediately and snapped his fingers, and his siblings followed him quickly.

"Call them back!" Ainsley ordered.

"No," Kimberly cried. "I won't let you hurt them."

"Kimberly, please," Ms. Collins pleaded, frightened as tears welled up in her eyes.

Kimberly thought about Pamela. "You've got to promise me you won't hurt them," she said to Ainsley. "Or kill any of them including Elizabeth. I'll turn myself over to you and you can kill me. The children will never have to know about the money, and Elizabeth will never tell, will you Elizabeth?"

Ms. Collins shook her head desperately.

"Fine, come here!" Ainsley ordered as he shoved Ms. Collins away and now pointed the gun at Kimberly.

Kimberly slowly came, frantically trying to figure out a way to get out of this. She hoped the children wouldn't see her die. The gunfire above was becoming louder and more rapid. Onyx and Jaelen had to have been running out of ammunition or were they dodging bullets by now? Would they come and save her and the children?

When she was an arm's length away, she thought about the last piece of the letter. Trust no one. What had Ms. Collins meant by that? She stopped and stood in front of Ainsley so he could hit no one, but her.

"Now, call the children," he ordered.

Kimberly bit her lip, hesitant. They had planned a long time for these moments. The self-defense classes, the hostage tapes Kimberly had studied, and the kidnapping case files she had read. Now, all that was coming into play, and this was one of the moments. She had ordered the children that in any instance when they knew her life was in danger, which they would never come out until the secret word was uttered.

To throw Ainsley off, she spoke gibberish with a Spanish dialect.

"Talk in English!" Ainsley ordered.

She called for the children as Ainsley ordered. "Please, come out." After waiting a moment, she shouted for them again, but they still didn't come. Kimberly put her best disappointment look on her face.

"Then I'll just have to kill you and then search for them, won't I, but I was hoping to kill them first, then you, so you can watch them die," Ainsley said.

"But you promised to not do that," she exclaimed angrily, slightly feeling her leg to see how many knives Onyx had left. There were two there and she knew if she could wrestle Ainsley, she could easily get to the knives and stab him somewhere critical in the upper torso.

He pulled the sheath back on the Beretta he was holding and prepared to shoot her in the chest.

"No," Jason cried, coming out of his hiding place. He was alone, but Kimberly was still upset he had ignored her order.

She ordered. "Jason, run. This has nothing to do with you."

"No," Jason said defiantly.

Ainsley smiled triumphantly. "Grab him," he yelled.

Kimberly watched in horror as Ms. Collins grabbed Jason's arm. Her son tried to desperately fight to get away by latching his teeth into her hand where she was holding him.

Ms. Collins screeched in pain. "Stop that, you mean little brat," she yelled, trying to shake him off. When Jason continued to fight wildly, she viciously slapped him several times until he was in a daze.

Throughout all of this, Kimberly screamed hysterically and tried to get to her son, but Ainsley was holding her in a death grip around her waist and when she fought too hard, he would squeeze so tight she thought she would burst from the pressure he put on her intestines.

"Why?" Kimberly demanded to know at Ms. Collins, who now held Jason like a rag doll by his arm. "Why are you doing this?"

"Don't you see?" Ms. Collins said. "I have no choice in the matter. You of all people should know this and understand. He'll have me put away forever. He conveniently killed the sheriff, who was working on the case, and he holds the evidence as blackmail. If I don't do this, he'll have me locked up, and they'll put Pamela in a home. You should be able to relate to this because you would do anything not to let them put Leroy away."

Kimberly's shoulders slumped in disappointment. "When? When did he get to you?"

"He found me in New Orleans. That's why I came back to Michigan."

Ainsley spoke up with his lips near Kimberly ear. "But I never had them and you at the same time, and you stopped letting her know where you were. So Beth kept her trust in you until the right time, which is now."

Jason had started to come to a little and was trying to pull out of Ms. Collins' grip on his arm.

Ms. Collins tone was filled with disappointment. "Now I'm so deeply involved in his illegal shit, I'll never get out, but at least I'll have Pamela."

"Kill him, now!" Ainsley ordered.

"No!" Kimberly yelled, but she was just ignored and held tighter.

Ms. Collins' long fingers wrapped around Jason's neck and proceeded to strangle the child.

Chapter 39

Kimberly screamed, "Please, don't! Please, stop!" Her cries were ignored as the life began to leave Jason's body.

Suddenly, Jaenae jumped from behind one of the canisters and sunk her teeth into Ms. Collins' inner calf. Blood spurted out, and the woman bellowed maniacally, trying the shake Jaenae off her leg while hurling Jason to the ground.

Jaenae held on tight until Ms. Collins sharply kicked her in the face, knocking the child unconscious to the floor. Kimberly was still trying to get over there, but Ainsley held her too tightly. Jason quickly recovered and jumped up from where he had fallen and chomped right down on Ms. Collins' thigh as he clawed her back at the same time.

The woman started yelping for help now. Ainsley aimed the gun in the children's direction, and Kimberly knocked his hand upward, just as the gun went off, then grabbed both knives in her hands driving them simultaneously in his neck and chest.

A look of pure shock entered his face as the gun dropped to the ground and his body followed shortly, pausing slightly to garble a word from his blood-filled mouth. Kimberly thought for him to say this word was strange, but she pushed that thought away as she turned to her son.

Jason was using the back of his hand to wipe the blood from his mouth. He was staring down at Ms. Collins' body, twitching in a horrible death dance as the bullet from Ainsley's gun had entered her head, shattering her skull on the opposite side, but it was taking a while for her body to realize it was dying.

Pulling him in her arms, Kimberly used her body to shield his eyes from that horrible view. He looked up at her with tears starting to well in his eyes. "I'm sorry I didn't listen to you, Momma, but I couldn't let them kill you. I couldn't let you give your life for us when you've done so much," he said, very upset with himself. "I'll understand if you punish me."

She held him tighter as the tears freely rolled down her cheek. "I won't, baby. You saved Momma's life. You and Jaenae did. I owe you everything."

He shook his head. "You're already given us everything." He looked over at Ainsley's body, which was lying face down on the ground. "Does this mean it's over? Can we stop being scared and stop running?"

She was almost too choked up to speak and had to force out, "Yes, baby. We can. Let's go check on your sister."

They went over to where Jaenae was laying on the ground, slowly coming to. Kimberly knelt down beside her daughter and checked for anything broken. "Does it hurt anywhere bad, NaeNae?"

"My mouth." The girl pouted. "She kicked me in my mouth."

"It wouldn't hurt so bad if it wasn't so big," Jason snipped, leaning in the way so his sister didn't have to see the two dead bodies behind him.

Jaenae cut him a sharp look, and then looked up at her mother. "Momma, I knew she didn't like me for some reason, but I didn't think it was that bad."

"She wasn't jealous of you, knucklehead," Jason protested.

Jaenae only shrugged as if she knew the real truth while Kimberly helped her up and they began to walk toward the office, where the other twins had ran.

"Where's Uncle Leroy, Momma?" Jaenae asked. "Is he all right?"

Jason looked just as worried. "He told us to run as soon as he opened the hatch to the car, and I took everyone to the hiding spot just like you showed me, Momma, but Leroy was trying to fight them to give us time to hide and he ran upstairs to make sure they didn't follow us. Then we heard Onnie and Mr. Gates arrive, but we didn't move."

Kimberly then realized the shooting had stopped and it was quiet. She signaled for the children to keep their voices low and hurry toward the office.

"Kim…ber…leeee," a faint groan said near the stairs on the first floor.

She stopped walking, not believing her ears.

"Kim-meeee," a desperate plea cried.

Jason and Jaenae looked up at her, and she whispered for them to go and get the twins while she left them and went to see if her ears were just hearing things. Moving around several containers, she followed the voice to a large body leaning against a container near the steps. Her eyes couldn't believe what she was seeing as he called out, "Kimmie? Is that you?"

Running to her brother, she held on to him tightly, but his legs started to give under her, and she was unable to hold him up and had to slowly descend to the ground with him until they sat slumped together.

Her brother's speech was slow and erratic. "Jaelen said you would come if I called."

"Are you okay?" she asked, seeing blood on the front and back of his shirt. Gently, she touched to see if there were any open wounds, but the only thing really bleeding was a wound from the back of his head, but it didn't look that severe.

"Jaelen says it's only a flesh would, but it hurts like a big one would, Kimmie," he complained, looking a bit disoriented.

Kimberly started to cry in joy, so glad to see her brother alive and knowing he would be okay. "You'll be fine, Leroy. Where's Jaelen and Onyx? Are they okay?"

"They're upstairs. He said they have to wrap things up and they'll be down." He suddenly gripped her as if he had just remembered something. "The babies! Are the babies okay?"

She nodded, using her hand to wipe the tears from her eyes. "They're fine. They're okay. Don't you worry."

His eyelids were starting to close, and she began to worry if she should let him sleep with that head wound. Lightly tapping his face, she awoke him slightly and he frowned as if he were seeing her for the first time in a long time. "I thought you were a dream, Kimmie. I thought they had killed you and I would never see you again. I wanted to die because I wouldn't have no one to help me with the babies."

"I won't leave you, Leroy," she promised.

"But you can't take care of the babies by yourself." Again, he grabbed her as if he had the most wonderful idea. "Mr. Gates can help you now. He promised to take good care of you and the babies so I can be an uncle and play with them again. Can I, Kimmie?" he asked weakly.

"Yes, Leroy," she answered, hearing police and ambulance sirens become closer and closer to them. "Try to stay up and wait. Don't go to sleep yet," she ordered. "Wait for the doctor, okay?"

"Momma, is Leroy okay?" Jaenae asked.

Looking behind her, she saw all the children peering around the corner worriedly at their uncle. Kimberly insisted they come closer so they could keep him up. Jaenae moved into her mother's place, and Leroy held all the boys on his lap.

Kimberly heard a double set of footprints coming down the steps. She tensed a moment, but then easily recognized Onyx's raven outfit with the long black mackintosh. Jaelen moved quickly to Kimberly and pulled her in his arms. It felt so nice to her, feeling his body close to her. He held her as if his life depended on it.

"I love you, Kimberly," he said.

The words were a shock to her system, especially just after the stress she had been through. Flabbergasted, she couldn't find the words to respond to his declaration, but the fact that she was speechless didn't faze him because he continued to speak.

"I don't want to wait, Kimberly. I want you and the children and Leroy in my life forever." He brushed his lips against hers. "Please say you'll accept my proposal."

She looked down at her children, who were intently listening to the conversation she and Jaelen were having. Jaenae and the twins were looking quite pleased, but of course, Jason had that obstinate look on his face. Despite this, she looked back at Jaelen and said, "Yes, Jaelen, I'll be your wife."

He hugged her even harder, and she looked over his shoulder at Onyx, who was staring right back at Kimberly, looking almost pleased, but a little confused, and Kimberly wondered could Onyx read her own frustrated thoughts.

Quickly, she looked away to hide her feelings. At least Jaelen was happy. Wasn't that all that mattered?

Chapter 40

Three days. It was three days before Kimberly received a full night's sleep at Lethal's home. Onyx didn't think it was safe for Kimberly and her family to be home, and Lethal insisted Kimberly stay there. The only person who didn't like this arrangement was Jaelen, especially since Lethal found great pleasure in kicking Jaelen out his home every night.

Deciding together, Jaelen and Kimberly planned for a wedding two weeks after the grand opening. She really didn't feel a part of all this, but went along with the motions. Kimberly had the honor of meeting Jaelen's father and knew where Jaelen's and Jason's sour disposition had come from.

Even though he seemed wary of Kimberly, the children enamored him. At the birthday celebration - postponed by the latter events by a couple of days - his father announced the wedding of Kimberly and Jaelen.

The grand opening of the club went as scheduled and was pulled off without a hitch. Jaelen even made a special toast, and Kimberly felt her heart go aflutter when he said, "To my bride to be, my partner in my business, my partner in life, and my partner forever."

Yet still, that doubting in Kimberly's mind overshadowed the feelings of her heart. Onyx was watching her so intently she thought Onyx's look would smite her as she stood. Kimberly carefully avoided the prying woman's intense gaze and looked at the crowd for just anything interesting. At that moment, her eyes lit upon Monica standing across the room on the arm of some council member old enough to be her grandfather. The lost and forlorn look on the woman's face made Kimberly feel a little better, but her spirits didn't perk up about the wedding.

Onyx had been right about Jaelen's attitude. If the man laughed or smiled any more, Kimberly was going to puke her own guts up. The man acted like it was Christmas every day. The children got along with him just fine, except for Jason, who upon Jaelen's visit would only sit in a chair in a far corner and look out a window or quietly observe while Jaelen would read to or interact with the children.

His mood was even better when he received news the night right before the grand opening, Edward had been caught. Lethal had sent Del using the tip Kimberly had left him at the front desk in Muskegon. Edward had been the one coming on the elevator when she had been getting off, and he had been found in the hotel. The woman he was with had not been the one that helped him at the bank, but when The Detroit Free Press published the capture of Edward Smith, the ex-bank teller had come forth feeling slighted by Edward since he dumped her in the middle of Nowhere, Michigan. She confessed to helping Edward embezzle from several different accounts - not just Jaelen's business.

After putting the children to bed the night of the grand opening, a bothered frown came to Jaelen's brow as he exited from the boys' room. Kimberly felt comfortable talking with him about anything now, except what was really bothering her, and could almost easily discern what bothered him.

"Will Jason ever like me?" he asked.

She almost wanted to laugh. For him to worry about the same thing she worried about from him seemed hilarious. True, he had expressed love for her with his words, but Kimberly had seen the worst side, and Jaelen and his behavior now towards her seemed too good to be true.

Yet, it wasn't Kimberly's emotions Jaelen was concerned with. "Jason just has a slight intuition about things, and he knew your animosity toward me prior to the admission of your feelings. He still thinks you're out to hurt me."

"But I'm not out to hurt you," he insisted. "Even you know that."

Kimberly wanted to ask, "Then what are you out to do, Jaelen? That's what we want to know?" Instead, she merely shrugged. "Jason has a hard time trusting people who just pop into his life suddenly. The others are receptive to you because they aren't as stubborn as Jason."

"Why would he think I don't love him? I've told him, I've showed all I can to prove it." Jaelen was frustrated and Kimberly really wanted to admit to everything. Her son would never let go of this behavior until he was assured his mother wouldn't be hurt, but Kimberly couldn't assure her son until she was assured herself, and no matter how much love Jaelen professed or showed, he never said he had forgiven her.

"Jason's been through too much. It's easy for him to assume the worst when that's all he's experienced, Jaelen." This was the same for her, but she wasn't going to say that aloud. "Give him time. He'll come to believe you and trust you."

"I'm an impatient man," he said, growling. "You speak to him."

"All right, tomorrow," she promised.

He shook his head and said, "Now. I want to hear what he has to say."

Before Kimberly could protest, Lethal called her name as he came around the corner to where Kimberly and Jaelen stood.

"We're busy, and it's not ten o'clock yet," Jaelen said, angry.

Lethal had implemented the house rule of guests being out by ten o'clock. Lethal had sworn Kimberly would be treated like a lady while she was under his roof, and Jaelen would be the perfect gentleman, or Lethal would beat it into him.

"This is important. I need Kimberly to come down to the living room immediately," Lethal ordered.

"I'll be there down in just a moment, Lethal," she assured him. "Thank you." She squeezed Jaelen's hand to hold his tongue. She had realized the power she had over this wondrous man, and it always amazed her to know this. A small look, touch, or whispered word made a difference in his turbulent emotions.

Lethal gave Jaelen a distrustful look, then walked away leaving them alone again.

Jaelen's eyes narrowed at Kimberly, and he leaned in close to her. "What was that for?" he asked, indicated the hand squeeze.

She backed up slightly and felt the wall against her back. He still held her hand, but his other hand moved to the side of her, seeming to block her in. Kimberly didn't feel intimidated - much. "I didn't want the two of you to start a pissing contest. Lethal's looking for anyway to shove his fist down your throat."

"And you wouldn't want him to hurt me, would you?" He smirked at her concern. "Don't think I could fight the big bully?" His lips moved over to her neck, lightly brushing the skin and moving up behind her earlobe.

"I … wasn't trying to protect you," she forced out, short-winded.

"Your concern is appreciated. Do you want to know how much it's appreciated?" His voice had gone very deep, and the bass reverberated, making goose bumps come on her arm and a flush come to her face.

Innocently, she asked, "How much?"

He licked a trailed around the nimble bones in her ear, then back down to her neck, suckling a sensitive spot in the crook of her neck near her shoulder, pushing the blouse she was wearing out of his way. His free hand had undone most of the buttons and was now working to get the bra that hooked in the front a loose.

Kimberly's heart began to speed up, and she was finding it difficult to breathe, swallow, think. Dear Lord was the last thought she remembered before his lips seized hers in a luscious lascivious kiss that could only mean one thing he was thinking.

By the time he drew away slightly, Kimberly's mind was miles away from what Lethal had asked her, and she was very ready for the suggestion Jaelen whispered in her ear about sneaking out of the house like a couple of teenagers and finding his car convenient enough to do whatever they wanted.

Lethal cleared his throat in annoyance down at the end of the hall. Jaelen's hand had worked its way between her legs, but his body shielded Lethal's eyes from seeing all this.

"One more moment," Jaelen snapped at Lethal.

"Thirty seconds and I would like to hear Miss Hawthorne's feet coming down these steps, Jaelen," Lethal threatened.

Jaelen gave her a moment to gather her wits before letting go of her. Teasing her, he asked, "Do you think I could show some more appreciation later?" He licked his lips greedily.

She gave him an annoyed look as she quickly fixed herself up.

"What was that for?" he questioned, a little amused.

"You know exactly what, Jaelen Gates." She finished with the last button and started toward the stairs. He gently grabbed her wrist and pulled her back in his arms.

"I want to hear you tell me," he ordered, his tone of voice quite calm, but the look of passion still in his eyes.

"Don't start what we can't finish."

"I would gladly-"

She placed her finger over his lips to stop him from his wicked suggestions and moved away from him. He allowed her to leave, but the look of frustration was evident since he had started something he definitely wanted to finish, but he and Kimberly had both agreed to abstain until the wedding. Although Jaelen felt he had been pressured into it since Lethal had made the suggestion.

Lethal believed the only person allowed to have sex in the house was the person who owned it. Kimberly really didn't feel comfortable imposing already on Lethal although he didn't feel to mind, and she wouldn't break the rules. Damn her goodness and sweetness and honesty and...

How could he damn something about a woman he enjoyed so much about? He followed Kimberly down into the front room where Lethal was standing in front of a man who had his back to the door, so he didn't see Kimberly and Jaelen enter, but a strange woman and Lethal had.

Onyx was watching from a corner, out the way, with a small bowl of popcorn.

Kimberly only cut her a glance before giving Lethal her full attention.

Lethal moved from the man to Kimberly's side as the man turned around. "Kimberly Parker, I'd like you to meet Thorin Lampkin and his wife, Cassandra Lampkin."

She hardly heard a word Lethal was saying because she was spellbound by the face on the man who looked at her with just as much shock.

"Alicia?" he asked bewildered.

"You look like my brother, Leroy," she admitted, stepping forward toward the tall man built just as brawny as her brother.

Understanding dawned on his face. "Kimberly. My God, you're alive."

Kimberly's eyes widened as she realized who this man really was. "You're my father?" she asked, unsure.

Chapter 41

The large man with Leroy's gentle brown eyes stepped toward her, but she immediately stepped back, not wanting him to touch her.

Everyone saw the painful, terrified look on her face. Jaelen moved up behind her and held her shoulders for comfort.

Lethal spoke up quickly. "Maybe I should explain everything, Kimberly," he said.

"There's no need," Kimberly said to Lethal, then looked back at Thorin. "My mother told you I was dead, and you didn't bother to come to a funeral of your child. If you had, you would have realized it was all a lie and..." It was becoming difficult to speak as she thought about her horrible life with Uncle Charlie. "You could have saved me from all the beatings, the black eyes, the broken bones, dislocated shoulders, the horrible nights when I thought I would never see the light of day again and the worrying that he would take my brother away forever..." She couldn't continue.

"Kimberly, I was too broke to come. I had left to find better work. Back then the city didn't offer too much to a black man with no high school diploma and a family to feed. I left the city to find work and found myself further and further away to make enough money to send home to Alicia. Every time I did come home, she got worse and worse. The drugs were taking over her life, and I didn't want to become involved in the life she was leading. I wanted to get you out of there even before you were born, Kimberly, you have to believe me.

"Six months before I got the letter, I came home to find she had moved out the apartment, cleaned me out of everything, and she and Charles were nowhere to be found. No one would help me because we weren't married, and she didn't put my name on the birth certificate so I could claim you. I went back to Traverse City, found me a great job, and then received the letter telling me you were gone. I couldn't leave because I was just getting back on my feet and didn't have the money to travel back to the city at that time, and I blamed myself for your death because I could have saved you.

"I still blame myself, Kimberly, because I know you would have rather been dead than to have rather suffered all that pain. I should have come back, but I was so ridden with guilt that I never wanted to come back and even try to find a gravestone. Please forgive me, Kimberly. Please forgive me for all that has happened to you. I should have tried harder. I should have tried to find out the truth."

Kimberly was shaking as she stood there with Jaelen's arms now wrapped around her. He wasn't just comforting her, he was holding her up so she wouldn't collapse to the floor in a heaving sob. She had thought all this time that this man didn't exist and now he was here. Now he was standing in front of her and asking for forgiveness.

Pushing gently away from Jaelen, she moved toward the large brawny man who was an exact older version of Leroy. There was so much suffering and guilt in his face, she couldn't help but feel pity for him. Reaching up, she cupped her palm to his cheek, and he leaned his scruffy bearded face into the warmness of her hand and closed his eyes, enjoying the comfort of her touch.

Thorin was too afraid to touch her until Kimberly moved closer to him and moved her arms around his neck, using her tiptoes to reach up all the way. He ensconced her in the tightest bear hug, his tears wetting her neck. She found herself comforting the large man, and the more she softly whispered her acceptance of forgiveness, he wept even harder.

The other people in the room were silent as they watched father and daughter hold on to each other for dear life; it was as if they were watching the past being erased and a new beginning start. The sight was wondrous to watch and almost too precious to break up.

Onyx cleared her throat, drawing Lethal's eyes to her. She nodded to Cassandra and indicated he needed to finish.

"Kimberly, you should be reminded of exactly who these people are. We got them down here with the insistence of meeting their son's killer," Lethal said, getting Kimberly and Thorin to look at him.

Kimberly gasped and looked over at Cassandra who looked rather displaced in all of this.

"He wasn't my son," Thorin admitted freely. "Unfortunately, he was my stepson."

Moving to the woman, Kimberly saw a lot of Ainsley's features, and she wondered had this woman taught her son to be so greedy and would the woman hate her for what Kimberly had done to save her life. "I'm deeply sorry about your son's life, but I had to defend myself," she said to Cassandra. "This explains your son's last words to me."

"What?" the woman said eagerly.

"I didn't understand it until now, and I thought I was maybe dreaming it, which is why I made no mention of it in the police report. He said, sister. I thought it was a dying man's shock, but now I knew that he knew who my father was and what relation I was to him."

Cassandra hung her head in disappointment. "Yet still he would have killed you and the children."

"You know everything?" Jaelen asked coming to Kimberly's side for strength and comfort. She gave him a look to let him know she was glad he was there.

Cassandra moved to her husband's arms. "Yes. The lawyers told me everything about what my son had planned and when they found out he couldn't pay the money they came to me. We didn't discover his lecherous plans from a secret taping the lawyers had done without Ainsley's knowledge until it was too late, and we had a horrible time trying to find out who to contact about it. Mr. Heart came to us and let us know what had happened, and I don't think a better ending could have come about for him."

This was rather startling to hear a mother talk of her son this way, but no one made a comment about this.

Thorin explained, "Thornton died barely leaving Cassandra with enough to live on, and Wescott was nice enough to give her the trust to help her out, but Cassandra could not raise the boy in Flint, Michigan, where Ainsley was born, so she sent him to Detroit to a brother where Ainsley quickly learned about the money to gain off the streets and ripping off rich folks. He was lazy and spoiled by his own greediness and his uncle. Cassandra tried to keep the trust information away from him, but he found out about it behind our backs and perused the matter without us knowing because she could have put a stop to his greediness a long time ago."

Cassandra stepped to Kimberly and took her hands in comfort. "It is I who owe you an apology, Kimberly. I know what you did to Ainsley was for your defense, and I would probably have done the same. Please do not feel any guilt for what has happened."

"I only feel guilty because he dragged a person who I thought was a good friend of mine down with him. She had a child who I'm going to take care of with no problem."

"And we'll gladly help," Thorin said. "Anything she wants just let me know. Forward all bills to me."

"That could become quite costly," Kimberly told him.

"Money should not be a problem," Thorin said proudly. "I've recently acquired some of my own fortune in the tourism business and have landed government contracts for luxury liners to travel from the UP to Detroit and Windsor, Ontario."

"Well then," Onyx said, "you shouldn't have a problem with paying for your only daughter's wedding."

Thorin smiled. "You're getting married, Kimberly?" he asked, taking her hand to see the ring Jaelen had placed on there at the birthday celebration weeks ago.

"Yes," she said, trying to sound as happy as possible hoping her father would not see the truth.

"And who is the lucky fellow?"

"I am," Jaelen announced proudly, shaking Thorin's hand. "It's a pleasure to finally meet you, sir."

"When is the wedding?" Cassandra asked.

"In less than a week," Onyx answered.

Kimberly cut her a look that clearly said, "Shut up," but Onyx wasn't about to stop.

"I just had a great idea," Onyx exclaimed. "Wouldn't it be great if your father could walk you down the aisle, Kimberly? I'm sure Mr. Lampkin wouldn't mind staying here for the week to get to know you and Leroy and the grandkids better."

Thorin was too excited for words to describe the immense pleasure it would be to do this, and Kimberly almost felt like an outsider as she watched Jaelen, Thorin, and Cassandra eagerly plan for the event. She couldn't feel the excitement they felt because all she could experience was trepidation about the upcoming nuptial. When she looked over at Onyx, she saw a woman studying her like a lioness moving in on the prey for the kill.

Kimberly felt lightheaded from the exhaustive day she had and decided to excuse herself for the night after about an hour of speaking with her father and Cassandra.

Lethal insisted that her father and stepmother stay in his extra guestroom - he had eight of them in all. Kimberly walked Jaelen to the front door and of course, as usual, he stole a kiss. Onyx was leaving with him, and Kimberly avoided the woman's stare on purpose. Onyx had probably figured out something was wrong, but Kimberly wasn't going to speak with her about it although it would have been nice to get another woman's opinion, but Onyx couldn't objectively speak like a woman when her nature was much too mannish. Kimberly would be forced to figure out her dilemma on her own, and she needed to hurry.

Chapter 42

The music outside her door was serene, and watching her daughter gloat about how she looked almost as beautiful as the bride made her laugh. Her father looked so handsome, and Cassandra was almost like a real mother, fussing over everything being perfect. Everything looked peaceful around Kimberly, but her insides were turning inside out. In thirty minutes, she would be Mrs. Jaelen Gates, and her heart was feeling as if the weight of the world was on top of it.

Onyx came in the room, and Kimberly's eyes actually went wide with shock as Onyx was wearing a white camisole under a long knee length black coat and matching black pants. This was as close as Kimberly would ever see Onyx actually making an effort to dress up, and Kimberly could actually see a beautiful female under all that rough exterior Onyx constantly tried to hide.

"It's almost time, and this little princess needs to go down to where they are preparing to walk out," Onyx said to Jaenae.

"Don't I look fabulous, Auntie Onyx?" Jaenae asked.

"You are gorgeous," Onyx said, playing along.

"We'll take her down and get seated," Cassandra said then kissed Kimberly's cheek after Jaenae gave her mother a hug and kiss.

Thorin only gave her a hug, knowing he'd get a kiss before he gave her away. "I'll give you a moment to yourself and meet you at the door," he promised.

"Thank you, Daddy." The word still felt foreign on her tongue, but she was becoming use to knowing she now had a father in her life.

When she was left alone with Onyx, she turned around to the mirror to check her makeup in an attempt to ignore her. Onyx made no move to start, and when Kimberly turned around to see why the woman was just standing there, they just stared at each other as if daring the other to speak first. Kimberly gave in first.

"What is it that you want to pry your nose in now?" she snapped.

"Pry? You don't think I should pry? I've never seen a woman so unhappy about getting married in my entire life."

"I'm not unhappy," Kimberly lied.

"Don't shit me, Kimberly. The closer this wedding came, the more miserable you became. You are going to tell me what the fuck is wrong with you, or we'll be staying in this room until you do."

Kimberly wasn't going to even try to challenge the woman, so she sighed giving in. "All right, go ahead and pry."

"Why don't you want to marry Jaelen?"

"Because I don't think his intentions are true. I think he still has animosity for me for what I did to him."

Onyx's nose crinkled in a "that's all" kind of look. She sat down in front of Kimberly. "Have you asked him?"

"Of course not. I shouldn't have to ask him."

"You don't think marrying you is a forgiving gesture?"

"I'm the mother of his children, he could be marrying me because of that, Onyx. He's an honorable man, and he does want to be with the children."

"Even his express concern for Hawthorne's children? He's gone to the trouble to adopt them as well as his own."

"That could be because he does care for me, Onyx, but how do I really know his love is true? Maybe one day, he'll get upset and remember how much he really hated me and then decide to make my entire life miserable."

Exasperated, Onyx asked, "So why are you even marrying him?"

"Because I do love him and the children-"

Onyx cut her off. "Only loving him won't make you happy, and don't you dare marry Jaelen as a sacrifice to your children."

"Then what do you think I should do? It's twenty minutes before I'm supposed to walk down the aisle."

"Dammit, get your ass down there and ask him, Kimberly."

"And if he hasn't forgiven me?"

"Then don't marry him."

"But-"

Onyx cut her off again. "Look Kimberly, your whole life you've been making sacrifices after sacrifices. When a woman is getting married, it is her time in life to be happy, adored, envied, and admired. If you don't feel like this when you go down the aisle, you will never experience true happiness for the rest of this marriage. If Jaelen tells you he hasn't forgave you, and you still want to marry him and be happy, you better tell him he needs to get over and forgive you."

"I should demand forgiveness?" Kimberly asked unsurely.

"Yes! And don't take anything less. This is your moment. Go down and take it." Onyx pointed toward the door.

Feeling a renewed sense of hope and strength, Kimberly arose and went to the door. "And if he has forgiven me? Should I let him know how doubtful I felt these last few weeks?"

"And make him feel like a fool for not noticing? Nah, we'll keep it between us."

"Isn't it bad luck for the groom to see the bride before the wedding?" she asked.

"Damn bad luck if it means you're going to be miserable for the rest of your life. Get down those steps and find out if that man loves you and forgives you," Onyx insisted.

"Why are you helping me like this?" Kimberly had to ask.

"Because I love Jaelen like a brother and I want the best for him." Onyx came over to Kimberly and handed her the train to her dress so it wouldn't drag on the floor. "And you're what's best for him."

"What about Lethal? Isn't he making sure no one comes upstairs?" Kimberly noted.

"I sent him off on a foolish errand that will keep him busy for the five minutes you will need to slip out," Onyx explained.

Looking back at Onyx one last time, she gave her a good luck wink before leaving the room.

Kimberly went down the small back staircase and peeked down the hall to see if anyone was standing there. Jaelen was close to the door peeking into a room right by the door Kimberly was to come out of. He was devastatingly handsome in his dark blue Christian Dior tuxedo.

Yet, he looked as if he were very bothered and sneaking to listen to the conversation going on in the office where she knew the kids would be sitting quietly waiting for someone to take them to the main chapel. She listened intently and could hear Jaenae and Jason arguing about Jason's past week's attitude.

"You'd better stop looking like that," Jaenae was warning. "He's your father, Jason, and you should be as happy as me and the twins."

"Why should I when I don't want him to be my daddy?" Jason asked.

"Why?" Jaelen asked at the doorway.

Jason looked at the man, narrowing his eyes to slits, but this didn't deter Jaelen from repeating his question adding on, "Why don't you want me to be your father, Jason?" He stepped into the room, going in front of Jason and kneeling to meet him eye to eye.

"Because you're only marrying my mommy to hurt her some more because you think she hurt you," Jason spat.

Kimberly quietly stepped into the hallway and snuck by the door to watch and listen to what was going on.

"That's not true, Jason. I love your mother."

"But she stole us from you. That's what I heard Uncle Lethal saying before Mommy agreed to turn herself in and you hate her for doing that," Jason protested. "How can you love and hate her at the same time?"

Jaelen took a deep breath. "I will admit I was very mad at your mother at one time when I didn't understand what had been done to me by her had been done under duress. When I really opened my eyes to see that she had no choice, and I opened my heart to see she in turned saved my life and has saved yours and everyone else she loves, I couldn't help but to turn the other cheek and forgive her. I love your mother, and if it takes the rest of my life, I'm going to fill every single second of hers with happiness. This, I promise you, Jason."

"Will you make us happy?" Jaenae asked.

"No doubt," he promised, giving her a playful wink and then looked back at Jason. "Your mother's happiness is my most important concern right now, and I intend to never hurt her for the rest of her life."

Jason stared hard into eyes just like his own. The boy's stiff resolve soon relaxed, and he moved his arms around his father's neck and kissed his cheek. "Thank you, Dad. That's all I needed to hear."

Jaelen smiled in relief, knowing whatever had been bothering the boy for the past few weeks was gone by just the promises Jaelen had just made. The boy just needed to hear what Jaelen was feeling. He left out the room, closing the door and almost backed into Kimberly.

"What are you doing here?" he asked making sure the office door was closed all the way. "Damn you look good!"

"I-I needed to speak to you, but-" Again she found herself too choked up for words.

He pulled her in his arms and held her close. "Is every okay?" he asked, concerned.

She could only nod feeling very emotionally overwhelmed and not wanting to cry. All her doubts had been erased by what she had overheard, and she felt so silly for not cherishing all the moments of the last weeks because of her silly misgivings.

"I wanted to speak to you before all of this, but I knew there was no way I could sneak up to your room with Lethal watching out from every damn doorway. I swear the man must have eyes behind his head," Jaelen said. "I know you have something old which is this remade dress Cassandra insisted you wear, that you look gorgeous in, and Onyx told me she loaned you her three-piece pearl set, right?"

Kimberly nodded self-consciously, touching the pearls that hung to accentuate the low cleavage. "What does this have to do with anything?"

"Well, I was thinking hard about this last night, and you needed something traditional especially since this wedding is rather rushed." He continued on to what he was previously pointing out. "The colors of this wedding is blue, which is why you have the dark blue shoes on."

"Yes, Jaelen, but-"

He cut her off yet again. "Let me finish." Reaching into his coat pocket, he took out a velvet red box. "You needed something new before you walked down the aisle."

"I just figured the ring you would give me would do," she said.

He shook his head, presenting the box to her. "This will do."

"What's that?"

"Open it and see," he insisted.

Warily, Kimberly took the box and slowly pulled it open then gasped. "What's this for?"

He took the box away from her and reached inside of it to take the platinum Rolex watch out with diamond studs at the numbers. It was the most beautiful watch she had ever seen. "I had it engraved just an hour ago. You can thank Onyx for helping me get it." He smiled proudly at himself. "I wanted to replace the rather cheap one you were so fond of. If you don't like it, we can leave right after the wedding and go straight to Wal-Mart and get you one just like the one I burned up. Do you like it, Kimberly?"

She was fighting to keep the tears from coming so she wouldn't mess up her makeup, and she ended up making the most awful face.

"Is that a yes or no?"

She could only nod, too choked up for words.

"Read the back," he ordered, turning the watch around for her to read.

Kimberly had to blink several times to see through the build-up of tears in her eyes to read aloud the italic engraving. "Kimber, always the captor of my heart, Jaelen."

A weird shriek came out of her mouth as she threw her arms around his neck and held on tight, trying her best not to ruin her makeup. "Thank you, Jaelen. Thank you for everything." She looked up in his eyes. "You've given me so much strength and love. I don't know what I would have ever done if I had never met you. I'm sorry for being so emotional right now."

"That's why I'm marrying you, Kimberly. I need your emotions to tame my devils, as Onyx says." He chuckled as he placed the watch on her wrist, and then lifted up his sleeve to show her the matching watch in a larger size.

Kimberly smiled at this man's astounding personality. He could love as passionately as he hated, and Kimberly was so glad to have his love in her life.

He kissed her gently, careful not to mess up her makeup and molded her body against his. "Can I ask of one more thing, Mrs. Almost Jaelen Gates?" he questioned.

"Anything, Jaelen," she said, kissing his cheek and loving the feel of him pressed against her. Now, she didn't care if her dress or her makeup messed up.

"I would like one more baby."

She looked up at him, confused. "Don't you think we have enough?"

"The more the merrier, but I want just one more to experience everything with you. I want to be there for every moment and cherish you even more as the mother to my children and most importantly, the woman in my life."

She smiled so brightly; she felt light as a feather. "Are you sure you want this?" she asked.

He nodded. "I do, Kimber."

As usual the name made her senses reel in pleasure. "Then you can rest assured the process is already taking place, and she should be here in about four and a half months according to my doctor I saw two days ago."

It was Jaelen's turn to light up brightly, and he picked her up and swung her around. "Another girl? Are you sure, Kimberly?" When she nodded, he swung her around again. "Thank you, Kimberly. Thank you." He kissed her face all over leaving her lips for last, which his delicious mouth lavished with the most wonderful kisses.

"It was nothing," she said modestly.

A wicked brow of his shot up. "I'll love you forever, you know this, right?"

"I know, Jaelen, and I'll love you forever," she promised.

With that nefarious handsome look still on his face, he asked, "Tonight, after the wedding, do you think you could tie me up again?"

She couldn't help but laugh and hold him close, knowing today was a new beginning for her life and from this day on, Jaelen would make her happy every second of the hour.

About This Author

D etroit Author & Founder of Motown Writers Network, Sylvia Hubbard has published over 40 books on suspense romance.

As a happily divorced mother of three, Sylvia has received numerous awards and recognitions for her work such as the Spirit of Detroit from Detroit City Council and State of Michigan Governor's Certificate of Tribute Emerging Minority Business Leader Award. She's spoken all over the United States and Canada about independent publishing, social media, 21st Guide to Marketing for writers and authors, How Readers can make money promoting their favorite authors and even how to be a single mom.

Recognized as an avid blogger by HoneyTech Blogs, Ms. Hubbard runs over five blogs including How To Love A Black and has had five #1 Best Sellers on Amazon. Her current work is Beautiful and she has two books coming up.

Related websites:

www.SylviaHubbard.com

www.MotownWriters.com

www.HowToEBook.org

Social Media:

www.facebook.com/sylviahubbard

www.twitter.com/sylviahubbard1

www.instagram.com/sylviahubbard1

www.youtube.com/sylviahubbard1

www.periscope.tv/sylviahubbard1

www.snapchat.com/sylviahubbard

www.goodreads.com/sylviahubbard

www.amazon.com/author/sylviahubbard

Related to Stealing Innocence:

(If you're trying to read my books in order, I couldn't tell you. Honestly. My brain writes in real time to the characters lives. One reader once told me follow Lethal Heart's hair length. Another one created a family chart and followed the "cousins." I just enjoy the ride they take me on.)

Stealing Innocence II: The Ravishment
Stealing Innocence III: Lethal Heart *(coming soon)*

The Hearts are weaved throughout my different stories and then there are the Hearts Of Detroit series. Jaelen has a close business friend, Ethan Black and he makes appearances in The Black Family Series as well. As always, enjoy…

To read more of this author's work, go to her website: www.SylviaHubbard.com.

Check out author's book list at: http://sylviahubbard.com/books

Support this author, by downloading or purchasing more books from her, reviewing this book from place of purchase and/or then sharing this author on your social network to encourage your reading friends to purchase her work. Thank you in advance for your support.

Connect Online to Sylvia Hubbard:
- Twitter: http://twitter.com/SylviaHubbard1
- Website: http://SylviaHubbard.com
- My blog: http://SylviaHubbard.com/blog

Or subscribe to her newsletter at:
http://groups.yahoo.com/group/SylviaHubbard
Want another book to read now?
http://sylviahubbard.com/fictionbooks

Happy Reading!

Made in the USA
Middletown, DE
16 August 2019